GW01445036

The Uncanny Valley

S.W. Campbell

Published by Shawn Campbell

The Uncanny Valley

The Uncanny Valley

ISBN: 978-0-9977105-4-0

To Adrianna, for telling me I should show people my stories, and to Mallory, for bothering me enough about this book to get it done.

The Uncanny Valley

Chapter 1

The America I was born in is dead. It's not that it was really much better than the one we have now, but at least we had the illusion, something to believe in. Anymore it's just right there in your face, something that can't be ignored. Maybe it's the technology that has done us in. That always seemed to be the limiting factor in the past. Hell, anymore everyone walks around with a little tracking device in their pocket. They can't leave it alone for a second, might miss a Facebook update or something. We're all connected. We're all together. We're all watched. How much longer until the curtain is drawn back? How much longer until the hood is opened and we're forced to look at all the gears? I don't know, but you won't catch me goose stepping with the crowd.

My left arm spasms, then my right. A sharp cutting pain in both that fades to the uncomfortable buzzing of a hit funny bone. My heart beats loudly in my ears, the slow rolling rhythm of lubs and dubs. The world shifts back into focus. Alice bounces across the desert at the nail biting speed of 30 miles per hour. Her aftermarket struts squeaking with every bump. Jostling across the flat sandy ground with the sagebrush and half dead greasewoods whipping past on each side. My mother's Saint Christopher medallion, hanging from the rearview mirror, flashes in the starlight. I sit in the driver seat, my hands gripping the wheel tightly, my head leaning forward so my nose is only inches from the windshield. Occasionally I jerk the wheel one way or the other. Trying to avoid an especially large rock, thick sagebrush, or imagined coyote. Every bit of my efforts are bent on keeping us moving forward into the bleakness of the west Texas wild.

Thirty miles per hour may not be fast on the highway, it's damn near illegal on the freeway, but it's on the edge of insanity when you're driving out across the desert. Even more so when it's the middle of the night, with a new moon, and your headlights are covered with transparent red packing tape. Why transparent red packing tape? Because red light doesn't ruin your night vision. Plus it's a lot harder for an observer to see at a distance. Now is not the time for stupid questions. There's not a lot to worry about on this patch of desert off of Highway 90. It's pretty desolate. My biggest concern is gullies, if we hit one of those we could all be fucked.

Off in the distance the lights of farmhouses glint like stars. Well, not really like stars. It's a clear night and no moon, so the stars really look like stars. The farmhouses are just poor imitations compared to the skies above. There is nothing like a clear moonless night sky in the middle of nowhere. It's something you don't get to see in the city. Cities are too bright. They're always too bright. There's no such real thing as darkness in a city. All those houses, headlights, lit-up signs, and street lamps create a dome of light, which only the biggest and best stars can push through. In a city the sky is a roof with a couple little lights twinkling. In the middle of nowhere the sky is a great emptiness filled with the wonders of the universe.

I have to be careful looking up. I keep getting drawn in, my brown eyes lifted upward. Millions of fiery balls of gas stretching their light over millions of years to reach us. The great cloudy band of the Milky Way stretching across the heavens. Bring me any asshole who thinks they're an important big shit, stick them out in the middle of nowhere with nothing but the night sky, and I guarantee they'll come back humbled. You can't help but feel insignificant. That's why people huddle together around the light in their man made jungles. Hell, even cavemen stayed close to their fires. It's all arrogance, not fear. They weren't afraid of any god damn monsters. They were just afraid of having to look up into the void. Afraid to realize everything about them doesn't mean shit.

Yep, the dome of light over our cities hides a lot of ugly truths about the universe. It also hides a lot of ugly truths about ourselves as well. When you're in the city you don't notice all the strange twinkling stars that move across the sky at a rapid pace. You don't notice all the damn satellites peering down at you with their camera lense eyes. Searching, tracking, and watching. When you're out in the middle of nowhere you can't ignore them because you can see them.

You can't pretend that you're all alone. You can't ignore the cold hard......

Something bounds through the red dimness of the headlights. I hit the brakes and swerve. My head bumps against the windshield. Not too hard. Thank god. Shit. I need to be watching ahead of me. Not gazing out at the stars like I'm god damn Galileo. This is no time to quit paying attention.

Lindsey's voice cuts through the silence of the cab.

"What was that?"

"Nothing. Looked like an antelope."

She looks behind us at the kids buckled in the backseat. Making sure they're all right. Both are still sound asleep. Those kids have been through so much shit that they could probably sleep through Judgment Day. I lean back in my seat and rub the sore spot on my head. My hand runs through my salt and pepper hair. Still thick despite my age. I have a thick skull. At least I didn't whack my nose. It's been broken enough times. More bulbous than Roman anymore.

"Where are we?"

"I don't know. We've been off the road for a couple of miles now.

"Are you sure you can find Mexico?"

"Of course I can find Mexico. It's just everything south of us. Can you grab me a beer?"

"Are you sure you should have one? You're driving."

The classic line of questioning to a simple request. God I wish she was still asleep. I love my wife, but sometimes I love the silence more. Besides, I really don't think she has the right to question me having one beer while driving. Not after all the shit she's pulled.

"Yes, I'm sure. Just hand me one and go back to sleep. It will be daylight soon."

Lindsey reaches back behind her, pulls a beer out of the cooler and hands it to me. I watch her bony frame out of the corner of my eye, and consider calling it a night so that the two of us can have some fun before the kids wake up. There's not enough damn time for that though. We have to keep going. We have to cover as much ground as we can. There will always be more time later. I have to stay focused.

I crack open the beer and Lindsey settles back in her seat and closes her eyes. I sip my beer, stare forward, and enjoy the silence. In my head I remind myself to mark down that I drank a beer. We're on tight supplies and everything needs to be kept account of. It's probably a little early to be dipping into my beer supply. Thank god we stopped in Marfa to replenish after the Big Bend didn't work out as planned.

We had six cases of beer to start with. I've drank seventeen beers so far, thirteen of which were needed to calm me down after all the shit at the Big Bend. We then bought another two cases at the store in Marfa. That would give us a total of seven cases plus seven extra in the cooler minus the one I was drinking. Twenty-four beers per case times seven cases is one-hundred-and-sixty-two beers.

Wait. Is that right. That doesn't seem right. Four times seven is twenty-eight, plus twenty times seven which is one hundred and forty. You add those two together and you get........shit. My mind is blank and for some reason simple math seems to be eluding me. My memory is shit but I usually have no problem with numbers. Granted I haven't slept in a while, I'm exhausted, a little strung out, and most definitely distracted. But this shouldn't be that hard. Maybe if I break it down differently. Twelve times fourteen. Two times four is....

"It just all seems so unreal doesn't it."

Lindsey's voice sounds loud in the silence. The only other sound is the hum of the engine, the squeaking of the aftermarket shocks, and the fizzing of my beer.

"What?"

"I said it just seems so unreal. You know, driving out here in the middle of nowhere in the dead of the night. Rushing about like a bunch of chickens with our heads cut off. Each day a blur so we can barely even think about it."

"We're doing the best we can. I never asked for this."

"I know. It's just....."

"Yeah?"

"It's just I wish we could have brought Roger Snuggleton with us."

God, this conversation again. It seems like every day since we threw everything we could get into Alice and got the hell out of Sweetwater she's felt the damn need to bring up that fucking cat.

"I know Linds. I know, but we couldn't find him and we sure as hell didn't have time to start looking for him."

"I know. I know. But still. We could have looked for him. We didn't have to be in that big of a rush."

My wife knows very little about the world. It's times like these that I have to remind myself that she's only twenty-seven. It doesn't help any that I've tried to keep her sheltered from the worst of things. I keep my mouth shut and hope that will be the end of it. I sure as hell wasn't going to put my family at risk for some god damn cat. Especially a cat, if I'm being honest about it, I never even really liked.

The most Roger Snuggle....whatever ever did for me was not claw my leg or vomit in my shoe. I would have put him in a bag and drowned him a long time ago except Linds and kids adored the shit out of him. Either way, a cat shoved in a car on this type of trip would have been way too much trouble. An uncontrollable variable at a time when everything needs to stay under control. I take another drink of my beer and hope Linds has fallen back asleep. All of this talking is distracting me from my driving. I look at the speedometer. Alice has dropped down to twenty.

"It's just that none of it seems real you know."

I grunt to let her know I'm listening. If I don't show I'm listening she'll just get mad, and that's not shit I really need right now.

"Sometimes I feel like none of this is real at all. That maybe I'm not real. Sometimes it feels like maybe I'm just some character in somebody else's dream."

I grunt again and take an extra large pull off my beer. I hate it when she gets fucking whimsical. I wish she would just shut up and go to back to sleep. Leave me alone with my thoughts. I have to do all the thinking for everybody 24/7. Don't I deserve just a little time to be alone with my own thoughts?

"Wouldn't it be funny if all of this is just some dream Roger is having? That all these weird things are just in his head while he's snoozing under the porch?"

I look over at my wife. She gazes out into the night, half of her face blackened by shadow. I hope the look on my face gets my thoughts of "what the hell" through to her, but apparently it's too dark.

"I can tell you one thing. If this is all just some dream Roger is having I guarantee he's probably all wiped out on catnip."

She giggles to herself. I look at my wife's gaunt face again and say nothing. I hope to god she's not back on the drugs again. We spent way too much time and money getting her cleaned up last time. If she's back on then I might as well dump her out right here in the middle of the desert. Don't get me wrong. I love my wife more than I love myself, but I love my kids more. They come first in all of this. They're the important thing.

We ride in silence for a while, both of us watching the shadowy terrain slide past. I finish my beer, crinkle up the can, and throw it on the floorboards. No roads, no worries about getting pulled over for drunk driving. I'm glad my wife isn't talking right now, especially if all she's going to do is talk about that damn cat. I like little pussy talk and little talk from pussy. I laugh a bit to myself.

"What's so funny?"

"Nothing."

If I tell her what I'm laughing at she'll just call me sexist and go off on some kind of rant. I'm not sexist. I believe women are capable of doing anything a man can do. I just enjoy a sexist joke now and again, that's all.

"Who laughs at nothing?"

"I guess I do."

"Whatever asshole. I don't really care anyways."

Blessed silence again for a few minutes.

"I wish we could listen to the radio."

"We went over this a hundred times. Anything that picks up a transmission can also transmit."

"I know. I know. I'm not stupid."

I think about pointing out that if she wanted to prove that hypothesis she needed to quit acting stupid, but I don't. Marriage is about love and compromise, but mostly about knowing when to keep your mouth shut. Silence reigns again and after a while I hear gentle breathing sounds indicating that Linds has returned to the Land of Nod. The well of words has finally run dry for the night.

I breathe a sigh of relief and lean back behind the seat to grab a second beer, reminding myself to take two off the inventory sheet in the morning. Can't forget to take them off the inventory sheet. There's not going to be anymore stops in civilization from here on out. We have to make what we have last. I open the beer and take a drink, then move my head back close to the windshield, and watch the suspicious satellites go round and round overhead.

Chapter 2

In 1957 the Soviets launched Sputnik, the world's first artificial satellite. Twenty months later the CIA launched Corona, the world's first spy satellite. Corona was a technological marvel, a five-foot camera, one hundred miles overhead, taking pictures on over a mile and a half of film. The film would be sent back to Earth via a re-entry capsule, which was hooked mid-air by a passing jet to ensure the top secret photos never fell into enemy hands. Over thirteen years, six generations of Corona were launched one hundred and forty-four times. The first generation could resolve images down to 40 feet in diameter. The second generation could do ten feet. The final generation, three feet. It's frightening to think of what they were capable of fifty years ago. It's even more frightening to think of what they must be capable of now.

There are some places that from looking at them you would never suspect that they are a drug house. They sit in nice quiet neighborhoods, painted an inoffensive color of beige. The house is always kept perfect. The lawn is neatly trimmed each week. The landscaping is impeccable and has the look of being professionally done. The curtains are never drawn and inside you can see a comfortable sitting room with a big flat screen television and large leather couch.

Sometimes as you walk your dog you see the owner getting his mail out of the box, or maybe retrieving the paper thrown into the bushes by the paperboy. He's a nice older gentleman with a full head of gray hair and bright cheerful eyes. He's kind of quiet, likes to keep to himself, but all in all that's not a bad thing. His wife is a lovely middle-aged woman who waves every time you see her. Sometimes the grandkids come to visit and you can hear them playing in the backyard, wrestling and screaming with rambunctious joy.

They seem like the perfect neighbors. You never have a problem with them and they never bother you. They seem like the nicest people you've ever met. The American dream in living color. Then one day you get back from work to find the entire house has been boarded up. The nosy neighbor that lives next door tells you that the police came by and took the old couple away for cooking and distributing meth. You're left stunned and dazed. All you can think is here you've been driving across town for meth, when you could have been buying it right next door.

The house just off Lancaster Avenue is not one of these hidden drug houses. It is most definitely a crack house. It has broken windows and peeling faded paint. It has piles of trash half covering the weed patches and bare dirt that had once been a yard. This isn't really the kind of place I want to be at. It's too much like the flashes from my past to be a good idea. It's too close to the old life I'm trying to avoid. I've been here before, not this specific house, but this type of situation.

I have a handle of tequila in my hand and four joints already rolled in my pocket. I'm ready to party. To be honest, I really didn't want to come out tonight, but Larry had hinted pretty heavy that he needed some alone time with his old lady. I could hardly blame him. I've been squatting on his couch here in Fort Worth for the past three months. Ever since they gave me my walking papers. Who was I to try and tell him that I didn't really want to go out?

This is most definitely a party. The flashing strobes through the windows and the constant vibration of the bass are a dead giveaway. Skeeter climbs up on the porch, opens the door, and walks in like he owns the place. I follow. Who am I to judge this house and the people inside? For Christ sakes, I've just gotten out of prison. I have no right to give a Sermon on the Mount.

The inside of the house looks much like the outside. It's overflowing with people who are most definitely not the right kind of people. Muscle heads in wife beaters and baseball caps with the tags left on. Fat girls wearing way too much makeup and way too little clothing, bellies and muffin tops hanging out over their waistbands. Human skeletons of both sexes with long stringy hair and bony joints sticking out at odd angles. Some freegan kids against the back wall, standing around with their greasy dreadlocks and patched dingy clothes. Black, caucasian, and Asian. All the major races represented. All but Mexicans. Mexicans usually go to their own parties.

By the looks of everybody the party has already been going on for quite some time. It's only 10 PM. The whole cast of characters is glassy eyed and jerky in their movements. Some dance by themselves. Some make out on shabby old pieces of furniture or in shadowy corners. Some shuffle around mumbling to friends only they can see. Some just sit and stare, comprehending the mysteries of the universe. Booze is everywhere. So are bongs, pipes, needles, and pills. There are even a couple of lines some little chubby Asian girl is snorting off the coffee table with a rolled dollar bill. No one is trying to hide anything. It's all out in the open and no one is giving a shit who sees. The liberated zombies of the modern world.

When Skeeter walks in everyone cries out his name like he just walked into his local bar. A couple wiggers in their baggy pants run up and give him a hug, slapping his back. One gives me the eye and whispers something in Skeeter's ear. Skeeter puts his hand on the wigger's shoulder and says something back. I can't hear him over the constant pounding of the bass, but I can see his mouth move with the words.

"He's cool."

It's just a simple check of credentials. Nothing to get upset about. I'm just some random dude. An unknown. Who knows who I could be. Maybe a narc, or maybe even a cop. This is not the kind of place you just walk into. You have to know somebody who knows somebody.

A kid like Skeeter is always loved at a place like this. He has something that a lot of these people lack. Money. Skeeter's real name is Roger Something Something the Third. His daddy is some big shit who owns a small chain of stores selling crap. His uncle is on the Fort Worth city council. Kids from money always end up either striving to prove themselves or giving up and just not giving a shit. Skeeter is the latter. We call him Skeeter because he is an annoying little shit who's always buzzing around. It doesn't matter, a kid with money can always find friends.

The wigger talking to Skeeter gives me a head nod, letting me know I am approved to stay in this den of degradation. I give a head nod back and sit down on the nearest stained couch. I take a pull of tequila, light one of my joints, and sit back to absorb the chaotic happenings around me. Say what you want about people who hang out at a crackhouse, but they're a generous lot. Within the first fifteen minutes I'm offered a buffet of narcotics. Hardcore druggies never want to get high alone. It's always better if someone else joins you on your journey. I politely refuse each offer and turn and give away drinks of tequila to show that I'm cool with the overall communistic vibe. It's been a long time since I've touched anything but pot, booze, and cigarettes. It's been a long and interesting road. One that I have no interest in walking down again.

The kids next to me are working themselves up into a frenzy of jabbering back and forth. One pimply faced guy with glasses keeps talking over all the others, pontificating to the crowd about the hidden world that only the dumb ass sheeple can't see.

"......and for another thing, jet fuel doesn't even burn that hot man. Only about 600 degrees max. The fucking melting point of steel is clear up around 1200. It doesn't make any god damn sense. They found fucking melted steel in the debris. Where the hell did that come from?"

I listen to his rant for a little bit, the preacher not even slowing down to take a breath. As long as you can keep talking without a break, no one else will ever get a word in. I can tell that several of the other kids want to break in, eager young pups, their heads filled with what passes for original thought, but he isn't giving them a chance. Stupid uneducated little shit. Thinking he's so smart without ever once having a single logical idea. Regurgitating some random crap that he read on the internet one day. I believe in live and let live, I'm a Libertarian, but that's no excuse for stupidity. I can't stand these kind of people. I stand up and walk deeper into the house.

I make two circuits and smoke my way through my second joint before I see her. Living room, dining room, kitchen, backyard, through a sliding glass door into a bedroom. You can go anywhere you want at one of these parties. As long as a door is open or unlocked, it's all free game. Nothing worth stealing except drugs anyways, and those are all freely given.

She's sitting alone on an old musty green couch on the back porch. There's a fire blazing in an oil drum surrounded by a variety of people in various states of reality. Some talking and some dancing around the flames. She sits with a beer in her hand, watching the fire, her pale blue eyes glassy and reflecting the fire. She's just a slip of a girl, thin almost to the point of gauntness. Her hair is dishwater blonde, long and straight. It frames a face with sharp features. The flickering flames in the barrel create a dance of light and shadows all around her. Her space never darkens. I catch myself staring. Here in this den of crackheads, surrounded by detritus slowly circling the drain, is an angel.

She looks away from the fire and looks at me, catching me staring. I don't avert my gaze. She's the most beautiful thing I've ever seen. I can't look away. I'm afraid if I do she'll disappear and I'll never see her again. She lowers her head, looks down at her feet, then looks up at me again. I've never been shy. I've been through enough that I'm pretty hard to intimidate. I'm not like these fucking kids. I smile and walk up to the couch. I see her give me the once over as I approach. I know what she sees. An older man. A thick head of black hair streaked with gray. A body more fit than most men my age. There's not much to do in prison except read and work out. I hold out the bottle of tequila and shake it. She looks up at me for a few seconds, doing nothing, then reaches out and takes the bottle. She swallows a healthy pull. I sit down next to her.

"Hi. My name's Paul."

"I'm Lindsey." Her voice is soft and quiet, a little hard to hear over the constant booming of the music.

"Nice to meet you Lindsey, is it all right if I call you Linds?"

"Why would you want to call me that?"

"I don't know. You just seem more like a Linds. Plus it's a hell of a time saver to cut off that extra syllable."

Her lips curl in a smile showing a row of perfectly white teeth. A short snort of laughter escapes from her.

"You're funny."

She hands back the tequila bottle and I take another pull to try and hide the fact that I'm grinning like an idiot. She looks up at me, her head slightly dipped.

"How do you know Davey?"

"Who's Davey?"

"The guy who owns the house. This is his party."

"Oh. I don't know Davey. Skeeter brought me here. I've been staying with my buddy Larry for the past few months and he wanted me to get out of the house for a little while so he could have some alone time with his old lady."

"Oh, that was nice of you."

"Yeah, well his old lady doesn't really like me much. Thinks I'm some kind of low life. But Larry is a pretty good guy. We were in the Marines together."

Larry's girlfriend has never actually come out and told me she doesn't like me. She doesn't have the guts to actually call someone a piece of shit to their face. She never says a word, but it's definite that she doesn't like me. She never tries to hide the look of disgust she always has on her face when she sees me. She never tries to hide her disdain. When I first moved in I tried to be nice to her. Tried to start a few conversations but only got curt responses back. I don't know why she doesn't like me. Anymore, the feeling is mutual. Both Larry and I had been pretty wild in our Marine days. Maybe she's worried that Larry's going to revert back to how he used to be.

The tequila and joints must be taking effect. I come back out of my own head realizing that Linds is asking me a question and expects some kind of response.

"What?"

"I asked why doesn't she like you much?"

"Probably because I was in jail for the past five years."

The words pour out of me. I don't even consider lying about it. I was in jail. It was something that I had done. I made some mistakes and I paid for them. I don't feel any shame about it.

She stares at me quietly for a little bit. Her eyes focusing and unfocusing. At least I think they are. It's hard to tell. My own vision keeps wavering on the edge of clarity.

"What were you in jail for?"

"Made some mistakes. Me and a couple buddies were cooking meth."

"Why?"

"At the time I was addicted to it."

I take out my third joint and light it, taking in a deep draw to make sure it's truly lit. I offer it to her. She takes the joint out of my hand and takes a deep drag. She lets out a short series of coughs. I smile as I take back the joint.

"I'm not addicted anymore, prison cleaned me up pretty good. To be honest, it was probably one of the better things to happen to me."

"So what are you doing now?"

"I'm working as a fabricator at an engineering firm. I was a combat engineer in the Marines. The engineers design it. I build it."

"Sounds like a pretty good job."

"Yeah."

Her eyes break from mine and look out over the scene of the dancers around the burning barrel. One is down on the ground, convulsing, and the others keeping dancing, careful not to tread on his flailing limbs. What is this girl doing here? What is this angel doing here in these ruins?

"Looks like Petey's epilepsy is acting up again."

"Is that Petey on the ground?"

"Yeah."

"Should we do anything for him?"

"No, he'll come out of it in a little bit."

"What are you doing here?"

"What?"

"You don't belong here."

"What?"

"You're too good for this place. This is the kind of place where if you hang out too long it's just going to drag you down into the shit. This place is quicksand."

"What are you doing here then?"

"I've been through enough shit that I know what to avoid. I've already made my mistakes."

"Oh."

"Do you want to get out of here?"

14

"What?"

"I saw a Pancake House about ten blocks up the road when Skeeter drove me here. Do you want to go get some pancakes?"

I can see the gears turning in her head. Calculating the risks of going off with a complete stranger she met at a crackhouse to go get some pancakes.

"Sure, why not."

I stand up, take her by the hand and lead her out of the house. Past the dancers in the backyard, past the couple having sex in the back bedroom, past the open market of drugs in the living room. Right out the front door. I hand the bottle of tequila to some random kid as we walk out. Linds stares and watches it disappear back into the depths. We go out into the night and start walking up the darkened street.

Her voice seems louder now that we're alone.

"How old are you?"

"Thirty-nine."

"You don't look it."

"No, everyone tends to look pretty young in my family. We never lose our hair."

"I like your hair."

"Thanks."

We walk for a bit in silence. Police sirens scream in the distance as we approach the more major streets. She moves lithely beside me. I eye her curves by the glow of the streetlight.

"How old are you?"

"Seventeen."

"Oh."

Shit.

Chapter 3

None of the 9/11 conspiracies ever made much sense to me. All of them are so fucking complicated and convoluted. Nobody on the planes. The towers getting brought down by controlled demolition. A cruise missile hitting the Pentagon. Shit. It's not really the lack of scientific understanding that bothers me, it's the total lack of thought about the number of people. The more convoluted the plot, the more people who are going to be involved. Some of the theories I've heard would require easily a thousand people keeping their mouths shut. Can you imagine a thousand people keeping their mouths shut? What's wrong with what we've been officially told? It makes the most sense. A couple of crazies, working with limited support, hijack some planes and fly them into some buildings. What's so hard to believe about nineteen men who believed in something so much they were willing to kill thousands of people and themselves for it. Extremists. The only question I have is whether or not we were told the truth about what those men believed. I don't know. Every group has it's fanatics.

David, Twerk, and I stand in the driveway in our underwear and watch the old farmhouse burn. The house's outer skin has already started to fall away. Blackened framing revealed like broken ribs, caressed by fingers of fire. I can't take my eyes off of the flames. They dance up into the sky, orange tongues twisting and turning with fiery whips snapping fifty feet into the air. Everything moves in slow motion. It's beautiful. By far the most beautiful thing I have ever seen. The rest of the world shrinks back and disappears. In my eyes there is nothing but the fire. My brain is enraptured. I feel as though I am seeing fire for the first time in my life. As though I've never before seen its wonderful chaotic powers of destruction. Nothing else matters. Nothing else is important.

Each buffet of heated air is a lovers embrace. Sweat beads on my forehead and bare torso. My eyes refuse to blink. They refuse to chance missing any of the splendor. The fire roars and throws itself into the air. A flaming sea assaulting the shore. A firestorm. A conflagration. It is as though the spirit of the house is escaping. Energy bursting forth from once passive molecules, screaming their defiance at the uncaring world. Knowing that soon they will be gone, consumed, but free at last. Potential energy to kinetic energy. Their physical forms dropping away as smoke and ash. Their spirits transcending into a higher plain.

I want to join them. I want to be free. I want to feel the shackles of my body drop away, releasing me from this cruel existence. I want to step forward into the fire. I want to join it, meld with it, be consumed by it. I want my spirit to scream as it breaks free. I want to fly upward into the sky and become one with the world around me. It all seems so simple. So very very simple. It's the answer I've been looking for my entire life. All I have to do is start walking forward. All I have to do is take that first step.

Both of my feet remain firmly planted on the ground. Somewhere deep in my addled brain remains resistance to the plans of my fevered mind. Down deep within is still the primal urge to protect my own life. The animalistic need to survive. I stand with my body and mind engaged in a civil war. One striving to move closer, and other trying to move farther away.

It had all started so small. A small explosion and then small tongues of flame across the kitchen. Some no bigger than the flames on the candles Diane used to light before we made love, or the ones she used to light on the back of the toilet to hide the smell of farts. The small flames had grown. They had come together. It hadn't taken long. It was as though a deeper consciousness controlled their actions, rallying and sending them forth on the attack.

We never really had a chance of winning. First went the kitchen, then the dining room, then the living room. By the time the attack was mounted on the second floor the three of us had given up and fallen back to the driveway where we stood and exulted in the beauty of our loss. We had created this from nothing. Where once an entire house had stood, solid in frame and foundation, now stood a growing mountain of flames. I feel powerful. I feel like a god.

I hear sirens. The second story collapses into the first. I'm surprised it's taken so long. The nearest neighbor is five miles away, but you would think a fifty-foot flaming pyre would be noticed a little quicker. None of us turn to watch the fire trucks and police cars drive up. They pull around us and park on the weed-filled front lawn, once verdant and green, once the pride and joy of my father, now left to its own devices and dying. It will look funny out here without the house.

The firefighters get out their hoses and start to douse the burning abode. David thinks it's funny and starts to laugh hysterically, his face contorted into a ghastly shape, his shrill giggles silent, muted by the fire's roar. The firefighters seem to get the idea and turn their hoses onto the walls of the other structures to cool them and keep them from being taken by the hungering beast. The old barn that my great grandfather built. The shed, still full of my father's lawn mower and tools. It doesn't matter. Everything is worn and broken. None of it holds any value.

Policemen surround us. Some walk slowly forward, their hands open and exposed, showing they are unarmed. Their steps are slow and exaggerated. I get the sense that time is not moving at the same rate for them as it is for me. For them, all their movements seem normal. Others hang back, their hands toying with the butts of their holstered pistols. I ignore them. They are just men. How can they compare to the depths of the inferno.

I recognize the police officer in front of me. His name is Tom. We went to school together. He'd been tight end on the football team in high school. He was a nice guy. His dad was a great man. Tom's face is tight and I can see the fear in his eyes. He looks like he's approaching a strange dog, and he doesn't know which way it's going to jump. I keep my eyes focused on the fire. I can't ignore it, but I smile in hopes that it will make Tom feel more relaxed.

"How are you doing Paul?" Tom's voice sounds like it's coming from a long distance away. It's slow and echoey. "Are you all right?"

I widen my smile even more, feel my face contort until my cheeks hurt. Tom needs to relax. Everything is okay.

"Yeah. I'm fine. It's one helluva fire."

"Yeah. It is."

One of the officers behind Tom says something I can't hear. Tom half turns his head to listen, but his eyes never leave me. He nods his head and says something back. He turns back to me and his voice echoes again across the distance.

"We're going to have to take you in Paul. Is there going to be any trouble?"

Take me in. The idea rattles through my head and gets lost in the vortex of my thoughts.

"Sure Tom. Take me in. No trouble at all."

I guess I'm going to jail. Probably about time. After all, we did burn down the house. Jail seems like the logical next step. It doesn't really matter. All that really matters is the fire. It's like looking god in the eye. Every synapse in my head is popping, trying to interpret what I'm seeing.

Tom takes a pair of handcuffs from his belt and walks forward. Every step is ridiculously slow. He moves behind me and I feel him take my arms and press them together behind my back. I feel the cold metal close on each wrist. I don't move a muscle. I don't even tense up. With the fire burning before me, how can anything be bad.

My accomplices don't take to the change quite as well as I do. As they handcuff David his laughter just gets louder and harder. He bends over double and starts convulsing, unable to get enough air between his gales of hilarity. For the first time since we came out of the house I notice that his eyebrows are burned off. I try to reach up to feel if mine are gone as well, but the handcuffs stop me. The movement makes Tom tighten his grip on my arm.

Twerk takes the change the hardest. As the handcuffs close on his wrists he lets out a howl of fury and pummels himself into the nearest officer. They go down in a tangle and he throws himself up and down, trying to use his body and head as a club to bludgeon the officer to death. Another policeman comes up behind Twerk with his gun drawn and gives him several hard whacks to the back of the head with the pistol butt. Twerk goes down like a sack of potatoes. His nose is bloody. He lays on the ground and cries like a child. I stand perfectly still. Tom seems to appreciate it.

19

They lead each one of us to a separate car and put us in the back seat. I stare out the window at the burning house. The entire structure has collapsed but it's still an impressive inferno. As long as I can see the fire everything is going to be okay. I can feel it keeping me calm. Drawing me in and keeping me safe. An officer climbs into the front seat and the car jerks and begins to head back up the driveway. I twist to try and look out the back window so I can still see the fire. We pull out onto the main road and the car picks up speed. I stare at the shrinking dot. A star brought down from the heavens.

The burning house disappears behind a set of low hills. I start screaming until I pass out.

The world flashes into wakefulness. The blackness fades away. I'm sweating heavily. One arm lays across my chest, the shirt underneath it soaked and salty. My throat feels raw. My whole body is sore. I feel empty. Drained out. The darkness of dreamless sleep beckons seductively for me to return. A crashing noise out of sight. I can't remember where I am. I feel a foam pad under my back and dry dirt covered ground under one of my hands. My head lays next to a brand new aftermarket tire on a large matte black vehicle. It's daylight, but the world around me is shadowy. A large tan tarp blocks out the sun, stretched slightly from the top of a 1987 Chevy Suburban to the ground in a makeshift lean to. Alice. The Suburban's name is Alice. The desert. I'm out in the middle of nowhere in the desert. I'm fifteen miles from the nearest highway. I drove out here last night. I drove out here in Alice. We left Marfa at one in the morning, at least that was what it said on the bank clock as we drove out of town.

What time is it? Obviously still day, but how late have I slept? There's no way to tell. We don't have a working watch with us. My grandfather's old wind up watch is in Alice's jockey box, but it hasn't been wound in years. It's been in there since Dad owned Alice. We did have a digital watch when we left Sweetwater, but Linds gave it to the kids to play with. I'm sure it's still somewhere in Alice. I just have no idea where. I can't sleep the day away. I have shit to do. I need to get up.

I sit up. A six year old child plays with an old doll and a pile of pebbles. Philip. For a moment I think it's Philip. No, that's impossible. This is Rachel. Little Rachel with the boy's haircut and the big brown eyes just like mine. Rachel who gets that gleam in her eye that you know means trouble. She's my favorite of the two kids. Stone looks more like her mother. Light blonde hair and blue eyes. No, not exactly like her mother. Linds has light blue eyes. Stone's are a much deeper blue, like the ocean off of Grenada. Rachel looks more like me. She looks more like Philip.

I must be tired. I haven't slept much in the past few days. Philip would be a grown man by now, twenty-one, legal to drink. Diane came to the jail six months after I got put in with prepared legal documents in hand. She'd been smart about it. She'd waited long enough for all the shit to get out of my system. It was the first time she had come to see me since I got put in. She didn't bring Philip. She didn't want him to see what I was. Diane wanted a divorce. By that time I was clean enough that I couldn't really blame her. I signed without hesitating. It was the best thing I could do for her.

When was the last time I saw Philip? God only knows. Most of those years didn't get saved. The few memories I have are fairly fuzzy. It's probably for the better. I can remember holding him as a baby. Playing with him when he was little. I can remember a birthday party where all the other parents took their kids home early and Diane started yelling like she always did. Was it the time I went to pick him up from school and he pretended not to know me? Was it the time I came to the house to surprise him and nobody would open the door? I can remember his little face peeking through the curtains at me as I beat on the wood and Diane yelled that she was going to call the cops. I guess it doesn't matter. It's been something like fifteen years since I've seen him. It just feels like something I should remember.

Rachel looks up from the game she's playing and and notices that I'm awake. She grins at me, her smile full of crooked teeth and gaps already paid off by the tooth fairy. I smile back.

"Hey Daddy, did you have a good nap?"

"Yeah Monkey, I did."

"You got loud."

"Sorry Monkey."

"My name's Rachel, not Monkey."

"I know that Monkey."

She giggles. "You're silly."

I look around at our shadowy world made up of bare ground, Alice, and the tarp stretched overhead. Rachel goes back to picking up the pebbles around her and putting them in a pile.

"What are you playing?"

"I'm helping Lucy find diamonds. Lucy wants diamond jewelry and some of these rocks have diamonds in them."

"I'm sure Lucy is pretty enough that someday somebody will give her diamonds."

"Maybe, but things are better when you get off your ass and get them yourself."

I smile a little wider and try to keep myself from laughing.

"Very true, but watch your language."

"Okay."

"Where's your mother?"

"She's sitting on the other side reading a book and having a smoke. She told me not to bother her unless I need to use the honey hole." Rachel puts down her doll and looks up at me. "Are you hungry?"

"Yeah. Would you mind grabbing me one of the MRE's out of Alice?"

"Sure. No problem-o."

Rachel gets up and walks around the back of Alice where the rear doors are open. I watch her go and hear her pull herself up and start rummaging around. It's so strange how easily she's taking to all of this. I guess everything is normal to you if you're a child. Even abandoning your home and camping in the middle of the desert. As long as Linds and I keep our cool, the kids should stay calm. As long as we act like things are normal, the kids will think it's normal.

Rachel jumps back to the ground and brings me a cup of water filled from the big tank and one of the many military surplus MRE's I bought for the trip. They're not supposed to be sold to civilians, but there's no actual law stopping it from happening. I purchased most of what we have on various internet sites. I found the rest at garage sales.

"Thanks Monkey."

"You're welcome Daddy."

I look at the MRE. Jambalaya. I try to hide my grimace. Rachel watches me until I open the box and give her the crackers inside. I've

22

never liked the crackers. She munches on them and goes back to her game of collecting pebbles, humming to herself happily. I fill the flameless heater pouch with water and let it heat the food while I eat the cereal bar and then chew the package of coffee grounds. I don't like coffee, but I need the caffeine. The jambalaya finishes heating. I open the pouch and choke it down as fast as I can. It tastes like dog shit. Definitely the worst of the possible flavors. I'm guessing whoever designed the concoction never actually tasted real jambalaya.

My meal finished, I scrub my hands with the provided moist towelette and separate the remaining items in the MRE into two piles. Matches and toilet paper back into Alice. The rest of the crap into a garbage bag to be thrown into the honey hole and buried when we leave. It's best not to leave any trace that we've been here. You never know who might be watching.

I pull my pocket knife out of my right pocket and go to cleaning my nails. The handle is worn. The blades are thin. It's an old knife. Close to forty years old. I've had it for a long time. Tom's dad gave it to me when I was a kid. A gift when I was ten. I've always taken good care of it. Kept it sharp. Kept it dry. Kept it clean. Age is just a number. If you take care of things they'll last damn near forever.

Chapter 4

A false flag operation is a military or terrorist attack where an attacker disguises themselves in order to gain a military or political advantage. Everyone has heard of the most famous example, Hitler burning down the Reichstag so he could seize total control of the German government. Of course we Americans are not so innocent ourselves. In 1898 the battleship Maine mysteriously blew up in Havana harbor, leading to the Spanish-American War. In 1915 German submarines sank the passenger liner Lusitania, drawing the US into World War I. The fact that the Lusitania was carrying arms was never mentioned until ninety years later. In 1941 Frankie Roosevelt ignored warnings that the Japanese were going to attack Pearl Harbor, giving him the support necessary to bring the US into World War II. In 1962 the US considered Operation Northwoods, fake terrorist attacks that would be blamed on Cuba to provide the provocation to go to war. In 1964 a warship fired at radar ghosts in the Gulf of Tonkin. The US government called it an attack by North Vietnam. US troops poured into the jungle. In 1991 a Kuwaiti girl gave testimony to the atrocities Saddam Hussein was committing in her home country. The testimony spurred the US to war. It was later found out that she was the daughter of Kuwait's ambassador to the US. How are things so different today?

The man, I think his name is Roy, at least I'm pretty sure it's Roy, yammers on at me. I half listen to his bullshit as I tinker with Alice's distributor cap on the workbench. I don't have time for this bullshit. I'm on a deadline. Roy doesn't give a damn. He's a government bureaucrat. A self-important county official who has the great state of Texas backing him up and a union membership card in his pocket. Both guarantee he'll never have to be in a rush for anything. Without warning I turn around and punch him in his skinny face. Not really, that's just in my brain. Physically I just stand there and nod, pretending to pay attention.

Roy, or Ron, or whomever, must have allergies. His nose wheezes with each breath. His voice is high and reedy. There is nothing about him that doesn't get on my nerves.

"So you can understand then, sir, why it is that I needed to come out here and give everything a look see. It's nothing against you personally, it's just that I have a duty to investigate situations when certain factors come together to suggest the possibility of wrongdoing."

God save me. He's one of those jack-off's who uses ten words when one would suffice. The kind of guy who thinks that he can hide his lack of intelligence by filling the air with big words. I quit fiddling with Alice's distributor cap, resisting the urge to throw it on the ground for dramatic effect, and turn to look at him.

"Look, the only thing wrong around here is you harassing me for doing absolutely nothing wrong. I'm not hurting anyone, cheating anyone, or whatever the hell else you think I might be doing."

The skinny little man blinks at me through his wire frame eyeglasses. "In my experience sir, people doing things wrong hardly ever hold the opinion that they're doing anything wrong. But the law works on absolutes, not personal opinions."

"Maybe in your opinion."

The weedy bureaucrat doesn't say anything. Instead his eyes start to rove across the barn again. Searching for the evidence that he knows must be there, hidden away amongst the scattered tools and auto parts. Alice sits in the corner on jacks with all four tires off. Next to her sits a three speed turbo hydromatic 400 transmission that I just took out this morning, right next to the four speed turbo hyrodmatic 700R4 that I was hoping to get in today. Other parts of her lay strewn nearby.

In various corners are other projects, some already finished. An engine for a 1978 Chevy Luv. A half put together automatic transmission for a Datsun. A pile of carburetors for various makes and models. If Roy had shown up a week earlier the barn would be twice as full and I would look twice as guilty. I haven't taken on any new side projects for weeks and the backlog is mostly cleared out. Parked just outside the open barn door is a freshly tuned up 1989 Pontiac Grand Prix waiting for its buyer to show up tomorrow. I follow his gaze as he looks around, noting everywhere he stops to stare. I laugh to myself when his gaze pauses on the nudey auto calendar on the wall above the couch that used to be Alice's third seat. Poor bastard probably doesn't get that much pussy. He comes back to me, his eyes meeting my nose. Little pissant can't even look me in the eye.

"I'm sorry for the inconvenience sir, but all we are trying to do is ascertain that you are not running an unlicensed mechanics or auto parts shop, and to make sure you're not running a commercial business in a place clearly zoned residential without the proper permits."

I laugh out loud, maybe a little exaggerated, but the whole thing is just too ridiculous.

"Look, I've already explained everything to you time and time again. All of these parts are either for my personal vehicles or are things I've fixed up as favors for friends and family. Sure, maybe some of them do some favors for me in return, but there's no law against that. I've given you a list of people to contact to verify that I'm working on their stuff. So why don't you do whatever it is you have to do and let me get back to work."

The bureaucrat lets out a little sigh. Even his sigh is wispy.

"That's what I've been trying to do. Now, if you just allow me to take some photographs I can be on my way."

"Fine, whatever you need to do."

I go back to work on Alice's distributor cap. Roy takes out a small camera and starts taking pictures of everything, even the junk pile. I ignore him. He's a suspicious wormy little bastard, but he's certainly not stupid. I am running an unlicensed mechanics shop, though theoretically everyone who comes in is at least a friend of a friend. I also buy junkers, strip them out, and then sell the parts on eBay. I don't have time for a real job, things are moving too fast. Everything Roy thinks is happening is technically correct. I just think it's ridiculous that a man can't start a business in his own home without dotting a bunch of i's, crossing a bunch of t's. Why should I have to pay a bunch of fees, fees that do nothing but guarantee some little shit has a job.

"I've taken all my pictures sir."

"Good for you."

"I'll be going now. I'll be back in a week or two after I get a hold of these contacts."

Roy sticks out his hand and looks at me expectantly. I stare at him and don't move a muscle. He stands there for a few seconds, unsure what to do, and then turns around and walks out of the barn. One or two weeks. All of the contacts are real people, but only a few are going to stand up to any scrutiny. It doesn't really matter. Anymore, one to two weeks is a long time.

With the bureaucrat gone I get back to work. First I install Alice's new transmission and then her new heavy-duty shocks up front. Things with Alice are coming along quite nicely. I've already installed heavy duty shocks on her rear and heavy-duty struts and axles. Four brand new heavy-duty tires lean against the barn wall. The check off list is getting smaller by the day. I still need to finish putting back together her electrical system, the clutch still needs to be rebuilt, the secondary pup tank needs to be installed in the back, and I want to go over the exhaust system one more time to see if I can't get her to run any quieter. Still a lot to do, and probably not much time to do it, but I feel confident that I can get it all done in time. The clock is ticking.

It's starting to get late. The last thing I do before calling it an evening is rip out the old AM/FM radio with cassette tape player and throw it on the junk heap. Anything that picks up transmissions can be modified to transmit. It's just safer to be without it. If the family gets bored on the trip we can always just have a sing-a-long.

I wash the grease off my hands in a bucket of water just outside the barn, scrubbing them with gritty soap to make sure they're clean. Linds doesn't like it when I go into the house with greasy hands. Sure the house is just an old single wide next to the burned out foundation of the original farmhouse, but for now it's still home. There's no reason to start fights over little things. Better to keep the waters smooth.

When I walk into the house the family is already at the small table in the kitchen. I go to the stove and pile dinner on a plate. It's cheap unnaturally orange macaroni and cheese with hot dogs mixed in. The kids love this kind of stuff. I don't really care. It tastes like crap, but it fills you up. Plus it's cheap. I sit down at the table.

"Hi Daddy," says Rachel.

"Hi Monkey." Rachel goes back to happily eating. Stone and Linds don't say anything. "Evening Stone, how was the book learning with Mom today?"

My eight year old with the pretty golden blonde hair raises her downcast eyes long enough to answer. "Fine."

We eat in awkward silence for a bit. I get up and grab a beer from the fridge and then sit back down. It tastes good after a long day's work.

"You should really come out and take a look at Alice, Linds, she's really coming along well."

Lindsey nods but doesn't say anything. Like Stone, she mostly keeps her eyes on her plate. Can't say that I blame her too much. It's pretty tiring caring for and homeschooling two kids all day. I wish she'd talk more. She's been pretty silent since we left Portland. I miss our conversations. I smile lovingly at her and go back to eating my chow. Rachel natters on about her day, the adventures and foibles of a six year old, and I nod and laugh appreciatively at the appropriate times, but my mind is really somewhere else. As my daughter talks about learning her addition tables my mind goes through checklists of supplies. What we already have. What we still need. Thinking about it for the thousandth time to make sure I haven't forgotten anything important.

The kids finish dinner and rush into the living room to play with their toys and watch videos on the VCR. Linds has been wanting to get a DVD player. The VCR works. VHS's are only a quarter at the Goodwill. Besides, everything here is temporary. I put my dishes in the sink, grab another beer, and go back to Linds' and my bedroom to use the computer. I plug the computer in, attach the ethernet cable, and turn it on. Having the computer on makes me nervous, but it's a necessary evil. It's not like I'm that hard to find here just outside Sweetwater.

I peruse eBay first, looking for things I might need. I find a seller with two cases of MREs available and I hit the "Buy It Now" button. I make a note on a scratchpad of $150 on the First National gold card.

28

Before we came back to Texas I never had a credit card. Now I have fifteen, all with varying limits, some under my name, some under Linds', even one under Stone's name. I have to write everything down to keep track. Overdrafting gets their attention. I don't need the attention. My mechanicing and parting out cars only brings in so much. I was raised to never believe in credit, but it really doesn't matter. Soon nothing will matter. It's not really stealing, at least compared to how much the bastards at the banks steal from us.

Seeing nothing else of interest I move on to the news websites. I have a whole list that I check every evening, none of the corporate controlled lackey sites, all independents. "Fed Secretly Discussing Further Quantitative Easing", "Government Continues to Adjust Statistics To Hide Growing Unemployment", "Big Banks Donate More To Congressional Coffers", "Debt Ceiling Expected To Be Raised Again." I glance at some, but ignore most of them. These types of articles are here every day. Evidence of widening cracks in the foundation. Proof that the whole thing is eventually going to come down.

"Surveillance Drones Sighted Over Major Cities", "Man Arrested For Blogging About Government", "President Signs New Executive Order To Protect Americans", "Police Declare Cincinnati a Gun Free Zone To Fight Crime", "Federal Reserve Doubles Gold Reserves In Past Six Months". These stories I pay a little more attention to, but again, I rarely read through all of them. This has been a step-by-step process since the signing of the Patriot Act. Every week brings new rules and regulations to protect our freedoms by slowly dismantling them. It's just further proof of the decay. Further proof of how afraid those in power really are.

A few stories stick out. One, "US Troops Moving Inland", details an increase in military convoys moving by rail and roads through the American heartland, largely noted by train spotters and other such hobbyists. Another, "Homeland Security Buys Five Thousand Armored Cars", leaves open the question of why the DHS needed such heavy fire-power? The final one to catch my eye is the most alarming. It's like a warning light flashing on the computer screen. "Government Raises Terror Alert Level". I read through it carefully, then read through it again. No reasoning for the increased alert level is cited anywhere in the article. I cross-check with a few similar websites. Same thing, higher alert level, but no reason why.

I plug the phone into the wall, pick up the receiver, and dial a number I have memorized. A landline is safer than a cellphone. Most people think it's the other way around. They're idiots. The phone rings once, twice, three times. I drum my fingers impatiently on the desk.

"Hello?" Larry sounds tired. I glance at the clock. It's already past eleven.

"Larry, have you checked out the news today?"

"No, I've been busy."

"Get online and check-out behindthecurtain.com."

"What? Christ Paul, not this crap again."

"It's all shaping up like I thought it would Larry. Something is building up."

"Damn it Paul, I really don't have time for this. Madeline had a ballet recital this evening and I'm pretty sure I'm coming down with something."

"Jesus Larry, there's some things more important than your personal crap. I think the shits starting to boil over."

"What's it matter Paul? I have an emergency kit laid out at the house, what more do you want from me? Even if the shit did hit the fan there's nothing we can do about it."

My hand tightens its grip on the receiver. Larry was more gung-ho about this kind of stuff six months ago. Then again, he has always had trouble concentrating on something for any length of time.

"That's your opinion."

"I gotta go Paul. We can talk about this tomorrow. I have to get up early and report in for a Marine Reserve physical."

I feel a cold bead of sweat drip down my back. "What did you say?"

"I said I have to go get a Marine Reserve physical. Something to do with the terror alert getting jacked so high."

"Damn it Larry. Why didn't you tell me? When was the last time you had to go in for a physical?"

"I don't know, probably, the last time the alert got this high, it's been awhile."

"Yeah, a long while."

"Listen, we can talk more tomorrow. I have to go to bed. Good night."

The phone goes dead before I have a chance to say it back. I hang up the phone, turn off the computer, and unplug all the wires from the wall. The room goes dark and I sit for a few minutes rubbing my temples and thinking. I get up and walk back out to the living room. The kids are already in bed and Linds is asleep on the couch. I don't wake her. I go outside and head for the barn. I have a lot of work to get done.

Chapter 5

It goes without saying that 9/11 changed everything. Within forty-five days of the towers coming down Congress began passing a series of measures that stole away the rights of the American citizenry in the name of national security. The President declared a state of emergency, giving the government the ability to suspend the rights of habeas corpus and to suspend the use of grand juries for trials involving military personnel. Several high profile anthrax attacks added further fuel to the panic. Congress passed the Patriot Act by a wide margin. Few actually bothered to read it. The Patriot Act allowed for indefinite detentions, gave law enforcement the ability to search a home or business without the owner's knowledge or consent, expanded the FBI's ability to do searches and wiretaps without a court order, and expanded law enforcement's access to personal records. In essence, as long as the word terrorism was used, the Constitution was little more than toilet paper. The state of emergency has been renewed every year since. The Patriot Act, originally only meant to last five years, was reauthorized in 2006 and 2011.

I duck under the tarp and into the bright Texas sunshine. The light is blinding after the dimness and it takes my eyes nearly a full minute to adjust. I stare down at the dry gray sand and bunches of yellowed grass at my feet until I can handle the brilliance of the world around me. Alice sits near a small knoll, its steep side blocking out my view to the north. To the east and the west the desert rises and falls like a frozen sea, sagebrush and greasewoods floating on the surface as far as the eye can see. To the south the land is the same, but on the horizon the land gets rougher, hills rise upward, topped by outcroppings of basalt.

I can hear Linds snickering back underneath the tarp. Her voice drips with sarcasm. "Have a good scouting expedition. Don't forget to put tin foil in your hat so no one can read your mind."

She snickers to herself again. I ignore her and adjust the backpack on my shoulders. A couple water bottles, a few granola bars, and a couple joints in one pocket to help me relax. A man deserves to relax, even when on the run. I can feel the comforting weight of my pocketknife in my right pocket. I look up at the blue sky, mostly clear except for a few long overstretched clouds. The blue hides what hangs above, but it doesn't matter. A single man walking through the middle of nowhere isn't an easy thing to find, even for them.

Eight year old Stone is kneeling in the shadow of the steep dirt hillside, poking something that I can't see with a stick. Her long honey blonde hair drifts lightly with the occasional puff of hot wind. She's skinny as hell, all knees and elbows. She'll probably grow up to be a beauty, just like her mother. That's why I named her Stone, as in stone cold fox. Her mother wanted to name her Cherry. I sure as hell wasn't going to let my daughter have a stripper name. I chose Stone while the epidural still had Linds. Linds had been mad, but I had promised she could name the next one. Thank god Rachel got a normal name.

I walk up to my daughter. "What ya poking at Stone?"

"Nothing, just an old dead rabbit."

"Well, be careful, it's probably full of disease."

Stone turns and looks at me with her deep blue eyes. She has the eyes of an old woman. A world weary look. Beth would have called Stone an old soul if she had ever seen her, but Beth had been long dead and rotting in the ground by the time Stone was born.

"I know Dad. I'll be careful."

Stone turns and goes back to poking the dead rabbit with her stick. She wasn't always like this. When she was younger she use to be a little chatterbox, always smiling and giggling. Now she rarely says anything, staying quiet and keeping stone faced. I worry about her all the time. She's much too young to carry so much on her shoulders, but I don't know what to do about it. Rachel was too young to really remember any of the shitty times. Stone wasn't so lucky. She's a tough little shit. I think about going up and hugging her, but decide not to. Stone doesn't like to be held.

I adjust my backpack and start walking south towards the distant hills. I pull out one of my joints and light it. After a few thousand yards I turn and look back towards the knoll. I can hardly tell the tarp covering Alice is there. The tarp is tan and covered in dirt and small stones glued on by spray can epoxy, plus a couple random weeds and bunches of grass I threw on top when we set up camp this morning. Close up the camouflage is pretty much worthless, but from a distance, or from the air, it's hard differentiate from the empty land around it.

We ran drills with the kids when we were still in Sweetwater. I'd throw the tarp up over the swing set and then make helicopter noises. The kids would run across the yard to hide under the tarp, Rachel giggling and Stone even smiling a little bit. They had thought it was a great game. Linds used to join us early on, but she soon grew tired of the game and wouldn't play anymore.

I turn back south and continue walking. I've pretty much memorized the topographic maps of this area, but maps are nothing compared to actually seeing it. It's important that I scout out the next night's route. The fact that I get to get away from Alice and the family for a little bit is just an added benefit. Out here in the desert I have no worries. As I walk my muscles unclench. I start to relax.

I don't hurry. I walk at a leisurely pace. I find an old watering hole in a depression. Cracked dried earth surrounding thick dark brown mud. A little bit of remaining water covered in bright green algae. Little brown birds flap around, playing in their receding oasis. I sit and watch them for a little while, finishing my first joint and starting a second, and then continue on my way. Insects chirp and rattle as I walk by, and the silence is occasionally punctuated by a bird song. It's a nice day.

I've always loved being in the outdoors. Walking out alone in the middle of nowhere is the closest thing to heaven for me on God's green earth. With each step I feel like I'm floating. I'm not tired at all, and after just three hours or so I'm already practically to the hills. The landscape around me gets rougher, and the frozen waves grow higher.

I reach the top of a shallow draw and let my gaze follow its softly rolling slope towards the bottom. Shit. I drop flat to the ground, my heart beating rapidly. Shit. I shouldn't have let my mind wander like that. I need to concentrate more. Now is not the time to be fucking around and feeling at peace. Below me, hidden from view until you're practically on top of it, sits a small farmstead.

I sit perfectly still for a full five minutes, just like they taught us in basic. I let my breathing slow, but my heartbeat continues at a mile a minute. Slowly I reach down and put my hands around the small pair of binoculars that hang from a cord around my neck. Slowly I raise them to my eyes, focus them, and examine the signs of civilization below me. My eyes move across the scene bit by bit. I let out a sigh of relief.

The farmstead is old, it's obvious that no one has lived here in some time. The big wooden barn sits mostly roofless, the walls bowed inward, collapsing in a super slow motion implosion. The two-storey farm-house is covered with peeling white paint. The chimney has fallen over and the roof sags. Most of the windows are broken. The remains of an old corral sits next to the barn, not a single fence still standing. Slightly away from the other buildings sits four stone walls in a tight little box except for an empty doorway. The whole thing is blackened by fire. Everything looks long abandoned. Maybe it's over a hundred years old. It's hard to tell out in the desert. The lack of moisture preserves everything.

I wait on my belly for another five minutes, looking for any signs of movement. Everything stays still, except for a few birds sitting on the remains of the corral. I can't stay here forever. Besides, my curiosity is piqued. I get up and walk down to investigate.

It's quiet in the draw. The hillsides protect it from the wind. I go to the closest building first, the four burnt out stone walls. I peak in the doorway. It was obviously once an outhouse, though the insides are just as burnt as the outside and the hole is mostly filled in. The soil around the outhouse is still discolored from the fire. It must have been one hell of a blaze. I feel uncomfortable, like I'm interrupting something that isn't any of my business. I move towards the house.

The porch of the house is rotten and crumbling. I watch my step as I walk across it. The door and trim is a vibrant green, the paint much better preserved compared to the white of the walls. I turn the door-knob and push. The door won't budge. The house has probably settled since it was last opened. I give the door a couple kicks and force it open halfway, then walk into the dimness, brushing cobwebs out of the way.

It's like walking into a museum. The furniture sits exactly where it was left a hundred years ago. A couch and two sitting chairs sit on one side of the room, the horsehair stuffing long since torn out by rats and mice, exposing rusty springs to the outside world. Two bookcases hold old leather bound books, their bindings rotting away. An old wooden chair and writing desk sit in one corner. Five square bottles sit on top of the desk. The other side of the room is dominated by a large wooden staircase that looks like it's about ready to fall in, and several closed doors that must lead to other rooms. Everything is covered in a thick layer of dust. The house smells musty.

I take a few steps forward, putting my feet down as quietly as I can. For a moment my heart begins to beat rapidly again and I tense to escape. There are footprints in the dust. My panic is just for a moment. The footprints are old, already filling with dust themselves. I walk across the room to the bookcase and look over the titles. I pick up an old copy of *Oliver Twist*. It comes apart in my hands, the pages falling to the floor.

Above the desk hang five portraits in round wooden frames. Two large ones of a man and a woman. Three smaller ones of children. The man wears a high collared suit and has a thick bushy moustache that hides his upper lip. The woman wears a dark dress that buttons up to her chin. She appears to have some Indian blood in her, or is it Native American now, or indigenous people, I can never keep up with the latest politically correct term. Either way she has the look, high cheekbones and dark black hair. All the children appear to be teenagers, though I'm terrible at judging age. The oldest has his mother's look and the wispy beginnings of a moustache on his upper lip. The next two, a boy around fourteen and a girl around twelve, both look more like their mother. All five portraits are unsmiling, and all have the hard look of people who have long faced the hardships of west Texas. Their eyes remind me of Stone's eyes.

I walk up to the desk and open one of the drawers. It's filled with dried up fountain pens and old letterhead. I pull one sheet out and read the top.

Kraus Cattle Company
Wilhelm Kraus, Proprietor

I close the drawer and open the larger one beneath it. Inside is a large leather bound book still in good condition. The drawers fit tightly into the desk, it's a very well made. I take out the book and open it. It appears to be some kind of ledger. Each entry is made in a strong and precise hand. All the entries are in German. I flip through pages. One catches my eye as the yellowed paper slips through my fingers.

2 Januar 1919, Pferdegeschirr Reparatur, Daniel Gibbs, $11.05

I flip through all the pages and then flip through them again. The ledger stretches from 1907 until early 1920. A financial history of some long forgotten cattle ranch, hidden away here in this abandoned museum of a farmhouse. Mr. Kraus was a true German. The ledger is perfectly ordered, everything in its exact and proper place. A man of precision. Near the end of the ledger the entries become more erratic, the handwriting more jagged and rough. The last entry is dated 4 Februar 1920. The description is smudged out. After that the pages are empty, except for one near the back. There, written diagonally across the lines, in a hand that is barely recognizable, is a short message.

Die kinder sind weg und Lilith hat sich in den hugeln verschwunden.
Ich habe alles verloren. Ich bin fertig.

I feel a cold drop of sweat dribble down my spine. I put the old ledger back where I found it and close the drawer. Nothing seems right in this place. This strange time capsule feels too unreal for me to be comfortable. Too many unanswered questions. I quietly walk out of the house and force the green door back closed. My body involuntarily shivers. I walk back up to the top of the draw. It's just an old abandoned homestead, nothing to worry about.

The sun is getting close to the horizon. I hold my hand up flat like I'm shading my eyes and then put my other hand flat on top of it. Eight knuckles between the horizon and the sun. Each knuckle is fifteen minutes so I have two hours before the sun goes down. I'll have to hoof it to get back to Alice and the family before sunset.

The finger trick is one that Tom's dad taught Tom and I when we were kids and he took us out camping for the first time. We were nine years old. It was real camping, with hiking, roasting marshmallows, and sleeping out under the stars in the Guadalupe Mountains. It wasn't like the camping that Dad would make me do. The kind where I slept in an old tent in the front yard. The kind where his friend Ruby would drive down from Fort Worth to visit. I guess I shouldn't complain. Those times were few and far between. Ruby didn't last too long. No one could ever stand Dad too long. It was better when he gave up on that part of his life. Accepted that it was gone. Camping with Tom's dad, that was real camping. I smile at the memory and look back into the draw, starting to fill with shadows.

Tom's dad was always good to me. I wish I could give my girls such a life. I wish this all wasn't necessary. That house down there really creeped me out. Our trailer back in Sweetwater is probably the same way. Everything sitting exactly where we left it, slowly getting covered by dust. A home abandoned, left perfectly intact as a museum of what once had been. It's probably going to be a while until anyone gets up the guts to go in and see if we're really gone. At least I hope so. It hadn't been a bad place to live. If we could have stayed we probably could have been happy there. The girls could have gone back to school. I could have fixed things up around there. Made them look like when I was a kid again. I could have given the girls the life they deserve.

A black speck on the far horizon catches my eye. A moving dot far off over the hills. I feel my hands clench and unclench. Heavy running footsteps. A voice yelling out my name. Cursing. The tight grip of fingers around my wrist. A bright light shining in my eyes. For a moment I'm weightless, floating up into the air. I know what it is as soon as I see it. It's too far off to hear the rotors whipping the air, but I know it's a helicopter. A black metal bird flying low and searching for something. It's a long ways off, and as I watch it moves farther away. I breathe a sigh of relief, reach into my left pocket, and pull out a small plastic container. I shake out a small yellow pill, pop it into my mouth, turn, and start walking back north. I need to stay alert. This is no time to let my mind wander.

Chapter 6

In the 1950's and 1960's American abstract expressionism exploded in the art circles of Europe. Names like Jackson Pollock, Robert Motherwell, William de Kooning, and Mark Rothko, long scoffed as hacks in their native land, found fame and fortune. America, once thought a cultural dead end, became the centerpoint of global artistic ingenuity. Even artists in the Soviet Union were influenced. By day they painted in the Soviet sponsored style of stark realism, promoting the power of the proletariat, by night with splashes of colors and dreams. Risking the gulag to unleash their creativity. The rise in abstract expressionism was thanks to various foundations spending millions to fund overseas shows and exhibitions. Where did the foundations get the money? In the Cold War, everything was a battlefield, including the world of art. The CIA was well aware that the cultural war was just as important as any actual war. America could not afford to be seen as an artistic wasteland.

The skin of the dead raccoon slides across the rotting muscle beneath with each poke of the stick in my hand. It's disgusting to watch, but yet I keep doing it, enthralled. The dead raccoon feels unnaturally squishy, and little bits of yellowish fluid come out of the wound on its side every time the stick presses it. The smell is terrible. I feel a little nauseous, a slight tightness in the back of my throat. The scraggly land between the cotton fields near my house rarely offer up things this interesting for a ten year old.

"Paul! Where the hell are you Paul! Beth says its time for dinner."

Cindy's voice is a shrill piercing ring that rushes its way across the empty lot to assault my ears. I look up from my poking and see Cindy's fat frame climbing down the steps from the back porch of the house. It's a windy day, but her curly blonde hair doesn't move, glued down by a can of hairspray.

For a second I consider jumping into the cotton field and hiding. I've done it a couple of times before. It had been great fun sneaking around and avoiding Cindy why she huffed and puffed, cursing under her breath. But the last time I had tried it she just went back into the house. I had hidden out in the cotton fields until it got dark and I got scared. I had run into the house at the first coyote howl to find that they had eaten dinner without me. No, it was better to just come when she called. I drop my stick and run towards the house.

"There you are. What the hell have you been doing?"

"Nothing."

I run up onto the porch and Cindy grunts. Her face, with it's layer of over applied makeup, twists into a look of disgust around the cigarette in her mouth.

"Christ look at you, you're filthy."

"I'm sorry."

"Not as sorry as you're going to be. Those are your damn school clothes."

Cindy takes the old broom leaning against the wall and starts to brush the dirt off my clothes. She doesn't do it hard enough to knock me down, but I have to brace my legs. She motions for me to turn around and repeats the process.

"It will have to do for now. You know how Beth gets if you're late for dinner."

"What's for dinner?"

"What were you hoping for?"

"Hamburgers."

"Well, then you're going to be disappointed."

I follow Cindy into the house. Beth stands in the kitchen, stirring a pot on the stove and smoking a cigarette with a long witch's tail. She looks just like her daughter, the same curly blonde hair and same make up slathered face, but where Cindy is fat, Beth is thin everywhere except her backside. Beth is my grandfather's second wife, at least fifteen years younger than he was, but her face is still covered in deep lines. I tried calling her grandma once. She got so mad I thought she was going to slap me.

I go to the sink and wash my hands. Beth continues to stir the pot and I see the long piece of ash fall off her cigarette into whatever we're eating tonight. I get out the plates, cups, and silverware and set the table. Cindy sits in her chair, her rolls overflowing the seat, reading some celebrity magazine from the grocery store checkout counter. I sit and quietly wait.

I don't remember much about my grandfather except that he was an older version of my Dad, only with a big bushy white moustache. About the only memory I have of him is falling down the porch stairs one day while he was watching me. I was probably only about five or so at the time. I started crying immediately.

"What the hell are you crying for?"

"I scraped my knee."

"That's barely a scratch. God you're soft boy. Your great grandfather had to live in a sod house and wipe his ass with a Sears catalog, you think he would cry over a little scratch?"

I hadn't said anything, just snorted back loose snot before it could fall from my nose, and stared down at my tears falling into the dirt.

"Jesus Christ, your great great grandfather was out chopping wood one morning when he got mauled by a bear, damn thing ate half his face before he could fight it off with his axe. Do you know what he did after that?"

My grandfather had always scared the shit out of me. It was rare that I could force myself to answer him, let alone look him right in his bitter hazel eyes half hidden behind overgrown white eyebrows.

"He went inside and made everyone coffee before they woke up, because that was what he did every morning. When his wife got up she looked at his ripped up face, took a drink of coffee and told him it tasted like shit. Do you know what he did then?"

I had answered with my weak little voice.

"No."

"He apologized."

My grandfather had burst into a wheezy laugh, which soon turned into a fit of phlegmy coughs which didn't stop until he was bright red in the face. A few weeks later he went to the hospital and died. For months afterwards I had nightmares of a man who looked like my grandfather with half his face torn off.

Beth carries two pots to the table and serves dinner. Spaghetti-O's and frozen peas. Every bite tastes like ash. I know it's probably mostly in my head, but everything still tastes like ash. Dinner is a silent affair. Cindy reads her magazine and Beth stares off into space.

"When's Dad coming home?"

Beth keeps staring at a picture on the wall. "Later, he's working late tonight."

Cindy snorts to herself. "Yeah, I'm sure he's working real hard."

She snorts again and starts miming drinking heavily from a bottle. I give her a dirty look. Beth takes a bite, chews slowly, and swallows.

"Christ, you can't claim the man doesn't work his ass off, I don't see any calluses on your hands. There's nothing wrong with getting a little bent now and again. A man who's been through what he has deserves to get a little loose."

Cindy stares at her mother over the top of her magazine. "A little? The way he goes at it you'd think that he had three wives go off to........"

Beth cuts Cindy off, her voice sharp. "Shut up Cindy. A man's wife running out on him is no talk for the dinner table."

The table descends back into uncomfortable silence. I try to lighten the mood. "I got a B plus in math today, and I beat Tom three times in a row playing tetherball at recess."

Beth turns towards me, one hand holding her fork, the other hand holding her cigarette. "You talking or you eating?"

Her tone suggests the right answer. I finish my dinner quickly, put my dishes in the sink, and go upstairs to take a shower. I prefer baths, but Cindy told me baths are just for little kids. Brown rivulets curl around my toes as the dirt washes off of me. When I finish my shower I go to my room and read a book I got from the library. It's filled with brave knights and beautiful princesses. Gallant deeds that end the tyranny of vile dragons and ogres. I can hear Cindy and Beth watching television downstairs.

The small clock beside my bed says ten. I hear the television shut off and footsteps come up the stairs. I can tell it's Beth, Cindy's footsteps and breathing are always heavier. Beth pokes her head in the door.

"It's time for bed. Your Dad will be home soon."

"Okay." I put down my book and snuggle underneath my covers. Beth turns out the light. My voice sounds small in the darkness.

"Good night."

Beth is already gone. I hear the front door open and close, followed by a car moving off down the driveway, taking Beth and Cindy back to their single wide in town. I lay alone in the darkness and listen to the house creak as it settles. My mind starts to conjure up nightmares. The front door squeaks as it opens. Light footsteps creep up the stairway, my heart starts to beat harder. I pull my covers up, hiding everything but my eyes. My door slowly starts to creak open. My breath quickens.

The girl who walks in is five years older than me. She's tall and thin. She has brown eyes and black hair. My older female twin. I can see her smile with her crooked teeth in the dim light from the window. I smile back. It's my sister Amy.

"Hey little brother, how ya doing?"

"I'm good. Where have you been?"

"Oh just out and about. Beth and Cindy already gone?"

"Yeah, they left a little while ago. Hey Amy guess what."

"What?"

"I got a B plus in math today and beat Tom three times in a row at tetherball. Oh, and I found a dead raccoon out by the cotton field."

"That's great kiddo. Sounds like you've had one heck of a day."

"I did, and quit calling me kiddo, I'm nearly eleven."

Amy laughs and playfully punches me in the shoulder. "You're always going to be kiddo to me. Is Dad back yet?"

I feel my smile fall away. "No, Beth said he's working late, but I think he's probably out getting drunk." Amy's smile fades away too. "I wish he wouldn't get drunk. I wish he'd be the way he used to be. Why does he drink so much Amy?"

Amy sits down on my bed and reaches out to clasp my hand. "We've talked about this kiddo. He's sad."

"Because Mom ran off?"

Amy gives my hand a little squeeze. "Yeah. He misses her."

"I know he does. I found a picture of her in the drawer next to his bed. I caught him looking at it and crying one time."

"You shouldn't go looking through other people's things."

"I know, but I had to look at it. All the other pictures are gone. Sometimes I worry that I'm going to forget what she looks like. I miss her too."

Tears fall across my cheeks. Tears fall down Amy's cheeks too, glinting in the moonlight. "I do too kiddo. I do too."

"Why did she leave?"

"I don't know."

"Was it because she didn't love us?"

"How could she not love a kid as great as you?"

"I hate it here. I wish she would have taken me with her."

"I know, but she didn't. So we have to make the best with what we have. We have to be strong for Dad."

Amy wipes a stray tear off my cheek and I take a deep breath in and out. "I know."

"You should get some sleep. It's going to be another day tomorrow, full of adventures."

"Just like the knights in the book?"

"Just like the knights in the book."

"Okay." Amy starts to get up but I grip her hand harder. "Amy, could you maybe stay here with me until I fall asleep. Sometimes I get scared."

I see the flash of white teeth again as Amy smiles. "Sure, anything for you kiddo." Amy lays down beside me on top of the covers and I snuggle up close to her, my back against her front. I feel her heart beating against my back, a comforting steady rhythm. Amy hums tunelessly to herself and rubs my hair.

"Good night Amy."

"Good night kiddo."

I wake up alone in my bed to the sound of a car pulling into the driveway. The clock says three thirty. I hear the front door open and close and unsteady steps work their way up the stairway. My father comes into view, a shadow in my bedroom doorway. The shadow sways back and forth, my father's face slightly illuminated by the red hot coal on the end of his cigarette. His entire body seems to sag into itself, as though he's a turtle trying to hide in his shell.

My father must be able to see my eyes in the moonlight. He walks into my room. "Hey Paul." His words are slurred like his tongue is too big for his mouth.

"Hey Dad."

"Were you good for Beth and Cindy today?"

"Yes sir."

"Did you get all your schoolwork done?"

"Yes sir."

"Good."

The dark shadow and the dim light of the cigarette turn and walk back out of my room. I lay in my bed and listen as the out of beat footsteps move up the hallway and the door to my father's room opens and closes. I close my eyes and fall back to sleep.

Chapter 7

The 9/11 terrorist attacks raised concerns over the domestic safety of the American citizenry. In response, the government created the Department of Homeland Security. The new department was tasked with ensuring the country's border, economic, transportation, and infrastructure security. In total, twenty-two different government agencies were put under Homeland Security oversight. Federal, state, and local governments became required to follow Homeland Security guidelines or face the loss of funding and possible legal action. Local law enforcement agencies were forced to step into line, and as a reward were given access to surplus military hardware, resulting in the militarization of the US municipal police forces. In less than a year the Department of Homeland Security became the third largest Cabinet department, with over 200,000 employees. A giant security edifice with little to no Congressional oversight over its activities as a whole.

I get back to the campsite just as the last bit of the sun is peaking over the horizon. As soon as I duck under the tarp Linds hands me an already hot MRE. I smile, Linds is a damn good wife to me. We may not always agree, but she's always looking after me. My smile grows wider when I see she's prepared beef ravioli, my favorite. The kids are already finishing up their meals. I wolf mine down with a hearty appetite. We have to be ready to move out as soon as it's dark. As I eat I can feel Lindsey's pale blue eyes on me. She looks dour and sour. I smile at the wordplay in my head, but her look kills it pretty quick.

I scrape the last bits of food from the MRE. "Did you update the supply list for these MRE's?"

"Yes."

"Did you also count those two beers I had last night?"

"Yes."

We don't have time to pussy foot arond the issue. "Is something wrong?"

She stares at me for a second and then lets her eyes fall to the ground. She crosses her arms and bites her lip. "Nothing."

Her body language gives everything away. We've been married too long for this kind of crap. I can read her moods like a book. I wish we could get past this kind of shit and just say whatever we feel needs to be said. Fuck. Maybe that's just a part of marriage. One more thing that has to be endured.

"Bullshit," I say gently, "it's okay, say whatever you feel you need to say."

She looks up at me and then down at the ground, and then up at me again. Her eyes flick for a moment behind me and I turn and follow her gaze to the girls. They're playing some game where their trash is planes, or spaceships, or god knows what. I raise my voice to be heard.

"Girls, would you please take the trash out to the honey hole and cover everything up with dirt. If you have to go to the bathroom use it before you fill it up. We have to get a move on soon."

Stone gives me a sullen look but Rachel is all smiles. "Okay Daddy," they say in unison, one excited and one just above a whisper. I hand the remains of my MRE to Rachel and the two of them run to the other side of Alice. I turn back to Linds. She's still staring at the ground.

"Okay honey, now will you tell me what's wrong?"

"It's," she pauses for a second, "it's," another pause, "it's nothing."

Fuck. Just spit it out already. I make myself smile to try and help her along. I keep my voice gentle and even. "Something is obviously bothering you. C'mon honey, you know you can tell me anything."

Linds stares at my shoes for a bit, lets out a loud exhale of breath, and looks up at me. "It's just that I wish we hadn't left Roger behind. He was a damned good cat and it was a damned shame to leave him."

Jesus Christ. This again. I try to keep from rolling my eyes. "I wish we could have brought him too hon, but we just didn't have time to look for him."

This seems like the most diplomatic answer. I don't like lying, but I'm sure as hell not going to mention how glad I am that we couldn't find him when we left.

Linds tries a weak smile, showing yellowed teeth. "I know, I know you're doing the best you can for us. But........."

"Yeah?"

"I don't know, maybe it isn't as bad as you think it is. Maybe we can just turn around and go back home. Maybe we'll get there and discover that the world is exactly the way we left it."

A sigh escapes my lips. My foot begins to tap the ground rapidly. We're too far along now. We can't go back. I take in a couple deep breaths to calm myself down. She's just scared. She doesn't know what she's talking about. Sometimes I forget how young she is.

"We've talked about this honey, we can't go back. There's nothing left for us back there."

"But what if you're wrong? What if we've abandoned everything for nothing?"

"We've talked about this so many times. You know what's happening back there. We didn't abandon anything. The world as we know it is going to disappear. Maybe it's already gone. I'm trying to do the best thing for you and the kids. I'm trying to keep you safe."

"I know. It just all seems so far out there. It's just hard to imagine that it can all be true."

"It is true. Everything has been building to this for years. There's going to be a lot of people caught by surprise, but not us. The best I can do for my family is to keep us out of sight and get us across that border as soon as possible."

"Do you really think it might have already started?"

"Probably. I saw a helicopter when I was out scouting today. A black one."

"Do you think it was looking for us?"

"I don't know."

Linds looks me straight in the eye. For a moment I think she's going to say more. Instead she takes a deep breath. "Okay. It's almost dark, we better get ready to head out."

"That's my girl."

We walk around Alice and load up the kids and the last few odds and ends still laying about. I check the honey hole to make sure the kids did a good job covering and hiding it. Things look good. I feel proud. They're smart kids. I probably had them dig and refill over a hundred holes in our yard back home. No, not home, Sweetwater. It's probably better to not think of it as home anymore. As soon as it's completely dark Linds and I take off the big tarp and fold it carefully before putting it in the back of Alice. It takes us less than five minutes. This is something else we used to practice at home. Linds got good at this part very quickly. She has clever hands. Oh boy, does she ever have clever hands.

We climb in Alice. The dome lights stay off when we open and close the doors. I took out the bulbs when we left Sweetwater. Better to avoid mistakes that might give away our position. The headlights go on and their red beams pierce the dark. I turn the key. The sound of Alice's engine is a roar in the silence, even with the high-end mufflers I installed. I put Alice into gear and we head out deeper into the desert.

The going is slower than the night before. The brush has become larger and thicker. The ground is more broken with gullies and ragged stones. Nothing is flat anymore. It's much harder to see obstacles in the filtered redness of the head-lights. A few times I get Alice up to twenty miles per hour, once even up to twenty-five, but mostly Alice stays in first gear, five to ten at the best. I wish we could go faster, but there's no use in risking a breakdown. We still have a long ways to go.

The kids and Linds fall asleep soon after we start out. I wait until their breathing becomes long and even, and then reach behind me and pull a beer out of the cooler. I have to remember to take one beer off the list. It's all about lists. We have to be careful. We have to make sure everything lasts for as long as possible. The beer tastes so good though, it's the perfect way to start a long night of driving. It gets boring out here. No one to talk to and no radio to listen to. I guess I could talk to Linds, but since we left Sweetwater it seems like all we do is fight. I know she isn't fully onboard with the whole thing. She pretends to, but she doesn't really understand. She's so young, closer to Stone's age than she is to mine.

I stifle a yawn. That's not good. We're just getting started. We have a damn long ways to go still. I reach into my pocket and pull out the little medicine bottle. I pull out one of the little yellow pills and wash it down with a mouthful of beer. There we go. Have to keep concentrating. Have to keep my mind on task.

Walter Jones. His chubby cherub face framed by lank greasy hair and an overgrown beard. Weird, I haven't thought about Walter in a long time. We used to be buddies back in Portland. I wonder what happened to him. Last I knew he disappeared down to Reno and was calling himself Carl to avoid going back to jail for breaking the rules of his parole. He was a good-hearted idiot. His only crime was never being able to take responsibility for his own stupidity.

When he got hauled off to jail was a prime example. He was doing ninety miles per hour down I-5, beer in hand, lit joint in the other, and a big bag of weed sitting on the seat next to him. He swore up and down to the cop that his medical marijuana card was coming any day. Walter could never get it into his head why the pig just didn't give a shit. The world was always against Walter. It was always out to get him. The way he saw it he was a boat adrift on an open sea, a person with no control over the world around him. If you don't take responsibility for your life, how can anyone hold you accountable when things fuck up? Poor little shit.

The slow pace is starting to get to me. My hands clench and knead the steering wheel. My left leg starts to shake. We could go a hell of a lot faster if we just used the normal headlights. This would be a snail's pace compared to what we could do if we drove during the day. Stupid thoughts. These aren't options. Bright light, whether from the sun or from the high beams, makes us too conspicuous, too visible, too noticeable. You never know who might be watching. You never know who might take an interest.

I finish my beer and put the empty in the cooler behind me. I think about chucking it out the window into the empty desert. What's the chance of anyone finding it or even caring if they did? No, we've been careful this long. No reason to fuck things up just because I'm in a cranky mood. The wheel turns lightly one way, then the other, dodging illuminated red obstacles. I feel like I've been driving all night, but it's probably only been a few hours. We haven't gone far. We could walk faster than this.

Alice starts pulling to the right. At first it's just a gentle tug but it soon becomes more insistent. The constant jerking of the wheel on my arm reminds me of Stone when she was younger, and a hell of a lot less sullen, tugging on my arm to get my attention. But Stone never made the thumping sounds like the ones coming from the front right corner of Alice. Shit. I bring Alice to a halt, take her out of gear, apply the emergency brake, and turn off the engine. Silence fills the world.

Linds opens her eyes and looks over at me sleepily. "Why'd we stop?"

"Flat tire."

"Oh."

"Could you hand me the flashlight out of the jockey box?"

Linds opens the jockey box and rummages around a bit before handing me the flashlight. It's a surplus military headlamp with a red light. I put the lamp on my head and open my door.

"Do you want any help?"

"No, I can handle it."

There's rustling from the backseat. Rachel's squeaky voice is loud in the darkness. "What's going on Daddy?"

"Nothing Monkey, just a flat tire. I'll get it fixed in no time. Go back to sleep."

I shut the door and walk around the front of Alice to take a look. It's cold out. Goose pimples rise up on my skin. When I kneel down the ground feels even colder, biting right through my jeans. It doesn't look good. The right front rim is damn near sitting on the ground. I can't see any obvious holes. It must have been a slow leak. Shit. This is definitely going to eat up some time. We're definitely not going to make it as far as I had hoped we would tonight. Fuck.

Alice is fully stocked and prepared for almost any eventuality. She's been modified to carry three spare tires, one on each of the back doors and one slung underneath the gas tank. There's also a small air compressor in the back, the cheap plastic kind that plugs into the cigarette lighter. It's not going to do much good. I don't want us to be in the same boat as we are now just a few hours further on. Never mind the noise. Sound carries amazing distances in the dark. Simpler just to put on a new tire.

I stand up and the red light of my head-lamp plays across Alice's windows. The shadows of my family watch me from inside, taking me in like it's some kind of theater production. Now on Broadway, see the musical extravaganza, *Dad Changing a Tire*. I kneel back down to look at the tire again. I feel uneasy. Something doesn't feel right. I crouch in close, my face just inches from the black rubber, my hands brushing against the rubbery surface. These tires are pretty much brand new. It seems strange that one would suddenly just spring a slow leak. Then again, it's not like we're doing highway driving out here. Shit happens. That's all there is to it.

The hair on the back of my neck stands up on end. There's a loud thump above me. The sound of flesh hitting glass hard. My whole body jumps and my muscles all tighten. I look up just as Linds smacks the flat of her hand against the window again. Her form in the window is just a shadow, but I can see her hand fold into a single finger which starts frantically jabbing at the window between us. What the hell is wrong with her? My synapses pop. She's pointing at something behind me.

I turn my head. The red light on my forehead swings around. Alice's matte black side. A nearby sagebrush. A nearby rock. Another sagebrush. Nothing but empty desert. Nothing but.......Shit! My whole body jerks around in a single motion. My ass hits the ground. My back presses back against the flattened tire.

Two red orbs glow in the darkness twenty feet away. The sound of soft footfalls reach my ears. The shadow around the red orbs moves closer. The movements are slow and careful. It's stalking me. Whatever the fuck it is, it's stalking me. I can hear it breathing, in and out. Breaths shift into a growl from deep within an unseen throat. There are no night time sounds. No crickets, no wind, no nothing. Just the growling monstrosity coming at me and the wild beating of my own heart. My hands scrabble for loose rocks on cold ground. I feel the prod of my pocket-knife in my right pocket. No good. I'll never get out in time. I'm helpless.

"Get the fuck out of here!"

My voice echoes off the distant hills. The shadow stops for a moment, just out of my light's reach. The red orbs rise up and then move slowly back towards the ground. It's getting ready to jump. It's getting ready to spring. I throw myself to the side, my boots tossing loose dirt as they struggle to gain purchase. I skitter around the front of Alice on my hands and knees, rip open the driver side door, jump in, and slam the door shut behind me.

My entire body shakes and I begin breathing for the first time since I turned around, gulping in panicked breaths. Fuck. Holy fuck. My heart feels like its going to burst out of my chest. For just a moment, I am one with my savannah ancestors of a thousand years ago, nothing but pure instinct and adrenaline keeping me from being the definition of prey. I lean over across Linds' lap and look out the passenger side window. Nothing. I can see nothing out there. Just the faint reflection of my own light shining back at me.

"What the fuck was that?" Linds' voice is rattled and full of panic.

"I have no god damn idea?"

We both sit still. Staring out the window, trying to spot a slightly darker spot in the night.

"Maybe it was just a coyote or a bobcat."

"It was too big to be a coyote or a bobcat."

"How do you know? It's dark as hell out there."

"We're you out there?"

"No."

"Besides, have you ever heard of a coyote or a bobcat stalking somebody?"

"No, but how do you know it was stalking you?"

"I could just tell."

"But…."

"Just give me a sec to think about this."

Silence, blessed silence. Nothing but the heavy breathing of my family. I've got to think about this. I've got to be the man of the family. If I panic, they'll panic. I take a few deep breaths and try to calm down a little bit. Whatever it was it was definitely stalking me. Linds can have her doubts, but she wasn't out there. She wasn't about to get pounced on.

Stone's voice floats up from the back seat, flat and emotionless. "Did you see how it's eyes glowed? Maybe it was a chupacabra."

Linds turns around to look at the kids. "A chubacabby what?"

"A chupacabra, a goat sucker. I watched a show about them on TV."

My daughter's voice seems to spark my brain back into full speed. Panic and fear subsides. Logical thought regains control. I am an adult. I have to assess this like an adult.

"Many animals' eyes glow when you point a light at them honey. Remember, just like the cat back home. Chupacabra's aren't real. They're like unicorns or dragons. They're just a story somebody made up."

My daughter's voice sounds insulted. "They are too real. Aiden said his uncle saw one last fall when he was out hiking."

"Aiden's uncle was mistaken honey. If he saw anything it was probably just a mangy coyote. Chupacabra's aren't real."

Rachel's voice is shrill and filled with fright. "I don't want to be here if a chubbycabby is outside. Make it go away Daddy."

"It wasn't a chupacabra Monkey. It was probably just a cougar."

Lindsey looks back at me. "Have you ever heard of a cougar stalking someone?"

Christ Linds, c'mon. I need you to be an adult too. It's bad enough that the kids are all worked up. I try to make my voice sound soothing.

"They do all the time. Remember Carol from down the road? When I was a kid it happened to her. She was taking a walk one evening when she ran into one. She had to walk backwards clear to her house until the dogs chased it off. Cougars will go after just about anything."

Linds faces forward and stares back out the window. There's a short moment of silence.

"So are you going to go back out there and fix the tire?"

The muscles in my back tighten at the thought of going back out into the darkness.

"Hell no, if that cougar's still out there then it wouldn't be safe."

"Well then, what the hell are we going to do? We can't just sit here all night."

Linds is right. This is no place to hide Alice. We'll need a good spot so I can fix the tire in the day-light. I'm pretty sure I know about where we are. I'm pretty sure I know the general direction. It will probably ruin the tire to get there, but it seems like the best option.

"I know a place."

Linds doesn't say anything. I lean forward and start Alice.

Chapter 8

In 1996 news reporter Gary Webb had the story of a life time. Thanks to several whistleblowers he had proof that the CIA-backed Contras, a paramilitary force fighting the spread of communism in Central America, had smuggled cocaine into the US throughout the 1980's to fund their operations. The cocaine was sold as crack throughout the Los Angeles area, fueling a widespread drug epidemic. The CIA was well aware of the transactions, and even President Reagan was involved, shielding inner city drug dealers from prosecution in order to guarantee the flow of money to the Contras who had been cut off from direct US funding by a Congressional order. The report caused a huge uproar and resulted in a strong backlash from the CIA and other groups within the US government, which pressured the American media to declare Webb a fraud. Webb found himself ostracized from the mainstream media and hounded until he committed suicide in 2004.

I sit on the edge of the bed in the hay loft and stare out the open barn door at the sun, striving to climb higher into the sky, slowly forcing back the remnants of shadows on the ground below. The air is cold. My breath steams out with every movement of my chest. My bare arms are covered with goose pimples. Two dots of black flash past the doorway. A pair of birds frolicking in the sunshine. All is right with the world. All is good.

The bed is not really a bed, though it serves that purpose just as well as any bed you can buy in a store. Plus I didn't have to wait for a sale. The bed is just a group of straw bales pushed together, covered in blankets. Several thick blankets below to protect our naked bodies from the sharp poking of the straw. More blankets on top to protect us from the cold. I had shoved loose straw under the bottom blankets to make it softer and more like an actual mattress. Lindsey had treated this simple idea as signs that I was some kind of genius. It wasn't anything, but I'm glad it made her happy.

The sun is near the top of the door. It's probably already past ten in the morning. Linds should have woken me up. Part of me is glad she didn't. We had a good workout last night. The extra sleep felt good. I stand and feel every vertebrae in my back pop. I'm getting old, but she makes my heart feel young again. Jesus, what a cliché, but it's true god damn it. It's true. The stiffness in my joints subsides as I walk across the old wooden floor, smoothed by countless long-past bales of hay, and lean against the door jam.

The world of my childhood home is shaded numerous variations of yellow. The plants have all gone dormant, awaiting the beginning of next spring. All is quiet except for the sound of Linds moving about on the ground floor below, and the random chatter of the birds. The November sun does nothing to warm the world. It seems almost poetic that while the world drops into the dark sleep of winter, my soul is already blooming with new life. A silly notion. I'm not a poet, but love does strange things to a man.

I stand in the old barn where I used to play and have adventures. It was once a castle, a space station, and the sight of numerous western shootouts. Now it's just an old barn in need of a new roof and fresh paint. I never imagined that it could be a home. Over there was the chicken coop where my mother used to keep hens. Now just a jumble of old boards and wire. The toolshed that smelled of gasoline and grease. The door now hangs open, showing the empty interior. There was the two-storey farm house where we lived. Now just a blackened foundation. It's been six years since the fire took the house. When I first brought Linds here she had asked what had happened to the house. We had been standing next to each other in the cold and I had put my arm around her to keep her warm.

"Meth heads," I had answered. "A bunch of meth heads thought they could save some money by cooking their own meth. But they didn't know what they were doing so they burned down the house."

I still have the scars on the back of my hands. It all seems like another world. Like it happened to someone else. In our defense, we never planned to sell it. It was only going to be for our own demise.

"Paul," I hear my wife shout, "Paul, are you awake?"

"Yeah, I'm awake. I'll be right down."

In front of me hangs the old cross tree, hook, and chain that once lifted the hay into the barn. Linds and I had used it to hoist up the straw bales we had bought from George. For a moment I see myself jumping onto the old chain and riding it down to the ground below, making a dramatic entrance. The rational part of my mind throws the idea away immediately. I'm not as young and spry as I once was. Besides, I'm pretty sure the physics wouldn't work out right. I turn and walk to the hole and ladder that leads to the ground floor.

The ground floor doesn't have much more than the upper story. A few folding chairs around a card table, cardboard boxes with canned goods from the local food pantry, and several red and blue plastic coolers. Near the back is an old workbench covered by my scattered tools and several small engines I'm trying to repair. Mostly ones from neighbors' lawn mowers. One belongs to an irrigation pump. A circle of rocks forms a fire pit near the open door. An old blue tarp hangs over the top of the door-frame to force the smoke outside.

Linds is leaning over a large pot on a portable propane cooker poking at something with a large fork. Her butt is towards me and I stare at its shape, just barely hidden by the layers of warm clothing, sweatshirt, and heavy coat. I walk up and press myself against her back. I smile as she presses herself back into me. I give the back of her neck a quick kiss and lay my chin on her shoulder.

"What's cooking?"

"Turkey. I'm trying to deep fat fat fry it. My uncle used to do it every year."

"It smells good."

"Yeah. It's going to take a little while. I'm not sure if I'm doing it right."

"I'm sure it will turn out great."

"I figured we could also make up some of those instant mashed potatoes and you could pick up some cranberry sauce when you went into town today. You know, have a real Thanksgiving."

I walk over to one of the coolers and grab a bottle of apple juice from the inside. No need for ice. It's too damn cold. I sit back and watch my wife as she works. My mind fills with dirty thoughts. I feel my body demanding for a basic need to be sated, but no, not yet. I have to get a few things done today. She's a spirited woman. If we get started we're liable to forget completely about the turkey. At best we'd have to eat it overcooked. At worst the whole barn would go up.

I'm proud of my wife and how well she's adapted to our current circumstance. I have no doubt that she loves me more than anything else in this world. She followed me into poverty. This isn't the way I wanted our marriage to start, but we're making the best of the situation. At least we have each other, which is good, because we really don't have anybody else.

My boss in Fort Worth had brought me into his office a few days before our wedding to tell me that he was going to have to lay me off. I was a damn fine worker he had said, but times were tough and I was the one with the least seniority. The whole seniority thing has always seemed pretty stupid to me. I had been a much better worker than most of those with seniority. Relative timing is a stupid way to measure worth. My first instinct had been to tell him such in as bellicose of a manner as possible, but I restrained myself. I knew I wouldn't change his mind, and I didn't want to screw up a good reference. Instead I had simply nodded, and taken my last paycheck.

The day of the wedding, Larry had given me the wedding present of telling me that his old lady most definitely did not want me and my, what she called "child-bride," living on Larry's couch. I was going to have to find a new place to live. The whole child-bride thing had been a bunch of shit. What a bitch. I couldn't really blame Larry. I think Larry really loves this one, and just me staying there had caused enough friction. He had given me some money, not enough, but what he could, to help us get a start somewhere. Skeeter had offered to let us stay at his place, but I had declined. He isn't the type of person I want my wife to be around. So out to the old stomping grounds we went. Linds hiding her disappointment behind a smile and treating it like it was some grand adventure.

My apple juice finished, I get up out of the folding chair. "I'm going to go into town and see if there are any messages."

"Okay. Don't forget the cranberry sauce."

"I won't. Do we need anything else? Maybe something like a pumpkin pie?"

Linds gives me an amorous look and an exaggerated wink and shake of her hip. "Don't you worry about the desert. I'll take care of that."

Damn what a woman. I go outside and walk over to Alice, her metallic blue paint shining in the cold November sunshine. Get in, start her up, flick the radio over to classic rock, and head off down the road towards Sweetwater blasting The Doors. I have to keep reminding myself that just because I feel young, doesn't mean I actually am.

The wedding had been a bit of a bust. I wish it could have been better, but the world didn't seem to want to cooperate. It had been in a church, though it had taken a little doing to find a minister, but the rest was mostly just a big mess. Very few people showed up. On her side there were just a few girl friends from high school and that epileptic kid named Petey, though he spent the whole ceremony glaring at me and I wished he hadn't come. None of Linds' family showed. Not one of her four sisters, or her mother.

Her mother despises me. When she found out we were going to get married the woman, who is around my age, called me a cradle robber and a dirty old man, amongst several other things that mostly seemed to be strung together curses. She swore up and down that I was lucky her husband wasn't still alive, because if he was, he would beat my ass into the ground. When Linds didn't back down her mother told her she was cut off. It really wasn't too much of a loss. All the woman had was a dilapidated two bedroom house in a shitty part of Fort Worth. She worked two jobs to keep it, and even then the elder daughters had to work after school to help out.

I really don't know why the hell she got herself all worked up. Sure, once upon a time I was a meth head and an ex-con, but that doesn't make me the devil. Her past isn't all that spotless clean either. Linds once told me that her mother had worked a short time as a stripper to help make ends meet, and that was when her father was still alive. If anything, Linds' mother should feel lucky that a man of my convictions wanted to marry her daughter.

Linds and I hit it off from the first moment we met. We knew from that first night that neither one of us wanted to be with anyone else. Sure, she was seventeen at the time, but I was willing to wait. I never touched that girl until we got married, and we didn't get married until she turned eighteen. Anyone who wants to question what kind of man I am can try doing what I did while the hottest seventeen year old you've ever seen does everything in her power to try and get you to fuck her. Sure the honeymoon was in the back of Alice on some country road, but what a honeymoon it was.

My side of the church was even more empty than Lindsey's, just two people. Larry was one of them. He didn't really seem to agree with what I was doing, but at least he showed up to support me. The second had been unexpected. Cindy was fatter than ever. She sat by herself at the back of the church. It was the first time I had seen her since Dad's funeral. She didn't say a word to me. Just slipped in after I had already walked down the aisle and slipped out after the "I do's." She did leave behind a envelope with a hundred dollars in it though.

Amy hadn't been able to make it either, but she did give me a call from San Francisco the night before the wedding.

"Hey kiddo, hear you're getting married tomorrow."

"Yeah, I am. Sorry to hear you're not going to be able to make it for the ceremony."

"Me too, but things out here in California are keeping me pretty busy. I hope you don't think too badly of me, especially since this is your second wedding I'm going to miss."

"No. You know I can never think poorly of you."

"Glad to hear. I'm sure it will be a good wedding. You just make sure this is the last wedding I'm given the opportunity to miss."

"I will. This one's different. I don't know how to explain it, but this one is different."

"Sounds like you made quite the catch."

"I'd like to think so.....but....."

"But what?"

"I don't know. Everyone thinks I'm doing something crazy because she's twenty-two years younger than me. Even Larry thinks I'm off my rocker."

"Do you feel like you're off your rocker?"

"No."

"Do you love this girl?"

"Yes."

"Well shit, that's all you need. Screw what those other people think. If you feel like you're doing the right thing and she feels the same, than screw everyone else. You only get so many chances for love in this world. When one shows up, you have to grab with both hands."

Amy's words had echoed in my head when I walked down the aisle and said I do. She was right. I did feel like I was doing the right thing, so the hell with everybody else. Lindsey looked beautiful when I put that cheap cubic zirconia ring, the best I could afford, on her finger and said the words. I knew I was doing the right thing, and five months into it, though we have nothing, I haven't changed my mind.

I pull up in front of George's Grocery and walk in. George smiles and waves as I push my way through the glass door. When I was a kid we always did our shopping at George's, and not much has changed, though George does look a lot more weathered and saggy these days. I like George, he's one of the good ones. Unlike a lot of the people in Sweetwater, he doesn't put himself on a high pedestal and pass judgment on others. George has done nothing but show me kindness since I got back into town. Letting me use his phone to call long distance without charge and letting me buy groceries on credit whenever money is tight. They don't make good people like George anymore.

I walk through the aisles and pick up two cans of cranberry sauce and a bottle of cheap wine to surprise Lindsey with. It is a holiday after all. George beams at me as I walk up to the counter.

"Hello Paul. Happy Thanksgiving."

"Happy Thanksgiving George. How are you today?"

"Just fine. How's your new wife?"

"She's doing good. Cooking up a turkey as we speak."

"Sounds delicious. Have you seen all the strange men in town?"

"Strange men?"

"Yeah, guys from some company called Vista or something like that. Had a few in the store. They were talking about maybe throwing up some windmills south of town, you know for the electricity."

"I'll believe that when I see it. I remember they used to talk about that kind of stuff when I was a kid."

"Who knows, but it would probably be a good thing for the farmers if they did. Hear they pay good money if they're allowed to build some on your land. Anyways, total comes to fifteen dollars and sixty-five cents." I hand George a twenty and he hands me my change. "You want a sack for that?"

"Sure." George shakes out a plastic bag and puts my purchases into it. "Have there been any phone messages for me?"

"Glad you said something. I nearly forgot." George feels around in his pockets and finally pulls out a piece of paper that he squints at. "A Mister Anderson called earlier to tell you that the job was yours if you wanted it. Was wondering if you could start next Monday. I'm guessing he's talking about the job you were telling me about up in Nashville."

Relief and elation sweeps through me. This is an unexpected holiday surprise. I've been sending out resumes left and right trying to find work. This one had been a long shot, a job I had found while perusing the internet at the Sweetwater Library. It was another fabricator job, similar to the one I had in Fort Worth.

"Yeah, it's the one in Nashville."

"Personally, don't know if I'd want to work for man who has the gall to call on a holiday."

"Yeah, but beggars can't be choosers." I stand staring at George. I know I'm smiling like an idiot. I can't wait to tell Linds the good news. Finally I'll be able to give her all the things that she deserves. She's never once complained, but I know things haven't been easy for her. I can feel it in my body. This is the turning point. Things are really going to get better.

George patiently watches me, a smile on his lips. "Congratulations Paul."

"Thanks George. Thanks for everything. Can I use your phone?"

Chapter 9

By 2002 it became apparent that the ongoing military operations in Afghanistan were not going to be enough to unite the country against a common enemy. No one really considered the most backwards country in the world as a real threat. Voices were rising in derision. Too many questions were being asked about what was going on at home. The US government needed a better overseas distraction. Something divisive. Something controversial. Iraq fit the bill perfectly. Though far from its hey-day, Iraq was still a power in the Middle East. Iraq's ruler, Saddam Hussein, had been the most recognizable enemy of American democracy for the past decade. It didn't hurt that Iraq sat on top of one of the largest oil reserves in the world. All that was needed was a reason. In October of that year the CIA reported that Iraq was building up its stores of chemical and biological weapons. In March of 2003, the invasion began.

Everything feels numb. There's a bright white light hanging over my head. It's shining downward straight into my eyes, forcing me to squint, blocking out any clear view of the room around me. The room is white, that much I can tell. White ceiling, white walls, and probably a white floor. Everything is white, too white. My eyes are watering. I blink spastically. Short flashes of comforting darkness, blocking out the terrible whiteness of the world around me. Each time my eyes open the world that I find myself in flashes back even brighter. It's painful to look upon. I want to hide. I want to escape. I don't want to face the light and its pain.

I try to raise my right hand to block out the light but it won't move. It's strapped down. My left hand is the same, as are my legs. I can't move. I try to turn my head to look around but two soft cushions hold it in place. Two soft cushions supported by something hard and unyielding. There is a strap across my forehead. I'm trapped. I struggle, but I can't get up. I can feel the leather against the bare skin of my wrists and ankles. A shadow on the edge of my vision. A calming hand reaches down and lays itself on my shoulder. It feels small and delicate, a woman's hand.

A voice, echoing from far away. I recognize it but I don't. "Calm down Paul. You need to calm down."

I lay in silence and the hand stays on my shoulder. I can hear my heart beating in my chest, long pauses between each lub and dub. I can hear myself breathing. Each inhale and exhale becoming more rapid and shallow. I don't want to be here. They have no right to keep me here. They have no right to tie me to this table. I brace my body and throw myself against the straps. Every muscle in my body strains to be free. I can feel my veins and arteries protruding. My back arches as high as I can lift it. The female hand disappears and a new shadow comes into view just outside of my range of vision. Two large callused hands, a man's hands, push on my shoulders, forcing me back down.

The voice is a booming one, counter to its soothing tone. "Paul, you need to take it easy. You need to quit fighting it. Everything is going to be okay Paul. Everything is going to be okay."

I ignore the voice and continue struggling, throwing myself against the straps that hold me down. I'm panicking. I'm losing control. The whole world is spinning out of control.

From far away I hear the female voice again. "Stop it Paul. Please stop it. Stop it. Stop it. Stop it."

The world fills with the sounds of screaming.

My eyes open. I see the interior ceiling of Alice. My body is lying in the driver seat kicked all the way back into the reclining position. My body is fighting to rise against the seat belt that holds me down. My hands fumble with the clasp and suddenly I'm free, sitting up and staring anxiously out the windshield. I'm free. I'm in Alice. I'm alone in Alice. It was a dream. It was just a bad dream. Saint Christopher on his medallion, hanging from Alice's rearview mirror, smiles at me sweetly.

The world rolls back into focus around me. Alice sitting inside the old half-collapsed barn. The old half collapsed barn at the abandoned farmstead I found yesterday. The tire, there was a flat tire. I came here so we would have a place to hide while I fixed it. I was so tired.

I must have fallen asleep as soon as we arrived. I didn't even take off my seatbelt. Everything makes sense again. Everything is okay.

My throat feels raw. I reach into my left pocket, pull out the small plastic container, and shake out a little yellow pill. I pop it in my mouth and swallow. Daylight streams through the barn doorway and the large gaps in the roof overhead. The barn interior is filled with dappled shadows. I can't believe I fell asleep so easily. Wasted so much time. I don't have time for sleep. I can sleep when we're safe in Mexico. I hope no one heard my screams. Night terrors, that was what the doctor called them when I was a child. They don't happen so much now. Just every now and again. Just a dream. Just a very bad dream.

I open the door and step out. Dust motes float through shafts of light, pushing back the shadows. Linds stands on the edge of one beam of light. For a moment it's not her. For a moment she is not my beautiful young wife. Her sharp features have become gaunt and bony. Her eyes have sunk in and loose skin hangs in bags beneath her eyes and chin. Her features have become soft butter, drooping downwards. Eyes bloodshot, teeth brown and rotting. Where once there was a young supple woman of twenty-seven, now stands a prematurely aged crone, bent by the hardships of life.

I blink and shake my head. Linds steps forward into the light and is herself again. She is not the same woman she was when I first met her. Nobody keeps the shape they were when they were seventeen, and motherhood takes its toll, but for me she has only become more beautiful. My graceful angel put here on Earth to make me a better man. I stare at her, drinking her in, taking in the radiance. She stares back, her pale blue eyes filled with concern and a hint of fear.

"Are you all right?"

"What?"

"Are you okay? I heard you screaming."

"Yeah, I'm fine. It was just a nightmare."

"What kind of nightmare?"

"I don't know. I can't remember. I was in a bright room. I wanted to get up but I couldn't for some reason."

"You can't remember?"

"No, it's gone. It just really scared me."

"Are you sure you're okay?"

"Yeah, just a bad dream. I used to get them all the time when I was a kid."

"It just really scared me."

"I'm sorry." I walk forward and take Linds into my arms. I hold her tight, feeling the bones of her shoulders underneath her skin. I feel her breathing in and out and hear her stifle a single sob. "It's all right. It was just a dream. Nothing to worry about."

We break apart and she gives me a pearly white smile before looking down at her feet. "I'm sorry. I was just worried about you. You know how much I love you. I'm just a little freaked out."

"I love you too. I never want anything to ever happen to you or the kids. You're the most important things in my life."

She looks me in the eye and smiles again. "Are you hungry?"

"Not really."

"You should probably eat."

"I'll eat before we leave tonight." The word leave makes her flinch a little. It's a small involuntary jerk. Barely noticeable. Something you miss unless you spend nine years of your life married to someone. I choose to not say anything about it. "Where are the kids?"

"Outside playing."

Thank god. Thank god I didn't scare the kids like I scared Linds.

Linds looks nervously towardsly the barn door. "Have you been in that house?"

"Yes."

"I went in for a little bit, but not too long. That place is really fucking creepy."

"Yeah, it is."

"Are you sure you don't want to eat?"

"I'm sure. You shouldn't have let me sleep so late."

"I'm sorry, you just looked so peaceful."

"We still have a long ways to go."

"You're pushing yourself too hard. Maybe we could stay here for a bit and rest."

I don't want to have this discussion again. I'm tired of having this discussion. It's like a damn broken record. I love my wife so much, but she's never been the quickest. She's never been able to fully understand. For me it's a matter of logic, for her it's a leap of faith.

"No, we gotta keep moving. Amy is waiting for us. We have to keep going."

"Are you sure you're all right?"

"Yes." We stand in silence for a moment. I turn and break my gaze. "I better get to work on that tire."

I walk away before Linds can reply. I don't have time to go nattering on all day. There is plenty to do before dark. Linds has always been this way, reacting more to feelings and basic wants and needs rather than actual thoughts. I wouldn't change her for the world, but I wish she could change that.

The drive across the desert on the flat caused more damage than I expected. The rubber is in shreds and I can tell just by looking at the rim that it's warped. Luckily, something like this was not unexpected. I take off the ruined wheel and replace it with the spare slung beneath the gas tank. For a moment I consider keeping the ruined tire, but what would be the point. I roll it into the darkness, deeper into the ruined barn, kicking up puffs of dust as it goes. I'll have to remember to update the checklist. One spare tire gone, two left.

While I'm changing the tire Linds keeps herself busy too. She takes a bucket out of Alice and walks out of the barn. A little while later she returns with it full of water and pours it into the big tank in the back of Alice. I watch her as she goes back and forth.

"Where did you get the water?"

"There's an old hand pump over by the house."

"Did you use the water test kit?"

"Of course I did, I'm not stupid. You think I want us all to have the shits?"

Linds goes back outside and sits on the porch of the old dilapidated house, reading some trash book about vampires, and smoking cigarettes. I wish Linds would read something better, something that was less mass produced crap, but I keep my trap shut. A wise husband knows to pick his battles. I stand in the barn doorway, glad to be in the fresh air and out of the musty interior. A joint would be pretty good about now, but better not. I never smoke pot in front of the kids. A cigarette will have to do. It's better than nothing.

It is peaceful here. It's a good hiding spot. Secluded from the outside world. The hillsides of the draw block the old homestead from the view of the world around it. You'd have to walk right up or fly over to see it. It's a good place to stop. Maybe Linds wasn't so far off. Maybe we could stay a couple of days. I inhale the last of my cigarette and stomp it out under my leather work-boot. That's all it is. Just a crazy thought. We have to keep going. South of the river we'll be safe. South of the river is the future.

Stone is walking low along the hillside, pausing and sweeping her eyes across the landscape, her hands blocking out the sun, peering behind random clumps of sagebrush. I leave the comforting shadow of the doorway. It's hot out. I don't take many steps before I feel myself start to sweat.

"Whatcha doing Stone?"

"Me and Rachel are playing hide and seek."

"You mind if I help you look?"

"Sure."

Together we walk back and forth across the hillside. Keeping our eyes peeled for signs of my youngest daughter. It's been awhile since I've had time to just play with the girls. I've forgotten how good of a hider Rachel is. Once when she was five, and we were still in Portland, she hid so well that we couldn't find her for over an hour. The smell of dinner cooking had brought her out of the bottom of the hamper where she had secluded herself under a pile of dirty clothes.

Stone and I walk in silence, but it doesn't feel like the usual dour silence. We search here and there for Rachel, taking our time, and basking in a feeling of contentment. I can tell Stone feels it too. The ways things used to be. The way things oughta be. The way I always want her to feel. As we search I reach down and take her hand. She doesn't pull away. I smile and let myself imagine that Stone is smiling a little bit too. I feel like I ought to apologize to her. I don't know. What would I say? It's not my fault the world is so shitty. It's not my fault her childhood got stolen away so soon. Maybe things can be better though, once we get to Mexico. Maybe there things will be like they used to be.

The slight breeze carries the sound of a giggle from behind us. Stone's face goes cross and she turns and runs back towards an old tree stump surrounded by stones overgrown with dry grass.

"Damn it Rachel, we agreed that no one hides near the graves!"

Rachel pops up from a thick layer of bunch grass caught in a fit of giggles. We had walked right past without seeing her. As I jog up behind Stone I see that what I assumed to be rocks are actually grave stones. Old markers knocked on their sides and slowly crumbling away. Stone and Rachel debate their agreed upon rules. I lean over and pull the grass away. The graves look like they've been knocked over by vandals, or maybe just cows rubbing up against them to scratch an itch. Only one is still readable, the others are too damaged, worn too smooth.

Felix Kraus

July 13, 1903 - March 14, 1919

Jetzt mit den Engeln

My skin crawls. I look at my daughters, Stone berating Rachel, and Rachel laughing at Stone. I feel sick to my stomach.

"Girls." They both fall silent, their heads snapping upwards. My voice was harsher than I meant it to be. "Let's go play somewhere else."

My two girls stare at me a moment, and then nod their heads. We walk in silence back towards the barn. Rachel breaks into a run as we get closer. The sun hangs high in the sky and soon I'll have to go out and scout the route for tonight. Soon we'll be in Mexico. Soon I will not have to be afraid.

Chapter 10

During the 1960's, psychologist Stanley Milgram ran a series of studies to try and show that people were generally inclined to follow the orders of authority figures. In his most famous study, participants were told they were part of an experiment involving memory. They were instructed to teach another person, out of sight in another room, number sequences and then push a button to shock them if they failed to remember the sequence correctly . With each wrong answer the voltage of the shock was turned higher. As the voltage was turned up and the sounds of pain increased, an authoritative figure in a white lab coat would prod the volunteer teacher to continue, telling them they must continue, and that they would not be held responsible. Though most were obviously uncomfortable, 65 percent of the participants continued to the point where the other person, if they had been truly shocked, would have been killed.

I know. The words are fully formed in my head. I can feel them in my mouth. I know what happened. Linds and I walk along the Cumberland River through the tall grass. A thicket of trees hides us from the rest of the world. We are alone, separate. Divided from the happy families galavanting through the park. When we first started walking she had tried to take my hand. I had let her hold mine at first, until we got out of sight, then I let it drop. I move slightly ahead. She follows in silence.

My entire body quivers. Some of it's anxiety, some of it's rage. It's all too much. Too many conflicting emotions. Too much swirling around in my head. I'm in pain. Not the sharp pain that I experienced a few weeks ago, as though someone had driven a knife into my chest. No, it's more of a dull pain now. Like an old tooth that needs to be taken out. My father used to tell me that my grandfather never went to the dentist. When he needed a tooth taken out he got drunk and ripped

it out himself with a pair of pliers. I can never remember my grandfather having teeth, at least not real ones.

I look back at my wife, following me meekly. A puppy that knows it's going to get yelled at. I'm surprised she agreed to come when I suggested we go for a walk. The last two weeks have been uncomfortable. She's not stupid. The discomfort in our home is enough that even Stone is picking up on it, and she's only four. She knows that I know. It hangs like a dark cloud over everything. I don't let myself think about it. I don't let myself brood. Everytime I look at my wife I feel torn in two. How is it possible to love a woman so much but yet still want to slap her as hard as you can? I don't know what to feel. I don't know how to act. I don't know what to do.

I know what you did. For the past two weeks I've been rehearsing what I'll say. Practicing speeches, trying out different reactions and facial expressions. In my mind I have gone over every possible scenario I can think of. All I have to do is push the words out of my mouth. All I have to do is say what I've been holding back. I stop walking. She stops as well. I turn and look at her. I can tell she's frightened. She looks tired. There are dark circles under her puffy eyes. She looks as though she hasn't been sleeping and has spent all the extra time crying. She looks older than her twenty-four years. She looks like she could be twice that age.

It's either now or never. I open my mouth and the words start to come. Linds leans forward, wraps her arms around my neck, and kisses me hard, stifling my speech with her tongue. I'm no fool. I know what she's trying to do. I know what it is that she wants. I will my hands to push her away, but instead they pull her closer and run themselves along her curves. The hurt and confusion of the past few weeks. All of my doubts since we moved to Nashville. Everything that has gone wrong. It is nothing. It is nothing compared to the lust I have for this woman. It is not something that I can ignore.

A part of me rebels. A part of me will not forget, even for a moment. I break the kiss.

"Not now. Not here. For god sakes woman, we're in the middle of a park."

She looks up at me, her eyes full of lust and desperation. She runs her hand through my hair. "Don't be such a fuddy-duddy. No one can see us here. I want you to take me. I want you to take me right here in the grass."

I try to pull back, but the resistance withers and dies. "God damn it woman. The things you do to me."

We embrace again, my hands fumbling with the clasp of her bra. Her hands fumble with my belt. Our clothes fall away, revealing our true selves. I throw her onto the grass and follow her down. She moans as I enter her and two bodies become one. God made me a man of strength and convictions, but he made me a man with weaknesses as well.

All the torment. All the anger. All the anxiety. It all comes out of me in a primal and ferocious explosion of hormones and animalistic needs. Linds' hands rake my back as I thrust harder and harder. My breathing is heavy. Linds is a ferocious mountain lion. Inhuman sounds escape her lips, somewhere between pleasure and pain. My hands run along her body. The body that has borne me two children. They have left no mark upon her. She looks younger than she is. She looks no different than the first time I ran my hands across her, when we could wait no longer and gave ourselves into our mutual needs.

Splashing in the river. I look up, but I don't stop. Six canoes full of boy scouts and loving fathers come around the bend. They can see everything. Linds does not notice. She is lost to this world. We are no longer part of it. The boy scouts gawk at the scene before them. Some of the fathers do as well. Others try to cover their children's eyes or paddle faster to get around the bend. One man stands up, the canoe rocking beneath him. He bellows across the river. I do not hear him. There is nothing else. Just Linds and I, joined as one.

Culmination. I collapse on top my wife. The boy scouts continue on their paddle trip out of sight. Linds rubs my back and coos in my ear before pushing me off of her. The world comes sweeping back in with all its troubles and pain. The moment of relaxation is gone. The anxieties are back. I look up at Linds as she pulls her clothes back on. I can feel the words forming in my mouth. I know. She turns and walks away. I sit for awhile, an eroding stone in a stormy sea. Coward. I'm a fucking coward. I get up, put my clothes back on, and meekly follow my wife's footsteps. I have waited two weeks. I can wait another day.

I push my way back through the thicket and walk across the cut grass to the blankets under the big elm tree. Three little blonde haired blue eyed girls run by. Stone in the lead, followed by Josh and Lacie's daughter, then Rikki's daughter bringing up the rear. Stone's hair is straight. The hair of the other two is curly. The three girls look similar enough that they could all be sisters. They laugh and shriek as they run, too young to know all the troubles of the world.

Linds is sitting by Rikki, sharing a marijuana cigarette and talking quietly, laughing at private jokes. Linds and Rikki are the same age. I gaze at Rikki, admiring the curves under her tank top and shorts. I don't have to imagine what she looks like. She and Linds are good friends. She's joined us many times before. Linds looks up and we stare at each for a few seconds. I can feel her challenging me with her gaze. Daring me to say something here in front of these people. In front of our friends. I say nothing, and she goes back to talking to Rikki.

I sit down on the blanket next to Josh. He's in his early thirties. He's fit. He goes to the gym a lot. I keep myself in good shape, but I feel pudgy next to Josh. He's a good looking man. Wavy blonde hair. Blue eyes like deep pools. He hands me a beer and I drink it quicker than I should. He nurses his own and gazes across the grass to where his wife Lacie sits nestled against the elm's trunk, holding Rachel and cooing at her happily. Lacie is always holding Rachel, every chance she gets. She wants another baby, but Josh doesn't. I finish my beer and Josh hands me another, gesturing towards Rikki's twin brother Ricky.

"What do you think he's thinking right now?"

The young man with the greasy hair sits ten feet away from the rest of us. He stares at nothing through his bloodshot eyes, staying perfectly still. I doubt Ricky can see anything. He tries everything he can get his hands on. Rikki once told us that her brother is impotent, because of all the drugs. I doubt that it's true. He's not impotent, just on a ride that's easier to get his hands on.

"I don't know. Probably not much."

Josh laughs and goes back to drinking his beer. I like Josh. He's a good egg. We work together, he's one of the engineers, but one of the good ones. An engineer who doesn't think he's better just because he's an engineer. Lacie is all right too, though at times a little melodramatic. They seem to get it. They seem to know how to relax. They're both swingers, just like Linds and I. They've offered to do a swap, but I've always declined. Linds and I are adders, we're not swappers. Still, it was nice of them to offer.

I could do without Rikki, and have absolutely no use for Ricky. Their parents must have been fucked up giving them both the same name like that. Lacie was the one who introduced Linds to Rikki. She thought they'd get along. She was right. Rikki is a fun girl. Both in between the sheets and just hanging out. I wish we'd never met her. Rikki's fucking crazy. There are no boundaries with her. No rules. No opportunity should be turned away. I think she's a bad influence on Linds. Linds hasn't been the same since they met. It scares me how easily Linds can be influenced. Sometimes I forget how young she is. Josh's voice breaks my isolation.

"Lacie was telling me you and Linds are thinking of moving out to Portland."

"Yeah, that's right. My sister Amy lives in Tacoma, out by Seattle. She's always raving about it. Lots of liberal minded people, pretty lax on busting people for dope, it seems like a good fit."

"I'll take your word for it man, one place always seemed just as good as the next to me."

I look at my wife. She and Rikki are whispering to each other. Linds' hand is brushing along Rikki's knee. The three of us are together in the back yard, sweating in the hot night, a convulsing pile of flesh and hormones. How many little bags of pills have I flushed down the toilet over the past few months? God only knows what she's been doing when I'm not around. What she's been trying. The house fills with the sounds of hysterical laughter before collapsing into tearful sobs that turn into angry yelling. Things are getting weird. Things are going in a bad direction. I feel more like her father than her husband. She looks haggard.

"I don't know. Just seems like time for a change."

"Restless soul, huh. You have a job lined out there yet?"

"Not yet. I've been talking to Mr. Sanders, he knows some people. People offering jobs similar to the one I have here."

"Well, here's hoping the best for you. Lacie and I are going to miss you two, and Emily is going to miss Stone, and Lacie is most definitely going to miss Rachel."

Josh chuckles and I follow along. He raises his beer and we clink our bottles together. We throw them back, letting the cool bitter nectar slip down our throats. I hold my bottle at face level, letting the sun sparkle through the green glass. Josh pulls out another pair of beers and I exchange my empty for a full.

"It's going to be a little while yet. I'm not moving until I definitely have a job. Can't risk it with the kids ya know."

"It sounds like you have it all planned out."

"Yep."

We sit and sip our beers, watching the three little girls running in circles in a game only they understand, and listening to the sounds around us. Rustling tree branches, Rikki and Linds quietly whispering, the girls giggling, and Lacie cooing at Rachel. It all seems so peaceful. It seems so strange that a single moment can be perfect and my mind can feel contentment when there is nothing but chaos in my life. I am in the eye of the storm. I appreciate the rest.

Linds pulls out her cell phone and shows Rikki a picture. The two of them laugh. My chest feels tight. Is it the same picture I saw two weeks ago? The one I saw when she left for the evening and accidentally forgot to take her phone. Two smiling younger men I don't know, naked from the waist down. My wife kneeling in between them. Her hands full. Her face twisted as though she's in pain. Her eyes look like she isn't entirely there. Who took the picture? Was it Rikki? Was Rikki there? Why is it on my wife's phone? Sometimes I forget how young she is. When was it taken? Who are these men? Why would she let them do that to her? My wife looks like a prop, a set piece. These men don't love her. They don't care about her. She's nothing to them.

"Is anything wrong Paul? You haven't seemed yourself lately."

Bodies convulsing against each other. My wife taken in ways I've never imagined as I'm forced to watch. She takes another handful of pills and motions for another man half my age to come join in the rapture.

I turn my head and force a smile. "No, nothing is wrong."

Chapter 11

The entire justification of the Patriot Act and the Department of Homeland Security depended on the fear of another terror attack similar to 9/11. Without that fear, people would start to question the foundation of the new order. However, the US government was faced with a problem. The countermeasures they had created worked too well. Most terror groups preferred to go after easier overseas targets. It wasn't that there weren't any possible terrorists in the US, it was just that they either lacked the resources, or were just plain too stupid to be any kind of real threat. The FBI joined forces with state and local law enforcement agencies to fix this. Undercover cops teamed up with would-be terrorists, taught them how to make their thoughts into reality, provided them money and materials, pushed them towards the unthinkable, let them push a harmless button, and then arrested them.

I shiver and pull my coat tighter around me. The night is cold in the desert. I hold my military flashlight with its red beam in my hand, the strap wrapped around my fingers, waving it back and forth as I move forward. This way doesn't look too bad. The ground is mostly clear and it's not that steep. Much better than the draw I had walked down initially. I head back towards Alice's red headlights, just visible in the darkness. I walk into their beams and wave my arms, motioning to Linds. She puts Alice in gear and starts coming towards me. I turn and start moving forward slowly, keeping myself just within the range of the headlights' muted beams.

The stars shine brightly overhead. The Milky Way arches across the sky like some forgotten bridge to the heavens. It's beautiful out here. Why do we spend so much of our lives locked away in cages? Why do we not revel in this beauty all around us, hidden only by our own creations? I sat under a sky like this when I was a child, up high in the Guadalupe Mountains. A fire crackled and snapped. Tom and I worked at making s'mores. Tom's dad told ghost stories. All was right with the world. All was good. What I wouldn't give to be back there now.

Things look much different in the dark. The land has changed since we left the old homestead. In my head I can see the topographic map in Alice's jockey box. I can see the land rising up into hills and then dropping back into flat terrain, then rising again before dropping twenty-five hundred feet to the river far below. I can see the country getting progressively rougher. This is going to be the hard part. It has already taken us too long to get this far.

I've been here before. When I went scouting this afternoon. I've already wandered these hillsides. It had been peaceful. Birds chirping and taking wing at my approach. In the daylight all the hills had been topped by rimrocks, their foundations sticking out for all the world to see. I had wandered the hills and draws, enjoying a smoke, looking for a place to get Alice up the hillside. The draws had all been full of juniper and greasewoods. The emptiness had been beautiful.

Getting Alice up the hill had been easy. All the landmarks had seemed familiar. We reached the top of the ridge in only an hour. Getting back down proved to be more difficult. The backside is steeper. There are fewer options for Alice to get down. Everything looks different in the dark. Nothing looks familiar. The world is just shadows that all look the same. I wasted too much time, driving back and forth, waiting for a flash of insight, my family staring at me, waiting. I had to do something. We have to keep moving. Maybe I'd do better if I were on foot? It had made sense at the time.

How long have we been at this now? Two hours? Three? We haven't made it very far. That's for damn sure. Alice creeps forward. I raise my hand to signal Linds to stop. The rumble of Alice's engine blocks out the night time sounds. I move forward out of the beams of the headlights. Three hundred feet. I think we made it forward three hundred feet that time. Maybe I should have used some ribbon. There's a roll of pink construction ribbon in Alice. I could have marked the route to make it easier to find. No. Jesus Christ. What the fuck is wrong with me? Yeah, sure, just lay some ribbon. Might as well just put up a sign to lead people straight back to Alice. Straight back to my family. Fuck I must be tired.

I'm sure I'm far enough out to be out of sight. Linds and the kids can't see me. I reach into my left pocket and take out a yellow pill. I've taken more today than I did yesterday. It's getting harder to concentrate. Harder to stay awake. I wish I could have a beer, but now is not the time. Is this the world or is this a dream? Shit man. I've got to keep it together. This is no damn dream. This is no damn time to start getting sketchy. I hope I have enough to make it to Mexico. Once we're in Mexico it won't matter. I can throw the damn things away and be done with it.

Things are looking better. We had to backtrack a couple times, but it looks like this route is going to work. If we're lucky we'll be able to follow this ridgeline on a steady drop all the way down. We should be able to move fairly quickly when we get to the flats. There will be none of this back and forth bullshit. We need to make up some time. Who know's how far along things are back in civilization. The clock is ticking, but I don't know how long we have. This is taking too long.

I missed the funeral when Tom's dad died. I was in prison. They wouldn't let me out. I can't remember if I sent a card. If I did I doubt the sentiment was really much appreciated. I was too far gone then. Too far down the rabbit hole. I was the prodigal son that no one hoped would return. Tom's dad had been a good egg. He didn't have to do the things he did. I wish I could have talked to him. I wish I could have thanked him. Thanked him for taking me out camping. Thanked him for convincing me to join the football team. Thanked him for suggesting the Marines. Thanked him for so many things.

I look up at the stars again. The same stars I looked up at when I was a twelve year old boy going camping with Tom and Tom's dad. I can taste the chocolate and the marshmallow in my mouth. My hands feel sticky, just like they did then. I look up at the stars and hear Tom's dad's voice as he points out the different constellations. The Big Dipper, Leo the Lion, Cassiopeia, and Orion. I can see his face, smiling behind his sandy moustache as he points out the stars that make up Orion's sword, giving Tom and me a wink from beneath the old fishing hat he always wore.

"They say it's a sword, but that's not what it looks like to me."

Tom and I had laughed though we had no idea what we were laughing at.

"There's Ceres, the Dog Star, and there's Arcturus. If you draw a straight line from the edge of the Little Dipper, that's Polaris, the North Star. Ancient navigators used it to find their way."

"What about that one?"

"That's not a star. That's the planet Venus, and over there is the planet Saturn."

"What about that red one? Is that Mars?"

"Yes."

"Someday I want to go there. Someday I want to live on Mars."

"Maybe you will."

Tom's dad looks down and smiles at me and I smile back up at him. He gives my shoulder a squeeze as we stare upwards into the never ending majesty of the heavens. It's strange to think about it. Strange to think back to the point where I realized exactly how fucked up my family was. When I got back I remember talking to Amy about it right away.

"Amy?"

"Yeah?"

"Have you ever noticed that our family is different?"

"How so?"

"I don't know. That maybe things don't have to be this way. That there are families out there where things are better."

"You're just now noticing this?"

"I don't know. I guess I never thought about it before."

"Things could be better, but they could be a helluva lot worse too. It's not like you're getting beaten, or sexually abused, or anything like that."

"I guess. I shouldn't complain, but it just feels like things could be better."

"Things can always be better."

When I think about what kind of father I want to be for my kids, I always think about Tom's dad. I wish I could have told him that. Just another regret in the pile. I lost the path for awhile, but I'm doing better. I just always have to do better.

Back and forth. Back and forth. Walking to where I can barely see Alice's headlights, then back again to lead her forward. The hillside steepens a bit and I get nervous. We've already gone too far. I think we're past the point of being able to put Alice in reverse and backing up. Dirt and small rocks slide downwards with every step. I can hear Alice behind me, sliding forward a bit every time Linds taps the brakes. I quit going back and forth. I just go forward, walking at the edge of visibility. There is no turning back. We can only go forward. I start walking slightly to the side, in case we get to a point where gravity takes over. I can see Alice in my head, brakes squealing as she slides down the hill, crushing my body beneath her weight.

The steepness of the hill lessens. Things start to level back out. I don't want to get my hopes up. No, things are definitely getting better. We've definitely made it. I wave my arm. Alice comes to a halt on flat ground. The swell of the hills sit behind her. I turn and start walking back towards Alice. Movement on the other side of the windshield. Linds scooching over, back to the passenger seat. It will be good to be out of the cold. Now we can make up some time. I place my hand on the latch of the driver side door.

Rustling in the bushes behind me. I swing back around, tracing my light through the darkness. There. Just on the edge of the headlight beam. A shadow detaches itself from its fellows and moves away, the sound of breaking twigs just audible over Alice's rumble. The shadow stops for a moment, turns its head, stares back at my light. Red eyes glow in the night. I stiffen. Chupacabra. Stone's voice rings through my head. My shoulders rise up. My knees bend. The shadow turns and walks away. I smile and laugh to myself. Christ I'm tired. What the hell is wrong with me? It was nothing, just an antelope, or maybe a coyote. It's amazing how your mind can play tricks with you.

The kids are asleep. Linds sits staring out the passenger door window at nothing. She has turned the console lights as bright as they will go. I twist the dimmer knob until they disappear from view. I turn and smile at the shadow that is my wife.

"Well, we made it down. That's the easy one over and done with."

My wife says nothing. I put Alice in gear and drive forward, slowly so I don't jostle the cab too much and wake the kids. The ground here is still rough. Lots of greasewoods, rocks, and depressions. After already losing the time to change one tire, it seems better to be a little more careful. I reach over and put my hand on

Linds' leg. She says nothing, just stares out her window at the inky blackness. My hand doesn't feel welcome. I move it back to my side of the cab.

"Still have probably another hour before daylight. We should be able to get across this flat area by then."

Silence. I wish Linds would say something. I wish she would understand why we are doing this. I've explained it so many times, but she just doesn't seem to get it. We were delayed an hour getting out of the old farmstead. I can see it now. I get back from scouting just as it's getting dark. I eat a MRE as quickly as I can and then load the last of our gear into Alice. For a moment, I consider taking the time to bury the ruined tire, but settle with hiding it in the corner of the old barn. Linds doesn't help. She just stands and watches me for a while and then takes a blanket and disappears. I get everything packed. I tell the kids to stay in the barn and head out to find her.

She's waiting for me behind house. Standing next to the blanket spread out on the ground. The last bit of sun peaks over the edge of the draw. For a moment, from a distance, she turns into a crone again. Sunken eyes and mouth. Thin greasy hair. Skin splotchy and sagging. A body bent with age. It's nothing. Just a strange trick of the light. I move closer and the mirage disappears. The crone turns back into my wife. My beautiful twenty-seven year old wife.

She says nothing as I walk up to her. I look at her, drink her in. She pulls me close and starts kissing me. Our clothes fall away like leaves in the fall. She pushes me down onto the blanket and mounts me, rides me, takes me all in. Our passions go wild and we become one. For a moment all of the time falls away and it's just the two of us making love on a pile of bales in an old barn again. No worries. No problems. No regrets. Just the endless possibilities of the future. A simpler world. A better world. A world I don't want to leave. With a jerk and a spasm it all comes crashing down.

Linds lays herself down on top of me. I hold her tight. We're both sweating heavily though the air is cold. My breathing is deep. I can feel her breathing heavily in time. She kisses me again and puts her lips down by my ear.

"I want to stay."

I push myself so we're both laying on our sides, looking at each other.

"We can't stay. You know that."

"Why can't we stay here? Whatever it is you have us running from, surely it can't find us here."

"We can't stay here. We have to keep going. We have to get to Mexico."

My wife stares at me silently. Her naked skin a beacon of white in the darkness. I get up and start picking up my clothes, throwing hers to her as I find them.

"C'mon, get dressed. We have to get going."

She stares at me for a few seconds, and then gets up and starts getting dressed. She rolls up the blanket and starts walking back towards the barn. I pull on my t-shirt and start walking after her. The last of the residual elation bubbles upward and into the night. It was all just a distraction. It was all just a ruse.

The shadows flow past on either side of Alice. I stare forward intently at the patch of red light in front of us. Linds stares out into the darkness, at nothing.

Chapter 12

In 1999 the Australian government admitted to being part of an international intelligence operation designed to intercept signals from telecommunication satellites. The program, known as ECHELON, operated 15 to 25 intercept stations around the world. The intelligence agencies of the United States, United Kingdom, Canada, Australia, and New Zealand, were all involved. Built in 1971, the network was originally meant to be used to spy on the Soviet Union and Eastern Bloc. Following the end of the Cold War, the program floated without a primary mission. Whistleblowers claimed that the system shifted to being used for widespread interception of private and commercial communication as well as industrial espionage. In 2001 the European Union launched an investigation of the system, which concluded that there was little or nothing anyone could do about it. The investigation's final report was largely ignored. Over the first decade of the twenty-first century most communications shifted from satellites to fiber optic cables, largely ending the threat to privacy posed by ECHELON.

"Usually we get another woman to join, but every so often we get another guy. I'm not gay or anything, but I do know how to please a woman."

The look on the faces of the couple I'm talking too is priceless. The man is obviously uncomfortable and would rather be talking to just about anyone else at the barbeque. The woman is feigning the same, but I can see a hint of interest in her eyes. A bit of curiosity at tasting just a morsel of what my wife and I have. The conversation lapses into silence and the couple find an excuse to move on and talk to someone else. I giggle to myself and take another drink of beer. I thought Portland was supposed to be a liberal town. Maybe that's less true out here on the far edge of Beaverton.

I check my phone for the umpteenth time since I parked myself on the porch within arm's length of the keg. I didn't feel it vibrate in my pocket, but maybe I missed it. Still nothing. Still no answer. Maybe I should call and leave another message. No, probably better if I don't. I've already left five, and if she hasn't answered any of them, it's doubtful that a sixth will do any good. I force myself to put away my phone. Our last phone conversation runs through my head.

"Hey, how's the barbeque going?"

"Good, you should have come, these are some pretty nice people."

"Sounds boring."

"A little, lots of small talk."

"They're having a party at the neighbor's and I'm going to head over."

"Which neighbor?"

"Jeff."

Jeff is a young strapping man who does construction. Linds had wanted to invite him over for some play, but I vetoed her. We both have the right to veto, that's the way it works. I don't like Jeff. Jeff is a douche.

"Are you still there?"

"Who's going to watch the kids?"

"Kathy said she would watch them until you get home."

"Are you sure that's a goo....." The phone line had gone dead at that point.

I should have gone home right away. I should have gone outside, gotten into Alice, and roared back to Gresham. Jeff's party is not a good place for my wife to be. I had been to one of Jeff's parties myself. A lot of young people in their mid-20's, with shitty jobs and shitty lives trying to fill the hollow parts inside with flirtation and experimentation. I know the feeling, I know the vibe. I can remember when I was just like them. Nothing is taboo and nothing is off limits as long as it brings a rush of endorphins and can help open up their minds by making them forget. A slippery path with no perceived consequences along the edge of a cliff.

My wife is so young. She doesn't have the benefit of my experiences, my mistakes. The things I've told her are just words and stories to her, tales from someone who made mistakes that she can't possibly make herself. I can see Jeff feeding her booze and pills, bringing her up, and taking her down in a cloud of smoke, powders, and crystals. I can see her out of control and Jeff on top of her grunting, her hands gripping him tightly, as the party crowd cheers them on.

I should have left immediately. Right when I got the bad feeling. I didn't. I told myself it was nothing and it was all just in my head. My wife loves me. I know she does. Yeah, there's been some growing problems, but me running over there won't help anything. I can trust my wife. I know I can trust my wife. The worry keeps working at my gut. My attempts to drown it in beer haven't been helping. Fuck it. I get up. My legs are woozy. Doesn't matter. I need to go. It's time to go. My host and co-worker, Other Paul, sees me make my move. He sets himself in front of me.

"I can't let you drive man, your way too drunk."

"Get outta my way Paul." My slur doesn't sound that bad. "I have to get back to Gresham. My wife is at some party."

"I don't care. You can sleep here tonight until you sober up. Just hand over your keys."

I want to push him out of the way. I want to punch him in the face. It would feel good to hit something. Other Paul is a big guy, but I'm pretty sure that I could take him. Doesn't matter. I'm a guest here, a stranger. Aside from some co-workers, I don't know anybody. Never good to punch the host. In that kind of situation most people are probably going to jump in on his side.

"Okay Paul, no problem." I hand over my keys and Other Paul smiles.

"Thanks."

"No worries."

If I'm not going anywhere, I might as well get drunker. I sit back down next to the keg, and start drinking again. My guts churn with anxiety and images of my wife servicing anyone within reach float through my head. I watch the other party guests slowly filter away as the last light of the summer sun falls away. I'm all alone by the keg, slumped boneless in a chair but still feeling tense. I doubt I can get up without falling down.

Other Paul helps me to the couch and puts a blanket over me. He goes into the back of the house and I can hear him quietly arguing with his girlfriend. I can hear enough to get the jist of it, but I don't let it bother me. If anything, it's like going down memory lane, back to the day's when I used to sleep on Larry's couch. I check my phone one more time. Still no messages. My head is a twirl and I doubt I'll be able to fall asleep. I blink. It's morning.

Other Paul is as good as his word. I get up off the couch. He and his girlfriend are in the kitchen, drinking coffee. Other Paul smiles warmly. The girlfriend, I can't remember her name, gives me a dirty look over her cup. Other Paul is a good egg. He offers me a cup of coffee and breakfast before I go. I decline. I need to get home. I need to get home as soon as possible. Alice's engine sings as I take her nine miles over the speed limit down Highway 26 and Interstate 84. I want to get home, but I don't want to have to deal with cops. Most cops only nab you for speeding if you're going ten miles or more above the speed limit. Besides, I don't feel entirely sober yet. My guts are all twisted up inside me.

Off at my exit, down the main drag, a couple turns this way and that, and then up into my driveway. I get out, slam Alice's blue and silver door behind me, and rush for the front door. The house is a cozy little two-bedroom ranch style in what I would call a nice neighborhood, though some high falutin people would probably call it so-so. There's a recession on and I'm doing the best I can for my family. I'll kick anyone's ass that says anything different. Maybe I should stop and compose myself before I go inside. Fuck it. The front door is unlocked. I barrel inside.

"Linds! Are you home Linds!"

"She's not back yet Paul."

Kathy is sitting on the couch watching television. She's a pudgy girl in her mid-twenties. She has a cute face. She's been living with us for the past two months or so, since Linds brought her back to our place one drunken night as part of my birthday present, helping out with the kids and around the house.

"What do you mean she's not back? She didn't come back last night?"

"That's what I said. Relax, it's not like you made it home last night either. Don't worry, I've been here the whole time. The kids are fine."

My head feels like it's on the deck of a ship in a storm.

"Where are the kids?"

"They're playing in the yard."

"I'll be right back."

I run back out the door and up the street a block to a squat two story apartment complex. I rush up the stairs to Apartment 2E, the douchebag's apartment, and beat on the door. No answer. I beat on the door harder. Still no answer. I beat on the door as hard as I can.

"Linds! Linds, are you fucking in there! Answer the god damn door!"

Everything stays quiet except for a barking dog. I can feel some of the neighbors peeking out of their windows at me. Nobody is home, or if they are, nobody has the balls to come to the door. My head is still spinning and my breath is ragged. Home. She has to come home eventually. I can't stand out here beating on the door until some Davey Do-Gooder calls the cops. I walk back down the stairs and back to my house. Images of my wife wrapped in another man's arms fill my head. I've introduced my wife to a lot of things, things she has taken to quite readily, maybe too readily.

Kathy is still sitting on the couch in a pair of shorts that hug her ample thighs. I notice how her t-shirt clings tightly to the roundness of her breasts and stomach. She looks good. Images fill my head of throwing her over my shoulder and carrying her back to the bedroom. It's something that we've done before. I don't. That would be breaking the agreement. We can only have sex with other people if the other person is there and approves of it. No solo adventures. I'm afraid, but I don't know how much is based on reality and how much is just my own fears. I'm not going to be the one to break the pact.

I don't want to feel right now. I want to be numb. I go back in the master bedroom and open up my sock drawer. The mason jar inside is empty, only a few particles left at the bottom. My hand involuntarily tightens around the jar and I just barely stop myself from throwing it against the wall. Fucking bitch. This is horse shit. You can come into a man's home and you can eat his food. Hell, you can even drink all of his beer. But you don't smoke all of his god damn pot. I put the jar back in the sock drawer and stalk back down the hall to the living room.

Kathy looks up from the couch as I walk in. She glances up at me from the television and then goes back to watching. I didn't notice it before, but the entire living room stinks of it. Stinks like a person spent all night getting high on my supply.

"Did you smoke all of my weed?"

She doesn't bother to turn around to answer. "What was that Paul?"

"Did you smoke all of my god damn weed?" The muscles in my neck are clenching so hard that I'm having difficulty breathing.

She turns her head to answer, her mouth half-way open. When she looks at my face she halts before a sound comes out. For just a moment there is a flash of worry in her eyes.

"You don't smoke a man's weed without permission, and you sure as hell don't do it when you're supposed to be watching his fucking kids."

She rolls her eyes and her face turns into a sneer. "I didn't smoke any of your god damn weed Paul. Why don't you calm down and watch some television."

"Bull shit!" The exclamation is louder than I expected. This isn't the first time she's pulled this kind of crap, and it's time for her to move on. I'm tired of Linds' so-called friends hanging around the house. I'm tired of these pricks lazing around and stealing shit. A little sex and free babysitting isn't worth having someone like this around. "Get your crap, you're leaving."

She turns around again. "What the fuck are you talking about?"

"This is my god damn house, and I want you out of it now." My voice is even and cold. It seems to have a better effect than yelling. I see all of the defiance melt out of her in an instant.

Kathy's voice is quiet and she mumbles most of her reply. "Fuck. What the fuck man."

"Quit dawdling, get your shit and get the fuck out."

Kathy doesn't own much. She pushes some clothes into a duffle bag in the corner, glancing at me like a wary deer. Like I'm going to leap up and attack her at any moment. Enough is enough. Does her duffle bag look fuller than when she got here? Is she stealing shit? It doesn't fucking matter. As long as she gets out of the house. I don't want people like her around my kids. She mutters to herself as she moves. A bunch of "fucking psycho" this and "crazy ass redneck" that. She gathers the last of her belongings together. I hold the door open for her. She gives me one last sullen look and I slam it behind her. I breathe. I start to calm down.

I make a phone call and then stand at the sliding glass door in the dining room. My girls are playing in the yard. Chasing each other around in circles. Stone with her long strawberry blonde hair whipping behind her, her face so cheerful and full of life. Rachel's short bob hair cut bouncing with every step and her giggle like church bells on a Sunday morning. They notice me looking out at them and I motion them inside and make them macaroni and cheese for lunch.

Stone looks around when she comes in. "Where's Kathy?"

"She had to go."

Walter shows up during lunch. We go into the backroom to make the exchange and take a few sample hits. I don't smoke much these days, but I feel calmer with the mason jar full. After lunch we take the girls to a nearby park. Walter likes the kids, maybe they remind him of when he was a kid. Maybe simple things just make him happy. He's kind of like a big dumb Labrador. I push Rachel on the swing and he pushes Stone. She keeps yelling for Walter to push her higher. Rachel holds on tight to her swing, afraid she'll fall out.

Even a simpleton like Walter has to be able to tell something is wrong. I can see it in his chubby whisker covered face, but he doesn't ask any questions. Walter is good like that. Instead he tells me about his latest legitimate job, selling Kirby vacuum cleaners door to door. I listen in silence as he brags about all the money he's going to make. I don't bother to point out all the things that aren't in his favor. I don't mention that we're in the middle of the worst recession since the Great Depression and nobody is interested in buying a thousand dollar vacuum cleaner. I don't mention that this isn't the 1950's and nobody buys things from door to door salesman anymore. I certainly don't mention that no discerning well-to-do person with any sense is going to let him in their house. Best to let him hold onto his dream as long as he can. The air feels crisp and fresh.

The afternoon grows late. We take the kids back to the house. I make the girls grilled cheese and tomato soup for dinner. Walter and I drink a couple beers, bullshit and sneak back to the bedroom to take another little sample. I feel more relaxed. More ready to face whatever happens. Where the fuck is Linds? Whatever happens, I now I can handle it. I'm glad I kicked out Kathy. There were some fun reasons to keep her around, but not fun enough. I let things slide too much, let too much garbage accumulate. It's time to start cleaning shit up. I took a pretty good first step this morning.

We watch a little television and Walter goes home. I put the girls to bed, read them a story about a train that never gives up, and kiss each of them good night. They promise to say their prayers before they go to bed. I stay up and have myself another smoke to help me relax. I watch a little television. I wait.

The front door opens. The VCR says it's just a little past 10:30. Her hair hangs limp and greasy. Her eyes are so bloodshot I can barely see any white. Her clothes are wrinkled too, like they've spent a lot of time wadded up in a corner and were only recently put back on. She's still in another place. I can tell. Her stance and gait are all wrong. Her eyes dart around, furtive and unfocused. Her bender isn't quite yet over.

In my head I can see my two girls laying in their beds. My two sweet angels. My redemption for all my past mistakes. I can see them pretending to be asleep with their eyes wide open. The front door opens and closes. There are the sounds of murmuring voices in the living room, quiet, but louder than the television. One is Mommy and one is Daddy. There is something wrong with Mommy's voice. I can feel their little hearts beating as the voices build into a crescendo until the two are shouting at each other at the top of their lungs. The sounds of their voices rises and falls, like the waves at the seaside which they saw for the first time earlier this summer. Only snatches come through, the rest filtered by distance, walls, and young ears.

"What's this…...you…...Kathy?"

"Where the hell were…..!?"

"Fuck off you…!"

"Can't do…!"

"…..own me!"

"....mother....!"

"Fucking.......old man.....!"

"Fucking slut!"

"Jesus Christ....!"

"Your.......kill......!"

I can see Rachel starting to cry, her wails carrying through the house. The sounds of a banshee. I can see Stone climbing out of her bed and climbing into Rachel's to comfort and quiet her. I can feel their tension. The same fear they might feel during a bad thunderstorm. Daddy's voice goes silent but Mommy's keep up a tirade of words they aren't allowed to say. Footsteps in the hallway. The bedroom doorway opens and Daddy rushes in, his worried face barely recognizable in the dim illumination of the nightlight. He bends over by the bed, making cooing sounds. Trying to tell them it's all right. Mommy rushes in behind Daddy. Her face is twisted and horrible to look upon.

"You don't fucking walk away from me shit eater!"

Mommy's arm whips forward and plate goes flying through the air towards Daddy's head. He ducks and the plate shatters into a million pieces on the wall above Rachel's bed. Stone throws herself across the screaming Rachel. Daddy looks down at the broken shards and his comforting face contorts into that of a second monster. He rises up into the air above them.

"What the fuck! You never endanger my kids! You don't pull this shit around my fucking kids!"

Daddy's voice is more yell than words. His voice shakes the ceiling. He moves forward and picks up Mommy like she's a rag doll. He carries her down the hallway in his strong arms as she screams like an animal, scratching and spitting. The front door opens and then slams. The sound of the dead bolt being shoved home with great ferocity.

Daddy's booming voice. "You can come back inside when you've sobered up."

Daddy's footsteps echoing back up the hallway and him walking back in with tears in his brown eyes. I can see it all through my children's eyes. I can feel their confusion and their fear. I can see Rachel huddled beneath her blankets, crying and screaming herself hoarse, her bed littered with pieces of broken plate. I can see Stone sitting and staring at the doorway behind her Daddy. One arm is bleeding slightly where it has been cut by a shard of plate. She isn't crying. She isn't screaming. She's just staring. I scoop both girls up and hold them on Stone's bed. Holding them as tight as I can, muttering soft and comforting words. Rachel quiets down and looks up at me, her eyes full of tears. Stone says nothing. Her eyes are dry and empty.

Chapter 13

In 2005 an intelligence agent with the NSA named Russ Tice became one of the most famous whistleblowers in United States history. Mr. Tice claimed that the NSA had overstepped its bounds in a wide ranging data surveillance operation that monitored the phone calls and emails of millions of Americans, including lawmakers, State Department officials, media figures, large corporations and finance companies, the Supreme Court, and members of the military. An investigation into some of his claims led to the US government admitting to illegal wiretaps on some international communication by US citizens. However, wider investigations were stymied by the operation's designation as a special access program, or in layman terms, a black-ops program. Mr. Tice was rewarded by having his character assassinated by the NSA and the mass media, questioning both his reliability as a witness and his mental stability. The American public erupted in anger, and then forgot about it as the news cycle moved on.

The cliff stretches for miles either way. A sheer drop of solid basalt a hundred feet high. Alice sits parked and covered only a thousand yards away. I didn't know about the cliff. I had no idea it was here. It's lucky we decided to stop when we did. Lucky that the sun started to come up. Who knows what would have happened in the dark. In the night. We probably would have driven right off the edge. Guess someone up there is watching out for us. It's not time for me to die yet. I've always felt like I'll know when it's time.

I hear a sharp buzz and stop my forward progress. My head snaps back and forth, searching the sparse grass and the exposed rocks. I hear the buzz again and I slowly move backwards. There. There in the shadow of that big rock. There's the bastard. He's a big rattlesnake, probably over five feet long. His body curls and tightens and the rattles on the end of his tail buzz again. My eyes rove the ground for rocks to throw. When I was a kid Tom and I used to collect the rattles. We kept them in an old film canister to show Tom's dad. It's been a long time since I've played that game. There's no reason to kill unnecessarily. This isn't the area around my house. This is his turf, his home. I walk around, giving the rattler a wide berth.

I've felt jittery all day. Jittery, but tired at the same time. I'm probably only getting four hours or so of sleep a night. Sometimes not even that much if I can't get my brain to settle down. I can't get it to pop it into neutral. I'm probably taking too many of these damn trucker pills. Necessary evil though. I don't have to do it for much longer. They're starting to make me feel a little strange, kicking my imagination into high gear. When I woke up today I could have sworn I heard Linds having a conversation with nobody. Just a one sided conversation. She kept saying she was worried about me, worried about the kids, and didn't know how much more she could take. Maybe she's starting to crack up again. She has that tendency. When she ducked back under the tarp I asked her about it. She said she was just out peeing and then gave me the look. The one I don't like.

When I got up we ate breakfast together. Or was it lunch? Do we call it breakfast because it's the first meal of the day, or because of the time of day we eat it? I'm not sure. It really doesn't seem important, but it's fun to think about. I had two beers at breakfast. I made sure to remind Linds to take them off the inventory. It wasn't wrong to have beers at breakfast. We had breakfast at noon. Loophole. I wonder how you say breakfast in Spanish. I know cerveza and bano. Seems like a good start.

My hands can't seem to stay still. I feel agitated. I pull the ziploc bag out of my pocket and roll myself a joint. I smoke it as I walk along the cliff. In the winter these hills will be filled with cows. Evidence of them is everywhere. Old cow pies dried out and crumbling in the sun. They must be in the mountains right now. Enjoying the sweet mountain grasses. They'll be here again come winter, but I won't. I hope. In my head I imagined this trip only taking three days or so. How long has it been now? Four days. Five? We still have a bit to go.

It's beautiful out here. I kick a rock over the edge of the cliff. It drops to the hillside below and starts rolling swiftly down the steep slope. Two thousand feet to the flat below. The flat is covered in yellowed grass and sagebrush. South of the flat is another low line of hills. Beyond that is the Rio Grande. The rock reaches the flat. Birds take flight. All we have to do is figure out to get past this cliff. We are so close. So close to being free. No more skulking around. We can just disappear. But first we have to get off this cliff. Overhead is just the wide blue dome of the sky. It looks empty, just a few wispy clouds meandering by. Little wisps of cotton. Wisps is a funny word. I wonder where it came from. I wish there were more than wisps. Clouds are good. Clouds hide us from the eyes. As we get closer it will get more dangerous.

Linds and I had a fight during breakfast. She brought up turning back again. She just doesn't seem to get it. There's nothing back to turn around to. I was patient at first. I tried to explain exactly what was going on, all the nuances, but she just didn't seem to get it. All I want is to be free. Free of worries, free of cares, free to live my life as I see fit. Once it all goes down that's all going to be impossible here in Texas, impossible in every state. I wonder if it's already started. Maybe it has, maybe it hasn't. We should've done this a long time ago, gotten off the grid. For the first time in I don't know how long, I don't feel like someone is watching me.

The debate turned into an argument. I ran out of patience. She started crying and then yelling. I started yelling back. She called me delusional and then crazy. I laughed in her face. Laughed for her belief in a world that only exists on the surface. The veneer coverings don't matter, it's the cogs and gears that matter. In Utah the government is building a facility that can store and process twelve exabytes of information, twelve thousand petabytes, twelve billion gigabytes. Gathering information is easy, processing and storage has always been the limitation. The facility has room for expansion and there's undoubtedly plans for more. The limitation won't protect us for much longer.

I whip my head towards the sound of rocks falling below me. I freeze and look down over the side of the cliff. Below me I can see a deer, a mule deer, if it was a whitetail it would have its tail up. It's an old doe, probably dry, I don't see a faun, maybe she lost it. How did she get down there? How did she get off the cliff? She stops for a moment and looks back up at me. We stare at each other for a moment. She breaks away first, turning and bounding down the hill. It's more like a hop than a run. It's beautiful. I wish Linds and the kids could be here. It would be good for them to see it. It's too dangerous. When we cross the river. Then they can see it. They have wildlife in Mexico too.

One footstep in front of the other. I finish my joint and squash the coal with my thumb and finger before putting the battered butt in my pocket. Don't want to risk a fire. That would be a shame. Everything out here is dry. A tinderbox just waiting to go up. Why do we use that term? Who still even has a tinderbox? I try to picture a tinderbox in my mind. I can't. The joint is helping. I feel a little more relaxed, less jittery, less on edge. That's good. I wish I hadn't fought with Linds. I know she loves me. I know she trusts me. We're all just on edge. Things will get better soon.

One foot in front of the other. The sun inches its way across the sky. It's hot today. Hotter than yesterday. Yesterday was nice. That old farmstead hadn't been that bad of a place to be. Little creepy, but not bad. So strange for it to just be sitting there alone and untouched. I wonder what happened there. How long can this cliff be? How far can it go? It seems like I've been walking forever. It can't go on forever. There has to be a way down. There just has to be. The topographical map in Alice, it showed things getting better this way. Just have to keep going. My eyes follow a low rise to my left, a low rise that builds back up into hills. Hills that spill over my path and rise up to the edge of the cliff.

What am I doing? This is crazy. This whole damn thing is insane. What are we doing out here? No, this isn't crazy. The whole world is crazy. This is just me reacting to the crazy. Doing the best I can with what I have. God damn it. I wish Linds would shut up about all this. Now she's got me questioning everything. What does she think? That I don't want the same thing as her? That I didn't want to stay in Sweetwater, or in Portland? Fuck her.

Rhythmic whumping fills the air. The sounds of blades slicing through the sky. My body spins. My eyes hunt through the bright blue. There it is. Down towards the river. A rapidly growing black speck. Coming fast. Coming right this way. The image wavers in the heat. The dot growing and shrinking. The horizon shimmers. The whole world seems to tremble. Cold air fills my lungs. My body goes rigid. Instinct takes over. I throw myself to the ground next to a big greasewood. I pull myself underneath its branches as far as I can go. It's been over twenty-five years since I've been on active duty, but the training the Corps gave me has never gone away. There's not enough time to find a better hiding spot. The helicopter is moving quick. The black dot rapidly expands into a familiar bug like shape. I hold my body perfectly still, one side of my face pressed into the hot dirt. Grit clings to the sweat on my body. I'm wearing a gray t-shirt and faded dirty jeans. Maybe they won't see. Maybe I'll get lucky.

The noise of the helicopter becomes deafening. I close my eyes. The ground beneath me starts to vibrate. The wind from the rotors whips around me. I try to empty my mind, think about anything else. Don't think about your current situation. Don't give into your fear. Just wait it out. They can't find me. They can't have me. My family needs me. My high school girlfriend pops into my head. Her big green eyes and permed blonde hair. She used to give me handjobs as we drove around the backroads after football games. She had long red nails and would snap her gum while pulling my pud and talking about her day. I always wanted to take it further, but she wouldn't let me. Her daddy was a baptist minister. After prom she let Bobby Jensen fuck her in the ass, to keep her other hole safe for marriage. At the time it had seemed like the end of the world.

What was her name? Shelley? Maybe Sally? No, those aren't right. The helicopter's right above me. I can hear and feel its roar. I open my eyes. Its right above me, banking hard in a turn. I can see the pilot and co-pilot wearing headphones and sunglasses. I'm right in view. I'm out in the open. Naked. Exposed. How do they not see me? The rotors kick up a dirty tempest that swirls off the edge of the cliff. The helicopter's tail whips around the axis of the lift rotor and it slingshots away into the distance, collapsing back into a black dot and then disappearing from sight.

I don't move until the helicopter is gone, then I get up and start jogging as quickly as I can. I don't know if they saw me, but it seems too much to be just coincidence. First things first, let the training kick in. You're in the middle of hostile territory, possibly spotted, move away from the original point of contact as quickly as possible. My first instinct is to run back to Linds and the kids. I ignore it. Maybe they didn't spot me. Maybe I got lucky. Either way I need to assess the situation. Find a place to hole up to see if anyone is coming for another look. I run the opposite direction of Alice. They know to hide if they hear a helicopter. I don't want to lead anyone right to them.

I run close to the hillside, away from the edge of the cliff. There's more spots to hide near the hillside. More places to disappear. Walking along the cliff had been stupid. I should have been more careful. My breath becomes ragged and my booted feet begin to feel heavy. I'm out of shape. I should have spent more time getting back in shape. Up ahead I see a good place to hide, a hollow between two rock outcroppings projecting from the hillside. A large juniper grows between the rocks, shading the hollow from the hot sun. It will be a good place to rest. A good place to wait.

I pull off my backpack and wedge myself onto a patch of bare earth beneath the juniper. It feels cooler out of the sun. The rocks to either side hide me except for directly in front. I have a good view of the edge of the cliff and beyond. I sit and let my breathing slow. I pull a water bottle from my backpack and take a few pulls. I sit and wait. No sound but the wind whispering through the grass. I pull out a granola bar, open it, and start eating. If nothing happens in an hour I'll move on. Go back.

The few clouds move lazily overhead. I drink a little more water and eat another granola bar. I'm hungry. It must have been all the excitement. My high school sweetheart appears in my head again. Holding me close as we dance in the gymnasium. Telling me I'll always be the only one she loves. Pastel cardboard castles sit nestled in a sea of blue balloons and the band in pink tuxedos plays familiar songs in unfamiliar tunes as they smoke cigarettes. Even the singer is smoking, holding the cigarette in the corner of his mouth as he mumbles into the microphone. I tell her I've rented a motel room and she gets mad and storms off. I stand in the middle of the dance floor and watch her go. I know I'm supposed to follow, but I don't feel like it. I still can't remember her name. I know it started with s-h.

Footsteps. Somebody coming from the left. No, two somebodies. They're moving quickly, a fast walk. They're trying to cover some

distance. My hand pulls a large rock next to my side and rests on top
of it. I sit perfectly still and quiet. I'm part of the ground, part of the
landscape. Two men jog into view along the cliff. They stop right in
front of my hiding place, breathing heavily and sweating profusely.
They both have dark brown skin and black hair. Mexicans. One is tall
while the other is short. Both are thin. Both wear old jeans with faded
sweatshirts tied around their waists and canvas bags over their
shoulders. The tall one is wearing a t-shirt and the other a pearl snap
open halfway down his chest. Baseball caps sit on their heads, pushed
back to let them wipe away the sweat. They look in front of them, at
the ground, back the way they came, and out over the cliffs. Every
which way but at me. If they just looked they'd be able to see me in
the shadows. Their movements are furtive, like hunted prey.

Illegal immigrants. If Dad were still alive he'd be angry, yelling in
a rare fit of patriotic pride. I don't really care. They have as much
right to a better life as anybody else. Who doesn't deserve that? Their
one mistake is thinking they can find it here. I sit still and watch them,
waiting until they move on. They're obviously spooked, most likely
by the same helicopter I saw. I've heard of mules smuggling drugs
across the border, but these two don't look like mules. They look like
two scared twenty-something day laborers. Harmless. If they made it
this far, they must have gotten past the cliff somewhere. I think about
calling out to them, but I don't. I sit quietly and watch. The tall one
looks out over the cliff, and the short one, breathing heavily, calls out
to him.

"Ve usted el helicoptero?"

"No, tiene que haber vuelto por el rio."

"Pense que estabamos atrapados por seguro."

"Creo que estamos bien ahora, pero deberia mantenerse en
movimiento."

The short one nods his head. "Si. Por donde?"

The tall one looks around a bit and points in a direction diagonal
from the direction I came. "Creo que por ahi. Debemos salir de este
acantilado."

The short one nods again and the pair jog out of sight. I wait
fifteen minutes then crawl out of my hiding spot. There is no sign of

them or any helicopters in any direction. I almost feel sorry for the poor bastards. They would have been better off staying in Mexico.

I continue my walk along the cliff. After about an hour the basalt drop melts back into the pale tan dirt of the hillside. An old gaunt cedar marks the spot. I stop and look down the steep slope to the flats far below. It looks treacherous but doable. It's good enough, plus the cedar will make it easy to find in the dark. I take my pocket-knife out of my right pocket and carve out a sliver of cedar to use as a toothpick. Nothing freshens your breath quite like cedar. Tom's dad taught me that. I turn and start jogging back the way I came. I'm going to have to hustle to get back to Alice before dark. Off in the distance I can hear the call of a quail. Soon we'll be off this cliff. Soon we'll be safe in Mexico. Sheila. The bitch's name was Sheila.

Chapter 14

The US government has never felt much need to tell its citizenry about its facilities, even when they pose a risk to those same citizens' health and safety. For instance, in 1962 the military built a facility outside Umatilla, Oregon to house 3,700 tons of chemical weapons, enough to kill ten million people. The 25,000 people who lived in the kill zone were never told. I'm sure their notices all just got lost in the mail. Even worse is the endless experimentation. The general population treated like lab rats. In 1949 an operation, dubbed the Green Run, released radioactive isotopes from the Hanford nuclear facility into the Columbia River to see if they could be tracked from the air. In 1953 the CIA experimented with LSD in Project MK-Ultra, which included dosing subjects unknowingly to see how they would react. Throughout the 50's and 60's the military spread cancer-causing zinc cadmium sulfide over numerous cities to simulate the use of chemical weapons. However, by far the worst was the Tuskegee Experiment, a forty-year study of the long-term effects of syphilis, using unknowing, poor Alabama sharecroppers as guinea pigs. Every time another atrocity came to light, the same excuse was always given. It was done for the greater good of all.

"It's nice to see you today Paul."

Her smile isn't a real smile. It's not the kind of smile you give when you're truly glad to see someone. It's the kind of smile you give because you know smiling puts people at ease. It's a professional smile, a mask, doing its best to hide the turbulence of personal emotions. I don't like her smile. It makes me uncomfortable. I give her a nod and settle myself into one of the old worn leather chairs in her office.

"Nice to see you too Doc."

She squints at me through her glasses. She has a bad habit of squinting, as though she actually does need corrective lenses. The one's she wears are unneeded. They are as fake as her smile. I know because I looked through them once when she left her office for a few minutes during a prior visit. I had my suspicions before. They're just like the smile, just part of the act, part of the show. We sit and stare at each other. This is part of the game too. I'm supposed to talk first. Initiate conversation. I know the rules, but I'm not going to play the game. I drove two hours to be here. I shouldn't have to put up with this kind of shit. I'm not the one in her care and treatment. She's supposed to be helping Linds. Not judging me.

We both wait. I let my eyes drift across her office. The two of us in overstuffed worn leather chairs. Wood wainscoting halfway up the wall with the other half painted a calming shade of misty green. A large wooden desk in one corner, a computer on top with a moving starfield screensaver. Several framed degrees on the wall. A picture sits on the desk of the doctor smiling and holding onto a broad shouldered man. They both wear white t-shirts splashed with varying primary colors. Some kind of color run or other such nonsense. A distraction for the well off. A few potted plants in the corners. The whole room is meant to make the visitor feel at ease.

I guess I shouldn't complain too much. It's a nice place. Much nicer than I had. The feeling of cold concrete on my cheek as I sweat and shake uncontrollably. The coldness of stainless steel as I vomit once every few hours into the commode. The laughter of my block mates and the cruel japes of the guards as they force me to go through the day's routine. Manhandling me out into the yard so I can suffer in the sunlight. Leading me into the canteen so they can force food into me that will soon come back up. No, this is a much better place. I'm glad it's different for Linds. I'm glad she's here. This was one of Walter's better ideas.

The doctor reaches down and picks up her mug of chai tea. She sips it through pursed lips. Her lips always seem to be pursed. She wears a blue sweater, modest skirt, and boots. A colorful scarf of green and golds hangs around her neck even though its already comfortably warm in her office. She reminds me of a peacock that has just bitten into a lemon. She stares at me. I stare back until her gaze breaks away and I claim victory.

"So I've been going over your wife's file."

"How is she doing?"

"Very well. We've had several breakthroughs in her treatment over the past several weeks. She's making excellent progress."

"Good."

"How was your walk in the park together?"

The birds singing their lazy songs as they hop from branch to branch. My wife's bony hand in mine as we walk. I tell her about the kids and make jokes. She tries to smile, but can't. My wife looks haggard. She walks beside me with her back bent, her eyes staring at the ground, and her shoulders pressed inward as though she's trying to disappear into herself. She looks much older than her twenty-five years. Her skin looks paper thin. I can trace the blue veins across it. An old crone walks beside me. I miss my young beautiful wife. I don't say anything. I know that she is on the mend, but that she's now to the hardest part. Breaking the use is the easy part. Facing what you did while you were a user is much more difficult.

"She seemed okay. She didn't talk too much."

"That's fairly normal. She's still processing a lot of stuff. It's going to take some time for her to feel up to it. When she's ready, she'll talk more."

"I know. I know it takes time. The waiting is just hard."

"How are your children holding up?"

I can see their faces the night I threw Linds out. Rachel screaming and crying. Stone holding her sister, staring with an intensity frightening to see on one so young. She doesn't cry. She doesn't scream. She just stares. Rachel bounced back, she's young and the young can get past anything. It's only when you're older that the damage becomes more permanent. Rachel acted out a bit at first, little things, arguing more, a few more fits, but soon settled into the new norm. I worry about Stone. My little girl doesn't laugh and play anymore. She broods in silence. She doesn't act out. She doesn't throw fits. She does everything she's asked to do. Her spirit is gone. She's always been the quieter of the two, but now it's as though she's a mute.

"They're coping fairly well. You know how kids are. They bounce back pretty easy."

"That's good. Keep an eye on them. It's often hard for kids to process things like this and it often leads to more long-term traumatization. There's some very good therapists and groups that work with kids involved in these kinds of situations. I could give you some references for your area."

"Okay, I'll keep that in mind. They seem to be holding up pretty well. They don't really seem to understand. They think their Mom is on some kind of vacation. They both miss her a lot."

"She misses them too. She talks about them all the time during therapy. I'd say they're the main reason she's made so much progress. You should think about bringing them down next time. It may help her a lot."

A roughed up clone of my wife stands in the doorway. She's filthy and stinks. Her clothing is ripped and covered in stains. It's the same clothes she was wearing five days ago when I threw her out of the house. None of her clothes seem to fit. She bought them just a few months ago. They hang off of her bony frame. I can remember her complaining that no matter how much she ate she was still losing weight. I should have paid better attention.

Her eyes are red and puffy, I doubt she's slept once over the past five days. One cheek is bright red. A string of fingertip sized bruises snake their way across the upper part of both arms. Her hair is greasy and clumped together. I stand in silence and she looks up at me. Her eyes are haunted with memories that I never want to hear. She looks very young. A scared little girl who knows she has done wrong, and is desperately hoping for forgiveness.

"You're going to rehab."

She stares at her feet and nods dumbly. I pull her against me and hug her as hard as I can. She hugs back with desperation. Clinging to a rock in the storm. I reach inside and grab a bag already packed. A couple changes of clothes, some toiletries, and a few personal items. The photo of the family she likes the best. All of us in bathing suits down at the beach along the river. Everyone's smiling. I knew she would come back. The waiting had been the hardest part, that and not knowing what to do. It had been Walter who had suggested rehab. Every now and again the fat fuck has a good idea. Within an hour of her return, after a quick shower and change of clothes, we were heading south on I-5 to Eugene. I didn't let her see the kids.

"I don't want the kids to see her this way. I don't want them to see their mother in this place with these people."

"These people are just trying to get help for themselves."

"I'm not going to bring the kids here. She can see them when she's better."

"Okay. I really think them coming could help her, but it's your decision."

"How much longer until she can come home?"

"At her current rate of treatment probably within the next few months. She really has made some incredible progress. Most of the work now is helping her get through the residual guilt. People who don't work their way through the psychological aspect are more likely to suffer a relapse."

Sitting at a desk writing on cheap paper in a choppy hand with a pen they'll take away when I leave the library. This letter is just like so many that I have already sent, and so many that I still have to send. The exact details are different but the spirit is all the same. I'm so sorry for the things I did while in the grips of my addiction. I want you to know that I'm getting help. I want you to know how sorry I am. I'm not asking you to forgive me. I'm just trying to make amends. One by one they get sent out. One by one the load on my shoulders gets a little lighter. Bit by bit my soul becomes a little more free.

"I know. I want her to get better. It's just hard, that's all."

"I know it's a financial burden and that things have not been easy, but it's best not to rush these things. The more we rush the more likely she is to have a relapse."

"It's not the financial burden. I just miss my wife."

I sift through the bills and try to choose which ones are more important. Which ones can wait for another late notice without consequence. The balance in the checkbook is much smaller than it used to be. It had been an unpleasant surprise. I should have cancelled the debit card as soon as I threw her out. It had taken eight years to build our savings up to the point of comfort, to a point of not worrying. So much destroyed in only five days. Who knows, maybe it had been longer. I should have paid better attention to the bank slips coming in, but it had always been Linds' job. I wish I could ask her where all the money went, but what's the use? It's all vanished into the empty oblivion that were her and her so-called friends. What little is left is rapidly disappearing to pay for her care. They say money is nothing compared to love, but love doesn't keep the kids fed and housed. You can't survive on good feelings and happy thoughts. Hand to mouth, an old feeling I once thought could be forgotten.

"You mentioned at an earlier visit that you lost your job last month."

That's the problem with telling these shrinks things. They save them up, wait until you're vulnerable, then spring them on you again. It's really none of her business. It seems weird for her to be this personal, but it also feels nice to have somebody to talk to. It had been the best job I'd had since leaving the Marines. Engineers gave me designs, I made them reality. My dream job. Good salary, health insurance, dental and vision, retirement plan. All gone.

"Yeah I missed too many days of work because of the kids. A few of the babysitters I got turned out to be flakes and I had to run home a few times in the middle of the day for various reasons."

"That sounds rough."

"Yeah. Can't blame my boss for letting me go. He worked with me as much as he could, but they're running a business."

"Have you been able to find anything else?"

"I have a couple side jobs here and there, but nothing permanent, and nothing I want to keep doing after all this is done."

"We all do what we have to do. It's okay to be mad and worried about the financial end of everything. It doesn't take away from you caring about your wife. It's all right to be mad at Lindsey."

"I know, my sister Amy says the same thing."

"Oh yes, you've mentioned her before. She lives up in Tacoma?"

"Yeah, that's right."

"Has she been able to help out much?"

"Not really, she's out a lot. She works as a stewardess, flies out of Sea-Tac overseas, Tokyo, Shanghai, places like that, but we talk on the phone all the time. She helps me cope when things seem bad."

"That's good. It's important to have a support system. People to talk to. It makes things a lot easier. If you don't mind me asking, who's been watching the kids when you come down here?"

"My buddy Walter has been helping out. He's a bit of a lunkhead but pretty good with kids."

"Hmmmm." The doctor is silent for a moment. Gathering her thoughts. "I was wondering Paul if we could talk a little bit about your home life? Lindsey has indicated in therapy that the two of you don't have a traditional lifestyle."

I do mind her asking. The sudden shift makes the whole line of questions take on a sinister tone. Why is she asking all these questions? Why is she so curious? When I first brought Linds in it had been nothing but mister this and mister that. Now this quack doctor treats me like we're old pals. I don't like it. When it comes time to pay the bills they call you mister. When they're trying to get your guard down they use your first name. What the hell is she getting at? These seem like weird questions to ask? She's not my friend. She's just some woman paid to help make my wife better. These seem like the kind of questions you get asked when they're trying to decide whether or not you're a fit parent. Is that it? Are they going to take my kids away just because we don't live the way people think we should?

"I really don't see what our lifestyle has to do with anything?"

"Please understand Paul, I'm not saying that the way you live your life is wrong. I'm just trying to better understand your wife's situation to help make it easier to root out some of the reasons she fell into addiction."

I can feel myself starting to get mad. I came down here to visit my wife. Not get the third degree. Who the fuck does this doctor think she is?

"I'm paying you to get my wife off pills, meth, and god only knows what else. Not to have you judge how we've chosen to live our lives."

"Please sir, I meant no offense, but the more information we have the easier it will be for the outpatient therapists to help her avoid a future relapse."

"Outpatient therapists?"

"Yes, outpatient therapists. It will be best for her to visit an outpatient facility for at least a year after she's released. Regular group and individual therapy is very important for a full recovery."

"Jesus Christ. Nobody ever mentioned anything about this."

"It's common practice. They'll work with both of you"

"Me? I'm not the one with the God damn problem."

"Spousal inclusion is very important for full recovery. Just as important as providing a stable home life free of temptations."

"Christ, what do you think I've been trying to do? Hell, I've spent the past four months scouring the house for any stashes like a fucked up Easter egg hunt. I've lost count of the number of pills I've flushed down the toilet."

"That's a good start, but you'll also need to remove any addictive substances."

"What the hell are you talking about?"

"She can't be around pot, beer, or even, ideally, cigarettes. Any one of those items could help push her towards a relapse."

"What the fuck. I'm paying you because she's addicted to pills. Not beer and pot."

"The substance abuse is just a symptom. Not the actual problem."

I can feel my blood boiling and my hands shake. I know my face is bright red. Where the hell does this woman get off? Alcohol and beer aren't like the rest. They have nothing to do with the problem. Her problem is pills and meth. I stand up to leave. What a bunch of bullshit. Just a bunch of shove it down your throat moralistic bullshit. It's not like I know nothing about this kind of stuff. Standing before her is a man who's been clean for twelve years, and who has spent those twelve years still enjoying the occasional drink or the occasional toke without ever once going back to the crystal. What more proof does she need that what she said is complete bullshit.

"I've had enough of this garbage for one day. I have to get home and take care of my kids."

"Paul, I think it's very important that you understand….."

I don't listen to the rest. I stalk out of the office and out the front door of the rehab center. Outside the sky is still blue and birds are still chirping. I get into Alice, start her up, rev the engine, and head for home. Those doctors with their big degrees and easy lives don't know shit. All I want is my wife back. All I want is my life back.

Chapter 15

In 2006 a former AT&T employee leaked to the media the existence of Room 641A at the communication company's fiber optic line hub in San Francisco. The room contained NSA equipment designed to intercept and analyze internet communications at very high speeds. More information on the project started to crawl out of the wood work. Pundits estimated that ten to twenty such NSA facilities were being operated across the United States since at least 2003. The NSA claimed the system was only being used to investigate foreign internet traffic. A class action lawsuit was brought against AT&T. The case was dismissed before it could go to trial after Congress granted retroactive immunity to all communication companies that cooperated with the US intelligence community. The story was front page news for a few days, and then disappeared in favor of the latest celebrity gossip.

The railroad signal starts blinking, the barrier comes down, and I sit and sweat inside the pissant old Camry I bought to drive until I get Alice put back together. Six hundred dollars, bad suspension, no AC. I lean back in the well worn seat and stare out at the world through shaded lenses, hoping for a miraculous cool cross wind to dance through the open windows. No such luck. I can feel the Texas sun baking my arm dangling out the window. The other drivers lounge in their metal boxes, fiddling with their radios and lost in their own thoughts of what to have for dinner and whether or not so and so still gives a damn about them. Not me. I sit and watch the train go by, counting.

This isn't a normal train, with the usual assortment of box cars, oil tanks, and hoppers. This is a special train, with only one cargo. One by one the two locomotives pull seventy-three flat cars past my windshield. Each car holds three Stryker light armored vehicles. Big hulking hunks of steel balanced on four axles and eight tires. The US

Army's go to vehicles for its mobilized infantry. One hundred and forty seven M1126 Infantry Carrier variants, twenty-two M1127 reconnaissance variants, twenty-two M1128 mobile gun variants with their oversized tank turrets and 105 millimeter cannons, twenty-two M1129 mortar variants, three M1130 command variants, and three M1133 medical variants. None of them have any markings beyond their dark green paint.

The train loaded with military hardware glides slowly past. I don't know why I bother counting, must just be habit. When I was still in Portland I would have eagerly thrown my findings up on a couple sites and forums, adding another piece to the growing proof of what's coming. No more though. I have to stay under the radar. I have to keep out of sight. This isn't the first of these trains I've seen pass through. Texas has never been the type of place to take things lying down. The powers that be must agree. The forums suggests lots of military hardware moving into all the red states. The hippies have always been easier to contain.

The train goes by, the lights stop blinking, and the barriers go up. I put the crappy Camry back into gear. My hands tap nervously on the steering wheel. It's not going to be much longer.

There's a strange sound as I walk back towards Alice, the desert lit by the late afternoon sun. It takes me a moment to recognize that the sound is coming from me. I'm whistling. It's been so long since last time I can really remember myself whistling. It seems weird at first, but then it hits me. I'm happy. I can't remember the last time I was really and truly happy. God, it's been at least since before we fled Portland. I feel completely relaxed and worry free. It's such a strange sensation. Such an odd thought to realize that it is a strange sensation. If I could see myself walking across that desert floor, I would have to describe my movements as jaunty.

Who would have thought that finding that way down over the cliff would change my mood so dramatically? It's such a little thing. I know that there are going to be more challenges ahead, bigger ones, but as of right now, I have no worries, and no concerns. Little brown birds flit from sagebrush to greasewood, tweeting a happy tune, and here I am, whistling along like I haven't a care in the word. For the first time in who knows how long I don't feel afraid. I don't feel the noose drawing tight. We've made it so far, and for the first time I really feel like we're going to make it all the way. Everything can go to hell, but me and mine are going to be all right.

Linds and the kids are gone when I get back to Alice. I check under the tarp and call out their names in a not quite yell. There's no reason to attract attention. There is no answer. My hands begin to shake. Where the hell are they? My anxiety drops off. There's a note slipped under one of Alice's windshield wipers, written in Linds' crooked loopy handwriting.

> Paul, girls were restless so took them out on a hike. We should be
> back soon.
> Love Linds.

What was she thinking? She should know better than wandering off in the middle of this desert, so close to the border. What if someone should happen upon them, or one of those damn black helicopters buzzes by overhead? It's an unnecessary risk. I need to calm down. I'm getting all worked up over nothing. It wasn't the best thing to do, but Linds is a smart girl, it's not like the old days, she doesn't need someone to hold her hand all the time, and the girls know what to do. I taught them well. Another one of the games. Drop flat, hide, don't make a sound.

I pull an MRE out of the back of Alice, beef ravioli, one of the better ones, and sit back against Alice's front tire under the tarp to enjoy my meal. As I eat I think about the two Mexicans I saw earlier today and chuckle to myself. Larry used to always talk about a scheister cousin of his when we were younger, a real bastard who was always looking for ways to make an easy buck off some sucker.

Larry's favorite story about his cousin had been the time he rented a U-Haul truck and went into Mexico to play coyote. He made some contacts with the locals and let it be known that he was offering a way across, and all it would cost was fifty bucks a head. He'd get thirty to forty people jammed into the back of the truck and drive them around the Mexican desert for a few hours before stopping somewhere out in the middle of nowhere and throwing the door up.

"America! America! Vaya! Vaya! Rapido! Rapido"

The would-be immigrants would scatter into the desert and Larry's cousin would drive away. It usually took them a little while to figure out that they were still in Mexico. He'd then give his local contacts a cut to keep them quiet and drive a hundred miles or so down the road and do it all over again. He got away with it about eight or nine times, making it all the way from Tijuana to Ciudad Juarez, before word made it ahead of him. He sneaked back across the border before any of his victims or their families managed to track him down. He was a bastard, but a clever little shit, at least until he got knifed in a bar brawl up in Fort Mac in 2006. Those oil sands boys could put up with cheating at cards and a couple scams, but women are in short supply that far north, and it's best not to let your eyes wander. Larry never seemed too upset about his cousin's untimely demise.

My meal done I lay the remains next to me and smoke a joint. It's dark and comfortable under the tarp. I feel like a child in a giant bed. Warm and safe. All is right in the world. My good karma is finally kicking in. I sit, sift through memories, and wait for Linds and the kids to return.

The man's hair is long and greasy. He hasn't shaved in about a week. His brown eyes are wide and won't dilate. A little boy watches through the window of the house as the man hammers and kicks at the front door, screaming at the top of his lungs to be let in. The boy watches in silence, his bright green eyes taking it all in, unable to comprehend or process the madness. The police come but the man ignores them. All he can see is the door, the barrier. The police grab him, throw on a pair of handcuffs, and start pulling him away towards their waiting squad car. Neighbors watch from their windows, and a few brave souls step out onto their stoops. The man throws himself towards the house, and screams as loud as he can.

"My son! I just want to see my son! Philip! Philip! I just want to see my son!"

The police push the man into their car and drive away. The last thing the man sees is the younger version of himself, staring at him from the house's front window, until a figure pulls the boy away.

I wake up with a start, my brow crusted with dried sweat. I shiver, partially from the dream, and partially from the colder air. I'm not the man I was, but there are some parts of the past that you can never repair. Echoes that will never fade. I hadn't meant to fall asleep. How long was I out? The shadows are much deeper underneath the tarp, and the air trapped underneath is stale. I slip back out into the fresh air and climb up the little embankment that Alice is parked next to. The reddish sun is laying on the hills to the west. The skies dazzle with their colors. Oranges and reds across the western horizon, blue above my head, and a steadily growing darkness to the east. The shadows of every rise and sagebrush have lengthened, and my own is a giant stretching out behind me.

Where are Linds and the kids? They should have been back by now. They would never stay away this late. What's happened to them? Something is wrong. Panic tightens its steely grip around my chest. Images flash through my head. My wife and children wandering aimlessly the wrong way into the desert. Linds with a broken leg, the kids crying and unsure what to do. Linds crying as she stumbles with Rachel in her arms, blood flowing from two fang marks on my little girls leg. Two Mexicans laughing to each other as they take turns raping my wife and discussing what they should do with the ninas. I want to yell and scream out their names, but I can't, sounds carry a long ways in the desert.

There's a tall hill just to the northeast. It has a commanding view of the surrounding area. They couldn't have gotten far, I should be able to see them. If I hustle I can make it. I grab my flashlight and my binoculars from my bag and start jogging as fast as I can. The hill is about a mile away. My lungs can't seem to sunk in enough air. It feels like hours have passed by the time I reach the bottom of the hill. It's nothing, they're just a little late coming in, that's all. My reassurances fall on deaf ears. I start scrambling up the side of the steep hill, rocks and loose sandy dirt falling back in my wake. The sun sinks slowly behind me, less than half still showing by the time I reach the summit, three hundred feet above the flats below.

I take out my binoculars and start scanning the desert landscape. Searching for any signs of movement. Any signs of life. My movements are frantic, rapid shifts and long pauses just long enough to ascertain that nothing's there. The shadows are getting longer and it's getting harder to discern the individual shapes. Every scraggly tree, every greasewood, every rock, they all look like the figures I'm praying to god I'll see. A flash of movement towards the west. No nothing, just a deer, an old doe jogging her way across the desert with two fauns in toe. I run across the flat top of the hill to look more towards the north, scanning to the horizon far beyond the walking range of a woman with two little girls. Where are they? The darkness is falling quickly. Where are they? They're gone. They're fucking gone. The world below me is empty. There is nothing there.

I don't see it, but I hear it. The hard whap of the rotors beating down the air. The sound of a helicopter moving at full speed. For a moment I don't care. I feel relaxed, out of touch. I'm not on the hill. I'm in my bed. No, not my bed, but a bed. It's warm and safe. The world drowsily flows past. It's somebody else. The buzz grows louder. Fuck. I need to hide. There's no cover on top of the hill. I'm completely exposed. The sounds are coming from the south. I throw myself down the north slope, take five giant steps, and my feet come out from under me. The world becomes a tangle of jumbled sights and shapes. I curl myself into a ball, one hand protecting my head, and the other trying to keep a hold of my flashlight. At the bottom of the hill I come to rest next to a giant sagebrush. My pants are torn, and my elbows and knees are bloody. I feel like I've been through a meat grinder.

The sight of the swinging blades at the top of the hill awakens me from my daze. My flashlight lays next to me. I grab it. My binoculars are gone, the string that hung them around my neck broke somewhere on the way down. I pull myself under the sagebrush as much as I can and hold my breath. God I hope it didn't see me. God let them not have seen me. The reflections. The reflection of light off the binoculars when I was looking. It must have been like a beacon from the top of that damn hill.

The helicopter hovers over the top of the hill and the shadow where I hide becomes deeper. I find myself both cursing and thanking god at the same time. The darkness will hide me better, but remove any chance of me finding my family. The helicopter swings back and forth, searching, hunting. I lay motionless, not daring to move. The sun dips below the horizon and the world is plunged into darkness. The weak crescent moon that replaces the sun in the sky provides no light. I can still hear the helicopter overhead. Do they have a searchlight? God please don't let them have a searchlight. The black monster swings around, and the sound of the unseen beast disappears into the distance. I lay beneath the sagebrush, my breathing out of control, my body shaking with tension. I can't see a fucking thing.

I lay still until I get myself under control, and then start to pull myself out from my hiding place. The stars twinkle overhead and the expanse of the Milky Way spreads itself from horizon to horizon. A twig snaps not far away. I freeze, my head whipping towards the sound. The light pad of a footstep, then silence. I slowly raise my flashlight, and flip on the switch.

It's less than ten feet away from me. The red beam of my flashlight illuminates everything. Fuck. It has almost no hair over its sallow gray skin, just a few tufts across the ridge of its back. A giant shaved rat mounted on four long legs, the back two shaped for power, the front two for support. The hairless tail behind it looks like a whip. Two pointed ears sit on an elongated head with two glowing red eyes. It has a lean hungry look to it. A macabre image from the depths of hell. We stare at each other for a moment, and then whatever the hell it is lets out a loud threatening growl from deep within its throat. It takes a step forward. I scream as loud as I can, scoop up a handful of rocks and dirt, throw them as hard as I can, turn, and start running.

The beam of the flashlight swings erratically as I run as fast as I can away from the nightmare at the base of the hill. I stumble over something, maybe a rock, maybe a little sagebrush, catch my balance and keep going. My feet keep pounding until my breath becomes ragged and my busted joints refuse to carry me any further. I fall to my hands and knees and start puking up my dinner of beef ravioli. Frantically I turn around, searching with my light for any sign of pursuit, a dark shape or those glowing red eyes. Nothing. There's nothing.

I turn off my flashlight and the world plunges back into complete darkness. I sit in silence getting my breathing under control. As the adrenaline leaves my body I start to shiver. I'm still just in a t-shirt, and at night the desert gets cold. I don't know where I am, I don't know where my family is, and I don't know where Alice is. I'm helpless. If I start wandering in the dark, god only knows where I'll end up by morning. The only thing I can do is sit, and wait for the dawn to make everything make sense again.

I pull out the little container of yellow pills from my left pocket and swallow one down. I doubt I'd even be able to fall asleep, but I don't want to risk it with that thing out there. What the fuck was that thing? My mind again fills with the horrible scenes of my family lost, scared, hurt, captured, or murdered. I try to push them out. Please god, please let them be all right. Let them be waiting for me at Alice tomorrow morning. I scrape the ground with my blind hands, gathering up larger rocks and piling them next to me. A sound in the darkness. My light blazes forth, revealing nothing. I try to slow my breathing. Another. I again flick on my light. Just an old doe, maybe the same one I saw from the top of the hill. Silence. Nothing but the wind. A twig snaps. I flick the switch again. My light turns on, dims, and goes dark. The batteries are dead. I should have changed the fucking batteries. My ears strain, trying to hear what my eyes can't see. Nothing. Just silence. I'm left alone in the darkness, crying where no one can see.

Chapter 16

Governments changing the rules to better the position of those in power is nothing new. Just look at any country in Central America. Nearly every single one has had a presidential term limit clause in their constitution at one time or another. Then along comes a popular politician, the clause gets voted out of existence, and poof, new dictator. The dictator gets overthrown, the people re-enact the clause, and the whole cycle starts again. Of course the US isn't innocent of monkeying around with its rulebook either. Between 1935 and 1936, the conservative Supreme Court struck down numerous portions of President Frankie Roosevelt's so-called socialist New Deal. In 1937 Roosevelt took the bull by the horns and had his flunkies introduce a bill that would allow him to pack the court with an additional three judges, which would sway control to his side. Roosevelt already had control of Congress, so it looked like an easy pass. However, one of the Senators championing the move died unexpectedly, the media got a hold of the story, and an angry public swayed the legislature to defy Roosevelt. The American system based on its division of powers was saved, at least for a while.

The nurse walks into the dark room and hands me a pink grub in a blanket. She stays just long enough to see that I know what I'm doing then leaves to help somebody else. I sit in an uncomfortable chair in the hospital room's corner and stare down at the sleeping form of my daughter, less than three hours old. I'd forgotten how small they are when they first come out. How fragile. Without thinking I gently rock the bundle in my arms, an old reflex from a past life. I brush my hand across the blonde hair on her head and quietly whisper down at her.

"Hi Stone. Welcome to the world. I'm your Daddy."

Linds lies deep asleep in the big hospital bed. Her thin blonde hair lies around her head like a halo. She looks exhausted, drawn out. We've been here since early yesterday morning, and now it's 3 AM.

She looks very small and slight. Too small. Holding the bundle in my
arms I can't help but notice how young my wife is, how childlike her
features. At nineteen she's already a miracle maker. Soon the baby
will wake up and with a loud cry remind the world that she has to be
fed, but for now, they both deserve their rest. I sit back in the chair,
feeling knots grow in my back, but I stay perfectly still. I stare at the
miracle in my arms and let my mind wander. She's another chance. A
chance to do things right.

The room morphs and changes. My wife's slight face becomes
rounder and older. Her blonde hair turns dark and curls. The baby in
my arms changes as well. Whiffs of blonde are replaced by a
smattering of black. The face, so like Linds' face, shifts and re-forms.
A larger nose, a blunt brow, and a thicker chin. I stare down at an
immature version of myself. An infantile copy which will soon wake
up screaming at the world, demanding to be heard.

I'm shaking and I can't get myself to stop. I don't dare move my
arms from the position the nurse forced them into before depositing the
pink lump into them. I'm not sure I'll remember how to hold him if I
do. I sit and stare, unsure. I don't know what I'm doing. I feel like
I'm staring down at myself. A helpless little piece of myself that I
know I'm not ready for. Part of me wants to put the baby down and
run away. Just walk out the door and never look back. God, I hope it
doesn't wake up. I hope it stays asleep. I'm scared. God I can't
remember the last time I was this scared.

"One, two, three, four, I love the Marine Corps. One, two, three,
four, I love the Marine Corps."

My voice rings with the rest in a steady cadence, timed to the up
and down beat of our jumping jacks. I feel sick inside. We haven't
eaten breakfast yet, but I already want to puke. The beat is slow and
steady, a constantly swinging hammer slowly knocking me flat bit by
bit. The sergeant in front is in no hurry. He knows that he can take his
time. He has all day to flatten us out. He knows we can't escape. The
sergeant is nothing but muscle and sinew, I can see his throat bulge
like a bullfrogs as his voice reverberates across the yard.

"Come on you pukes. Drop and give me fifty. Double time. No
one eats until we get done with our morning warmup."

I drop with the men around me, obedient as dogs, and start pumping out push-ups to the steady baritone dirge. I keep my eyes to the ground. I don't want to look at the men around me. I'm afraid that if they look me in the eye they'll know how afraid I am inside. This was a mistake. This was most definitely a mistake. I should have stayed at home and gotten a job. I should have gone to community college. I should have done anything but this. I wonder if anyone heard me crying in my bunk last night. I wonder if any of the strangers around me cried as well. I know I can never ask. We're all on our own private islands. Moving upward and downward within feet of each other, but separated by much greater distances.

My arms grow tired and weak. They've never before been put to this kind of test. I feel them turn to mush and my body doesn't lift with the rest. The drill sergeant is on me in an instant, a booted foot catches me in the ribs and I instinctively roll into a ball.

"What the fuck do you think you're doing you lazy shit of a shit?! You think there's any laying down in my Marine Corps?!"

The booted foot shoots out again, and the contents of my empty stomach flow up my throat and onto the ground. The rest continue with their pushups around me.

"Quit stalling you piece of scum. This is no fucking time to take a nap. You get up and finish your fucking pushups."

I want to shrink down until I disappear. I want to get up and run. I want to cry. None of these are an option. I can't escape. I can't retreat. I can only go forward. I force myself onto my chest and struggle to raise my body with my arms.

"Maybe you want to go home you faggot? Maybe you want to go back to sucking dick behind the gas station in whatever fucking hick town fucking shat you out."

Hate wells up inside me and I feel it flow down my arms, filling them and forcing them to extend. My body rises and a voice screams from my mouth.

"No sir."

"Damn straight you fucker. You wanna be a Marine you damn well better not puss out now. I will fucking end you."

I can do this. I can survive. Happy thoughts. I just need to think happy thoughts.

"Paul, it's time for breakfast, get your ass down here."

The woman's voice from downstairs is like a half forgotten song where the tune is recognized but none of the words are remembered. The entire house smells of pancakes, eggs, and bacon. The boy abandons his nest of warm blankets and pulls a giant blue t-shirt, emblazoned with "Houston Astros" on the front in orange, over his head. The shirt reaches down to his knees. He opens the door to his bedroom, and runs down the stairs, his four-year-old legs taking a leap of faith as he leaves the step above before making contact with the step below.

In the kitchen a piled high plate waits for him. Bacon, crisp, pancakes drenched with syrup, and eggs scrambled with a sprinkle of pepper. A woman stands at the stove with her back to the table, flipping pancakes in a frying pan, a long brown braid falling between her shoulders. As she works she hums to herself. A man sits at the table, sipping orange juice and reading the Sunday comics. An ashtray sits nearby, smoke curling from a cigarette balanced on its edge. The boy smiles, sits down, and proceeds to eat.

The food is delicious. Every bite better than the last. The bacon is devoured, the pancakes are nibbled bit by bit, and the eggs are left to cool on the edge of the plate. The boy turns towards the woman to ask for more bacon but she is gone. The back door of the house is open, swinging on the hinge, letting in the noises of the outside world. The boy gets up and scrambles for the door. His eyes scour across the yard, searching for the elusive figure of the woman, but she is gone. Dejected he turns back into the house. The man sits at the table in his t-shirt and boxers, cigarette hanging from his mouth, and a can of beer in his hand. His eyes are locked on the wall in front of him, staring at something the boy cannot see.

"Fuck you Paul."

The woman in the tube top behind me, I think her name is Amber, backs further down the sidewalk away from the door. Diane's curly hair is frizzed out around her head, giving her a demonic demeanor only aided by her attitude. The world seems to be swimming all around me and I'm having a hell of a time keeping everything in focus.

I know it won't help the situation, but I feel my lips pull apart in a smile and a little laugh escape my lips.

"That's the idea baby."

Diane doesn't seem to get the joke. In my head I see her pulling her bathrobe open and grabbing onto me, just like she used to. Instead she just pulls the robe tighter around her. I can feel my legs sway underneath me, normally reliable, they seem to have turned to jelly. I try to smile again, but the angry look on her face kills it before it even begins. I feel like I'm underwater, or maybe one of those space probes where all commands have to be made several minutes in advance because of the interstellar distances.

"What the fuck is the problem?"

"What the fuck is the problem. Are you fucking serious? You drag some tavern tramp back here at two in the god damn morning, drunk as hell and whacked out on god only knows what, and you want to know what the god damn problem is."

I try to put one and one together, but they don't seem to add up to two. Though that is the answer to what I thought was going to happen when I had allowed the woman with the big tits, who I had shared a marijuana cigarette out behind the dumpster with, to drive me home in my car. Things did not seem to be moving in their expected path. Diane glares at me and I happily stare through the doorway at the lamp behind her head, enthralled by its vibrance. I sniff and rub my finger under my nose. It feels dry. It seems strange that it feels so dry, but then I remember the line of coke I did in the bathroom thanks to the generous help of David. Good guy that David. Good one to have around. It takes me a moment to realize she expects me to say something.

"So you going to let us in?"

"No."

"C'mon. We'll have some fun."

"I told you, I'm not doing that kind of shit anymore."

"You used to do it, you used to have a pretty good time doing it."

"I'm not doing it anymore."

"Why the hell not?"

"Because I'm a mother now. You're a father."

"I don't see what that has to do with anything. There's nothing wrong with it."

"I don't want to live my life like that anymore. Our son is more important than that shit. I want him to grow up to be good people. To be respectable."

I know what she's implying, but I don't let myself get riled. She has no fucking right to say that kind of shit to me. I work a good job. I'm a good provider. Who cares if I like to get a little crazy every now and again? Who's it hurt to have a little fun? It's nobody's damn business what a man and his wife do together. I'm not going to pretend to be something that I'm not. I take a step forward and try to force my way past her. She braces herself against the door jam. I paw at her robe and she slaps my face hard enough to twist my head around. My hands close into fists.

"You fucking bitch."

From deeper in the small house a three year old starts screaming for his mother.

"Come back when you're fucking sober."

Diane gives me a hard shove and slams the door in my face. I hear the dead bolt ramming home. Amber steps forward and helps me up. I look at her, makeup applied with a trawl, and shrug my shoulders. She stares at me for a bit, her expression a mix of sad and bored, like an old hound dog, and then leads me by the hand back to the car. I go with her willingly. It will be a while before I come back down, and one is better than none.

The movement of the creek gives tiny tugs on the fishing line, giving the illusion of something biting. Such movements might have tricked me when I was younger, but I know better now. This isn't my first fishing trip. I ignore the gentle pulls of the current and hold my rod just right to keep my line in the shade of the willows over growing the other side of the creek just eight feet away. Tom is about two hundred feet up stream, and his dad is fishing in the area just between us. I can hear Tom's dad singing softly, and the occasional gust of wind bends the grasses along the shore and increases the volume of his tenor in my eleven-year-old ear.

Old black Joe, old black Joe,
Where will he go,
Can't use a plow and can't use a hoe,
Ain't got wool where wool outta grow,
Poor old black Joe.

The line moves away from where I'd like it to be so I reel it in and cast again. The hook and nearly invisible line fly through the air and unceremoniously wrap themselves around a low hanging willow branch. I curse, the words like my cast, stronger than expected. The singing upstream abruptly cuts off and I hear footsteps working their way across the round river rocks towards me. Tom's dad walks nonchalantly, carrying his pole and whistling. He tips his fishing hat back and wipes his brow with the back of his hand. I wait impatiently for him to arrive.

"Everything okay Paul?"

His sandy moustache wiggles with every word.

"My line is stuck in that God damn tree."

Tom's dad looks down my pole and his eyes slowly follow the line, beaded water glinting in the sunlight, to the willow across the creek.

"Certainly looks that way. What are you going to do about it?"

"I guess cut the line."

"Bullshit, that line doesn't look too tangled. You should probably just go untangle it."

"But then I'd have to get in the creek."

"You ain't made of sugar. If you want to go fishing sometimes you gotta get wet."

I stare at him, his steel gray eyes, his curly brown hair poking out from a fisherman's hat that hides his bald head from the sun. He stares back for a few moments before taking my silence as me not getting the message.

"Don't look at me Paul. I'm not the one who got my line tangled in a willow tree. We all have to deal with our own shit in this world. No one else is going to do the hard stuff for ya."

Tom's dad starts walking back up the creek and I stand staring at my tangled line, cursing sullenly to myself and wondering how cold the water is. When he's about twenty feet away Tom's dad turns back and looks over his shoulder at me.

"Sitting and staring at it isn't going to change anything. Best to just get it done with."

I grimace at his retreating back, sigh to myself, and start wading out into the water. Above my splashing I can hear the tenor voice singing once again.

Jiggaboo jiggaboo where are you,
Out in the woodshed hiding from you.

The baby sleeping in my arms feels hot, so hot that it's making my chest sweat. I'd forgotten how warm babies are. It's been so long. So many things I've forgotten. My memory is fried. I know I don't remember everything as much as I should, but I remember enough. As I hold her sparks ricochet through my mind, lighting up dark recesses, the good and the bad, some real and some just half imagined. The little baby in my arms is more than just my daughter. She's so much more. She's the most beautiful thing I've ever seen. I lean forward and kiss her on the forehead, whispering so only the two of us can hear.

"I'm going to do it right this time Stone. I promise that this time I'm going to get it right."

"Hello?"
"Amy, it's Paul."
"What's up?"
"It's happening."
"What's happening?"
"What we talked about the other day."
"Are you sure?"
"Yeah. All the pieces are falling together, it's going to happen within the next couple days. If we want out, we're going to have to get out now. I've been loading Alice up all day. Linds doesn't seem so sure."

"Take it easy on her. You know she hasn't been watching this stuff like you. What's with all the noise in the background?"

"I'm on the last pay phone in Sweetwater, the one at the truck stop. I tried talking to Larry too. I left a message, but lately he hasn't been getting back to me."

"You can't save everyone Paul."

"I know. Amy?"

"Yeah."

"You believe me don't you?"

"Of course I do kiddo. Of course I do. I'm going to call my boss at the airline as soon as I hang up. I'll tell them an uncle died or something, nobody will ask any questions."

"Good."

"I'll see you in a couple days."

"I love you Amy."

"I love you too kiddo. See you on the other side."

Chapter 17

The internet is the greatest invention of mankind. It represents an artificial brain which contains the sum of human knowledge. No other tool has provided a greater access to learning. To navigate this new brain we have search engines, complicated algorithms that sort and prioritize information. While on the surface this might seem like the key to a golden age of enlightenment, the question must be asked. If the algorithms tell us what's important, than who controls the algorithms? Even if the algorithms work as we are told they do, that it is simply based on the sum of all past searches, there are still problems. These algorithms not only control our search engines, but also our news feeds, and what advertisements we see. They filter the world into the reality that we want to see, blocking out any information that conflicts with our world view. Constantly telling us that we are infallible until we actually believe it. Is it any wonder that today's population is so polarized?

It had all started out as just a hobby. Something to distract myself with while Linds was locked away. I've always been good at noticing things. I've always been a detailed observer of the world around me. The amount of information available was staggering. I would find myself up all night, reading, learning, trying to put the dots together. Lists, updates, schedules, sightings, and documents. All adding up to some greater truth. Posted by anonymous patriotic crusaders. It didn't take me long to join their ranks and start posting. For the first time in a long time, I felt like I was a part of something. Flying high enough to put together all the details that when seen below, mean nothing. Looking past the things that they want us to believe, and the things they hide just to distract those who refuse to accept their truth. Things were moving fast.

Smooth69 was the first one to disappear. The regular posts on the various forums just stopped without warning. No more updates from the Fort Leavenworth area. The silence was deafening. Next to go was FlagWaVer, then GhostRecon, then Pig69Pork, then HanCOCK. All the top posters, one by one. The flow of data slowed. What was once a torrent became a trickle. We were close to seeing the truth, but all the sources were running dry. Around us people slept, blind, unable to see.

Files started appearing on my computer. Hidden away in the folders that contain the nuts and bolts, the rarely looked into areas under the hood. You can find anything on the internet, learn anything, even proof when something does not belong. I deleted them. They reappeared. Numerous forms of anti-malware, anti-spyware, anti-virus. The files always reappeared. JefferSon went offline. I smashed my computer with a hammer. A week later we left Portland for Texas. Linds didn't want to go. I promised her that we could get a cat when we got to Texas. She was always hassling me to get a cat.

Once when I was a little boy, Mom and Dad loaded up the car and we took a four and a half hour drive to Marfa to try and see the famous Marfa Lights. My Mom had read about them in a magazine and somehow convinced my Dad to make the trip. Mom had always been into that kind of stuff. What she called the world behind the world. We camped alongside the highway. Mom and I stayed up all night in the pitch black, sitting in lawn chairs, covered by blankets to stay warm. Mom told me about the basketball-sized balls of light that the magazine had described to her. As she talked my eyes strained through the darkness, desperate to see.

The stars twinkled in the heavens, broken in two by the cloudiness of the Milky Way. The world seemed so big. There was plenty of room for a bit of magic like the Marfa Lights. They never appeared. The next day we drove back to Sweetwater. The car trip was silent, except for me asking once for a stop so I could get out to pee. Dad stopped alongside a gravel pile, and when I got out I noticed how suffocating the interior of the car had become.

Sitting in the darkness, my flashlight long dead, popping yellow pills into my mouth every time I feel my head drop, my eyes searching through the darkness, hoping to catch a view of the lights I failed to see forty-four years ago. My head swims through a haze of worry, anxiety, and expectation. The entire world is buzzing just an octave below my hearing. I can imagine my family, all the terrible things happening to them, but my eyes can't leave the wonderment of the skies above me. I'm small, oh so very small. It's impossible to look up at the heavens, and not feel so very small. In the cities you can grow big, the skies are hidden away, but out here, out here it's impossible to grow. The whole of the universe is pressing downwards. A great weight which none of us can escape.

It all seems so much like foolishness. My troubles. This trip. The reason why I run. It's all so god damn small compared to the celestial grandeur of the heavens. What am I doing? What have I done? What do I do now? None of it seems to matter. Even the cold that makes me shiver. It is nothing. It is all just nothing. I'm just a pawn, a tiny meaningless pawn in something too big for me to understand. My body begins to vibrate, changing speeds until it becomes in sync with the buzzing of the world around me. For a moment it all becomes clear and the curtains are drawn back. But then the sun bursts above the eastern horizon with the ferocity of a springing lion, and all falls back into the mists of my mind, forgotten.

As soon as it's light enough to see I get my bearings, just as the Marines taught me, and start walking back towards Alice. The daylight world seems suffocating, like the car on the drive back home when I was five, but there is no way to get out. There is no way to escape. The temperature quickly moves its way upwards and by the time I get to Alice I've gone from shivering to sweating.

I duck under the tarp hiding Alice. No one is here. I'm not surprised, but I'm still disappointed. During my walk I had refused to let myself think about it, but a part of me had still hoped that my family would be here when I arrived, and everything would be okay. My body turns to jelly and my legs collapse underneath me. I sit in the dirt and cry. Great heaving sobs that haven't escaped my body since I was a child. They're gone. They're gone. Good God they are gone. My sobbing does nothing. I sit for a while waiting, and finally accept the fact that my mother isn't going to appear to tell me that everything is going to be all right. I stand up, brush the dirt off of my legs, and push myself back out into the sunshine.

I climb to the top of the small rise hiding Alice. A small group of red cows with white faces graze nearby. Wandering aimlessly, their heads down. A gentle breeze whispers in my ear, pushing down the grasses and rattling the greasewoods. It's picturesque. I spin in a full circle looking in all directions for any sign. Willing my eyes to see what I know they will not. I don't know what to do. My body and brain feel numb. It's as though my mind has become overloaded, running slow, a computer put to too many tasks at once.

My family. I have to find my family. Everything else can wait. I can see my sister Amy, with her long black hair, waiting and worrying. This journey has already taken longer than it should have. The entirety of the world is against me. I'm fighting something so big that it's too massive to even see. Amy will just have to sit tight. I have to find my family. Linds with her soft kisses and thin body pressed up against mine. Rachel with her laugh like little bells. Stone, beautiful little Stone, with her sad blue eyes that have seen too much. They need me. They need me to protect them.

I slip back under the tarp and start replenishing the supplies in my backpack. I don't know where to start looking, but I have to try. Freshly topped off water bottles, a handful of granola bars, and new batteries in the flashlight. I'm just about to push my way back out into the open when the image of red eyes floats before my face. I climb back into Alice and pull a small plastic box out from under the driver side seat. I set the box on my lap and open it. Inside sits a 22 caliber pistol. Small, quiet, but more than capable in the right hands. I put the pistol in my backpack, close the case, and put it back under the seat. I reach over to open the jockey box to grab the box of shells. My mother's Saint Christopher's medallion glints in the sunlight. The holy man's face looks sad. My eyes catch a black cord. Fucking bitch. I stop breathing.

The cord hangs from the open ashtray, next to a half smoked joint. One end loose, the other plugged into the hole normally reserved for the cigarette lighter. It's a cell phone charger. My hand reaches forward and gently pulls it out. I sit back in the seat, staring down at the black rubber coils on my lap. My fingers run across it. Feeling, but not believing. No communications. It was the first thing that got cut off when we headed out. No phones, no radio, no nothing. We had to disappear. We had to become invisible. How could she do this? How could she do such a thing?

My breath and heart rate become rapid. I'm hyperventilating. I'm drowning. How could she? How could she? The half dreamed sounds of one-sided conversations. The acts of a petulant child, not wanting to go. She's taken them. She's taken them away. Oh god. Rachel. My little monkey. Stone. Sweet little Stone with the blonde hair like spun gold. Where are they? How could she do it? Fucking bitch. How could she do it? My hands begin to shake and the cord drops to the floor. A mixture of hatred, grief, and relief. They're okay. They're okay. Nobody has taken them. No one has hurt them. Fucking bitch. How could she? She's taken them from me. That fucking bitch.

The world spins around me. Somebody is screaming at the top of their lungs. Cursing. Crying. Air. I need fresh air. I pull the latch, fling the door open as hard as I can. It flings itself back at me and I kick it away. I try to get out but my legs have turned to jelly. My body flows out of the open door, depositing me on the hard dusty ground below. Rivers flow from my eyes and my fists pound the earth in frustration. Bitch. Fucking bitch. How could she? Why? Why? Why? My family. My fucking family.

Linds never understood. She never understood what I was trying to do. She could never see that I was trying to save us all. Give my family a chance. Give them a chance to live free without fear. To live their lives without someone always looking over their shoulder. That bitch. That fucking drug addled bitch. After all the shit she put me through. After all I did for her. The audacity. The fucking audacity. My girls. She's taken the god damn girls. My family. My daughters. My life. She's taken my fucking life.

I push myself up onto my arms, grab the open door, and pull myself to my feet. The fucking bitch. Nobody takes my family away from me. Not again. I won't let her. I won't let her. Rage turns my body of jelly into a construct of steel. I reach in and grab my backpack. The pistol still lies on top, just where I left it. I zip up the backpack and put it on. What the hell is she thinking? How many miles have we crossed? How can she expect to get two little girls across the desert? She can't have gotten far. It's been less than twenty-four hours. I push aside the tarp and step out into the sunshine.

This is crazy. Everything about this is crazy. None of it makes any fucking sense. I take my first step back north.

Paul-paul-paul-paul-paul-paul-paul-paul.

Voices talking. Voices talking about me. The volume just below the point of hearing. My back stiffens. I don't see it, but I can hear the whap of the rotors. Not now. Sweet Jesus not now. I don't pause to think. I act. I jump back under the tarp as a shadow races across the desert towards me. Everything sounds like it's a long ways away. I lay in the dirt, just inside the tarp, and listen to the battering of the air above me. I don't move. I don't breathe. I don't blink. It's right above me. I can hear it right above the tarp. Hovering. Hunting. It's hunting me. Did it see me? Dear god, please, please let it miss me. Let the tarp be convincing enough. It's not meant for close scrutiny. It's only convincing from a distance, or maybe a quick fly-by. Not this hovering bullshit. They know. They must fucking know. They must have seen me. The man on top of the hill. They must have seen him last night. They saw me last night. My hands cover my ears, trying to drown out the horrible rhythmic repeating of my name.

The pistol. I need the pistol, but I don't dare move. They're not going to take me. They're not going to take me without a fight. They're not going to put me back in a cage. I've done nothing wrong. All I want is to be left alone. All I want is to be allowed to live my life. Why can't they leave me alone? Someone is praying. It takes a moment to realize it's me. Hail Marys and Our Fathers. Please god repeated again and again in a never ending litany. Let it end. Just please let it all end.

The assault on the air above changes its tone. The sound of the helicopter shifts and begins to move away, off into the distance. I lay still and count to three hundred, and then slowly push my head out from underneath the tarp. The sun is shining and the cows continue to graze nearby. It's a beautiful summer day. In the distance a black dot moves over the ground, lateral to my position, just close enough that the breeze occasionally pushes the sound of the blades cutting through the air. Not near, but too close for comfort.

I pull my head back underneath the tarp and drag myself over to Alice. I pull off my backpack and lean back against Alice's rear tire. My body refuses to unclench. It vibrates like a freshly plucked guitar string. The note dark and mournful. Calm. I need to be calm. I need to think. I need to think this all out. I reach into the front pocket of the backpack and pull out a bag of joints I rolled yesterday morning. I take one out and put it in my mouth. A pacifier. My hands are shaking so badly that I have trouble getting it lit. After three tries it finally takes and I puff it down as quickly as I can. I don't wait for it to take hold. I light another one and suck it down just as quickly.

My body starts to unclench a little bit, but my hands won't stop shaking. I pull myself back over to the edge of the tarp and stick my head out again. The black dot is out of my field of vision, but I can still hear the steady beat of its rotors in the distance. I pull myself back over to Alice and stand up. Calm. I need to stay calm. I need to think. I can't let myself spiral into another panic attack that will do nothing to help. I open up Alice's back and look through the boxes of supplies. Everything seems to be in its place. Nothing is missing. Even the small bags with the girls' extra clothes are still here. What the fuck was she thinking? What did she think she was doing?

The cooler with the beer in it stares up at me. I pull it open and take a beer. All the ice has melted into tepid water. I open and drink the warm beer. Some of the beer runs out the sides of my mouth. I rub it away with the back of my arm. The movement feels stiff. A stab of pain. The beer's not bad so I have another. As soon as the helicopter is gone. As soon as it's gone I can go out and look for them. Soon. Soon my girls will be back in my arms. I finish the second beer and make a note in my head to mark them off the ledger. It's important to keep track. It's important to keep track of what has been consumed. Linds is gone. The ledger was her job. I'll have to do it. I can't go forward now. I can't go forward without the girls. This was all for them.

I crawl back over to the edge of the tarp and stick my head out again. I still can't see the black dot of the helicopter, but I can still hear its slow movements across the emptiness of the desert. The constant yelling of my name repeatedly.

Paul-paul-paul-paul-paul-paul-paul-paul.

Chapter 18

In 1948 the CIA's Office of Policy Coordination launched Operation Mockingbird, a coordinated effort to infiltrate every major media outlet in the country. The plan was a resounding success thanks to the journalists being surprisingly easy to bribe, whether by patriotism, money, or blackmail. Within the first few years of the operation over 400 high ranking reporters were recruited from all three of the major television networks and the majority of the major sources of print news. By 1953 the CIA had a major influence over 25 newspapers and wire agencies. This network of reporters avoided reporting about certain CIA plots, such as the overthrow of the governments of Iran and Guatemala, and spread pro-US government propaganda both nationally and internationally. As they always do, things quickly got out of hand, leading to the directing of editorial support for pro-CIA political candidates both domestically and abroad, and threats of smear campaigns against those who threatened to expose the operation. The program was shut down by Congress in the 1970's, or so the story goes.

I look down at a weak man lying in the middle of his cell, shaking uncontrollably, sobbing. He's not sure why he's crying, he just feels the overwhelming need to. The floor around him is covered in puke. The remains of a meal too quickly eaten by teeth that are still loose in his skull. When I close my eyes I can see through his. The vomit covered floor. The blank concrete wall. The underside of the stainless steel toilet in the corner. A sense of shame. A terrible feeling of remorse. Hunger. Desperate hunger. Fatigue. Praying to God to let him sleep and maybe not wake up this time.

My eyes open and I'm looking down on him once more. His body is covered by a sheen of sweat even though the air around him feels cool. I've watched him now for nearly a year. When he first came in they had strapped him to a bed and fed him a steady diet of antibiotics to destroy a staph infection brought on by untreated abscesses along his arms. He had railed and screamed against his restraints, shouting threats and collapsing deep into restless nightmare filled sleep. Several times he emerged from such derangement and was sent out into the general population. Each time he collapsed back, turning violent until they were forced to separate him once again. He craves his candy. He craves it with his entire soul. It's surprisingly easy to acquire candy in this box of refuse.

The man shifts and his shadow skitters along the floor. He catches sight of it in his peripheral vision and whips his head around violently, back and forth, trying to catch sight of something that isn't there. Watching. He can feel them watching him all the time. He wants to scream. He wants to rant. He wants to demand that they show themselves. But he barely has the strength to fill the emptiness in his center when they bring him food and drink.

Abandoned. The man has been left alone in a world that does not care. No family. No friends. No one to tell him everything will be all right. He has fallen to the darkest depths, and the sides of the pit are slick with guilt and depression. The only one that still acknowledges his existence is a sister who never calls, and refuses to pick up when he dials. She only talks to him when he's clean. She calls it tough love. She has promised to be there when he reaches the other side.

The tears dry up and the shaking ceases. I watch as his breathing slows, becoming more steady and even. His mind can take no more, and has thrown him back into the more peaceful limbo of the land of Morpheus. Even there he will not find peace. Nightmares of burning houses, dying old men, and shadow creatures skittering on the walls. I look down at a man fitfully sleeping in hell, trying to feel pity, but feeling nothing. He has brought it on himself.

I look up as three Blackhawk helicopters buzz by, their downdraft shaking the palm trees, moving into the interior to be greeted by the distant sounds of explosions and machinegun fire. All of my brother combat engineers look upward as they move by overhead, knowing that they are headed for the big show, and wondering when it's going to be our turn. Lieutenant Spicer doesn't look up. He keeps his eyes roving across his platoon of the 22nd Combat Logistics Battalion of the 22nd Marine Amphibious Unit.

It has been ten hours since we first landed on the white sand beaches of Grenada, emerging from the turquoise sea like a well-oiled machine of death and destruction. Ten hours since our fellow Marines charged off into the greenery of the interior, anxious to secure their objectives, leaving us to await their call for support. Ten hours of sitting in the hot sun. Ten hours of waiting for Spike the radioman, listening to his tinny canned voices, to call the Lieutenant over. Except for us, the beach is empty, just as we found it. The sound of machinegun fire has been steadily moving further away, and still we wait.

The quick pace of the well-oiled machine has slowed and the parts have drifted. Several members keep vigilant, crouched behind sandbag walls, constructed in the first hour, eyeing the edge of the jungle, guns at the ready, waiting for action. The rest of us have spread out along the high point of the waves. Smoking cigarettes, cracking jokes, and conjecturing on the current state of our inland brethren. Two of my brothers have dug a hole in the sand to a depth where it slowly fills with water. They pull wet gobs of sand from the hole and squeeze them to add to a growing drip castle. The spindly minarets, their foundations built by collapsed past versions, are already as high as my knee.

This could be called a tropical paradise. Even with the knowledge that there are men trying to kill each other just a few miles away, it is still beautiful. My rifle in my hand gives me a sense of calm I might otherwise not have. A little ways down the beach Larry takes off his boots and climbs a palm tree like a monkey. When he reaches the top he knocks down several coconuts and follows them back to the ground. He breaks one open with the butt of his rifle and drinks the water inside.

Lieutenant Spicer looks disgusted. His round black face is curved downward in an unfamiliar looking scowl. He turns and marches over to the ever-growing drip castle, stomping it to oblivion with his combat boots. He bawls out the two Marine builders and orders them to take their turn behind the sandbag wall. Larry laces back up his boots and walks back towards us across the white sand, carrying the

remaining coconut in one hand, his rifle in the other. I adjust my
helmet and light another cigarette.

The music pounds through my head, each note digging its way
through my ear to the center of my brain, reverberating from one end
of my skull to the other. It's not the kind of music I would usually
listen to on my own. Jackson, Bowie, Prince, Hall and Oates. I'm
more of a fan of Waylon, Johnny, and Willie. Music with a twang that
moves ya right down to your soul. This shit is okay, but it's not great.
I love Larry, but the man has bad taste in music. It's his night to pick
the records.

It doesn't fucking matter. Nothing fucking matters. Diane throws
her head back, laughing like a banshee. Her bright green eyes
sparkling. I nibble her ears and kiss her neck. One hand grabs her
curly locks and pulls gently downward. The other tips the silver
bullet, depositing an uneven line of white powder between her bare
freckled breasts. A sheen of sweat covers her body, the little house is
packed, the atmosphere is a little too warm for my tastes. I lean down
and snort the powder in a single movement, leaving behind the ragged
remains of the line mixed with the smell and the taste of her body.
Susanne, sitting next to Diane on the couch, leans forward and licks up
what I left behind. I throw my head back and howl at the ceiling, and
the whole party lifts their drinks and scream in return.

I lean back on the cushions and stare outward at the seething mass
of half dressed people undulating around me. Someone takes the
silver bullet out of my hand. It doesn't matter. It's nearly empty. The
room is filled with the intermingled smoke of cigarettes and joints, and
even one or two cigars. Everything in the house, so dingy and dirty
this morning, seems bright and new. Everyone looks good. Everyone
looks happy. I love the jive of the whole scene. Ha. The scene. Who
came up with a phrase like the scene? What a stupid description.
What a weak way to tell it. Giggles erupt from me. Uncontrollable.
Diane doesn't notice. She's too busy kissing Susanne. She doesn't
forget about me though. Her left hand runs down my bare chest and
rubs against the bulge of my jeans. I look down and feel myself
mesmerized by the twinkling of the diamond on her ring finger.

Larry comes in from the kitchen. He's wearing nothing but an old pair of green athletic shorts, tube socks, sandals, and a poker dealers green tinged visor. His lips are curled around a smoking joint. In one hand he holds the blender pitcher, full of some kind of fruity booze laden concoction. His other hand holds a knit cap that jangles as he dances across the room.

"Keys, keys, turn in your keys! Has everyone turned in their keys?!"

The crowd screams out their affirmations, pushing forward a wave of sexual tension.

"Hosts first. Hosts first."

Larry thrusts the hat towards me, holding it at just above eye level. I raise one hand, amazed at the amount of thought the simple movement takes, and rummage around through the contents of the hat. When my hand comes out it holds a set of keys that I recognize. They're mine. The crowd hoots and hollers, some calling for a redraw. Larry laughs. I flip off the crowd and pull Diane up with me as I rise from the couch. I lift her easily over my shoulder and push my way back towards our bedroom. Susanne starts to follow, but Larry holds her back.

"One per key. One per key. Those are the rules. Who's next?"

"Sir, I'm sorry, but at this time we're not looking to re-enlist older out-of-service Marines. If you would like some information on some volunteer organizations here stateside, I can provide you with those."

The Marine recruiting station in Dallas isn't much. A small two room rental space jammed between a dry cleaner and a hair salon in a strip mall just off Highway 30. It's cold outside, but uncomfortably hot in the little office. As hot as it must be for our boys over in the Gulf. The December wind blows through the bad seals in the glass door, creating a background hum that rises and falls at random. A few strings of Christmas lights hang along the upper edge of the walls, in sharp contrast to the usual plethora of recruiting posters. Duty. Honor. The Marines. The recruiter behind the small desk is a bull necked woman about my age. I'm willing to bet she's probably a dyke.

"Whaddya mean older Marine. For Christ sakes, I'm only twenty-eight. I want to sign back up and help in Kuwait."

"Your patriotism is commendable sir, but what I have told you is the current Marine Corps policy."

My head hurts. I shouldn't have imbibed so much the night before. At least I know my eyes aren't red like they were when I woke up a few hours ago. Half a bottle of eye drops took care of that. Why's she being so difficult? What's so hard about getting me back into uniform to fight the good fight?

"I'm in excellent physical condition."

I had been working out, doing my drills, since it had become obvious the US was going to get involved. All those Cold War generals sitting around with their thumbs up their asses, just waiting for an excuse to use all their pretty hardware.

"I'm sure you are sir, but…"

I can tell she isn't going to listen to me. I drop to the ground and start doing pushups in rapid succession. The litany that was pounded into me at the time of my rebirth escapes my lips, as automatic as the motions.

"One, two, three, four, I love of the Marine Corps."

"Sir, please get up."

I continue my pushups, staring downward at the floor. I can feel my arms shake though I don't feel fatigued.

"Sir, I'm going to have to ask you to leave."

"I'm not leaving until you sign me back up. I need this. I need my family."

"Sir, if you don't leave I'll be forced to call the police."

I stop my pushups and look up at her from the floor. She is staring down at me. Short cut hair and cold eyes. She doesn't look like someone who is fucking around. Of course she isn't, she's a Marine. Something I used to be. I get up and stand at attention. I salute. She stares at me and doesn't salute back. I wheel and march back outside, around the corner, and to my beaten old rust bucket of a car. I unlock the door, sit down, and put the key in the ignition.

Tears fill my eyes. The Marines had fixed me up once before. They could have done it again. Once a Marine, always a Marine.

What a bunch of bullshit. People walk by, but they politely ignore me, balling like a child in my car.

I can hear the phone ring on the other end and I grip the receiver tightly, praying that she'll pick up. She always does. She always has, but somehow every time I call I find myself filled with the same fear that this time she won't. That she's abandoned me like everyone else. I can feel the fear start to overwhelm me. I can feel my body start to shake. The other end connects.

"Hello?"

"Amy, it's Paul."

"Paul. I'm glad you called. How are things going little brother?"

"As well as they can be. How are you?"

"Doing well. It's a good thing you called today. I volunteered for the Tokyo run, heading out tomorrow and I'm going to be out of contact for a little while."

"The Tokyo run. That's great."

"Damn straight it is. How about you? Still working in laundry?"

"No, they finally wisened up at last a couple of days ago and agreed to transfer me over to the shop. Finally working with my hands again."

"See, I told you once you proved that you could stay clean things would start to turn around."

"Yeah. Things still aren't that great, but at least it's helping make things a little more tolerable."

"You still having any trouble with your cellmate?"

"No, he got in a fight with someone else in the cafeteria. Got sent back to maximum. I got a new roomie. Some little shrimpy white collar who was embezzling money from his father-in-law's used car lot."

"Sounds easier to get along with then some gang banger."

"A lot easier."

"Sorry I never get over there to visit. Bastrop is a long ways from Tacoma."

"It's okay. I know you're busy. It's just good to have someone to talk to."

"Nobody still coming to visit?"

"Larry came about a week ago. I wrote him a letter letting him know I'm clean now."

"That's good. How's Larry doing?"

"Lot different then he used to be. He looked pretty clean cut. Said he has some new girlfriend that he met at his church."

"Larry at church?"

"Yeah, I know, crazy isn't it?"

"I'm having a hard time visualizing Larry in church."

"He claims he sits near the front. Likes to sing along with the choir."

"Well son of a bitch. Old crazy Larry up front in church."

"Yep."

"How's everything else going?"

"Not bad. I'm still going to group three times a week. A lot of them are nothing but a bunch of whiners who will probably fall back as soon as they get out, but it looks good on the record."

"Been having any problems of your own?"

"A few twinges, but the books I read said that it's pretty normal. Don't worry, I'm not going to fall back again."

"That's good kiddo. I'm proud of you."

"Thanks. I'm glad somebody is."

"Any word from Diane?"

"No."

"I'm sorry."

"I try not to think about it. I've sent her a few letters trying to let her know that I'm clean now."

"Yeah?"

"They've all come back unopened. I don't know. Maybe she moved or something."

"I'm sorry Paul."

"Yeah, I'm sorry too. I fucked up Amy. I fucked up big time. I wish I could fix it."

"Some things you can't fix Paul. Some things you just have to live with."

"I know."

I hear a beep on the phone. The signal that I only have another minute. "I have to go Amy. It was good talking to you."

"It was good talking to you too little brother. Give me a call two Tuesdays from now. I should be back by then."

"I will."

"Stay strong."

"Thanks."

"I love you."

"I love you too."

Chapter 19

It's a little known fact that the Executive Branch of the US government has a legal loophole that can be used to dismiss court cases against it. Called the State Secrets Privilege, it allows the government to refuse to cooperate in a court case if by doing so it would threaten national security. While the idea sounds all well and good. The reality is much different. First invoked and upheld by the Supreme Court in 1953, the State Secrets Privilege has since become a heavily abused power, often being invoked to cover up political missteps that might embarrass the sitting or past administrations. The use of the privilege, once rare, has more than quadrupled since 9/11. Cases challenging the government's use of abductions, torture, the breaking of habeas corpus, and illegal surveillance have all been silenced over the past decade. Each and every one dismissed before they could ever go to trial.

"Paul."

At first I think it's the helicopter coming back.

"Paul."

The voice is one I recognize from memory, but it does not sound the way I remember it. I open my eyes. The desert has gone. As I slept hundreds of cottonwood trees had taken root and lifted themselves into the sky above. I lay in a hundred years worth of fallen leaves surrounding by a cloying mist that hides away the world of moderate distances. The air seems thick and heavy, an old wool blanket owned since childhood.

"Paul."

I sit up at the sound of my name and gaze at the white trunks around me. Bits of cotton float lazily in the air, in no hurry to finish their journey to join the detritus on the ground below. I hear the titter of laughter to my left. I turn my head and there she is, naked, smiling coyly as she peeks around a tree. Pink nipples flashing in the dappled light. One finger bashfully twisting a lock of long blonde hair. It's not the body of the woman she has become, but of the woman she once was. Supple and unmarked. No longer ruined by the fount of corruption that is her's by birthright. Not yet ravaged by the ugliness of the world.

"Hello."

My voice sounds small in the stillness of the air, swallowed up before it can spread its wings. She titters again, turns, takes a few quick steps away, stops, motions for me to follow, and then starts to slowly bound deeper into the mists. I rise up to follow. My body feels heavy and unwieldy, but I jog after as best I can.

"Wait."

My voice is lost before it even gets to my own ears.

"Paul."

The voice again, a wave of sound that ripples the mists as it travels. The nymph capers just on the edge of sight. A shadow in the mist, moving on ahead, stopping only to turn and motion for me to follow. Ahead a light grows brighter. A rising sun trying to break through the clouds. My feet feel weighed down. I try to kick off my boots, but looking down, discover they are already gone.

"Paul."

The force of the voice drives me to my knees. The nymph skips forward out of sight, unaware that I've fallen behind. My hands touch the ground. The dirt begins to cover them and pull them downward. I struggle to rise, but with every jerk find myself more entrapped.

"Paul."

"I'm trying. I'm trying."

My mouth moves but no sounds come out. The light begins to move away.

"Paul."

The voice is growing more distant. I lunge against the shackling ground but my body has become lead and I am too weak to lift it. The light fades and the last tinkling of far off floating laughter echoes through the trees. Tears fill my eyes and I begin to weep and wail, a scared child lost and all alone. A gentle hand comes down upon my shoulder.

"Paul."

It's a different voice. A voice I recognize instantly. I turn and see an ageless face with the same features as my own, wreathed by long jet black hair.

"Amy. Amy I'm so fucking scared."

She envelops me in her arms, and holds me tightly to her chest.

"It's okay Paul. I'm here. I'm always here."

My eyes are gritty and dry when I open them. The muted illumination of twilight leaves everything under the tarp in shadow. I blink my scratchy eyes and stretch. My legs brush aside empty beer cans, some crushed in bitter anger and frustration. I rise from my resting place, an old blanket on the ground next to Alice, and look about my dim hiding world. I hadn't meant to fall asleep, but I'm glad that I did. Time to sleep. Time to heal. Time to get my thoughts in order. The chaos of the raging storm in my mind has given way to clarity. I know now what I have to do. I stand up and dry swallow a yellow pill from the container in my left pocket. The world seems to sway and undulate around me. Now is not the time for sleep. Now is the time for action.

I run my hands through my greasy hair. My cheeks are covered in stubble. How long has it been since I last showered? When we were at the abandoned homestead we took turns pouring water over each other, washing our bodies with a bar of soap and an old washcloth. How many days ago has that been? Everything is blurring together.

I've been abandoned. That cunt has always been trouble. She could never see what was going on. Never understand what it was I was trying to protect them from. That fucking bitch. That fucking selfish bitch. I was blind. I could see it from the day we set out from Sweetwater. Hell, I could tell from the moment we left Portland. She didn't trust me anymore. She didn't believe me. She took the easy path. It's so much easier to put on the blinders. So much easier to play pretend. It's hard to force yourself to see the truth. It's hard to stare straight up at the sun.

My kids. Why did she have to take the fucking kids? I was doing this all for them. So they could live in a world where they could be free. So they could live a life free from tyranny. Where they wouldn't have to be afraid. If she wanted to go, fine, but she didn't have to take the kids. Stone, my precious Stone. Rachel, my precocious Rachel. Gone. Gone. Just like Philip. Oh god, I'm so sorry. I did everything I could, but once again I've failed.

Betrayed. I've been betrayed. All day I tried to go out and search for them. But every time I peeked outside of the tarp the helicopter was there. Sometimes close. Sometimes far away. But always there. All day the helicopter flew in a pattern that I recognized. A grid search pattern. They are looking for something. They are looking for someone. They are looking for me. What else could they be looking for? There is nothing but desert for miles around. Thank god Linds has a shit sense of direction. She could get lost in our driveway. No pattern recognition. They haven't found me yet.

Time. It's only a matter of time. I spent days working on the tarp. I started with one a light tan color. Splotched it with various shades of gray and brown paint. Covered the whole thing in epoxy and threw buckets of dirt over it of the same type I knew we would be driving through. The tarp was the most important part. We had to stay hidden during the day. Hidden from prying eyes. Hidden from those trying to find us. Every time we stopped for the day I would always add more to the permanent camouflage. A few buckets of loose dirt, a couple rocks, any loose branches I could find. Dig up some bunchgrass and lay it on top. Anything to add to the illusion. It's never enough. It's only meant for casual glances. It was never meant for too close of scrutiny.

I've been lucky. There's no denying that I've been lucky. Why they haven't seen the tarp for what it is yet is beyond me. Somebody up above must be watching out for me. I can't stay here. Alice has already been parked here too long. As soon as it gets dark I have to leave. I have to move. They can't hunt me in the dark. Keeping on the move is my only hope to avoid getting caught.

I can't go back. All day I sat hiding under my tarp. Ranting, raving, planning, and plotting. I want to get my kids back. I want to punch my wife in the face for betraying me. I want my family by my side. I'm being ripped in two. I had a few beers to calm my nerves. They didn't work so I had a few more. What a waste. I knew what I was going to have to do as soon as I saw that fucking cell phone charger. I just didn't want to face up to it. If I go back they'll just throw me back into a cage. I'll disappear like so many others, never to be heard from again. They can do that. They can make you never exist. I can't go back. In a cage I'm no use to anyone.

The only way left is forward. I don't want to abandon my children, but what choice do I have? If I can get to Mexico I can disappear on my terms. I can be safe. I can be free. Forward is a future with possibilities. Linds will do the best she can for them. They'll grow up slaves, but slaves can still be happy. I know I can't survive as a slave. It's not in me to live such a life. They are young. They can adapt. Someday I will come back for them, but for now, I have to look out for myself. It seems my entire life I've had to look out for myself. No one ever stands beside me long. Except Amy. Amy has always been there, and she's waiting. Waiting for me. I rebuilt once. I can rebuild again. I'm only forty-nine. There is still a lot of living left to do.

The twilight fades towards darkness. I pick up the empty beer cans and make a mental note to take seventeen off the list. Linds was the one keeping track of everything. I'll have to do it now. Tomorrow during the day I'll take a thorough inventory. Make double sure that nothing is missing. When I checked earlier everything looked okay, but it's always best to be sure. I hurriedly eat an MRE, this one chicken tetrazzini, and finish loading Alice and cleaning up the camp site. The last thing to be loaded is the tarp, but not until it's completely dark. It's hard going. The tarp is big, heavy, and unwieldy. I have to fold it by myself with just the red light of the flashlight strapped to my head. A thin crescent moon smiles down at me, a demented Cheshire cat.

With everything loaded I get in and start Alice up. Her engine sounds loud in my lonely ears. I look at the seats that once contained my life. For a moment I waver. My grip on the steering wheel tightens. Now is not the time for such things. I take a beer from the cooler and crack it open. The first drink washes down another yellow pill. I need to stay alert. Eighteen. I need to take eighteen beers off the inventory. I put Alice in gear and start slowly moving forward, blind to the world except for the muted red beams of Alice's headlights.

The cliff rolls by on my right. I try to keep my mind on my task, though I can feel the storm surging just out of sight. I have to make sure I don't miss the way down. Everything looks different in the dark. Guilt. Anger. Hate. Sadness. Combined with a tinge of elation. I am only responsible for myself. Maybe that is the way it's supposed to be.

The going is slow. It's hard to keep my concentration on the task at hand. I keep seeing my kids in the rearview mirror. Sleeping soundly, their mouths partially open. Every time I look back they are still gone. Tears are always on the edge of falling. My eyes are floating in their sockets. Madness. This is all madness. Alice continues rolling forward. I don't see Linds in the seat next to me. After all that I have done for her. For her to do this. She is dead to me. Fucking dead. In my right pocket my pocket-knife digs into my leg. The knife Tom's dad gave me. I know what he would say about all this. I know what he would want me to do. I clumsily dig into my pocket and adjust the knife into a more comfortable position.

There. Even in the shadows I recognize the gaunt cedar. I was so glad to see it the first time. So happy. This is where I go over. I stop Alice and get out to take a look. It's just the way I remember it. A steep slope, but it should be manageable. I rebuilt Alice for this kind of stuff. It's only steep for about a thousand feet, then the slope becomes more gentle for the rest of the drop to the flat below. I get back into Alice, chug the rest of my beer, and put her into gear.

The way down is slow going. I keep her in first and ride the clutch and brakes, occasionally sliding forward slightly out of control on patches of loose dirt and rock. I grip the steering wheel so tightly that my hands hurt. Every time Alice starts to slide my heart starts to beat like mad and my foot applies a little more pressure to the brakes. My eyes refuse to blink. Sweat pours down my forehead. My underarms are soaked. It's a hot night. Bit by bit. Little by little. I work my way down the hill.

My eyes keep getting drawn to the rearview mirror. Little flashes of two tiny forms sleeping soundly that disappear as soon as I concentrate my vision on them. I brush my brow across the sleeve of my t-shirt without letting go of the steering wheel. My left eye stings with salt. Outside the stars twinkle down peacefully, trying to coax my eyes away from the task at hand. My whole body is shivering. Perhaps it's not as hot as I thought it was. I reach over and put on my seatbelt.

"Dad, when are we going to get there?"

I jerk my head and look at the passenger seat. Philip sits next to me, illuminated by the stars outside. His little face looks up at me, bored and tired, his green eyes filled with curiosity. I look back out the windshield and then look at the seat again. He's gone. A hard lump drops to the bottom of my stomach and begins to grow. I begin to shake uncontrollably. Fuck. What the fuck. Desperately my eyes search the right side of the cab, searching for the apparition that was there just a moment before. The pocket-knife starts to jab my leg again. I take one hand off the wheel to adjust it.

Alice starts to slide again. I jerk my attention back to the outside world and recoil in horror at what I see. Illuminated in the dim beams of light stands a creature of familiar characteristics. The thin hairless body, the upright ears, the whiplike tail, and the red glowing eyes. Old instincts take over. Actions without thoughts. Memories of a youth spent bajaing through the desert and harvested fields, punching the gas to run down rabbits, badgers, and any other varmints unlucky enough to be in our path. My foot shoots forward and punches down on the gas. My mind catches up and moves the foot to the brake in a hard motion. Shit. It's too late.

The tires lock up. Alice lurches forward and starts to gain speed. Gravity overwhelms the forces that I can control. The brakes seem to do nothing. Alice picks up speed and hits a large bump. I'm thrown upward, held down only by the seat belt. My head hits the top of the cab and my foot comes off the brake. Things fall apart quickly. The entire world speeds up and I'm jerked violently in all directions, strapped down, but out of control. Loose beer cans and everything else not strapped down clatters around me. Something hits the back of my head. Loud curses echo through the cab. My foot desperately scrambles for the brake. The two can't seem to connect. The bottom of the hill comes rushing forward. My eyes fix on a dry creek bed at the bottom, anchored despite the chaos around me. The entire world stops moving. The windshield rushes at my face.

Chapter 20

Martin Luther King Junior was one of the most pivotal figures of the twentieth century, catapulting the issue of civil rights and equality for all races to the forefront of the American conscious. But to the FBI and other groups, Mr. King was nothing more than a degenerate who was attempting to rip asunder the fabric of American society. Believing that King was under the influence of communists, the FBI kept him under constant surveillance, bugging buildings and phone lines in a wide sweeping attempt to prove their suspicions. While the word communist was never uttered, they did learn about King's extramarital affair. This was later used in a threatening anonymous letter sent to King by the FBI, suggesting he commit suicide before all his personal secrets were revealed to the public at large. The FBI harassment of Martin Luther King Junior didn't end until his assassination in 1968.

Her leg kicks around the pole as she swings herself in a long slow arch. The movement is not graceful. It's obvious by her technique that it once was, but now the stiffness of her joints holds her back. It makes it sadder to know that she once had talent. Her hand reaches back and she lets her top fall, but nobody pays attention. Her body is old and bony, her breasts droop, and her belly is loose and paunchy. A c-section scar sits as an indentation down the left side of her stomach, a gift from her second child. As she dances she sees herself as young again, back when she was beautiful, and all the Marines came into the Spice Rack to see her. Life was a party back then. As she twirls a single tear falls down her face. I'm the only one that sees.

It's a slow night. Hazel only dances on slow nights, or when someone doesn't show up for their shift. She has been part of the afternoon B-Squad for as long as anyone can remember. An old wreck that got caught up on the rocks and never fully sank below the waves. Hazel isn't a bad type, just getting old. She usually tends bar, and always serves strong drinks as long as you're a good tipper. She treats all us leathernecks like we're her children. Probably because her's never call. I wish she wouldn't dance. It's not a pretty thing to see. But she doesn't like being behind the bar. She still wants to be out where everyone can see. I take a couple dollar bills off my pile and lay them on the stage.

"Christ man, just give it to me if you want to waste money. Try saving a little for the real talent."

Skunk's voice is shrill but still amazingly loud. I know Hazel can hear, but she ignores him, preferring the world of twenty years ago in her head. I can feel his squinty ferret eyes in his little weasel face staring at me, but I don't turn my head.

"Shut up Skunk. If I wanted your opinion I'd squeeze your head."

Larry looks over from the other side of Skunk. He's holding a daiquiri in one hand while the other brushes along the curve of the half naked cocktail waitress' leg as she walks away. Few Marines would dare order something so fruity, but Larry has never been one to care. The cold glass is sweating. So is Larry. It's 11 PM, but it's still hot as hell in the squat cinder block building on the edge of Jacksonville, North Carolina. The fans on the ceiling do little more than mix the hot muggy air with the cigarette smoke rising from the dozen spectators. My tan service uniform is already sticking to my back. I can tell by the smell that Skunk is sweating too. Skunk stinks terrible when he sweats. Larry takes a pull of his daiquiri and lays two dollars up on the bar next to mine.

"I can't fucking believe you two." Skunk's shrill voice is like a drill bit right down my ear.

Larry laughs. "Shut up Skunk. You're just sore because you wasted all your damn money on lap dances from Sage hoping she'd give you a handy."

Larry and I both laugh. Skunk doesn't say anything, but his head turns to watch the tall blonde cocktail waitress in baby blue lingerie move back behind the bar. Larry and I laugh again and Larry punches Skunk in the arm.

"Poor old Skunk. Always reaching for the clouds. You see my friend, you'd be better off giving your money to good old Hazel. She may not be much to look at, but I guarantee she knows a thing or two that would knock your socks off."

"Shut up Larry."

Hazel leans down to pick up the four dollars on the stage, her sad tits swaying, and pushes her face close enough for us to see every wrinkle and to smell the cigarettes and Jim Beam on her breath. Her voice is that of a woman who has spent her entire life in smokey bars.

"Yeah, c'mon Skunk, if you close your eyes all hands feel the same."

Skunk turns beat red. Larry and I burst out laughing, Larry's horse laugh echoing across the club. A couple of Marines sitting off the rack at a nearby table laugh too. Hazel picks up her clothes and saunters off the stage. Sage comes back around and I order another round of beers for me and Skunk. Skunk thanks Sage politely when she lays them on the table. The beer seems to help with his ego, though it probably does nothing to help his libido. Sage gets up on stage and takes her turn. Skunk eyes her hungrily, but doesn't have any money left to show his affection. Larry tips large so Sage pays more attention to him. I know he's just doing it to get under Skunk's skin.

Sage leaves the stage after her two songs and I get up to get another round of drinks for everybody. Hazel pops the tops off the bottles and hands them to me.

"Thanks for the tips up there honey." Hazel's voice slurs around the cigarette in her mouth.

"No problem Hazel."

"You'll like this next one. She's a new girl."

I give Hazel a twenty and she hands me back a whole mess of ones. I carry the beers back to the rail by their necks and pass them out. Larry is going off on one of his favorite conspiracy theories. Something about the CIA taking extra large condoms, marking them as regular, and dumping them over the Soviet Union. Some convoluted plot to lower the morale of the common Russian soldier and weaken the loyalty of the motherland's female population. I've heard it all before, so I don't bother to listen.

ZZ Top's *Legs* starts playing over the speakers, and the next stripper comes out onto the stage. Hazel was right about her. I do like this one. She isn't one of the great beauties of the world. Her body is a little pudgy and she has Charlie Brown cheeks and thick tightly curled brown hair. She has a pretty face, and moves that can only be described as lithe. It's as though her body is made of water. She bends around the pole as though she has no joints. Every movement smooth and unbroken. Larry keeps blathering on to Skunk about the various foibles of the CIA in their secret war with communism. I stare at the girl on the stage.

Her eyes are what draw me in. Most strippers are out of the moment. Lost in their own thoughts. They look like workers on an assembly line. Their bodies carry out the task, muscle movements memorized by constant identical iterations, while their minds go through the list of things they'll need to do when they get home. They are here to do a job and earn some money. If that means taking off their clothes for a room full of perverts, so be it. The only ones who really look at you when they dance are the newbies. Those too naive and too young to recognize that they've fallen into a trap that they'll likely never escape from. Those too dumb to even recognize they're being exploited.

This dancer is neither of those. This dancer stares back in defiance and puts everyone in their place. Her eyes lock onto yours and you're the first to look away because you know you are the weaker one. Her look screams out to the world. Declaring that yes, I am a stripper, I take off my clothes for money, so pay up. She is not being exploited. She is exploiting us perverts. Suckering us into paying to see something that everyone has. Her clothes fall from her body without hesitation. No delay. No shame. Her nakedness is natural. Watching her I get the sense that if anyone caused any trouble, she'd handle it before Buck the bouncer could even get his fat ass off his stool by the door. There is no doubt that she is the one in control. I've never been so attracted to a woman in my life.

The pile of singles handed to me at the bar rapidly disappears. I want this woman in front of me. I want her dancing for me. Not for any of these other knuckle dragging jarheads. She's a curvy woman, but I hardly even notice. Her eyes demand all the attention. A bright shade of green flecked with yellow, like an unwatered lawn at the start of summer. The last chords of Michael Jackson's *Beat It* flows across the club. Wait. When did her first song end? God what a woman. She leans down to pick up her money, and walks off the stage.

"Ain't that right Paul?"

I stare at her retreating ass, thick and round with dimples where it connects to her back. Her curvaceous hips roll like a boat on the ocean. As she goes through the door marked private she looks back at me for a second with a flash of green.

"Paul."

I'm breathing hard. Jesus Christ. No woman has pulled at me this hard before.

"Paul!"

I turn my head as the door swings closed. Larry and Skunk stare at me. Larry is smirking and Skunk is grinning like an idiot.

"What?"

"Christ Paul, don't stare too hard. You'll fall in."

Larry and Skunk start laughing. I start to blush.

"I've gotta get some air."

I get up and walk out the door, past Buck reading an old faded copy of *Hamlet* by the light of the little flashlight he uses to check ID's. He doesn't even look up. It's hotter outside than in. The North Carolina summer is humid, even at night. Walking feels like swimming and you find yourself constantly fighting off the feeling that you're drowning while you breathe. The gravel parking lot is mostly empty, lit by the neon sign above the door, and occasionally fully illuminated by the lights of a passing car rounding the corner on the highway.

I walk around the side of the building to a concrete patio covered in an assortment of garage sale bought chairs. I stand there and light up a smoke, fighting off disappointment for the loss of a stupid hope. I had hoped that the green-eyed girl might come out to the patio after her dance. Some of the girls did sometimes, to escape from the smoke and cloying heat of the club. It was stupid. Too damn hot outside. No damn breeze. It's cooler to stay inside. I finish my cigarette and go back inside. Buck's eyes stick to his book.

Larry is up by the bar, talking to the green-eyed girl. My whole body stiffens. She's wearing an old University of Miami tanktop and cutoff shorts. She's laughing at something Larry said. What kind of game is Larry playing? He's my friend but he can be a real ass. When he had figured out how much Skunk liked Sage, he had slept with her just to annoy Skunk. Things like that were easy for Larry. Women just liked him. He didn't have to work at it like the rest of us. When we we're in Grenada it hadn't taken him long to get to know the locals. It was common knowledge that he had planted a few seeds. Things had been the same in Lebanon. Larry had a twisted sense of humor. Skunk made sense. Skunk was a little shit. But me? We had always been pretty tight.

Larry looks up and notices me. He motions for me to come over. He's smiling like a cat that just caught a mouse. I walk over and the green-eyed girl with the curls turns. Her eyes give me the once over, but her smile is friendly.

"Paul, I want you to meet Cinnamon. Paul, Cinnamon, Cinnamon, Paul."

We shake hands. Her hands are surprisingly dainty, but she has a grip.

"I was just telling Cinnamon what a big fan you are."

I feel myself blush and think about punching Larry in the throat. Cinnamon looks at me and I look at her, but I don't know what to say. Hazel, behind the bar, hands Larry two beers.

"Well, I'll leave you two to conduct business. Skunk will be wanting this beer."

Larry walks back toward Skunk at the rail, leaving me next to the green-eyed vixen with the made up name. I try to think of something to say, but my brain doesn't seem to be working right. Cinnamon grabs my hand and starts pulling me back towards the booths where they do the private dances.

"What are you doing?"

"Your friend bought you some dances. C'mon Marine, hup two."

I let her pull me into one of the rooms and push me into a chair, my brain still fumbling as she pulls shut the heavy curtain. My eyes run across her curves, illuminated by a single red light bulb overhead and a straight line of light where the curtain meets the wall.

"You know the drill. Hands at your sides."

She starts swaying in time with the sound of the music out at the main stage. Rubbing herself against me and slowly and seductively pulling at her clothes. I feel myself rise to attention. I feel myself start to sweat. Nothing escapes her eye. She seems to find the whole thing rather funny.

"How long you been in the Marines Paul?"

The question ricochets in my brain. The last bit of clothing falls off of her body, revealing all the majesty that I had seen on the stage. Her ass plants itself in my lap, and moves rhythmically.

"A little over four years. Since I was eighteen."

"Hmmm….Short timer then?"

"Yeah, only a little bit longer."

"Seen any action?"

"I was over in Grenada and Lebanon. Never fired a shot. Saw some shit though."

"Nervous?"

"Sometimes. The waiting was always hard."

"What about now?"

My face flushes even redder. The gears of my brain aren't catching. I'm having a hard time catching my breath. My hands are gripping tightly onto the edge of the chair. She puts a leg up on my shoulder. Every movement she makes is seductive.

"Got any plans for when you get out?"

"Not right now. Maybe go back to Texas, that's where I'm from."

The music of the song ends and another starts. She keeps going. I wonder how many songs Larry paid for. For fuck sakes. I'm acting like a love sick kid. I need to regain some control over the situation. I force words out of my mouth.

"Where are you from?"

"Florida originally, but I'm working my way north to New York."

"Why New York?"

"Things are better in New York."

"What if they're not?"

"Then they'll at least be better than Florida."

"How old are you?"

"Kind of a personal question, don't you think?"

"Not really, given the circumstances."

"Twenty-two, same as you."

"Don't take this the wrong way, but you don't have the eyes of someone who's just twenty-two."

She stops and stares at me for a second, and I feel the full power of her gaze on me. I feel my confidence withering, like a flower beneath the hot sun.

"You don't have to be in the Marines to have seen some shit Paul."

She goes back to dancing. The second song ends and a third one begins. Cinnamon gets on her knees in front of me and starts tugging at my belt. My entire body tenses up.

"What the hell are you doing?"

"Your friend paid for something extra."

The illusion in my head shatters into a thousand pieces. Where just a second before there had been an angel, now kneels a sodden siren. I grab at her hands working at my belt. She looks up at me. I've never been good at hiding what I'm thinking. Her face becomes cross.

"For fuck's sake Paul. It's just a fucking blowjob."

"I....I.....I've never paid for one before."

"Christ Paul, it doesn't make it any different. Your willing to pay to see someone take off their clothes but you draw the line at paying someone to suck your cock?"

"I guess I never thought much about it before."

"It's not demeaning to me if that's what you're worried about. Fuck. I'm not going to fall in love with you or anything. We're just two people exchanging money for a service. It's no different than paying for a massage or anything else."

"It just seems wrong."

"According to who? You, or just what everyone has been telling you? I'm here of my own free will. I need the money to keep heading north, and it's a hell of a lot easier to get it this way then to work behind the counter at some shit little store. I'm not a victim, and I don't need you trying to protect morals that quite frankly I don't have or want. It's just fucking flesh Paul. Now do you want this fucking blowjob or not?"

I don't know what to do. The little room behind the curtain feels stifling hot. I feel like I've done something wrong. I feel like by saying no I'd be insulting her. I'm so damn confused. I don't know what to do. This woman isn't how I envisioned her, but holy shit she is so much more. I've never been so turned on.

"Okay."

Her hands undo my belt and pants, and pull them down around my boots. Her head nestles in my lap, a mound of frizzed out curly hair. I feel awkward staring down at her head, so I stare at the line of light at the edge of the curtain. The third song ends, and in the silence I let out a moan louder then I mean to. I hear laughter out in the main room and then Larry's tenor booming out a ribald tune.

> Who's got penis breath?
> She's got penis breath.
> Because you've been suckin on ding-a-ling.
> Suckin on ding-a-ling.
> Slobbin that knob like its corn on the cob.
> Sucking on ding-a-ling.

The entire club erupts into laughter. I can see them all in my mind. Staring at the heavy layer of fabric that divides me and this woman from the rest of the world, pointing and making dirty gestures. Cinnamon stops her efforts and looks up at me.

"Your friend's an asshole."

"Yeah."

I pull up my pants, walk out into the main part of the club, and punch Larry in the face.

Chapter 21

The election process has never been all that fair. Hell, just ask anyone who knows a thing or two about gerrymandering, the act of redrawing representative districts to make it more likely that certain candidates or certain parties will always win elections. Really the secret to all of it isn't just gathering up all of one's supporters, but also dividing up the supporters of your opponent. It's a whole picture kind of game. You don't need to win in a landslide. Just by enough of a majority to guarantee you always win. Of course once your chosen representative is in, they're not really even your representative anymore. After the vote, the control gets ceded back to the lobbyists and special interests. Those with the cash and influence get to call the shots.

Everything is dark except for a circle of light far above my head. I'm in cold water up to my knees. The walls around me are of smooth stone, covered by years of slime and mold. The light above is blinding. I can't look up at it for more than a few seconds at a time. I can't get out. The walls are too slippery to climb. I can't find any foot or hand holds. I try to keep myself calm. Try to think. Nothing is insurmountable. There is nothing that can't be done with the right attitude and enough persistence.

The hole isn't that wide. If I wedge myself, I can probably force my way to the top. It won't be an easy climb, but what other choice do I have. I press my back against the wall, feeling the wet slickness soak through my shirt. I put my feet on the rounded side opposite me, and start to push my way upward. There are small projections on the wall. Places where the stones don't fit together tightly, just a few millimeters to gain a little purchase with my feet and hands. Inch by inch. Foot by foot. The light gets brighter. It's getting harder to look at.

A tiny head appears at the lip of the well. I can't see any features, just a silhouette.

"What ya doing?" A child's voice. Philip's voice.

"Philip. It's me. It's Daddy. I'm trying to climb out. Go get help."

The silhouette disappears for a moment. I force myself up a few more feet. The shape of my son's head reappears. He throws something down the well. A rock falls past me, splashing in the water below.

"Hey, what are you doing? Don't throw those down here. You almost hit me. Go get help. Please, go get help."

Philip says nothing. Another rock comes down, ricocheting from wall to wall, barely missing my head. I try to find better purchase for my hands and feet. My legs are starting to shake from the effort of pressing against the smooth stone wall. A small rock comes down and hits my thigh.

"God damn it. Cut it out."

Philip ignores me. Two more silhouettes join his up above. Their voices are high and shrill, excited little girl voices that I recognize instantly. I hear my daughters up above, talking to Philip.

"What ya doing?"

"Throwing rocks down this well."

"Why are you doing that?"

"My Momma told me to. She said I'd understand when I was older. Do you want to do it too?"

"Okay."

I look up at the dark forms above, squinting my eyes against the brightness.

"Stone. Monkey. Don't throw any rocks. It's me. It's Daddy. Go get help."

They act as though they don't hear me. Rocks start coming down at a rapid rate. One hits my head. One hits my knee. One hits my hand and I nearly fall, catching myself just in time.

"Stop. Please stop. Why are you doing this?"

My children up above start singing a song, the words jumbled and incoherent. More rocks come down, pelting me. I suck in a breath to yell again, but then I'm sliding, and then falling. The children laugh up above as I hit the dark water below.

Bright. The light is so bright. It glows redly through my eyelids. The front of my head hurts, a dull pounding ache sitting at my hairline. My face feels stiff and hardened, as though I'm wearing a rubber mask that has grown brittle with age. My face twists in pain and I can feel the outer layer of skin crinkle and shatter. I reach up and run my hand across my forehead. Flecks break away with the friction of my hand, exposing wetness to the open air. It's hard to focus. The pistons in my brain are just starting to turn over.

My body is lolling on a car seat. It's the driver's seat. I can feel the bottom of the steering wheel pressed up against my right leg. Feeling returns to my body one piece at a time. Alice. I'm sitting in Alice. Her every curve is known to me, comforting. There is resistance to me opening my eyes, but the muscles in my lids breakthrough whatever is holding them closed. Bright. God it's so damn bright. The hot August sun dazzles me. Cracks spiderweb across the windshield, centered on a splotch of red directly in front of me. I rub my hand across my eyes to clear them. Flecks of dried blood, mixed with the bright red of fresh newly exposed layers and the salt of dried sweat, come off onto my hand. I try to sit up, but I don't have enough control yet. The hell bringing sun shines down. I'm sweating profusely. All the windows are closed. I'm in an oven. I'm trapped in a god damn oven.

My hand fumbles for the door latch and gets it after two or three tries. My arms feel weak, but with some help from my foot I manage to get the door open. The air outside is hot, but it feels like a spring breeze compared to the stifling heat of Alice's interior. Bright. It's so fucking bright. Fuck. Bright. Sunshine. Exposed. Alice is sitting on the bottom of the hill out in the open. Helicopters. Fucking helicopters. Her matte black paint is visible as hell amongst the tans and browns of the surrounding desert environment. Hide. I have to hide. Cover up. Need to make a plan. First things first. Tarp. I need to cover Alice with the tarp.

I throw myself out of the driver seat and collapse onto the ground. My legs are spaghetti. I sit on my hands and knees and wait for the world to stop spinning. I feel like I'm drunk. I don't have time for this shit. I have to hurry. My luck won't hold forever. Maybe they've already seen me. God, I don't know. I have to hurry. I lurch to my feet. The dry creek bed where Alice came to rest last night rolls like the deck of a ship in a storm. Despite my lack of sea legs, I force myself to Alice's back and pull out the tarp. Everythings a fucking mess. The tarp is heavy. I've done this a hundred times before. Drilled myself until I could do it in my sleep. Unfold the tarp. Make sure the right side is up. Pull it over the top of Alice. Lay rocks randomly on the edges. Shovel any loose dirt around on top. Throw on a couple of random branches. The world swims in front of my eyes. Out of focus.

With the tarp in place I crawl under and pull a bottle of water from my backpack. The bottle is worn and over reused. The plastic has started to decay. I chug half the water and splash the rest onto my face. Dirt, sweat, and dried blood come away with my hands. I refill the bottle from the big tank in the back of Alice, and splash more water onto my face. The world is becoming more clear. I lean against Alice's side, my shirt front soaked, catching my breath. Safe. I'm safe now. I take a yellow pill out of my pocket and dry swallow. I need a clear head. I need to think.

I feel a craving for chocolate milk. It's strange the little things that change in your life when you have kids. The little things you never think about until they're no longer an option. One day you find yourself standing in the grocery store aisle, staring into the cooler at a bottle of chocolate milk. You want it, but you know you can't have it. You can't have it because the moment you grab it the two kids with you will start howling out requests to have one too. You're a god damn adult. You should be able to have a god damn chocolate milk if you want one. But you can't, because it would spoil the kids' dinner. Instead you just collect the items you're supposed to get, pay, and leave.

When I was a kid chocolate milk was one of the few treats I ever got. Dad never kept much food in the house, and Beth sure as hell never brought over anything as frivolous as chocolate milk. But Beth used to send fat Cindy out to do the shopping, and she'd make Cindy take me if I was just sitting around. I never much liked Cindy, but she did have a sense of fairness. She'd always get herself something to add to her growing girth, and I'd always get a bottle of chocolate milk.

Linds never wanted the kids to have chocolate milk. She thought it would make them fat. I never argued the point, even though my own level of fitness was living proof that her hypothesis was a bunch of bullshit. Sometimes you have to choose your battles. We never kept it around the house, but I would sneak myself a bottle every now and again when I was out running errands. As things got more stressful it became one of my few comforts, a memory of when things used to be simpler. Some evenings I'd make an excuse, drive into town, buy a bottle, and then drink it at the end of the driveway.

Stone was the only one that caught on. She was always clever. One evening she walked down the half mile of the driveway and calmly climbed into the car and sat staring at me. Together we drove back into town and bought a second bottle. After that it was always our thing. Two nights before we started running we sat in the car and watched the sun slowly dropping below the horizon, sipping out of our bottles.

"Dad?"

"Yeah?"

"Can me and Rachel go back to school in September?"

"No honey."

"Why not?"

"I don't like the bullshit they're teaching you."

"I miss school. You used to let us go to school in Portland."

"I know, but you were younger then. Things are changing fast. Things are starting to get bad."

"Will they ever be good again?"

"Yes. I promise. I promise they'll be good again."

"Okay. I want things to be the way they used to be."

"Me too."

She sat quietly, watching the vivid orange on the horizon slowly turn to red. It was the most I'd heard her say in one stretch in a long time. We sat for another fifteen minutes, long enough for the brightest stars to start poking their way through the sky. My eldest daughter alone with her thoughts, and me planning for our escape.

I shake my head and stand up. There are things to be done. I can't think about the kids. I can't think about the past. I'm on my own now. I can't think about Linds. That fucking bitch. I have to think about the future. Alice. I need to make sure Alice is okay. She's the key. She's the key to my future. My escape. My freedom. She's never betrayed me. I walk around her, looking for damage. There's a lot of new scratches marring her matte black finish. Silvery random racing stripes. The front fenders are both pretty beat up. The right front tire is flat. Her front is buried up to the bumper. She's in a dry creek bed at the bottom of the big hill. The banks of the creek bed are sudden steep drops. Alice went in okay, but she sure as hell didn't make it out. The climb back out was too steep. A perfect vertical stair step at just the right height.

Mostly cosmetic damage. I drop down to check her undercarriage. Her guts. Things don't look so good. The right side of the axle hit a good sized rock. A stony iceberg. Just a bit sticking out. God knows how much hidden in the dirt of the bank. All the right side linkages are bent and broken. The u-joints are busted up too. She's leaking oil. That must have happened when she came down the other bank. I can't fix this. I don't have the parts. I don't have the means. Alice is broken. I can't save her. I've had her for seventeen years. My Dad had bought her new. The only new thing he ever bought in his life. She was Dad's pride and joy. Tears start flowing down my cheeks. I lay in the darkness under my long time companion, and sob like a little baby, my head hidden in my tear soaked arms. It's too much. It's all too much.

I crawl back out into the muted sunlight. I don't know what to think. I don't know what to do. I've lost everything. I've fucking lost everything. Why? Why? My body is running on automatic. I go to the back of Alice and pop open a beer. It runs down my chin as I chug. It tastes good. I have another. It tastes good as well. I roll a joint and light it. I open another beer. Dear god. How did I get here? How did it come to this? What am I supposed to do? The dope and booze works its way through my system. I start to relax. I need to calm down. I need to think. I get into the passenger side of Alice. The door sticks a bit and makes a horrible squeal when I force it.

I sit and look out at the underside of the tarp. I finish the beer in my hand and throw the can behind me. I take the inventory notebook out of the jockey box. I open it and look at the figures, the list of slowly depleting supplies. Ridiculous. It doesn't fucking matter. I pull a lighter out of the jockey box and light the notebook on fire. I watch it burn for a bit, mesmerized by the flames. I let it drop out the door onto the piles of rounded rocks below. Nothing fucking matters. I get up and grab more beers. Go back. Sit down again in the passenger seat. I drink them one by one as the brightness of the sun works its way across the tarp above me. Occasionally thoughts of the kids or Linds flash through my brain. I banish them. I keep my head in the moment. I stare at dust motes floating through the air. I wait for the sound of helicopters. Fucking bitch.

I knew she didn't want to go. I knew she never understood. But I never thought she would fucking betray me. Turn me in. All I ever wanted was to be free. Not have big brother looking over my shoulder all the time. Computers, cell phones, smart phones, the internet. Each step forward knitting the world a little closer together. Each piece of additional technology just one more way for them to watch you, track you, listen in. No privacy. No freedom. All given up in the name of public and personal safety. Statistically speaking the world has never been safer, but that is not the message they feed us. Afraid, be very afraid. You need us. Rapists. Murderers. Terrorists. The red Chinese. Give us your freedom. Give it up freely. Hand it over to your government. You can trust your government. We are the one's that can keep you safe. Yeah sure, the government cares. Just like the generals cared about us grunts in the Marines. We were never people. We were just numbers. Statistics. Pawns of the powerful. Those in control. Why couldn't she understand?

My hands moving across a pale thin body. Brushing across the rough xylophone of ribs as she lets out a moan and calls my name. The dust motes. Concentrate on the dust motes. Floating through the air. That fucking bitch. Two little girls laughing in the park. Asking me to push them on the swings. Higher and higher. Jumping back and forth between the two, getting in a rhythm. No. Can't think about these things. Can't think about them at all. Lost. All lost.

The beer cans are all empty. I get out, walk to the back, and get more. Drown the memories. Drown the reason. Drown it all. I get back into Alice's passenger seat. The cooler is empty. These beers are warm. My body feels sore. For the first time I feel old. I'm in good shape. Damn good shape for a man of forty-nine. Why do I feel so God damn old? Why do I feel so damn empty? What am I gonna do? Where am I gonna go? I can't go back. You can never go back. The world keeps on turning. That fucking betraying bitch. That whore. After all I did for her. After all I sacrificed. Nothing. I have nothing left.

I sit and finish the warm beers, then get out and get more. The sun works its way across the sky overhead, hidden by the tarp. I pee on all four tires. At the third one I start laughing uncontrollably. Nothing is funny. I just can't stop laughing. I'm losing it. I know I'm fucking losing it. More beers. I yawn. I take another yellow pill, wash it down with beer. That bitch. That fucking bitch. I have nothing. I pound my hand against the dash until the sun dulled plastic starts to crack and my hand starts to hurt. Sleep. Can't let myself sleep. I undoubtedly have a concussion. You're not supposed to sleep if you have a concussion. What the fuck am I doing here? What the fuck have I done? In the distance I hear a sound. So soft I can barely hear it over the wind. I recognize it instantly. A steady drummers beat.

Paul-paul-paul-paul-paul-paul-paul.

I need to get up. I start to rise, but two strong hands force me back down. I lay back and brace myself. The pressure of the hands softens. I throw myself from the passenger seat. My left arm jerks like a marionette on a string, but then breaks lose. Pain shoots up both my arms. My legs don't hold my weight. Down I go, sprawling onto the ground, my knees cracking against the round rocks, my beer a dark splash across the light gray. It's stifling under the tarp. Suffocating. Dear god. I'm suffocating. I can't breathe. I need to get out. No you damn fool. Shut the fuck up.

I rise up and crawl out from under the tarp. I stand up on the creek bank and stare out at the distant black dot working its way across the horizon. I stare in the direction of the river, of Mexico, of Amy. A place to be safe. A place to be free. A place to disappear. Where there are still places where a man can live without anyone noticing or caring. A place where things can be just like they used to be. Fuck that bitch. She can't control me. She can't stop me. I raise up my right hand with my finger placed in the universal salute. I scream my defiance. A guttural animal sound with no words. The emptiness washes out of me with the scream. The black dot flies sedately in the distance. I collapse and start puking. My body spasming uncontrollably.

Chapter 22

In 1968 psychologists John Darley and Bibb Latane wanted to find out why so many people stand by and do nothing when witnessing a crime. The pair put together a study where volunteers sat in an office to fill out a survey. Halfway through the task, harmless smoke was released into the room. The study showed that those taking the survey alone would report the smoke much faster than those who took the survey in a group. The individual recognized that they could only depend on themselves, so they acted. The people in groups just stared dumbly at each other, waiting for, and expecting, someone else to take the lead.

"Sir, your apartment is listed as Mr. Jones' last address."

"Yeah, I was letting him stay here a bit."

"When was the last time you saw Mr. Jones?"

"It's been a few weeks."

"How long?"

"Three weeks."

Cold winter air blows past the cop with the shaved head, through the open door into the apartment. His thick sausage fingers grip a pencil and pad. He pauses to scribble some notes. I stand in the doorway and try to keep my face bored and passive. Try to hide my annoyance. The cop is treating this all like a friendly house call. A friendly house call with him carrying a gun on one hip and a taser on the other. Gresham Police Department is emblazoned in white letters across the dark blue of his light duty bullet proof vest.

"What was the nature of your relationship with Mr. Jones?"

"We've been friends for a couple years."

More writing in the notepad. He looks up again. His two beady eyes, sitting in a fireplug head, sweep across the apartment behind me. It's a small apartment, not much to look at really, not near as nice as the house we were renting when I still had a steady job. Living room, dining room, and kitchen; only divided by a change of flooring from carpet to linoleum and a rack of counters at bar height. Two doors lead off to one side, one to a bedroom, and the other to a small bathroom. It's anything but luxurious, but the complex tends to stay fairly quiet, and we can afford it.

"Do you know the reason that Mr. Jones was evicted from his last place of residence?"

In my head I can see Walter and I drunk off our asses, smoking blunts, and throwing ourselves around his apartment in a near approximation of dancing as his speakers shred themselves on the heavy bass beat of a death metal album. The walls shake with the noise and it takes a full three minutes of pounding before we notice that someone is at the door. Walter goes outside and gets into a screaming match with his landlord. It's fucking 3 AM, blah, blah, blah. Quit being a fascist dickweed. We're just having a good time. Shut that shit off. Fuck off. Things after that are a bit hazy.

"No. I just knew he needed a place to stay for a while. Didn't really seem to be any of my business."

More scribbling, and then more looking over my shoulder. I stare straight ahead. I can feel the cop's eyes going over our belongings. An old musty couch with a stained cover, a coffee table that's seen better days, an old television with a built in DVD on top of a milk crate, a twin mattress covered with blankets where the girls sleep, and a half rebuilt transmission on a tarp in the dining area where a table should go. His eyes rest on the transmission the longest, or maybe the silhouette of Linds through the blinds covering the sliding glass door. A shadow on the balcony, lounging and smoking.

The cop's nostrils flare and I pray to God the place doesn't reek of marijuana. I only smoke it out on the balcony, and I make Linds do the same, but sometimes some of the smoke sneaks its way in. Since it's been getting colder I've caught Linds smoking in the house several times. Usually in the bathroom, blowing the smoke into the fan. I wish she wouldn't be so blatant about it. I don't like it when she smokes around the girls. The cop sniffs again and writes something else in his notebook. Panic fills my system. What the fuck could the pig be writing? He points with his pencil at the half rebuilt transmission.

"Doing some side work?"

More like my only work. I'm doing any side job I can get to keep my family afloat. I could go back to the stuff I was doing while Linds was in rehab, it was good money, but I don't want to. That shit was too risky. I've got to keep things on the down-low. Stay under the radar.

"Naw, just doing some rebuilding on my transmission."

The cop's lips turn upward in a strange approximation of a smile.

"Yeah, my Dad used to be really into stuff like that. He was always tinkering with something. My Mom hated it."

I manage a half smile in response. Standard operating procedure. Find something in common. Get them to let their guard down. Get them to reveal more than they otherwise would. Fucking pigs. The cop keeps smiling and then looks back down at his notepad. I hear giggling and the sounds of light horseplay from the closed bedroom door. The cop doesn't seem to hear.

"Okay, if you hear anything from Mr. Jones or remember anything else that might be important, please let us know."

He hands me a business card and I nod my head in understanding.

"Will do."

The cop turns and walks away. I watch him go down the stairs back to his car. As he drives away a white Ford panel van drives by. I feel myself tense up. Three o'clock. The van drives by every day at three o'clock. I shut the door, and lock it. I walk over to the bedroom and open the door. Stone is sitting quietly on the edge of the bed, her face blank, staring at nothing. Rachel, as soon as she sees me, stops jumping on the bed, landing on her butt in the middle of the rumpled comforter.

"Were you jumping on the bed Monkey?"

She smiles her bright smile of youth unencumbered by the troubles of the world.

"No Daddy."

"Are you sure?"

"No."

Stone looks up at me, no emotion showing on her face.

"Can we come out now?"

"Yes honey."

"Is it okay if we watch a movie?"

"Yes, just keep the volume down."

The girls rush into the living room. Rachel starts bouncing on the twin mattress. Stone sets up the television and VCR. I go out onto the balcony. Linds is sitting on a plastic chair, smoking a joint and staring out at the line of warehouses down the hill behind the apartment complex. As I pull the sliding glass door closed, she passes me the joint, but does not look up. Her pale green eyes stare at nothing. She looks haggard. Tired. She has a little more meat on her bones, rehab at least did that for her, but since she got out two months ago, a lot of the old spirits been missing. I know I shouldn't complain. She cooks. She cleans. She takes care of the kids. I just wish she would do more with her day than sit on the balcony and smoke pot. Sometimes I feel like Rachel and I are the only two left with any life in us. I take a hit and pass the joint back to her. She takes it without a word.

"The cops are gone."

"What did they want?"

Her voice is flat, monotone, like she's bored or just doesn't give a shit anymore.

"Just asking about Walter again."

"Hmmmm."

"The girls are watching a movie."

"That one with the unicorn again?"

"I don't know."

"I'm sick of the movies we have."

"I'll grab a few new ones when I can."

"I wish we still had cable."

Black Arial letters on a glowing computer screen flash through my mind. Pig69Pork's last message before he disappeared.

SOMETHING IS GOING DOWN. I THINK THEIR ONTO ME.
I'M BEING WATCHED.

I don't say anything to Linds. This has been a back and forth since she got out. She doesn't seem to understand that anything that transmits can also record. She doesn't seem to want to understand. I look down at the overturned plastic bucket next to her. Her cellphone, a cheap flip phone, sits next to her ash-tray.

"I thought we agreed to keep the phones in the closet when we're not using them. You know, between the towels."

She doesn't look up.

"Sorry, I must have forgotten."

Another running battle. Another unresolved conflict. Another game my wife seems unable to understand. I can't say anything. Not now. You never know who might be listening. I need a distraction.

"I'm going to walk down to the store. Do you need anything?"

"Grab a gallon of milk."

I reach down and pick up her cell phone. I go back inside and put it in the closet next to the bathroom, nestling it in the middle of the stack of towels. The girls are sitting on their mattress, enraptured by the television. They should be outside playing, but there's nowhere to play around here. Besides, the world outside is a dangerous place. I go in the kitchen and pull a bag of frozen burritos out of the back of the freezer. I pull a twenty and a couple ones out of the bag, put it back in the freezer, and mark off the amount on a ledger sitting on the counter. $2,183. I pull on my coat, walk outside, down the steps, and start my walk to the store.

It's cold outside. The air hits my lungs like a hammer. The sky is dull and gray. Cloud cover hugging close to the ground. There's three stores that sell milk within walking distance. A mini-mart, a drug store, and a large grocery store. I went to the mini-mart last Sunday, and the drug store on Tuesday. I should go to the grocery store this time. No wait. Scratch that. Got to keep it random. Someone could be watching. I need to be careful. Patterns. Patterns are how they get you. It's best to establish good habits now. Train myself. Make it all second nature. Got to look ahead. Got to plan ahead. I walk past Alice in the parking lot. Her dull blue paint is chipped and peeling. She's getting to be a pretty roughed up lady.

The winch on the front of Alice still needs to be worked on. It's still conked out from my last adventure with Walter. I had gone on a trail run. Three weeks back. I've been trying to get back into shape. I've never really been out of shape, but I want to be in Marine shape. I have to be ready. Ready for when the shit hits the fan. Rock climbing at the gym on Monday, free weights at home on Tuesday, trail running with a local club on Wednesday, resistance training on Thursday, drinks on Friday, cardio on Saturday, and Sunday with the family. Each week, every week, for the past three months.

Three weeks ago Walter decided he wanted to come to my trail running club. I had told him we usually have a few beers afterward. I'd been surprised. Walter's only shape is round. This ain't a beer belly, it's a gas tank for a sex machine. He looked ridiculous in his wife beater and basketball shorts. We ran up in Forest Park, just on the other side of Portland. Great place to run, you can forget you're even in the city. Little bit of snow, everything was pretty soft and muddy. I've been getting faster. Walter spent the whole time in the back, sweating like a pig.

All the cars were parked on a dead end. When we tried to get Alice out she slid partially off the road. I tied the winch cable to a tree across the road to pull her out. The winch took a shit. The cable was too tight to get off the tree, a big old bastard fir. All the other cars were blocked in. Everyone was mad. Walter was panicking. I just laughed. The whole thing was hilarious. Maybe it was just the pot. One intelligent fucker named Donovan finally had the bright idea to call his redneck friend who owned a truck. After about an hour the redneck showed up and pulled Alice back up onto the road. We got the cable off the tree, and rewound it onto the winch by hand. I gave the redneck a couple joints. He seemed to think it was a fair trade.

The air is extremely still. I can feel a charge of static electricity. My primal mind is screaming out in warning. Watch out. Something's up. Keep your eyes open. There are nothing to worry about. Just walking to the store. Just a nobody. What about that car coming up from behind? It's nothing. Just some jack ass going about his business. There are eyes everywhere, but nobody is watching me. There's no reason to watch me. How would I know if someone is watching me? There are too many eyes to watch them all.

The night kept going downhill after the winch adventure. Walter and I went to a bar on 82nd to try and find a playmate for me and Linds. Walter usually makes a pretty good wingman. He's too stupid to be considered a threat. That night he was too drunk. He kept scaring all the women away. Yelling about this and that. We gave up around 1 AM and went home. The kids were both dead asleep on their mattress in the living room. Walter usually sleeps on the couch. Linds was in the bedroom waiting. She had already polished off a twelve pack. I like it when she drinks. She's more like her old self when she gets drunk. Can't have her getting drunk all the time. Just like how I can't be drunk all the time. Just every now and again. Just for a treat.

Linds seemed disappointed with our failure. We smoked some pot to calm her down. Opened up a bottle of vodka. Had ourselves some drinks. It was cheap vodka. Bottom shelf cheap. Linds got flirty. Things got weird. Real weird. Everything onward is pretty hazy. Looking at my wife's naked back. Looking up at Walter's fat face with his greasy moustache and stubbled cheeks. Saying something to Walter. I can't remember what. He gets mad. We start yelling. The kids wake up crying. Walter storms out. The sound of his shitty car revving up and peeling out of the parking lot. I pass out.

Walter disappears. Two weeks later, one week ago, I get a postcard from Reno. The postcard is signed by one Carl Anderson in Walter's sloppy handwriting. The note apologizes for what happened. It tells me that my friend Walter got in a little bit of trouble and he had to get out of town. Parole violation. He doesn't want to go back to jail. Big fucking dumb animal.

The mini-mart door slides open automatically and greets me with a beep as I walk through. The Asian owner, I think he's Korean, at least he looks Korean, eyes me like I'm going to steal something, then goes back to watching some Asian show on his laptop. Everything in the store looks grimy. I go to the back and grab a gallon of milk off the shelf. I think about buying a snack, but decide not to. I don't need it, and we can't afford to waste our money on frivolous things. I walk up to the counter and the Asian guy rings me up. Four bucks. What a ripoff. The guy peels off the bills slowly and precisely and hands them to me. I pocket them. Cash only. No credit cards, no debit cards, and no checks. They were the first to go. Easiest way to track somebody. Besides, people like dealing in cash. Cash opens doors.

As I walk out the door I glance at the newspapers in the rack. Rescue package agreed to for Ireland. Europe is going to shit. More diplomatic cables released by Wikileaks. The internet forums have been abuzz with each new discovery. I've been trying to keep up, but the sheer volume is overwhelming. Spying, gossip, backroom deals, and corruption. A good effort, but nothing compared to what all is out there. The economy is still sluggish. Things are not getting any better. Drone attacks. Some asshole a thousand miles away kills with just the push of a button, like he's playing a god damn video game.

The cover of *Busted* catches my eye. I stop and stare down at the rows of mugshots printed on cheap newspaper and start laughing. Unfucking believable. I buy a copy and start walking back home. I need to get back to work on that transmission in the living room. Once it's done that's another thousand bucks in my pocket. Cash money. I'll show Linds the copy of *Busted* when I get home. That ought to get a laugh out of her. Then maybe I'll send it down to Reno. It's not every day you see someone you know on the front cover of *Busted*.

Chapter 23

The failure of the Republicans in the 2008 election, losing not only the presidency, but also numerous seats in both houses of Congress, combined with the worst economic crisis since the Great Depression, led to a schism in the Republican party. A so-called grassroots campaign, dubbed the Tea Party movement, spread across the country, with thousands attending hundreds of public protests nationwide. The group had only one goal. Smaller government and lower government spending, no matter what. Over time the protests shifted to political rallies which succeeded in electing numerous far right candidates in 2010. These newly elected Tea Party members refused to compromise their beliefs in any way. Congress became more polarized, and the gears of government ground to a halt. Public approval ratings for the US Congress plunged to all time lows. Investigations later showed that that Tea Party organizers took in millions of dollars in donations from several prominent corporations.

She lies on her belly, he lies on top of her, pumping away. They're both covered in sweat. Linds' face is contorted as though in pain. Her pale green eyes roll back and she is lost to the world, riding a wave of ecstasy only held in check by the physical limitations that created it. He is a stranger to me. A younger man with dark curly hair and a body not softened by age. He has to be at least fifteen or twenty years younger than me. One hand snakes beneath my wife, the other grips her hair, pulling her head up, keeping her face fully in my view. My wife moans loudly with every thrust.

"You like that? You like that you little slut?"

"Oh god yes."

"Better than your husband?"

"So much better."

The stranger kisses the back of Linds' neck and looks me in the eye. His eyes are a beautiful shade of bright green. His face looks like it was chiseled from granite. He smiles at me. My wife is not the part he enjoys. He enjoys the fact that she is not his. I want to charge forward and rip him limb from limb, but I can do nothing. I'm stuck. I'm forced to sit and watch as he takes her.

I open my eyes. The world is hazy. My shirt is soaked with sweat. The taste of vomit is still on my breath. My head is pounding. I haven't slept long, only an hour or two. I sit up in Alice's driver's seat and dig the pill container out of my left pocket and dry swallow two. I can't sleep. I can't let myself fall back into nightmares. I have to stay alert. I can't stay here forever. I have to decide what to do. It's hot as hell under this damn tarp. Usually the night brings relief, but not this one. This one feels just as hot as the day-time. My belly growls. It's feeling better than it was. No reason to starve myself. I have to keep up my strength.

A few minutes work and a long pee leave me with a heated MRE on my lap and three full beers sitting on the dash. I eat the food slowly, taking sips of beer between bites. The ache in my head dulls as I refill my tank. The taste of meatloaf with gravy covers the flavor of vomit in my mouth. It doesn't taste good, but it's better than not eating. It's hot as hell. So damn hot. I can't stop sweating. The air inside Alice is stifling and stinks of body odor and hot garbage. I roll down the driver and passenger side windows. It does little to help. The world under the tarp is trapped. Contained. Separate from the outside world around it. I finish my meal and lay the remains between the two front seats.

I sit back, my t-shirt front covered in gravy, and let out a belch. I start shaking. I can't stop. My body settles back into stillness. It's all been too much lately. One has to expect a little anxiety here and there. I drink my beer and stare out at the underside of the tarp, barely visible in the darkness. The beer is warm. It does little to help the heat. One by one the cans surrender their contents to me. My eyes sting. I pull up my t-shirt and use it wipe the sweat out of my eyes. The windshield ripples in a nonexistent breeze.

My head is swimming. I feel like I'm running on a delay. I'm an automaton driven by a tiny little man hidden away in my cranium. Everything is running, but only at an idle. It feels like time is running slower than normal, or maybe faster, it's hard to tell. My time seems to be at a snail's pace, but the world's time seems to be moving at a blur. Everything is hazy, out of focus. I'm not part of the world around me. I feel separate. Lost. Alone. But not scared. Nothing seems to matter. All I have to do is just let go. Release my fingers from where they hang on the precipice and let myself fall into the warm embrace. I'm just a single speck on a spinning rock that is a single speck in the universe. None of it matters. Not one bit of it matters. I just need to let go. What's my pain and hurt against the infinity of the cosmos.

"What the fuck are you doing?"

I turn my head towards the passenger seat. A woman in her early thirties sits next to me. It's a face that I haven't seen for a long time outside of memory. The rounded cheeks. The brilliant green eyes that look older than they should. A body, thickset, but shapely. Slightly fattened and worn by the trials of bringing life into this world. Her face is stern and cross. Exasperated and tired of repeating itself again and again. Diane.

"What the fuck are you doing here?"

"That's not answering my damn question."

"It's really none of your fucking business."

"The hell it isn't.

"You really want to know what the fuck I'm doing?"

"Yeah I want to know. I wouldn't have asked if I didn't."

"I'm waiting to die. There, you happy? I'm waiting to fucking die."

"What the fuck is wrong with you?"

"What isn't? I'm out in the fucking middle of the desert, Linds is gone, the kids are gone, Alice is all busted up, I'm getting hunted down like I'm some kind of wild animal, and now I'm sitting here all fucked in the head, talking to my ex-wife for the first time in over a decade. Things aren't exactly going all that well."

I whack the steering wheel in frustration. Diane stares at me. She looks pissed, but then again, she always did.

"Jesus Paul, you still don't get it do you?"

"What Diane, that I'm a loser, yeah I get it, I'm a fucking loser. I guess I'd have to be though. Only a loser would get involved with people like you and Linds."

"Fuck you Paul."

"No, fuck you Diane. Fuck you for always being such a bitch. Fuck you for taking away my son. Fuck you for abandoning me when I needed you the most."

"You're not being fair."

"Yeah, well it sounds pretty spot on to me. You were all I had. You and Philip were all I was living for."

"Christ Paul, you burned down your own damn house. What the fuck was I supposed to do?"

"Gee, I don't know, maybe help me get some help. Maybe stand by your man. Maybe live up to all those vows you said on our wedding day."

"Yeah, what about you Paul, what about your vows? I did stay. I stayed as long as I could. You didn't want help. You threw yourself off a fucking cliff then got mad because I wouldn't jump over after you. For fuck's sake. I loved you. I loved you more than I ever loved anyone before. I gave up my dream for you. I gave it up because I wanted to be with you. But you went away. You went places where I couldn't follow."

Hot tears run down my face. My voice is echoing through the cab.

"That fire was an accident."

"I'm not talking about the god damn fire."

"You took my son away."

"Yeah Paul, I did. I took your son away. What the fuck was I supposed to do? With how you were could you really blame me?"

"You took him away from his father."

"Who left who Paul? I don't remember me or Philip high as shit all the time. Philip and I didn't spend all our money on meth. Philip and I sure as hell didn't get hauled to jail by the cops. Who left who?"

"I needed help. I know I was fucked up, but I needed help."

"Tell me I didn't do the right thing Paul."

"You had no right to take away my son."

"Tell me I didn't do the right thing.

Her green eyes pierce right through mine. I don't know why I'm arguing with her. I know she's right. I was fucked up. Every bit as fucked up as Linds had been, if not worse. What if Linds hadn't gone to rehab? What would I have done then? Would it have been any different than what Diane did? No. The answer is no. I know it is. I would have done whatever I needed to do to keep my kids safe. My throat feels tight, invisible hands around my neck. A big gob of snot rolls down the back of my throat. Diane keeps staring. I can't meet her gaze. I look down at my hands in my lap.

"You did the right thing. I'm sorry Diane. You did what you had to do. I was a fucking mess. I had no business being around you or Philip. You did the right thing."

Diane's face softens. Her eyes are wet with undropped tears. She reaches over and gives my leg a squeeze.

"I know you're sorry Paul. I know."

"I got better though Diane. You have to admit that I did get better."

"Yeah Paul, I know. I know you got better."

"Then why did you disappear? Why didn't you ever come back?"

Diane looks away. Her eyes trace across the starburst pattern on the windshield, resting for a bit at the dark stain at the center of the break.

"I don't know Paul. I guess it seemed like the best thing to do at the time. There was no guarantee that you'd ever come out of it. No guarantee that you'd ever be the man I loved again. Everything with you was just wrapped in pain. I had to break free. Not just for me, but for Philip too. I just wanted Philip to have the chance to grow up to be normal. You know, not like us. I wanted his life to be better."

"I've never been ashamed of my past."

"Yeah, but tell me you don't want better for your girls. Tell me you don't want to save them from having to make all the same mistakes you did."

I don't say anything. We both know the answer. Everything Diane did for Philip, I'd do for Stone and Rachel. Silence, stretching through time and space, just a moment, but endless.

"I'm sorry Diane. I'm sorry for everything."

Diane doesn't say anything. She just stares out at the unseen world around us.

"Tell me you know that I'm sorry. Tell me you forgive me."

Diane reaches over and squeezes my leg again.

"Yeah Paul, I forgive you."

The back of my t-shirt is soaked through. I can feel it clinging to me and sticking to the back of the seat.

"What the hell am I supposed to do now?"

"I don't know, I guess what you've always done."

"What the hell is that?"

"Keep fighting. Right or wrong you always put up a fight. You were never the type to just lay down and die."

Diane smiles at me. The smile she used to always give me. The one I saw on our wedding day. The one I first saw the night I punched Larry in the face for her.

"I don't know what the hell I'm fighting for anymore. Linds is gone. The kids are gone. I have nothing left."

"Bullshit Paul."

My eyes start to sting. I use my t-shirt to wipe my brow again. A sense of nausea clings to the back of my throat, slowly working its way up. There's a sound in the distance. Maybe it's the helicopter. I don't know.

"I don't know what you're seeing Diane, but it's just you and me in here, and I'm pretty sure I'm the only one who's real."

I turn and look out my window. Nothing but darkness. The world outside Alice does not exist. I turn back. Diane is gone. In her place sits a woman with long black hair and a Roman nose. Her eyes are hazel, just like our grandfathers.

"Amy, what are you doing here?"

"Hey kiddo, just thought I'd better check up on you. How you doing?"

"I don't know Amy. Everything is fucked. Linds took the kids and disappeared. She told the border patrol, or the cops, or god knows who where I am. Alice is all fucked up. I was just talking to Diane a second ago. I think I'm cracking up."

"Yeah, that sounds like a lot of shit to hit all at once."

"For god's sake Amy, weren't you listening. I was talking to Diane. I'm fucking losing my mind."

Amy looks me up and down, appraising me from top to bottom.

"I don't know little brother. I'm willing to bet though that I'd be seeing all sorts of crazy shit if I was downing those trucker pills like they were candy."

"I don't know what I'm doing Amy. I don't know what to do. Everything is just so out of control. For god's sake, I've lost my family again."

"Well, if you don't know what to do, what is it that you want?"

"I don't know."

"Bullshit. Why are you out here then?"

"Because they're after me. They're mad because I won't live by their rules. Do what they say. Think what they want. I had to leave. If I didn't they would have locked me up."

"So what is it that you want?"

"Fuck Amy. You know what I want. I want to be free. Is that too much to ask? Just to be left alone. To be able to live my life without some other asshole deciding I'm doing it the wrong way. To not have some pencil pushing bureaucrat trying to take the place of god, telling me what's wrong or right."

"So what's any of this have to do with your family?"

"What was I supposed to do, just leave them?"

"Can you go back Paul?"

"No. I told you, they'll lock me up if I go back."

"Is there anything you can do about your family right now?"

"No."

"Can you go back and get them?"

"No."

"Do you even know where they are?"

"No."

"Then maybe you should just concentrate on the things you can do."

I can't seem to stop sweating. God, how many beers did I drink. I feel drunk. No. Somewhere closer to hungover. I can still hear the throbbing sound of the helicopter. It's right up in my brain. Pulsing in time with my heart.

"What about Alice? She's all busted up. She's not going anywhere."

"Fuck Paul, it's a god damn Suburban."

"Yeah, but…."

"You want to be free Paul?"

"Yeah."

"Then you're going to have to let it go. Part of being free is being able to let go. Right now you need to get off your ass. Go back or forward. It doesn't matter. You just can't stay here. There's nothing here."

"I can't go back. They'll get me if I go back."

"Then the decision is pretty damn easy, isn't it?"

I look forward out the windshield. Out into the darkness. Shapes just out of sight move and intertwine in an endless dance of chaos and uncertainty. She's right. I can't stay here. There's nothing for me here. No matter what I do, I have to move on. I can't let myself get stuck. I can't let myself get trapped. I have to let go. It's all just baggage. I can drop it anytime I want to. I just have to let go. Fuck it's hot. I swear I can see heat waves coming off the dash. I turn back to look at Amy. She's gone. There's nothing in the seat next to me. Fuck it's hot. My hearts beating like mad. The fucking helicopter is still flying around inside my head. My temples are throbbing. My body is shaking. The entire world is twisting as though god is wringing it out like a towel.

Heat stroke. What the fuck am I doing? I'm giving myself god damn heat stroke under here. I'm killing myself. Idiot. Stupid fucking idiot. I know better than this. Air. I need god damn air. I push open the door and grab my backpack as I climb out. I feel dizzy. I can barely stay on my wobbly legs. It's still hot as hell. Fresh air. I need to get out from under this fucking tarp. I crawl out from under the tarp into the starlight. It's still hot out here, but compared to under the tarp it feels cool. A slight wind pushes the air around me. A muggy shift better than any spring breeze. I feel sodden and sticky. Everything feels chafed and out of sorts. I climb out of the creek bed and sit with the blackness of the hillside behind me, the majesty of the heavens before me, bridged by the nebulous span of the Milky Way. Beautiful. It's so fucking beautiful.

The world around me is all dark shadows. The only differentiation is where the starlit sky meets the horizon. I navigate by feel and unzip my backpack. I pull out a bottle of water and chug it. I pull out a second and drink it slower. I don't want to drink too much too fast. It would just make me puke again. I sip the second bottle and feel my heart rate slow. The world begins to solidify around me. My hands slow their shaking. That was close. What the hell was I doing? Stupid bastard.

I feel around my backpack in the darkness, and pull out the plastic bag of joints and my lighter. I take out a joint, spark the flame, inhale, and feel the last tensions in my body ease away. Calm. Just sit here and feel calm. Nothing to worry about. Nothing to be scared of.

A rustling to my right. Something crawling through the bushes. Slowly. Start and stop. Something stalking its prey. Something stalking me. My heart rate spikes again. Adrenaline courses through my body. Panic. Don't panic. Stop. Think. Don't be stupid. I reach slowly into my backpack and pull out my headlamp and hold it in my left hand. My right hand closes on the grip of the 22 pistol. I slowly pull it out and cock it. The click is loud in the darkness. More rustling. I stare at the point where the sound is coming from. Maybe twenty feet away, but closing. I'm not scared. Not tonight. No fucking way.

I hold my breath. My left hand clicks on the light and the red beam illuminates the world in front of me. Red eyes raise up in surprise, sharp ears snap back against a naked head, a bony hairless body turns to run. The pistol cracks three times in quick succession. My ears ring. The light from the muzzle blinds me. A terrible animal scream of pain cuts through the night amongst the sounds of desperate running. My dazzled eyes clear and I shift the light around, searching, hunting. The prey has become the predator. The bastard has dogged me since I came into this fucking desert. The monster in the dark. Fucking chupacabra, or whatever the hell it is. I'm not scared anymore. I'm not fucking scared. Silence descends around me. My ears quit ringing. I search a bit more with the light, and then turn it off. I sit with the pistol in my hand, my ears searching the darkness. I sit and wait, a smile on my face. My name is god damn Paul, and I'm on the top of the god damn food chain.

Chapter 24

In 1965 the psychologist Martin Seligman mistreated numerous dogs to test the perception of control. Several puppies were placed in a large crate with a low barrier. A shock was administered which could easily be avoided by jumping over the low barrier. The dogs of course quickly figured this out. The good doctor and his associates then took a second group of dogs, and administered shocks that were unavoidable. The dogs were then put in the box with the low barrier where the shocks could be avoided. Despite the shocks, not one dog tried to jump over the barrier. Each assumed that the shocks were unavoidable, despite their changed environment, and just sat and cried. The shocks were seen as something that had to be endured. They were seen as a normal part of life.

Mabel, Dad's old '61 Chevy Suburban, bounces along the dirt road at a constant rate, neither speeding up at the straight aways, or slowing down for the rough patches. The beams of the headlights bobble in time with the bounces, creating a jittery view of the darkened landscape. Dad sits behind the wheel, illuminated by the glow of the dash lights and the coal on the end of his cigarette. Mabel's ash-tray is full of smoked down filters. Occasionally Dad erupts in a wheezing cough that makes my lungs hurt. I try to sit as far away from him as possible. I alternate between staring sullenly out the window at the gleaming stars and invisible desert landscape, and picking randomly at Mabel's chipped and scratched metallic mint green interior.

Bastard. Fucking bastard. Tomorrow is the first day of deer season. I could be on my way with Tom and his dad to the Guadalupe Mountains right now. Just like for the past four years. I could be sitting in a '75 Ford pickup, pulling a travel trailer chock full of food and camping supplies. I could be cracking and laughing at dirty jokes. Telling stories about previous hunts. I could be anywhere but here. Fucking asshole. Why? Why now? Why this time? The asshole hasn't gone hunting in over ten years. Why has he suddenly taken such a god damn interest in my upbringing? He had my whole childhood to give a damn. It's not fair that he's decided to do it now. Hell, even after Beth died five months ago things didn't change. I just learned to cook for myself, do the laundry, and keep the house clean.

I stare at my dim reflection in the window glass. I hear Beth's hoarse voice in my head.

"Paul. Come closer Paul. There's something I gotta tell you. Something you need to know."

The hospital room is not comforting. Nothing but harsh metal lines, drably painted walls without decoration, and multiple beeping and hissing machines, all on wheels to make it easier to move them to the next patient when Beth expires. Beth lies in the bed, an oxygen hose in her nose, the lines on her face deeper than ever. Gray roots are starting to show on top of her head. Beth looks old, far older than she should at sixty, and a hell of a lot older than she looked just a month ago. Before there'd been any pain and shortness of breath. Before any damned doctors had mentioned anything about lower respiratory infections. Dad had gone off to buy some pops from the machine down the hall. Beth had motioned for me to get my ass closer.

"I always meant to tell you when you got older, but it doesn't look like that's going to happen. Your father never wanted you to know, but you deserve to know the truth."

I walk forward, but stay back beyond the edge of the bed. I don't want to get too close. Being too close makes me uncomfortable.

"The truth about what?"

Beth's body convulses in a series of terrible wracking coughs that shake her skinny frame and bring tears to her eyes. She lays back in the bed and stares at me with half closed eyes.

"God I wish they'd let me have a cigarette. Doesn't really fucking matter anymore. Bunch of over educated bastards. Just have a smoke and go out dancing like I used to. God I had some good times. I never thought it would be like this."

I stand silently, unsure what to say. My curiosity grows to the point that it's overwhelms my disgust. I step closer to the bed.

"The truth about what?"

Beth looks at me, a renewed spark of recognition crosses her face. Her weak skeletal hand clamps down around my wrist.

"Why don't you shut up so I can tell you?"

Dad gears down and turns onto an even rougher dirt road. He's acting like he knows where he's going, but he's not fooling me. He has no god damn idea. He hasn't had any idea since we had dinner in Fort Stockton. He just keeps picking random roads. Left off Highway 385 up into the hills. Drive through a giant oil patch. Right through an open gate with no signs. Just keep going until it looks remote enough. That's part of hunting, isn't it? Going some place remote? I stare at my father until he glances over. I turn and look straight ahead. I want to tell him I know. I want to raise my cracking voice and scream to the world what a bastard my father is. That I know what he did. That I know how he lied to me. I've been wanting to say something for the past five months. I just keep losing my nerve. Not this time though. Not this time.

Mabel pulls off the road and comes to a halt. Dad cuts the engine and turns off the headlights. The world goes dark except for a sprinkling of stars not blocked by clouds. He stabs his cigarette out in the ashtray, lets out a sigh, and turns in his seat towards me.

"Well, this spot looks as good as any. Better catch some shut eye."

We stare at each other for a bit, his gaze steady, mine quivering with anger. I break away first, climbing over into the back seat where I lay down and cover myself with an old blanket. Dad reaches around to the floor-boards next to my makeshift bed and pulls another blanket over the back of the seat. He stretches himself out on the front bench seat. He's snoring within minutes. If I was with Tom and his dad we'd be sitting next to a roaring fire. Goulash cooking in the dutch oven, sourdough biscuits cooking on the lid. We'd be playing cards while we waited. Five card draw, gin rummy, three hand cribbage. I usually do the best at cribbage. Tom does the best at rummy. Tom's dad always lets us win at five card draw. What do I have here? Just a couple old blankets and a few bags of canned goods. I lay and stew until sleep takes me.

It's still dark out when Dad shakes me awake. He hands me an opened uncooked can of pork and beans with a spoon in it. I sit up and start shoveling the beans into my mouth, sullenly staring at the back his head. He eats his own can of beans and glances back at me through the rearview mirror.

"Everything okay?"

"You said I would get to drive."

"What?"

"In Fort Stockton. You said you'd let me drive as soon as we were off the main roads."

Dad is silent for a bit. Staring back at me. His brown eyes desperately trying not to roll.

"I forgot. Guess I was pretty tired."

"Yeah, I guess so."

"I'm sorry."

"Whatever. I guess I don't ever really need to get any practice in. Lots of people pass their driver's test without ever getting behind the wheel."

"I'll let you drive when we leave."

"I guess we'll see."

Dad's eyes look annoyed but he doesn't say anything. He opens the door and gets out, shutting it just hard enough to show his frustration. He opens up the back and starts rummaging around. I wait a few moments and get out and join him. It's cold. Dad's already wearing a bright red sweatshirt. He hands me another and I slip it on. I stamp my feet to stay warm. Dad loads up two backpacks with granola bars, bags of trail mix, boxes of bullets, a roll of toilet paper, old military surplus canteens, and a pint of Jim Beam. Dad hands me the backpack without the bourbon in it and then the 308 Winchester. He hoists his own bag and takes the 30-30 Springfield. Without a word he starts walking away. I fall in behind. The sun starts to peak over the eastern horizon.

Both the rifles are old. They belonged to my grandfather and have spent the past decade gathering dust in the coat closet. Dad had cleaned and oiled them before we left. The 308 is the newer of the two, lever action, open sights. The 30-30 is older and in much rougher shape. Bolt-action with a peep sight, a crack in the stock held together with layers of wound electrical tape.

We walk for quite a while. Down a hill into a canyon, up the other side, and then across the ridge. Past greasewoods and sagebrush. Some only waist high. Some above my head. Every now and again I step on a twig that snaps or accidentally roll a rock down a hillside. Dad looks back, but doesn't say anything. Dad tries to act like he knows what he's doing, but it's just like the drive out here. There's no one else around. Not even the distant sound of rifle fire. I'm pretty sure we're trespassing. Finally tiring of the game, he stops on a hillside overlooking a canyon, sits down on a rock, and motions for me to sit too. He points below us.

"We'll wait here for a while. See if any deer come down this canyon."

We sit and wait. No deer come. He tries to start up a few conversations in a quiet whisper. I give him back only grunts. I'm not in the mood to talk right now. He might be able to force me to come out to god only knows where, but he can't make me talk. If it makes him uncomfortable, too fucking bad. Dad gives up after awhile. He lights a cigarette and slowly starts chain smoking his way through his pack. We sit quietly and stare at the empty canyon as the sun rises higher in the sky. After a couple hours Dad gets up and motions for me to follow.

We start walking aimlessly again. Down into the canyon, up the other side, along another ridge. It starts to get hot. We both take off our sweatshirts and tie them around our waists. Around noon we eat granola bars and trail mix. Dad takes a couple swigs off the whiskey bottle. I'm kind of surprised he's made it this far through the day. Dad looks at me, and then holds out the bottle. I eye it warily like it's some kind of trick. I take the bottle and swallow a gulp, feeling the burning liquid roll down my throat. I force my face into a grimace. This is not my first time. Tom's dad often let us have little nips off his bottle. Sometimes you'd have to pull stray moustache hairs off the rim. It seems best to pretend. Dad puts the bottle away and we move on to sit overlooking the same canyon from this morning.

We sit and watch the sun move towards the western horizon. Late in the afternoon I see movement up the canyon, out of range. Dad is a little further down the hill, in amongst a thick sage bunch, taking a shit. It's a deer, maybe a forked horn, or maybe even a three point. It moves with slow careful grace, entirely unaware of my presence. I work the lever action on my rifle, sit perfectly still, and wait. Step by step the deer gets closer. Unaware of its impending demise. I slowly raise my rifle to my shoulder, advice from Tom's dad runs through my head. Wait till you have a good shot. Shoot on the exhale. Squeeze the trigger, don't jerk it. Be sure you line up your sights right. There's a big juniper down in the bottom of the canyon. I use it as my mark. When the deer pulls even, that's when I'll shoot. The deer continues forward. My finger tightens around the trigger.

The wracking cough is deep, loud, and full of phlegm. Birds take off from the trees and the deer throws itself around and starts running back up the canyon at top speed. My rifle swings around. The shot is wide to the left. The loud crack leaves my ears ringing. Out of the corner of my eye I see Dad running up the hill toward me. I work the lever action on my rifle, the empty shell comes out smoking. My second shot is wide to the right. I work the lever action again and the mechanism jams. Fuck. My curses echo down the canyon as I work to clear the jam. I bring the rifle up again, just in time to see the deer disappear over the hill. I sit and stare at the place it once was.

The ringing in my ear stops. The old man is on his knees hacking away, struggling for breath. His face is bright red and his brown eyes are bulging out of his head. For a moment I feel a pang of pity and worry, but it doesn't last long. He's a selfish lying bastard. He doesn't deserve pity.

"You scared the fucking deer."

My words echo across the canyon. Dad looks up, but doesn't say anything. He sits crouched over for a bit, catching his breath. He takes out the bourbon bottle, has a pull, and then walks up to sit next to me.

"Was it a big deer?"

"Not really, just a forky."

Dad nods, picks the two brass shells off the ground, puts them in his pocket, gets up, and motions for me to follow. The sun is below the horizon by the time we get back to Mabel. Dinner is another can of cold beans. Dad makes an excuse about it being too dry for a fire. I know it's just an excuse because he doesn't know how to make one anymore. It gets cold fast. The sweatshirts go back on. We huddle under blankets on our respective bench seats in Mabel. Dad turns the key so we can listen to the radio for a bit. He sits with his back against the passenger side door, the window open, smoking a cigarette. I sit and stare up at the ceiling of the cab. Working up the courage to say what needs to be said.

I wish Amy was still around. It would have been a hell of a lot easier to talk to her first. She always had a good perspective on things. She always seemed to know what to do. But Amy's been gone for two years. The moment she turned eighteen she high tailed it out of Texas. Ran off and got herself a job as an airline stewardess so she could see the world and have adventures. Do all the things we used to talk about back when we were kids. Amy had made her escape, but left me behind. My sister has always been the lucky one. She calls every now and again, but the calls are few and far between. If I'm going to say anything, it's going to have to be on my own. I sit up and stare at the shadow of my old man.

"I know that Mom didn't run off."

Dad turns his head to look at me, his expression hidden by the darkness. I can feel my body shaking. I plow forward before I lose my nerve. I will the words to come out smoothly.

"I know that you put her in the state hospital up in Wichita Falls. I know that she died up there."

Dad reaches forward and turns off the key, killing the radio. He looks back at me, his face quiet and sad.

"Who told you that?"

"Beth. The day before she died."

Dad stares forward at nothing. Our breathing is loud in the silence.

"Well, is it true?"

"Yeah, it's true."

"You always told me Mom ran off. That one day you woke up and she was just gone."

"That was true in a way. You were probably too young to remember. The screaming. The yelling. The paranoia. The seeing things that weren't there. By the time I had her committed, there wasn't too much of the woman I married left."

"She was right there. Right there the whole time. Just two and a half hours away. Why didn't you ever take me to see her? Why did you lie? Why did you lie to me?"

Dad sits quiet for a bit. Gathering his thoughts and watching the smoke curl from the end of his cigarette. I sit straight, as if there is a rod in my spine. My hands clench the seat to either side of me. I can feel moisture building in my eyes.

"Your grandfather had a sister named Gloria."

"What?"

"She was his favorite sister. When I was a kid we use to get loaded up in the car every month to drive up to Wichita Falls to see Aunt Gloria. We never had much money back then, but we always made the trip. When Gloria was still a teenager she got the sleepy sickness. No one remembers the sleepy sickness, though it killed over a million people. It happened at the same time as the big Spanish flu. From what your grandpa said, one day she woke up with a sore throat and a fever, started acting funny, and then fell asleep for a month. Most people died then, but not Gloria. She woke up as though everything was just fine."

"You've never talked about this before."

My father doesn't hear me. He's off lost, somewhere in his own little world.

"Gloria wasn't fine though. She became pretty bad tempered and started acting funny. She'd make suggestive comments to the neighbor boys and disappear for hours up in the barn. She started getting the shakes. She started having problems staying upright. Her balance got all fucked up. Every muscle in her body would tighten up. Your great grandfather didn't know what to do. They took her to some doctors, but nothing seemed to work. So in the end, he took her up to the state hospital and had her committed."

Dad takes a deep breath and pauses for a moment. Seeing things that only he can see. I sit quietly and wait.

"It always creeped me out when we went up to visit her. Her face looked like a damn kid's face. You never get any lines or wrinkles if you never have any facial expressions. She was pretty much catatonic. Just sat in a wheelchair all day, staring at nothing. Her head was always twisted at a weird angle with one arm up over it. The staff would wheel her out and your grandfather would sit there and talk to her like she was a normal person. Tell her all the news of the family, all the local gossip. He acted like there was still someone in there. Like she wasn't just a living corpse. You could get her to do some things. If you told her to raise her hand she'd do it, or if you played some old ragtime on the record player she'd jerk around a bit. Dad always got mad when we did that kind of stuff though. He felt like we were stealing her dignity."

Dad lights a new cigarette. He takes the first puff and lets out a deep set of coughs.

"Hell, those monthly visits are probably why we're all so fucked up. Your Aunt Linda was the first to run off. The moment she hit eighteen she was gone. Ended up stripping down in New Orleans. Lives over in Arizona now, selling magic crystals or some such shit. Sends a Christmas card maybe every other year. I ran off and joined the Marines to go to Korea. Your Uncle Pete lied about his age and came too. I came back. He didn't. I think we all just wanted to get away. While I was in Korea Aunt Gloria died. Choked on her own tongue or something like that. Your grandfather got easier to deal with after that, though it was too late to keep your grandma in the picture. The whole thing creeped her out too. She'd usually just wait in the car during our visits. After Pete died she filed for divorce and remarried a guy up in Tulsa. Got killed in a car accident the same year you were born. I roved around a bit then came home. Like I said, your grandfather was a lot easier to deal with after Gloria died."

I don't know what to say. This is the first time I've ever heard Dad talk about his past. There are always stories to be heard, stories told by others. But this is the first time I've ever heard anything directly from the horse's mouth. Hell, this is the most he's ever talked to me in my life.

"When things went bad and I had your mother committed, I decided not to put you through the same thing. It seemed better to tell you that she ran off. Better to have you think that than to know the truth. Hell, they had her doped up to the gills so often that she wasn't that much different from Aunt Gloria. That's probably why I didn't go up much either, though I wish I had."

"But why did you have to commit her? Why did you take her away?"

"I didn't want to do it Paul. When we first got married there were no hints that anything was wrong. She was a little quirky, a bit of a beatnik, people used to say she was very spiritual, but nothing that rang any alarm bells. I don't know. She always used to talk about things we couldn't see. Maybe I was just young and dumb. It happened gradually. She'd have to lock all the house doors even though we lived in the middle of nowhere. Sometimes she'd wake up screaming in the middle of the night. Wouldn't calm down for hours. We started getting into fights all the time. The doctor gave her Valium, but it didn't seem to help. She just got worse. Started talking about shadows like they were people. Claimed they were out to get us. She refused to turn out the lights. One morning I woke up and found her standing over you sleeping in your bed, holding a kitchen knife, muttering that she wasn't going to let them get you. It freaked the shit out of me. What was I supposed to do? I had her committed the next day."

I can see the glint of tears as they roll down my father's ragged cheeks. He looks old. So much older than he should. A life-time of punishing himself and trying to forget etched across his features. I don't want to ask, but I know I have to. I have to know. I have to know how it ended.

"How did she die?"

"She killed herself. You were about eight. They were trying out a new medication. One where they wouldn't have to keep her so doped up all the time. It seemed to help. The first thing she did was sneak into the kitchen and slit her own wrists. I had her cremated and spread her down at Padre Island. She grew up there. It was her favorite spot."

Too much. It's all too much. I want to scream. I want to pound on my Dad in frustration. The world around me disappears. I'm aware that I'm crying, but have no idea when I started. I feel like I can't breathe. All the hate and anger is washed away. All gone. Replaced by nothing but darkness. Escape. I have to escape. To get away. I throw open Mabel's door and start to run into the night. I hear the sound of the front door opening and slamming shut behind me.

My boot catches on something and I go down onto hands and knees. I
sit down and curl into a ball, snot and tears flowing out of my face.
Running footsteps behind me, then the feel of arms around me,
enveloping me. A head against mine. A voice in my ear.

"Paul. Paul. I'm so sorry Paul. I'm so sorry."

With one arm I try to push the body away, the head with its wet
face, but the arms just hold me tighter. I cling back like a rat on a
piece of garbage, flung free from a sinking ship. I sit in the dirt and
cry like I have not cried in years, clinging to a stranger for comfort. I
violently push him away.

"No. Get away from me. Get away from me you bastard."

My father sits in the dirt. Tears streaming down his face. He
reaches out his arms towards me. I throw myself to my feet and run
into the darkness. I run. I run as hard as I can, the sound of my
father's wracking cough fading behind me.

Chapter 25

Lobbyists and special interests, with their silver tongues and loads of money, might have always run the country. But at least in the old days they had to stay out of the elections. They weren't able to put money directly for or against any particular candidate. That all changed in 2010 with the Supreme Court decision Citizens United vs. Federal Election Commission. Political commentary was recognized as a form of free speech. Corporations and unions were given the right to have their voices heard. Sure, they couldn't give directly to the candidate, but they sure as hell were allowed to shovel all the money they wanted into ads supporting or deriding as they pleased. Money flooded in, and those who didn't get in line soon found themselves swept out of office. The American public completely lost control. Duped by a shit ton of cash, and their own inability to think for themselves.

The priest's words, flat and monotone, float over the wooden box adorned with wreaths and flowers. A picture of my father sits on top. An old black and white of when he was young, his eyes still full of hopes and dreams. A face unlined and unworn. It looks nothing like the man I knew. The priest's words sound like jibberish. Like his tongue keeps getting stuck to the roof of his mouth. None of it seems real. I want to start laughing, but I stifle it. People are already uncomfortable enough with my presence. I compromise with a little smile that I hide behind my hand. With my aviators on people will probably just assume I'm crying.

It's been three days since I got the call. I haven't slept in that entire time. Three days of searching the cosmos, looking for answers. I waited until I could feel my feet brush the ground, then made the three and a half hour drive from Dallas to Sweetwater. I spent the entire trip drinking Mountain Dew and listening to my Best of AC/DC cassette on repeat. Made it through nearly four times. When I arrived with just a couple of hours to spare the people at the house freaked out. They threw me in the shower, combed back my long greasy hair, and threw together an acceptable funeral outfit for me. The sport coat and button down blue shirt belonged to Dad. They couldn't find pants that fit so they left me in my old pair of dirty ripped blue jeans. They hadn't liked how bloodshot my eyes were, even after several doses of Visine. They had argued until settling on me wearing sunglasses in the church as the best option.

The family showing is light, but then again, there have never been that many. Dad was never big on keeping track just because of blood. On one side of me sits fat Cindy. Her blonde hair pulled tight into a bun on back of her head. Her face slathered with makeup as usual, the lipstick a dark shade of red because it's a funeral. On my other side sits my Aunt Linda, who I've maybe seen three times before now in my whole life. She's the complete opposite of Cindy. No makeup. Skinny as a stick. No decoration except for a large crystal on a necklace. Lined up down the pew next to her sit a couple of cousins I don't really know. Two of Linda's kids, I'm not sure how many she actually has, and a couple others which I'm pretty sure are somehow tied in through one of my grandmother's siblings. Strange for them to come out of the woodwork now.

Most of the pews are filled up with people from town. Drinking buddies from the bar mostly I'm guessing, but a couple of the more respectable. A little ways behind me sits George from the store. Near the back in matching suits sit Tom and his dad. It's been awhile. Tom's dad looks funny without his fishing hat on. His chrome dome reflecting the church lights. I had waved when they walked in, but they, like the rest, had not bothered to acknowledge my existence. They were here to pay their respects, not impart sympathy on the wayward son. It's weird to think about. Dad lying dead there in that box. His face plastered with makeup. His innards pumped full of formaldehyde. The world around me is twisting. Christ, I'm spiralling down hard. Hell of a time for a three-day joy ride to end. I can feel myself in the box with my Dad, stinking of chemicals, stuck in the dark. I can hear them lower us into the ground. The sound of dirt coming down on top. The sides of the box rotting away and worms digging their way into my cheeks.

"Oh god."

The moan is loud. The priest falls silent. All eyes turn towards me. It takes me a moment to realize that I was the one who made the noise. The room keeps spinning. My belly starts to spin with it. Down there. In that box. That's what's going to happen to Dad. That's the end. Nothing left. Just a memory better left forgotten. Everyone's still staring. I'm sweating like a bastard. Like a whore in church. I bite back a chuckle. I'm going to be sick. I push my way past Cindy and into the aisle. Down past all the staring eyes, out the door to the entryway, into the small bathroom. The puke is neon yellow from all the Mountain Dew. It comes out easy. Nothing solid. Just liquid.

I wash my mouth out at the sink. I spit. It's the color of old blood. A tooth rattles around the basin. Another molar. That makes three so far. All in the back. Nothing to fuck up my pretty smile. I look up and grin, my tongue probing the new hole, my face twisted into an unrecognizable shape in the mirror. I start laughing, but everything bends and the giggles shift into sobs. I wait for them to subside, and then head back out. Cindy is waiting for me. She grabs my arm with her sausage fingers and brings me to a halt.

"Hold on Paul. I don't think you should go back in there."

"The funeral. We're right in the middle."

My voice sounds funny in my ears. All the words are mumbly.

"I know, but it would probably be best if you headed home."

"But Dad. I should be there for Dad."

"Trust me Paul. This is better for everyone."

She pulls me by the arm and I don't resist. Outside the sun is shining. Everything is green and new. A world engulfed in the smell of recent rain. She puts me in the passenger seat of her car, gets behind the wheel, and starts driving back out of town towards Dad's place.

"But what about Dad?"

Cindy doesn't seem mad. Just weary.

"Christ Paul. Would you look at yourself. You're a god damn mess. Your fucking thirty-two years old. When are you going to get your act together?"

I stare out the window at the passing scenery. City giving way to newly planted cotton fields and run down farmhouses. It's why I don't come home. I can hear Dad saying the exact same thing over the phone last time we spoke. That was a while ago. How long? Must have been at least a year.

"God how your Dad worried about you. Especially these past few years. I hadn't seen him worry about you that much since you still had those imaginary friends in middle school. At least you grew out of that one. Hell, all that damn anxiety probably didn't do him any good."

"He should have saved himself the trouble. We've barely spoken in years."

The car pulls up the driveway and comes to a stop next to the front porch. Cindy turns and looks at me. Her big brown cow eyes boring into mine.

"Your dad loved you Paul. He wasn't the best at showing it, but he loved you a bunch. He was so damn proud of you. For joining the Marines. For getting married. He used to say that the day you phoned to tell him you got hitched was one of the best days in his life. Hell, he's left everything to you. The homestead, all his money, his car."

"Alice?"

"Whatever the hell he called this one. All he ever wanted was a good life for you, and all you're doing is throwing it away."

"Cindy...."

"Just shut up and go into the house. I'll bring the lawyer by later today so you can sign the papers."

I get out of the car and it pulls away. It starts to drizzle a bit so I hustle across the well kept green lawn into the house. Even when he was getting sick, Dad never stopped working on the damn lawn. All the lights are off. All is quiet and empty. I sit down in Dad's easy chair. Several old National Geographics sit on the side table next to an old rotary phone and an ashtray. In amongst the burnt out filters I see a flash of metal. I dig my hand in and pick it up. It's an old Saint Christopher medal. The patron saint of travelers. I recognize it. It was my mother's. Jesus Dad, hell of a place to keep it. A flash of anger washes over me, then subsides. What's the point? What's the point of being angry at a dead man? I put the medallion in my pocket, pick up a National Geographic, and start reading. Several hours pass. I'm halfway through the third when the phone rings. I pick it up.

"Hey kiddo. Just got back in on the red eye from Tokyo and heard the news. Thought I better call."

"Hey Amy, thanks. Just got back from the funeral."

"How you holding up?"

"Okay I guess. I think I'm still a little stunned by everything."

"Hard to imagine the old bastard dead."

"Yeah."

"What got him?"

"The smoking. I guess some kind of respiratory infection. Just like Beth."

"Well, it was going to be either that or the drinking."

"Yeah, I guess."

"You sound a little funny kiddo. You're not out of your gourd or anything are you?"

"Just coming down, that's all."

"Christ kiddo. When are you going to get off that shit?"

"Not now Amy. I've already heard it today from Cindy. I really can't take it right now."

"Okay. Okay. How's the family doing?"

"I don't know. Diane kicked me out again a couple of months ago. I'll probably stay out here for a while."

"Well, that's part of what happens when you're doing that kind of shit."

"Amy."

"Sorry. You know what I think. I'll drop it. You doing okay?"

"I don't know. Cindy said worrying about me helped kill Dad. I'm feeling pretty low."

"I'm sorry kiddo. I wish I was there to give you a big hug."

"I didn't think it was going to hit me this hard."

"Good and bad, he was a big part of your life."

"He left me everything."

"Fine by me. I'll never be back. Besides, he always liked you better. To him, I pretty much never existed. What are you going to do with it all?"

"I don't know. Maybe stay out here for a while. Is it okay if we talk about something else?"

"Sure, what do you want to talk about?"

"Tell me about Tokyo?"

Amy and I chat until Cindy gets back with the lawyer.

The body of the so-called chupacabra is smaller than I expected. It's so skinny that I can count all its ribs. It's early morning, but the flies are already swarming. People in olden times used to believe that fly grubs were inside living things all the time, only emerging as flies when something died. Fucking idiots. About as fucking stupid as I've been. The monster I've built up in my mind is just an old coyote with severe mange. Everything looks funny without its hair, and this poor bugger pretty much had none left. Nothing supernatural or weird about it. I've been a fucking moron. Shine a red light into an animal's eyes, what do you get? A red reflection. Who knows why it kept following me. Probably been digging up our trash holes and eating our shit. Who knows, maybe it was rabid. That would at least explain why it had been so aggressive. Sad mother fucker.

I kick the body with my boot, raising a swarm of flies, and start walking back to the corpse of Alice three hundred feet away. The bastard hadn't lasted long after he got hit. A pretty good shot in the dark. The morning is warm, but not yet too hot. I didn't sleep a wink last night. I feel more relaxed then I have in days. Acceptance can do wonders. Acceptance of the things that I can't control. Acceptance of the world around me. Warts and all. No more feeling sorry for myself. No more wishy-washy feelings. I know which direction I need to go.

Alice sits in the creek bed under her tarp. She's not going anywhere. She'll have to be left behind. I wish it didn't have to be this way. The two of us have had a lot of adventures together. By far the best thing Dad ever left me. But facts are facts. Without a major overhaul she's not going anywhere. I had thought about burning her. Giving her a good viking funeral. Siphoning out the gas. Lighting her up. Leaving nothing but a burnt frame. I had let go of the idea pretty quick. Sending up a big smoke signal wouldn't be the best way to avoid the people after me.

Better to just leave her under the tarp and move on. I'm sure they'll find her eventually, but not for a while. Besides, they'll have a hard time connecting her to me. All her papers have been burnt, and we removed and buried her license plates the first night we started going off road. When I rebuilt her I chiseled off all the VIN numbers. Engine block, transmission, driver side dash, frame under the driver side door, and frame by the inner side of the right front wheel fender. Not the glorious end I'd like to give her, but it will have to do. Who knows. Maybe someday I can come back and get her running again. Doubtful, but who knows.

I spend a good part of the morning throwing more loose dirt and random desert debris on top of the tarp. Setting it up better for long-term hiding. As I work a small lizard watches me from its perch on a sagebrush. It's a brownish gray with black stripes. Only about as long as my finger. It reminds me of the lizards I used to catch as a kid. I push the shovel upright into the dirt, wipe my brow on my shirt, and take a step towards the lizard. It scurries across the ground to a sagebrush a little further away, freezing in an attempt to hide. I walk slower this time. Moving my arm less than a foot a minute. I rest my hand on the dried woody branch next to the lizard. It doesn't move. It just stares up at me with its tiny black eyes.

A shadow crosses overhead. The lizard panics and runs. I look up and see the shadow's source riding the thermals next to the hill. A locust hawk. White belly and brown chest. Tom's dad taught me how to identify all the birds. He had a head full of that kind of stuff. Beautiful bird. It swoops back and forth overhead. Not hunting. Just enjoying being alive and flying free. Soon that will be me. Flying free. My eyes fall to the hillside that Alice came down. In the daylight you can see some skid marks if you know where to look. I take my shovel and climb up the hill to scatter dirt and the such until they disappear.

No more crazy time. No more fucking around. No more shit. Time to start thinking rationally again. When you lose your shit, that's when they get you. Can't worry about the past. Gotta keep trucking towards the future. I walk back down the hill. It doesn't seem as steep on the way back down. It's definitely a hell of a lot less steep than the night in Alice. I climb under the tarp and make myself my favorite

MRE. Beef ravioli. I eat it slowly, savoring every bite, and then drink my fill of water. I won't be able to take any MRE's with me. My backpack is too small. I should have brought my old Marine bag. I never thought I'd be abandoning Alice like this. Should have thought about it more. Oh well. No use dwelling on it.

I fill my backpack with bottled water, granola bars, the flashlight, extra batteries for the flashlight, a couple extra pairs of socks, a spare shirt, my whetting stone, wads of toilet paper, lighter, my bag of weed and rolling papers, needle and thread, and all the cash from the metal box built into Alice's frame. One bunch of hundreds, two bunches of twenties, and two bunches of fives. Fifteen thousand dollars, plus the petty cash from the jockey box that I don't bother to count. My grandfather's pocket watch is in the jockey box as well. I leave it. If I'm going to leave Alice, I might as well leave it all. Hell, I don't even know if Dad really wanted me to have it. It was in the jockey box the first time I ever drove Alice.

The backpack is mostly water. You can go longer without food than you can water. Into my left pocket goes the container of little yellow pills. Into my right pocket goes my pocket-knife, the one Tom's dad gave me. I tie a sweatshirt around my middle. I pause for a bit to think about the pistol. In the end I take one bottle of water out to fit it and a box of bullets. Better to have and not need, then to need and not have.

I lock the passenger door and slam it shut. I do the same with the all the others. When I reach the driver door I get in and sit behind the wheel one last time. It's still sweltering hot inside the cab. My fingers brush across the well worn steering wheel. My butt relaxes into the familiar ass grooves on the seat. She feels good. She's been better to me than any other lady in my life. The passenger seat sits empty. I glance over at it. I can't believe how dumb I was. Sitting drunk in an overheated cab. Heat stroke. Jesus fucking Christ.

I leave the keys in the ignition. Maybe somebody will find her and make her useful again. I think I'd like that. Shame for her to rot away out here. My mother's Saint Christopher medallion softly rocks on the rearview mirror. I take it down and put it in my left pocket. He's the patron saint of travelers. I could probably use the luck. No time like the future. I get out, lock the door, and slam it shut. I pull my backpack over my shoulders. It's heavier than I'm used to, but nothing like what we used to carry in the Marines. I climb under the tarp and emerge into the bright sunshine of early afternoon. The distant horizon to the south shimmers in the heat, but it feels cooler out in the open. I put one foot in front of the other, and start walking. I don't look back.

It's a pretty easy walk. After a couple of hours I look back. I can't see Alice, but I can guess where she probably is. I wish it didn't have to be this way. I wish I could just go back and fix it all. A familiar sound starts to whip the wind. It starts faint, but builds as the black dot on the horizon comes closer.

Paul-paul-paul-paul-paul-paul-paul.

I duck down and pull myself under a large greasewood. A sharp twig jabs me on the inside of my right elbow. My arms jerks and it jabs me again, drawing blood. My heartbeat slows. My muscles relax. No use in the thinking about such things. I'm on the path I'm on. All that's left is to finish the journey. I can't go back. I can only go forward. Change is always hard. The helicopter passes by overhead, moving towards the hillside to the north. I wait until it returns to the size of a small black dot, then get up and start walking south again, whistling a jaunty tune.

Chapter 26

In 1971 Dr. Philip Zimbardo ran his famous Stanford prison experiment to study the effects of power. A group of volunteers, all thought of as good people, were found for the two week experiment and randomly assigned the role of guards and prisoners in a simulated prison environment. Within six days the experiment had to be stopped. The guards almost immediately began to abuse their power, which led to the prisoners resisting, which in turn led to further abuse and psychological torture. Over the course of the study the guards became more sadistic while the prisoners became extremely stressed and depressed. Though they could do so at any time, only a few of the prisoners quit the experiment early. All of the guards were disappointed when the experiment was ended. The Stanford prison experiment was later used to help explain the prison torture abuse by US military personnel at the Abu Ghraib prison in Iraq.

My head hurts. I raise up my fist and hammer on the locked bedroom door. The wood shakes in its frame. My bruised knuckles flare in protest and a sharp pain shoots its way up my forearm. From the other side there is no sound of movement, just the rattle of my father snoring through his broken nose. A good son would say that he was in a deep sleep, but that wouldn't be the truth. Passed out drunk is the more accurate term. I hammer away one more time, then turn away in disgust, and walk down the stairs to the kitchen.

The kitchen is a mess. Beer bottles and cans litter the counter and table along with a couple half eaten pizzas and several opened bags of chips. The whole place stinks of cigarettes. The ashtrays are overflowing with butts. I open the cupboard to get a glass. It's empty. All the glasses and mugs are dirty, spread amongst the empties and the dead soldiers. I shove some of the higher stacked dishes in the sink out of the way and dip my head under the faucet. I swirl and spit the last dregs of vomit from my mouth before sucking down as much water as I can, stopping at the point where I start to feel sick again. I lean against the counter, eating a slice of cold pizza, and looking out the window at the back lot and cotton field bathed in morning light. It's going to be the last time I see it for a while. I might as well drink it all in while I collect my thoughts.

The living room is less filled with the remains of last night's festivities, but its condition is little better. Everything is covered in a three-year layer of dust. Cobwebs, both old and new, hang in all the corners. The furniture is grimy and worn. The whole room is a time capsule from my childhood. The late sixties decor a monument to a lost world. Dad and I don't use this room much. Only every now and again to sit and watch some television a bit. The wind has the habit of knocking the antenna awry, and neither of us ever seems to have enough gumption to climb up on the roof to fix it. Easier I guess to just force our way through the snow and static. Dad probably gets enough TV at the bar, and I've never had much of a compulsion to watch. At home both of us tend to spend most of our time reading books in our individual rooms. History books for me. Mostly Longarm novels for Dad.

Rimjob Robertson lays passed out on the couch, his shirt, emblazoned with Go Mustangs, rides up, showing off his gut. Last football season he was a wall of muscle at middle linebacker. Seven months of beer and burgers have taken their toll, or maybe it was just the realization that all he had worked for didn't mean shit after high school. Rimjob was predestined to work at his father's cotton warehouse. It just wasn't until he walked out of the locker room for the last time that he realized it.

I don't bother to try and wake him. Rimjob lost his license a month ago for drinking and driving. None of the seven cars parked in front of the house are his. All have been abandoned by their inebriated owners with plans to return to retrieve them once levels of intoxicity drop to acceptable amounts. My own car is not an option either. In the barn is a hunk of twisted metal that was once a 1972 Chevy Nova named Abigail. She was in cherry condition until I took a 90 degree corner too fast while drag racing with some friends two months ago. It goes without saying that liquor was involved. I got out with just a few scratches, probably thanks to my more relaxed than normal condition.

The judge had wanted to throw the book at me, but took it easy when he found out I was scheduled to head out to the Marines. No sense in letting a little childhood frivolity get in the way of defending the country.

I could always say fuck it and just take Mabel. It would be Dad's own fault for being too drunk to wake up. She's sitting out behind the house where Dad always leaves her, but that would probably end up being more trouble than it's worth. The last thing I need on the day I ship out is to get into it with Dad again. Last night was bad enough. That leaves only one other option. One I know will always come through. I walk back into the kitchen and pick up the phone.

Tom's dad drives up about twenty minutes later in his old Ford pickup. He lays on the horn and waves at me cheerfully as I come out the door with my duffel bag slung over one shoulder. I run across Dad's immaculate front lawn, a patch of green surrounded by gray, and throw my bag into the back and climb up inside. Tom's dad is smiling, the curve of mouth hidden beneath the bush of his moustache, his eyes hidden by a large pair of reflective aviator sunglasses. When he sees my face his smile drops for a moment, but quickly returns.

"Hey Paul, need a lift?"

"Thanks for doing this."

"No problem."

He puts the pickup into gear and we head down the driveway.

"That's quite a shiner you got there."

"Yeah."

"How'd you get it?"

"Got into a little tussle."

"The usual?"

"Yeah."

"You want to talk about it?"

I stare forward at the old fishing hat sitting on the dash.

"No."

We turn onto the main road. I look back at the old house, desperately in need of a fresh coat of paint, until it disappears behind the rise. As the house vanishes I feel my body lighten, as though my hangover has magically been instantaneously cured.

"How did the goodbye party end up?"

"Pretty good. Wish you could've made it."

"Never been one for that kind of stuff. Tom looked a bit rough this morning. Glad it was a good time."

"Yeah, right up until the end."

We both sit silently as we drive into Sweetwater. Tom's dad licks his lips a few times.

"You excited."

"Yeah, part of me is. The other is pretty nervous."

"Well, I'd say that's pretty normal."

The pickup pulls over to the sidewalk outside the bus depot. Tom's dad puts it into park and turns to face me. He seems unsure what to say. Unsure what to do. After a few seconds I stick out my hand.

"Well, thanks for the lift Lou. It was much appreciated."

Tom's dad takes my hand in his and gives my arm a couple quick pumps. I start to turn to get out, but he doesn't let go.

"Just wanted you to know Paul, I'm proud of you. Joining the Marines and all. Nothing but good things can come from this decision."

"Well, I could always get shot."

Tom's dad smiles at me.

"Yeah, there's always that."

I get out of the pickup and grab my bag from the back. The bus station seems bigger than it ever has before.

"Paul."

I turn back and see Tom's dad leaning over, his hand out the passenger side window, holding a twenty dollar bill.

"So you can take a taxi when you arrive in Dallas. Easier than trying to figure out the city bus system."

I take the twenty from his hand.

"Thank you. Thank you for everything."

"You just go make something of yourself."

I smile and turn away. I force myself not to look back as I walk into the bus station, but I can feel him watching me until I disappear through the door.

I only have to wait fifteen minutes before we board. An old lady fusses about her bags and pleasantly bitches out me and a group of other waiting passengers when we don't offer to help her get them to the platform. By the way she moves she doesn't seem that decrepit, and nothing beyond her age makes me want to offer her any help. We all shuffle on board soon after and spread out across the half filled seats. The bus stinks of rancid farts, body odor, cigarette smoke, and the overly strong cologne of the bus driver. I go near the back, stretch myself across two seats, and try to get some sleep. I can feel the twenty dollar bill in my pocket, nestled next to my pocket-knife. The coughing of the old lady a few seats ahead makes it difficult to sleep. After a bit I resign myself to groggy wakefulness, and spend the rest of the trip reading. The book is about the early Marines during the Barbary Wars. All the books I've read over the past three months have been about the Marines. It's always good to know what you're getting into.

It takes four and a half hours to get the three hours to Dallas. Our progress is slowed by stops at Abilene, Cisco, Weatherford, and Fort Worth. The countryside along Interstate 20 whips past. I hardly pay attention. I've seen it all a hundred times before. The same flat never ending landscape of scattered fields and drought stunted trees broken by the occasional house or business that grow thicker as we move through the towns. As the day wears on the inside of the bus grows hot and sticky. It's an older bus with no air conditioning. Just my luck. Several people open their windows the small amount allotted, and all other sounds are drowned out by the roar of the hot wind.

The tall buildings of Fort Worth come marching forward, we go in amongst them, and then back out the other side. The creations of man lose height and then spring up again as we move into downtown Dallas. The Reunion Tower shines like a new nickel. Tom's dad took me and Tom up in it when it first got built a couple of years ago. It had been a nice view. We'd gone to Dallas to see a Cowboys game. The tickets Tom's dad had bought from a scalper had turned out to be fakes. I'd never seen Tom's dad so mad. It had still been a pretty good trip. We cross the Trinity River and the bus pulls up out of the freeway. Traffic is heavy. Our movement slows to a crawl.

We pull slowly through an intersection. A midget stands at the corner, waiting to cross. I try not to stare, but catch myself stealing glances repeatedly. He's a round little man with short arms and legs.

A man in a suit walks up behind him to cross the street. The man in the suit stops five or six feet behind the midget. I can tell by the look on the suit's face that he's uncomfortable, that he doesn't want to stand next to the little man The look on the midget's face shows that he knows it too. It's a combination of anger, exasperation, and sadness. The midget refuses to look back. I feel bad for him. I want to get out of the bus and smash the suit's face in, or at least yell at him and let him know what an idiot he is. The bus pulls forward, and the pair disappear behind.

The bus station is busy. People mill about here and there. A hill of ants. Everyone looks dirty and beaten down. Worn out like an old shirt put through the wash too many times. Half look like they're drunk or high. Several look like they're homeless. I pause for a moment to buy a Coke out of a machine and use a quarter to buy a handful of peanuts out of a dispenser. I'm feeling hungry again. A dirty disheveled man approaches me, obviously homeless. He's wearing a faded Carhartt coat and a red stocking cap. I feel myself tense up.

"Hey buddy, can I have some money?"

The directness of the question makes me mad. Who the fuck does he think he is?

"No, sorry, don't have any."

The man stalks off back into the crowd. I can hear him mumbling to himself as he goes.

"You're sorry? You'll be sorry when I shoot you in the back of the head with my laser eyes."

I go outside and wave down a passing taxi. The inside smells like bean burritos. The Mexican driving turns down his mariachi music when I get in. He gives me a funny look when I give him the address. The drive is only two blocks. I would've just walked, but Tom's dad gave me money specifically for a taxi, so there you go.

The Federal Building is a block of concrete and white brick. I shoulder my duffel bag and walk in. It's as quiet as a tomb. I ask a white haired man behind a desk in the lobby for directions. He points to a sign with arrows on the wall. I follow them through several twists and turns before walking into a small office. I drop my bag, stand at attention, and salute.

"Reporting for duty."

A bored looking Marine sits behind a desk reading a magazine. He looks up at me lazily, has me sign a couple of forms, and then sends me to the back where a doctor gives me a quick physical to make sure I haven't become unhealthy in the two months since I joined at the base in Fort Worth. Beats me why I couldn't report for duty there. I don't ask. Probably best to keep my thoughts to myself. The physical is done in less than five minutes. The doctor motions for me to go through another door. Inside is a waiting room filled with neat rows of metal chairs half filled by an assortment of random young men. A few, who obviously know each other, are playing cards. A couple are chatting. Most sit straight backed and silent, facing front, waiting. I sit down by myself and gaze at my surroundings. The ceiling tiles are stained, the tile floor chipped, and the tan walls dirty and in need of another coat of paint. My back hurts. I can't seem to relax. My foot taps nervously until a big bruiser gives me a dirty look. I force it to stop.

We wait three hours. More nervous looking eighteen year olds trickle in. One or two older guys as well. Finally a big Marine sergeant stalks in. A tank on legs. I brace myself for the tirade that is sure to commence. The sergeant doesn't say anything. He just motions for us to follow and heads back out the door. We pick up our belongings and follow him down a long hallway outside to a waiting bus. We file onboard and it heads out to the airport.

We're marched through the terminal, go through security, and then wait beside a gate under the watchful eye of a couple of sergeants. There's about thirty of us or so. A couple guys nervously walk up to the sergeants and ask if they can use the restroom. The sergeants nod in approval. The rest of us sit tight. After an hour we board a plane mostly filled with civilians. I sit next to the window and watch with trepidation and amazement as the ground drops away below. I've never been in a plane before. The surge of acceleration as we takeoff sets my heart to fluttering. I feel free. Like all the troubles of the world have dropped down below.

Some of my fellow recruits get chatty with each other again. The guy next to me falls asleep. I spend the flight staring out the window. Everything seems unreal. I keep looking up as the stewardesses walk past, half expecting to see Amy. I know it's a waste of time. Amy flies out of the West Coast. The world grows dark and we land at Atlanta and transfer onto another plane that takes us to Savannah. It must be around midnight by the time we arrive. We are led off the plane and through the airport to a bus waiting to take us the hour drive to Parris Island. The bus is already mostly filled. We take whatever seats we can get. The bus door closes, it grinds into gear, and the bus lurches into motion. The sergeant's start screaming at us.

Chapter 27

In September of 2011 the madness of our country hit a melting point. Anti-government and anti-corporate protests spread across every city. Tired of groveling before the ivory gods and their almighty dollar, the people rose up and demanded to be heard. They gathered in parks and town squares, refusing to leave until there was change. The movement spread across the western world. For a few months the force of the people was behind the movement and it seemed like real change was possible. Things quickly began to fall apart. Some protests became violent, buildings were vandalized. Conditions in the camps deteriorated, rapes and assaults became common. The movement began to fragment. Rumors spread of provocateurs amongst the ranks. General support vanished. On November 14 a coordinated police crackdown took place worldwide. Most of the camps were broken up. The movement kept going for a few more months, but it was already over, disintegrating back into the fringes of society.

The silver cylinder of the oxygen tank sits on a small two wheeled cart that he drags behind him. The squeaking of one wheel creates a harmony to the bass beat of the air hissing through the hose in his nostrils. His hair is a dead gunmetal gray. All of the black of youth is gone. It looks like a bird's nest on top of his head. Bits and pieces floating about. Loose feathers in the breeze. His face is loose and hangs from his skull. A portrait of a once strong man, splashed with water until the paint runs. Despite the decrepit state of his body, and his shuffling walk, he keeps up with my every step. Pausing only to release a hacking cough or to light another cigarette. This was what my father looked like the last time I ever saw him alive. A vivid memory shambling along beside me. I try my best to ignore him. I know he's not here. I know he can't be here. Yet, here he is. The same twisted bitter old soul, fighting for a life it doesn't even want. My head hurts. My temples pound with the power of an angry miniature strong man, trying to burst his way free. The afternoon desert sun beats down on the two of us, yet I am the only one soaked with sweat. I'm the one whose breath is ragged. I stop for a quick breather, and take a quick swallow from one of the water bottles in my bag. The moment I stop moving, the familiar croaking words begin to spew forth.

"What the fuck are you doing with yourself Paul? Is this the kind of man you want to be? You're a failure Paul. Nothing but a fucking failure."

I've heard it all before. These were the last words my father ever said to me, more than a year before he died. The last refuge cut away, and a lost soul left to float on the great stormy ocean alone. Dad had gotten in the last word. His breath stinking of the remains of his last meal between his teeth and cheap whiskey. My brain had been too spongy then to come up with any sort of reply, but not this time. No, not this time.

"Fuck yourself Dad. Just go fuck yourself."

"Oh ho, look at the big man. Speaking up for himself. Telling his old man to fuck off. Why don't you take that fight and put it towards something more useful than this."

"Yeah Dad, what the hell should I be doing?"

"Turning back for one. Giving up all this bullshit and going back. Find your damn family. Christ Paul, this isn't how I raised you."

I give out a loud bark of a laugh that's swallowed by the empty landscape.

"Really Dad? How you raised me? It's pretty damn hard to raise a kid when you're passed out drunk on the floor of the Pheasant. Not a lot of quality parenting going on there."

"I kept you fed and housed, made sure you had everything you needed. What more do you want from me?"

"Gee Dad, I don't know. Maybe just somebody to be a little nurturing. Somebody to act like they gave a damn about me."

"Oh boo hoo, you didn't get enough hugs. Welcome to the world. My old man only showed love and compassion to his vegetable of a sister. But did you ever hear me complain? No, because he made sure we always had enough. That's how he showed that he loved us."

"Shut up Dad."

I start walking again. The old man follows. The squeaky wheel drives a finger into my brain. His raspy voice closes the small distance between us.

"You're just a stubborn idiot. Fighting as hard as you can to keep moving, but never raising your head up to see where you're going."

I don't answer. I just start walking faster, hoping to leave him behind.

"You know, for all my mistakes, at least I stayed. At least I never ran away."

"You were a shitty father."

"I did the best I could with what I had. Yes, I was a shitty father. I admit it. I was so wrapped up in my own crap that it made me a real son of a bitch. I should have taken you out to ball games, taught you how to throw, read stories to you every night, but I didn't, and you're just going to have to get over it. Just because you had a shitty dad doesn't mean you have an excuse to be one too."

I spin around, my fists clenched with rage.

"You have no fucking right. I've been ten times the father you ever were."

"Yeah, where are they now? Where's Philip? Where are your two girls? Where the fuck are you?"

"I can't control what Linds did."

"No, you can only control yourself. It's all your choice Paul. All your fucking choice."

"Bullshit. I......."

Paul-paul-paul-paul-paul-paul-paul.

A gentle hand holding mine. The soft caress of fingers. An insistent repeating of my name in a droning litany of desperation. The entire world melts, a landscape painting, still wet, the colors all running together. The helicopter comes sweeping in overhead. I jerk away. I dive beneath a large sagebrush, the stiff branches clawing at my arms. Tearing at my skin. Jagged red bloody lines. My old man stays where he is, staring upward at the black insect, the wind of the rotors lifting his wispy hair around his head. It's the sixth time since I left Alice. They keep trying to catch me when I'm not paying attention, keeping my mind focused on the task at hand. The dark shadow moves slowly. I bury my head in my arms and keep as still as possible, holding my breath and praying that they don't see me. The sound of the helicopter begins to move away and I dare to look upwards into the sky. It's moving in the distance, but not yet far enough away to risk moving. The ghost of my old man is gone, blown away with the wind.

Gnarled branches claw at me with twisted fingers. Bugs crawl on my body, their many legs creating unpleasant tickling sensations. The smell of sage is overwhelming in my nostrils. My pocket-knife, at an awkward angle in my right pocket, digs into my leg. I want to move, I want to shake, I want to get up and stop wasting time, but I dare not while the helicopter is still in view.

When I was around ten I used to sit like this, bury myself under a bush until the bugs saw me as no different than the dirt and plants. I would wait for the wildlife to forget that I was there so they would come close enough for me to snatch. I wanted to be a mountain man, or a wild Comanche. Living off the land. Knowing everything there was to know. I read countless books about surviving in the wild. Anything I could get my hands on. I was old enough to know that I would need a career when I grew up, but not yet old enough to know the limitations.

Once I caught a rabbit, a skinny little thing infested with lice and ticks. I had never caught anything before. I had been laying in the cotton field near our house. He hopped right up and sat less than a foot away from me, scratching his ear with his large back leg. The mistake most people make is starting out their movement slow. It all has to be fast. One sudden quick motion. My hand shot out and grabbed his leg. The rabbit twisted around and bit my hand. I squeezed tighter and whipped him against the ground, stunning him long enough to grab his neck and give it a quick twist. The little body went still.

I carried him back to the house and laid him out on the porch. I pulled out my pocket-knife, the one given to me by Tom's dad for my tenth birthday, and cut a slit along his belly. The guts left a dark stain on the bleached wood of the porch. I did my best to skin him, loose hairs sticking to the blood on my hands. As I worked I envisaged myself making my living, trapping animals and tanning hides. I could live my life alone in the hills, coming down only to sell my wares and buy supplies. The once living creature became a sodden pile of ruined meat and fur. The hide too full of holes to ever be useful. I looked down at the mess with a deep sense of failure and shame for the waste. Beth soon after drove up to make dinner. When she had seen the rabbit she hadn't said anything. She just threw it back into the cotton field and drove me to the clinic for a tetanus shot.

That fall was the first time Tom's dad took me and Tom out deer hunting. I got too excited and accidentally shot a fawn. Tom's dad had put his hand on my shoulder and told me it would be all right. It was a mistake. Nobody knew. I was forgiven. Nothing was wasted. Everything is consumed by something. We moved on. That first time Tom was the one who got the deer. His dad showed us how to do it right.

The helicopter moves on. I shift myself out from under the sagebrush and adjust the knife in my pocket. I wish Tom's dad were here. If I'm going to hallucinate from a lack of sleep and an overindulgence of uppers, I'd rather it be of him than my old man. He'd be standing over me with his fishing hat tipped back on his bald head, his t-shirt tucked into his jeans, his middle swelling with the start of a beer belly that would grow throughout his life, smiling at me through his moustache. He'd reach out a hand and help me up. Dark clouds sit on the eastern horizon, fat with rain and blown in by Gulf winds. Tom's dad looks at them, and then smiles back at me.

"Hey Paul, where you headed?"

"Down to Mexico."

"Hmmm. I guess Mexico is a good as place as any to be going. It looks like rain."

"Sure does."

"Better find some shelter."

"It looks like there's some junipers just a little further south a bit up on the rise."

"Good call. Better get moving if you want to stay dry. No use sitting here gawking."

I nod and adjust my backpack. I take the little white cylinder out of my left pocket and pop another yellow pill. Tom's dad watches me, disapproval written across his face.

"What are those for?"

"Helps me stay awake. Stay alert."

"Hmmmm."

"You're not mad, are you?"

"No, just disappointed."

I look at the cylinder guiltily and put it back in my left pocket.

"I promise that I'll quit once I'm in Mexico."

"Okay. I wish you would do it sooner, but you're an adult. I trust you."

We start walking across the flats. The gentle rise, the last climb before the steep drop to the river, slowly moves its way closer. The wind begins to pick up, bending the grass and sage. The smell of rain grows thick in the air. We walk in a comfortable silence. Tom's dad looks at me from time to time, and I can see concern in his eyes. Thoughts bubble in my head. Things I wish that I had said. Things that I wish I had done.

"How've things been going Paul?"

"It's been a real mess of late. It doesn't seem like I can do anything right."

"Well, that's going to happen from time to time."

"I don't know. I just wish life were simpler. It just seems like everything is rolling out of control."

"Control is just an illusion Paul. In my experience a lot of things are only as complicated as we make them."

"It doesn't seem that way. Sometimes I just want to sit down and not get back up."

"We all feel like that sometimes. Hell, you want to sit down and you wonder why you even bother to get up. The world is just going to knock you down again. Then you realize, it's because you have to. It's because the only other option is nothing. You do it because it's all you have."

We walk in silence for a while longer. The dark clouds get bigger. The wind pushes them across the sky, blotting out the sun, and covering the world in a dark wooly blanket. Tom's dad whistles one of his old racist tunes.

"Did you know Paul that the Yellow Rose of Texas is actually about getting with a mulatto girl?"

"Yeah, you've told me before."

"Funny what people let themselves forget."

"I guess so."

"How's your wife and kids?"

The suddenness of the question catches me off guard. The quick shift in mental gears. A smattering of fat rain-drops begin to fall from the sky. The front lines of the coming storm. It's been awhile since it's rained here. Each drop sends up its own little plume of dust. Miniature wet craters across the barren land.

"I don't know. Linds ran off with the kids."

"Why did she do that?"

"I don't know. I guess she didn't really believe in what I'm trying to do."

"What are you doing out here Paul?"

"I want to be free."

"Nobody is free Paul. Nobody is an island."

"That's not what I mean."

"Isn't it?"

"She was probably scared."

"I'm guessing she isn't the only one that's scared."

Paul-paul-paul-paul-paul-paul-paul-paul.

The soothing hand back over mine. A cool wetness drawn across my forehead. I shake my head violently. My eyes jerk towards the west. The helicopter is racing straight at me. A growing black dot in the remaining blue of the western sky. There's nowhere to hide. The sagebrush all around me are too small. The wind from the east begins to pick up. Dust spins upward into the air. The raindrops increase in size and quantity. For a moment I feel like I'm weightless. Floating just above the ground. A curtain of falling water is fast approaching, spurred on by the sound of a thousand snare drums. The land behind it seemingly alive, as though a million locusts are following in its wake. I make to run, but the voice of Tom's dad stops me in my tracks.

"What's wrong Paul?"

"I've got to run. I've got to hide."

"That rain is coming fast."

"No, not that, the helicopter."

"What's wrong with the helicopter?"

"They're after me."

"What?"

The black dot grows bigger and bigger. The curtain of water moves closer and closer. The two racing to catch me first.

"They'll put me in a cage."

"Why would they do that?"

"Because I broke their rules. Because I know what they are."

"How do you know they're not trying to help you?"

The helicopter rotors, yelling my name, roar in my ears. The wind howls in protest, demanding my attention.

"You don't understand. Nobody understands."

Tom's dad frowns through his moustache, adjusts his fishing hat, turns, and starts to walk away.

"I think I do understand Paul, the question is whether or not you do."

"Where are you going?"

"I figured since I'm around I might as well see how Tom's doing."

"But what am I supposed to do?"

"That's really up to you Paul, I wish you the best."

"Wait."

The figure turns, affection in his steel gray eyes.

"Yeah Paul?"

"You're not mad, are you?"

"No Paul, just disappointed."

The figure turns away and disappears, his words echoing in my head. In another minute the helicopter is going to be here. What am I doing? Am I doing the right thing? Why am I doing this? Is it really all worth it? Is it worth losing everything? I just want to be free damn it. I just want to be free. Is it really so much to ask of the world? I'm standing in the middle of the desert. Abandoned and alone. I've come so far damn it. I've come so far. Just over that rise, down the canyon, and across the river. That's all I have left. In Mexico. In Mexico things will be better. In Mexico I can be free. In Mexico I won't have to worry. How can I turn back now? I start to run towards the rise. I run as hard as I can. The storm catches me first. It washes over the landscape and soaks me to the bone in an instant. The dark spot of the helicopter veers away, intimidated by the wall of water. It's gears, electronics, and lifting force no match for the unleashed fury of mother nature. It circles for a second, and then retreats back the way it came, back towards the rapidly disappearing piece of blue sky on the far western horizon. I run and laugh. Laugh in pure unfiltered joy. Run damn you. Run away. You can't have me today. You'll never have me. I'll never be a slave. Everything is going to be okay.

I reach the start of the rise and clamber up, water flowing down the slope. I throw myself under the first large juniper that's still dry underneath. I sit and laugh, watching the storm blowing past. The rain slackens, but does not stop. Raindrops splashing in puddles across the flats. When Stone was three there was a big drought in Tennessee. A big rain came one day. She rushed out to splash in the puddles, and laid in the grass just to feel the drops upon her face. She had squealed with delight and you'd think she'd burst with a joy too big for her little body to contain. Linds stood in the doorway and yelled for her to come inside. I ran out, grabbed Stone's hands, and twirled her through the air. The two of us laughing like banshees.

"Hell of a storm."

I turn my head at Larry sitting next to me. Bone dry and fit as a fiddle.

"What are you doing here?"

"Seemed like as a good a place as any."

"You should have come with me Larry."

"Did you really expect me to?"

"You know as well as I do what's going on. What's going to happen."

"Sure I do, but what did you expect, for me to just kiss my wife and daughter goodbye and run off with you?"

"You could have brought them."

"Yeah, sure, Jen would be down with that. C'mon honey, lets just leave everything behind, grab Madeline, and head off across the desert with that friend of mine you don't like."

"You don't think I'm crazy, do you Larry?"

"Fuck Paul. You really need to get off those pills. I'm just a figment of your fucking imagination. I'll say whatever you want me to."

"Tell me I'm not crazy."

"Fine Paul, you're not crazy."

Chapter 28

In 1951 Dr. Solomon Asch conducted a psychological experiment on group dynamics. In the experiment individuals were put in with a group of actors and set to the task of verbally stating which line was closest in length to a reference line. After numerous sets of lines, the actors, under orders from Dr. Asch, all switched to giving the same wrong answer. Despite the lines being right in front of them, 75 percent of the participants joined the group and gave the wrong answer. For them, it was better to conform than to ostracize themselves by being a single outlier. An individual alone.

I walk down the steps of the rehab center past a row of skeletons and carved jack-o-lanterns on every step. The bulk of the old renovated Victorian broods over me. The air is cold. Colder than it normally is this time of year. My breath steams in front of me. On the sidewalk I pause to zip up my coat, reach into my pocket, and light a cigarette. Once upon a time I had quit smoking. For Christ sakes, it's killed about everyone even remotely related to me, but here I stand, lighting up. It's comforting. A gentle pat on the shoulder by an old friend. I need some comfort. I'll quit again when this is all over. I'd rather have beer or marijuana, but those are out of the question. I have a long drive ahead of me.

I exhale my first puff of smoke and look back up at the freshly painted old house. She's standing at a second story window, watching me. She still looks old and tired, but the color is starting to come back to her cheeks. She doesn't seem so beaten down. She's definitely not as bony as she once was, but she's still not my wife. The spark is gone. The energy. The thirst for life. Where has it gone? Will it ever be back? Her eyes are like doll eyes. Shiny and bright, but dead inside. She's going to get out soon. Not too much longer. Just another month. It's probably just this place. Who could feel much joy in a place like this? It's just like a hospital. Full of sickness. Not a good place for the healthy. Linds sees me staring up at her. She stares back for a moment, then turns and walks away.

I walk across the street to Alice, climb in, and crank her up. The engine burps a few times, and then roars to life. Her voice sounds a little rough, like she's been smoking too. I haven't had time to tune her up of late. Just been too busy. Just another thing to fix when this is all over. I'm getting close. Not much longer. Just got to keep going at it. Keep my head down and keep moving forward. Nothing to it. The clock on the dash says 3:47. I need to hurry. I can't be late. I put Alice into gear and head down the street.

I don't go far. Just across the freeway to the Arco Station on Beltline Road. I park around the side of the building, leave Alice unlocked, and go inside to buy a soda. By the time I get back he's waiting. He's a bigger fella, with a neatly trimmed goatee and bad teeth. He looks like any nobody who makes a living pumping gas, a rarity across the country except for here in Oregon, or tending bar at a dive where most of the money comes from video poker. He's leaning against an old rusted out blue Pontiac Grand Prix. He nods at me and I nod back. I have no idea what his name is. In my head I call him Leroy.

"How ya doing?"

His voice is higher pitched than you'd expect.

"Pretty good. How about yourself?"

"No complaints. Just another day in paradise."

I open the back of Alice and he opens the Grand Prix's trunk. Six black duffel bags pass between the two. The moment I close Alice's door I start to feel nervous. My brain begins to demand constant vigilance. It's a strain to keep my head from swiveling back and forth. Don't look guilty. Don't look suspicious. Just two friends exchanging some bags. My anonymous friend looks calm and comfortable. Nothing seems to faze him.

"Next week the Bi-Mart in Cresswell."

"Okay. Look though, you need to pass it down the line. Three more runs, then I'm done."

"Are you sure? Things have been going pretty well."

"Yeah, I'm sure. Three more and I'm done."

"Okay, I'll send it back up the line."

Leroy gets into his car and starts her up. Before he pulls out he unrolls his window.

"It's going to be a shame to have to break someone else in. You've been good to work with."

I nod. Leroy rolls back up his window and heads towards the southbound freeway ramp. I get in Alice and head north. I put in a Billy Joel CD. I'm not much for the soft stuff, but anything amped up is the last thing I need right now. My fingers drum against the steering wheel. My eyes constantly dart from the windshield, to my mirrors, to the speedometer. Sixty-five. Keep it going just at sixty-five. Left lane just to pass trucks and campers. Keep it even and keep it legal. That's the problem with most of the young ones. Their adrenaline gets pumping and before too long they're pushing ninety. Might as well just call ahead to let the cops know you're coming. That had been Walter's problem.

My cigarette burns down to the filter, I use it to light another and stub it out in Alice's overflowing ashtray. I never smoke before a visit. I always come in smelling fresh and clean. It's only on the way home that I need the comfort. There's a huge knot between my shoulder blades. I can't get comfortable. I try not to think about the six bags in the back. It's usually six. Sometimes more. Sometimes less. I think the bags are weed. I'm pretty sure they're weed. I don't know. I've never looked in them. I don't want to know what's in them. God, what if it's worse than marijuana? How long would I go away for? How long would they put me back in? I won't even let myself do an internet search to try and find out. I'm sure that kind of search would raise up a red flag. It's one thing to be a malcontent, it's another to be a criminal.

Calm. I need to stay calm. Best not to think about it. Just a man on a drive. This is my ninth run. No, that's not right. My tenth. Everything is fine. I've done this before. Nothing to be scared of. Nothing to worry about. Flat farmland rolls past on either side of I-5. The Cascades rise up to the east, and the shorter Coast Range to the west. Time flows slowly by.

The outlet mall at Wilsonville rolls past. Rows of identical concrete boxes surrounded by a colorful sea of cars. A black Crown

Victoria comes down the onramp and merges just behind me. I can see it in my rearview mirror. It's staying back a safe distance, but keeping close enough that no other cars try to fill the space between us. What the hell is he doing? Calm. Calm. Need to stay calm. It's just a Crown Vic. There's a lot of them out in the world. Nothing to worry about. It means nothing at all. I can see the driver. He's a heavy-set guy in a dark t-shirt, his eyes hidden by aviators.

Mile after mile. The Crown Vic stays right on my ass. Part of me wants to romp down on the gas, get away as fast as I can, throw the bags in a ditch out in the middle of nowhere. I can't do that. There's no proof that this car is tailing me. Fuck, even if it was, if I dumped the bags Jerry would probably kill me. What the fuck am I doing? I know I need the money, but is it worth going to jail again? Is this the kind of person I want to be? I've done a lot of shitty things in my life, but never anything as bad as this. Fuck. I can't speed up, but I can always slow down. I ease Alice back to sixty, then fifty-five, then fifty. The Crown Vic doesn't roar past. It slows down too. This is bad. This is definitely bad.

Urban sprawl replaces farmland. The I-205 exit comes up, I take it. My follower takes it too. I speed back up to sixty-five. He speeds up too. My palms are sweaty. I keep rubbing them dry on my pants, but it does little to help. What have I gotten myself into? Sure the money's been nice. Hard to find a job in this economy. Each week, $2,000 in cash. Steady pay, just like a real job. It's a well run outfit. Nothing out of place. Fuck ups need not apply.

Walter was the one who hooked me up with it. He's been running little errands for Jerry since he got out of prison. Mostly delivering cash around the city. Walter claims he did a couple solids for Jerry's nephew while in prison. I don't know if it's true. Really none of my business. I've never actually met Jerry. Hell, Jerry probably isn't even his real name. It doesn't matter. None of it matters. I'm soon going to get fucked. It's not my fault. What the hell was I supposed to do? Let my kids starve? Not take my wife to rehab? The few side jobs I've managed to get sure as hell aren't paying the bills. What a system. What a world. Fuck.

I pull off the exit into Oregon City. I consider driving past. I don't. What the hell woul I do if I did? The Crown Vic doesn't follow. My tense muscles go limp and my body melts into my seat. Just coincidence. Nobody watching. Nobody knows. Safe. It's okay. Everything is going to be okay. Alice comes to a halt in the parking lot of a rundown Kentucky Fried Chicken. I pull up next to a familiar looking older model Ford Taurus, white chipped paint, and a faded half ripped off Vote For Kerry bumper sticker.

Lenny comes out of the glass door of the KFC with a bucket of chicken in one arm. His name isn't Lenny of course, like Leroy, it's just the name I use in my head. Lenny is a little shrimpy guy, looks like a high school English teacher. He wears glasses with old style blocky frames, has a molester style moustache, and his hair is kept long to hide his ever increasing baldness. Lenny is newer than me. When I started ten weeks ago there was some Mexican fellow. In my head I called him Pedro. After three weeks Pedro disappeared. He either got arrested, stole, or quit the business. Again, not really my business. Lenny doesn't say much as I unload the duffel bags into his trunk. He's a nervous quiet guy, can't even get himself to look me in the eye. I slam the trunk shut and look at my partner in crime.

"Next week, the Safeway in Oak Grove."

Lenny nods his head in understanding. His voice is meek and quiet.

"Okay."

"Also send it up the line. I'm quitting after three more runs."

"Okay. I will."

I look at Lenny for a sec. He looks at his feet. Three more weeks. Three more weeks then I can pretend that none of this ever happened. I get back in Alice, get back on the freeway, and head north for home. With the bags gone I feel looser, free. The world feels like a better place. Dark clouds gather on the horizon. It's probably going to rain tonight, but for now, things are a-okay. Linds will be out of rehab soon. Then we can start worrying about the big stuff. I've already started making plans. Plans for the future. Plans for a better life. Things are going to be better for my family.

The drive to Gresham doesn't take long. I pull into the parking lot of the apartment complex and let myself in. Stone and Rachel are sitting on the couch with Walter, munching from a bag of chips, watching a movie. Rachel squeals with delight and jumps up into my arms. Stone walks over and gives me a loose hug. Walter gets up and wipes his greasy hands on the back of his pants.

"Were they any trouble today Walter?"

"Nope, not a bit. Went to the park, had some lunch at McDonalds, and just hung out and watched movies."

Rachel tugs at my hand insistently, shoving a cheap piece of colorful plastic upwards for me to see.

"Look Daddy. I got a Megamind in my Happy Meal. Stone got a Metro Man."

"That's awesome Monkey. Just let me talk to Walter for a sec. Why don't you kids play in the bedroom."

Rachel runs into the apartment's only bedroom, Stone follows, closing the door behind her. Walter is smiling. Part of me wants to ask him what toy he got in his Happy Meal, but I don't. The babysitting is pro bono.

"How was the run today?"

"Good. No problems."

"Linds still doing okay?"

"Yeah, they still think it will be okay for her to come out in three weeks."

"That's awesome man."

"Yeah. I'll be glad to quit doing this kind of shit. The girls give you any trouble?"

"No, no trouble at all. Rachel was cheerful as ever. Stone was pretty quiet as usual, didn't really want to play or do anything. I'm no kid expert or anything man, but I'm pretty sure that's not normal."

"Yeah, I know. I've been hoping she'd snap out of it soon. I don't know."

"Maybe you can take her to some kind of therapist or something."

"I don't know. I'm having enough trouble with the ones at the rehab center. I really don't want to subject her to that kind of bullshit."

"Your kids man, just saying."

"Yeah I know. Thanks again for watching them."

"No problem. I'll be by in a few days with your cash. Talk to you later."

"Talk to you later."

Walter heads out. I make the kids dinner. Mac and cheese plus some frozen pre-formed hamburger patties I fry up on the stove. After dinner they take their baths while I watch a movie, one of the ones I haven't already seen a hundred times. After bath time I tuck them into either side of the couch and read them a story, using all the funny voices Rachel loves so much. She's asleep before the story is even over. Stone is still awake, watching me.

"Dad?"

"Yeah?"

"When is Mom coming home?"

"Soon honey. She'll be home soon."

"Okay."

"Did you have a good day with Walter?"

"Yeah, it was okay I guess. Dad?"

"Yeah?"

"Are things going to be okay when Mom comes back?"

"Yeah Stone. Things will be okay. Mom will be all better, just like she used to be."

"Okay."

"Now get some sleep. Tomorrow's a school day."

"Okay. Good night Dad."

"Good night Stone."

I turn off the light and go into the bedroom. I boot up the computer and go through my ritual of running a myriad of anti-spyware, malware, and virus programs. I open up the running programs list and start to go through them, Google searching any I don't recognize, deleting those that don't belong. There are only a few this time. It all takes about an hour. The housekeeping done, I start searching through the forums. Reading posts. Taking down notes. Looking for patterns. Something big is coming down the pipe. Something bad. The clock is ticking. Nobody is saying what needs to be said. Nobody is stating what is right in front of all of us. I open a new post and type in a series of bullet points, checking each off of my written notes as I get them down. In the subject line I type: *Government takeover?* The cursor on the screen scrolls down, my finger clicks, and my thoughts become a post.

Chapter 29

Six corporations control ninety percent of the media. Back when I was in the military, this would have been more around fifty or so. Not anymore, regulations have been removed in the name of free markets, deals have been made, and we've been left with six. Six companies that entertain us and tell us how to think. Radio, television, and internet. The whole shebang. It's not just what our brains consume either. In America today ten corporations control almost every food and household product that we consume. Candy bars, soup, fast food, soaps, detergents, chocolates, and all the rest. Just ten companies. It gets worse. Just five banks control over half of all financial assets, and despite the largest recession since the Great Depression, keep just getting bigger.

The line moves slowly up the road under the desert sun. The tar pavement has turned soft and radiates heat like an oven. Everyone is tanned, sunburned, and freckled. People stand alone or in groups. The man in front of me, in Bermuda shorts and a tank top, keeps drumming his fingers on his legs and humming Margaritaville. I've been waiting for more than an hour, slowly moving forward, one step at a time. Up ahead an old swinging bridge stretches over a dirty brown river at the bottom of a canyon. Men in tan uniforms, wearing flat brimmed campaign hats, guard the bridge. They all wear matching aviator sunglasses that give them the appearance of insects. Their patches and badges identify them as US Border Patrol. One checks passports at the head of the line. Two others lounge lazily on either side, shotguns loosely held by sweaty hands.

A fourth Border Patrol agent works his way up the line. Giving helpful tips to move the line faster. Sometimes he stops and asks a pointed question. A cold trickle of sweat rolls down my spine. It's funny. It's funny how even when you have nothing to hide authority figures make you nervous. Of course, I have plenty to hide. I have lots of reasons to be nervous. The agent talks to the man in front of me. I will my clenched hands to loosen. The agent starts walking back towards me. Christ. How should I hold my arms? What looks the most casual, relaxed? Just letting them hang seems weird, crossing them too aggressive, hands in pockets to casual. I settle for clasping my hands behind my back.

The agent is a bigger fella. Tall and going to fat. A thin dirty line of a moustache graces his upper lip. Beads of sweat trickle from under his hat. I can see my face mirrored in his sunglasses. I look worried and suspicious. The agent looks bored. I try to smile disarmingly. Just going for a little vacation. That's all. Just off to have some fun.

"Good afternoon sir."

The agent's voice is as flat as the surrounding countryside. My brain is out of gear. The words of my reply forgotten. It takes a few heartbeats for the popping of my synapses to re-form into a response.

"Good afternoon to you too. How are you today?"

"Fine."

Silence for another couple of heartbeats. It feels like an eternity before the toneless voice starts up again with its automatic set of questions.

"Just making sure you have your valid passport out and ready to help speed this line along."

"Of course, of course. I have it right here in my pocket."

My words sound too fast.

"Anyone else travelling with you today sir?"

"Four. Me, plus the wife and kids."

The agent stares, looks at the people to the front and back of me, then reverts his attention back to me. He pulls his glasses down a bit and skewers me with two very green eyes.

"Sir, are you okay?"

The world around us comes to a screeching halt. I try to answer, but my throat is too dry. I swallow and try again.

"Yeah, sure, everything's just fine."

"Sir, maybe you should come with me?"

Shit. Shit. Shit. I need a second. I need a second.

"What's that now?"

"I said maybe you should come with me. It's pretty hot out here."

My panic turns to pure high octane adrenaline, my brain shuts down, and the automatics kick in. I flail wildly, knocking into the people ahead and behind me before charging right at the very surprised border agent. He tries to jump out of the way but doesn't make it far enough. I feel my boot come down hard on his leg and he starts screaming. I run as fast as I can back up the road. Back the way I've come. Faster. Faster. Run. Run. Escape. Shit. Shit. Shit.

The cat jogs across the landscape, stopping right in front of me. He's a big cat. Gray fur. Big green eyes. I know this cat, but there's no way in hell he could be here. We left him back in Sweetwater. I rub my eyes and the cat's still there.

"Get out of here Roger Snuggleton. I've had enough of this bullshit. Get the fuck out of here."

My voice evaporates into the emptiness before me. I throw a handful of dirt and rocks at the furry fiend. He jumps away, looks at me again, and then turns and runs across the flat. Disappearing from sight into a sagebrush grove. Quiet. The world is quiet.

What the fuck am I doing here?

I'm alone. Completely and absolutely alone. My wife is gone. My kids are gone. I have no home. The place that I once lived sits an empty shell, filled with random belongings that hold no meaning. It was never my home anyway. Just a stopping off point. Just an old trailer in a place haunted by the memory of an old house, a place I once called home, a place that my old self burned to the ground. Now even Alice, the last connection to that past life, is gone. Discarded like a piece of trash whose use has run its course. At least I'm no longer shivering.

The sun hangs low in the eastern sky, but already it's warm. My damp clothes feel clammy and cold against my skin. My back rests against the juniper, which proved to be a less than adequate shelter against the storm. The world outside is steaming. Every bush. Every tree. Every rock. Even me. Off of all our backs the memory of the storm is evaporating into nothingness. It has been a long time since it has rained here. The ground is thirsty. It sucks up the water with a voracious appetite. There are only a few areas left that could be described as mud, but just barely, and shrinking rapidly. Maybe a few puddles here and there, but not for long. By noon no evidence will remain. It can be forgotten about, and both I and the world can continue our movement forward.

I've lost everything. All of my connections to the old world have been severed. No more responsibilities. No more obligations. No more dependency. It's all gone. Is this what freedom means, giving up everything that you've had? Is that the bloody sacrifice that is required? No innocent virgin or prized goat? No ceremony or celebration? Simply the willingness to let it all go. To leave it all behind. Is this the cost? To lose everything you love and cherish? Who would pay such a price for an idea that can be boiled down to seven letters?

Far off by the cliffs, the black dot of the helicopter moves against the blue sky. Too distant to hear, but hanging within sight like a herald of doom and despair. It moves from right to left. I sit and sip from one of my water bottles. I stare at the distant spot where I know Alice is, hidden out of sight under her tarp. You would've thought that with all the rain the camouflaging dirt would have been washed away. You would think she would be easy to find. If she is, the helicopter sure as hell doesn't seem to notice. Maybe she is visible, and they just don't care. Maybe they've already seen her. Maybe they've already had their dirty hands inside of her, pawing around, looking for clues. It doesn't matter now. It really doesn't matter.

What have I been doing with my life? I've known what I've wanted for a long time. Hell, I've spent the last few years getting ready. Is it really so much to ask? Is it really too much of a thing to want? To be free. To be able to live one's life by one's own rules. To know that there isn't someone out there watching over your shoulder all the time. Waiting for you to make a mistake. Fuck. Aren't we all human? Don't we all make mistakes? Shouldn't we all get a chance to do better? Is it really too much to ask?

I can see every step of the journey. I've come so far. I've sacrificed so much. I'm so close to stepping out of the shadow and into the sunlight. Am I really willing to throw it all away now? Am I really willing to turn my back on everything I have gained? Two little faces float in my brain. One that looks like her mother, and one that looks like me. Two ghosts that now float alongside a brother that they have never met. I could care less about their bitch of a mother. I've been in love twice in my life. I'm not too old for a third time to be inconceivable. She was a chain around my wrists. With her gone I no longer have to worry. I don't have to wonder about whether or not she loves me. About who she's sleeping with or what she's taking. She's gone, and it's for the better. The shackles are gone.

The girls were chains as well. A source of constant worry. Will they grow up to be okay, or has everything permanently fucked them up? Have I been a good father? Have I done everything that I could do? Will they grow up to be happy and successful? Will they turn out better than me and Linds, or fall back into the same ancestral pit from which neither of their parents could escape? By moving forward those chains will drop as well. The real people that they represent, will simply become thoughts which one can learn to ignore over time until they are no different than any other thought.

But what about the good times? All the giggles and all the smiles. All the holding them tight and telling them stories until they fall asleep. The hopes and dreams. The feeling of pride when I look on the best thing I've ever done in this world. Is this what freedom is? Losing all of this? Is this the price? Is this something I can pay? Here I am on the cusp of freedom, and what do I have? Nothing. Absolutely nothing. Just what I can carry on my back. Soon to be free, but for what? This was originally all for them? But what is it for now? What use is freedom when you're all alone?

It all seemed so simple not that long ago. It all seemed so right. Where has that man gone? Where is that man who knew what he was doing? Who knew what had to be done? When did the world get so complicated? It's not that I doubt my reasons. It's not that the shadow of the bureaucrats is not lengthening. Those pencil pushing self styled kings, ruling over their little kingdoms from their thrones of tin. The leering eyes of Uncle Sam gazing down. Forcing everyone to dance to his tune with a twist of marionette strings. Telling us all that it has to be done for our own good. To keep us safe. Piece by piece. Bit by bit. It's no world to live in. Say the right things. Act the correct way. Think the right thoughts.

Mexico. Mexico is a place where a man can still be free. Where a man can still stretch his legs and his mind. A country where the government prizes the illusion of power more than the actual fact. A place where a man can live his life free from big brother's expectations. Where judgment is not a government mandate. Sure, there's problems. Nothing's perfect. In Mexico law and order is a joke. A man can only depend on himself to defend his family and what's his. Law of the wild. Everything has a price. Everything has a cost.

Who am I doing this for now? Now that my family is gone. Vanished out of my reach. The helicopter moves across the horizon. Part of me wishes it would turn back. That it would find me under my tree. I could stand up and wave my arms. They could take me away and do what they will with me. No more running. No more hiding. No more worries. No more doubts. Would it be such a bad thing? Would it be so terrible to admit to myself that the cost is too high? Is freedom worth a fucking thing if there's nobody left who cares if you're alive or dead? What is it that is ahead of me? Not my girls. I want to see my girls again. I want to hold them in my arms. I want to have them tell me about their little adventures. I want to go back. I want what I once had.

The helicopter floats across the sky, and disappears from view. What am I thinking? What am I doing? Go back? Insanity. It doesn't matter if I go back. I'll never see my girls again. I've gone too far down the rabbit hole. Made myself too much of a target. I've gone past the point of no return. I'm a dissident in a world where that is no longer acceptable. I'm a marked man. I can't go back and make myself disappear. I can't rewrite history. Things can never be like they once were. Maybe they'll let me out someday, when my mind is broken and reshaped into acceptable dimensions. But then what? Will my girls still love me then? Will they still remember who I am? Will they be just like Philip? Remembering only the bad parts that they have been told. Avoiding me at all costs.

I'd go back if I could. God, if I could go back I would change the things I did. Keep quiet. Live under the radar. Dance their dance to the tune their pipers play. I'd be there for my girls. I'd live the life of a thrall for them. But that ship has sailed. It's no longer an option. At least forward I won't be in a cage. At least forward I won't have to bow or scrape. What do I have left behind? Nothing. The world has taken everything. But fuck, can I live with such a cost? Can I live with such a memory? I've always been a fighter. I've always had to fight. But which way do I fucking swing?

I put away the water bottle, climb out from under the juniper, and start climbing up the hill. I can't stand to sit anymore. I can't stand just doing nothing. It doesn't matter what I do. I just have to do something. I'm alone. So fucking alone. No dreams. No hope. No nothing. It doesn't take long to reach the top of the rise. Fifteen hundred feet below the muddy snake of the Rio Grande twists its way through a canyon filled with the green of cottonwoods. On the other side lies the promised land, rising upwards out of the canyon and into the distance. A mirror image of the craggy brown lands that I have crossed to make it this far.

Amy. Somewhere over there is Amy. Waiting for me. Waiting for me just like she promised. The only constant in my life. The only person who has always been there for me. The only person who's always cared, even when I was at my worst. The only person who ever gave me unconditional love. The only person who never asked for anything in return, never tied her love down with caveats and agendas. Going forward I give up everything. I drop behind the chains of my past life for the promise of a brand new day. My thoughts are just weakness. Hopes with no connection to reality. My goal is within sight. Of course not everything will be easier once I cross the river. Yes, sacrifices have to be made. Things have to be left behind. I'll miss my girls. Just like I miss Philip. But what use to them will I be if I go back? You can never go back.

I take the plastic tube from my left pocket and shake a yellow pill into my hand. It rattles all alone. The last one. It doesn't matter. Soon I won't need them. Soon I won't need to be wary. Soon I won't need to be afraid. Soon I'll be able to sleep again like I used to. Like I did when I was in my childhood bed. My head nuzzled in Amy's arms. My head full of dreams of a better day. That's what lies ahead of me. That's what I can't find on this side of the river. Hope. I drop the empty plastic tube, and start my way down the hill.

Chapter 30

When I was fifteen Jim Jones and his followers drank poisoned Kool-Aid, convinced that it was the only way to escape from the oppression of the US government. None of the people involved were kooks, at least no more than the rest of us. Most were well educated. They were all just looking for a better life, one with a little more meaning, one worth holding onto. No cult ever starts out bad. They just tend to slip under the waves of sanity, members clinging to the guardrails, refusing to let go. What happens in cults is an example of cognitive dissonance, a loophole in the brain's wiring. For the brain, the world has to make logical sense. When we do things that don't make sense, the brain has a hard time accepting that it did something illogical. Rather than accepting the truth, it instead warps our perception of reality, forcing us to accept the unacceptable. We don't think about the world around us, our brains won't let us see how far down things have gone, because deep down, none of our brains can accept that nothing of the way we live our lives makes sense.

It's funny how quickly you can let your guard down. How easy it is to get yourself into a groove where you get to pretend that everything is good and that the world might turn out to be a mighty fine place after all. Then pop, some crazy Arab halfway around the world sets himself on fire and an entire country descends into chaos. Before you know it the flames spread and an entire region of the world goes up just like that. Dictators that long thought themselves secure, find that their thrones are actually tinderboxes.

What's this have to do with me? Absolutely nothing. But such things make governments nervous, even those that at least try to keep up the illusion of being different. You get enough people out in the street anywhere in the world, and you can bet your ass everyone else will start looking a little inward. Time to contemplate one's own buildup of dead wood and brush. Time to be a little more proactive about smashing out any little sparks that might set the whole thing to burning.

You can let yourself believe that the world is a good place all you like, but patience on the part of the other side is not the same as forgetfulness. You can try to tell yourself that it's only coincidence that the police happen to start coming around more often again. Faceless men dressed all in black, looking like turtles in their flak jackets. Snapping turtles, armed to the teeth and itching to try out all their toys. More stormtrooper then protector. They ask all the same tired questions that they asked before.

"Have you seen or heard from Walter Jones? We know this was his last reported place of residence. No. Okay. Sorry to have bothered you."

It would be easy to assume that Walter just isn't doing a very good job of keeping his head down, or that he really has anything to do with the renewed scrutiny. You have to know how to read between the lines. To hear the things that aren't being said.

"We believe that Mr. Jones was involved in the running of narcotics. We have several reliable sources of information. Would you know anything about that? No. Okay. Sorry to have bothered you sir."

How much do they know? It doesn't matter, because you can bet your ass they sure as shit don't give a damn about circumstances. They sure as fuck don't care about the wrongs that the system has done. Hell, it isn't even that. If it was just that they would have dropped the hammer long ago. No, this is an impulse to set things right. To smash those sparks before they become big flames. An excuse to do what it is they actually want to do. You have to pay attention. Those who fail never make the same mistake again.

It's almost never a big thing, usually just a bunch of little ones that add up. A plumber's van that shows up one morning on the corner, and then never leaves. Jehovah's Witnesses showing up every other day, more interested in glancing in your house then spreading the good word of their god. Your computer crashes for no damn good reason and nothing you do can bring it back from the dead. All with logical explanations. Just a series of correlations and bad luck. But they eat away at you. They wiggle in your brain as you stand in line at the grocery store one evening, right in front of two non descript, overly average looking guys talking in voices just a little too loud to be natural.

"Crazy all the stuff you read in the papers these days."

"Yeah, really makes you think about what's important."

"Sure as hell does. I got my family and I got my freedom. Sure as hell couldn't ask for much more."

"Nope. World's a scary place. I'm sure as hell glad we got someone watching over us."

"Damn straight. I don't care what anyone says. This is the best damn country in the world."

"You remember my buddy Paulie?"

"The dark haired one from down south?"

"Yeah, that's the one. Crazy asshole got all caught up in conspiracy theories. Started spending all his time cruising all sort of kook forums on the net."

"Crazy son of a bitch."

"Yeah, he was convinced someone was after him. Always watching. Quit going to work, quit leaving his house, quit doing everything. Lost his job, wife left and took the kids, landlord evicted him. Pretty much disappeared."

"Christ, what a nutter."

"Yeah, I heard they sent him down to a home in Salem. Keep him laid out pretty much 24/7."

"Probably for the best. Can't have people like that just running around."

"Hell no."

They aren't talking to you, but you can feel their eyes digging into the back of your skull. Only an idiot could miss the message. So what do you do? You pay for your groceries, you rush home, and you start packing everything you can.

Alice roars up the Columbia Gorge, hungrily eating up the miles of freeway. The radio blasts classic rock, the girls sit in the back and read books, and Linds stares out the window, refusing to look at me. She's mad at me as usual. It's okay. At least we're on the road. At least we're not screaming at each other anymore. Fat drops of spring rain flood the windshield. Too fast and hard for the wipers to keep up. The river off to our left looks choppy. The howling wind kicks up a lot of breakers. Trucks, their warning blinkers flashing, sit on the side of the road, waiting out the storm. Some cars have done the same. Not us, no way in hell am I stopping now. The more miles the better.

Rooster Rock. Multnomah Falls. Bonneville Dam. It's a weird reverse deja vu. The mood is reversed too. Three years ago we drove this route the opposite way, full of hopes and dreams. Now here we are running with our tail between our legs. Shit, I can still remember Linds laughing.

"It sure as hell don't look like a rooster?"

"I don't think that was the original name."

"What was it then?"

"I'll give you a clue. It's another name for a rooster."

"What?"

"Just look at the shape of the damn thing."

"Ha. Oh shit. That's awesome."

When the hell was the last time I heard Linds laugh? It's been a long damn time. Too damn long. The lush and green turns to yellow and barren. Plan. I got to stick to the plan. It was one thing to rush around like an idiot when we were packing up everything we could carry, throwing garbage bags full of stuff into the back of Alice, Linds crying and screaming, the girls taking her cue and joining in. But now, now it's time to get my head in order. Start thinking again. Things have to be put in motion. Things have to be readied before we arrive.

I get off the freeway just after The Dalles and pull through a McDonald's drive thru to get some breakfast. The kids bounce excitedly in their seats. Linds keeps quiet. Four egg sandwiches, two coffees, and two milks. I don't want the coffee, but I need the caffeine. I top off Alice's tank at a gas station across the street and then pull all the way to the back of a cheap hotel's parking lot. The lot sits next to the river, with a nice view of a The Dalles Dam and a pink bridge over the Columbia. The spillways on the dam are open, turning the river into a white frothing beast. The sun is peeking up over the eastern horizon. The rain has eased up, just a trickle. I open my door and get out.

"I'll be right back."

Silence. I pull a plastic bag out from under my seat and close the door. Inside are the remains of my computer's hard drive. Scratched by a screwdriver, fried by a full minute in the microwave, scoured by a speaker magnet, and smashed with a hammer. I doubt anyone could get anything off of it, but better safe than sorry. I walk over to the cliff edge, open the bag, and sprinkle the contents into the river below. I jog through the drizzle back to the gas station. I throw the plastic bag into the nearest trash can. Along the outside wall, under the awning, sits a pair of pay phones. You don't see that many pay phones anymore. Hell, they're probably all bugged, but the call has to be made, and it sure as hell is safer than using a cellphone. Besides, both Linds' and I's are in pieces back in Gresham. More victims of the hammer. I pick up the receiver, and hold it a little bit away from my ear. The receiver feels greasy in my hand. I push in a couple quarters and dial the number.

"Hello?"

"Hey George, it's Paul."

"Christ Paul, it's not even eight yet."

"Sorry. Is there anyone in the trailer?"

"The one we put up at your Dad's place?"

I wince. I wish he hadn't said that.

"Yeah."

"Got some welder living in it. Short timer. Been working out on all the windmills they've been throwing up."

"I need him out by tomorrow."

"What?"

"Linds and I are showing up some time in the next couple days. I need him out by the time we get there."

"You okay?"

"Yeah, everything's fine."

"I don't think I can just kick him out without notice. I'm pretty sure that's illegal."

"Just offer him his money back for the last few months. Do whatever you have to do."

"Okay. Okay. Are you sure you're okay? You sound kind of funny?"

"Just get it done. Thanks George. Bye."

I hang up the phone before George can reply and jog back to
Alice. Sweetwater isn't a destination. Just a stopping off point. Just a
good place to get ready. It's never really been a place I've wanted to
go back to. At least it's a place I can live for free. The trailer is
theoretically mine, though I've never seen it. George had it drug in
about a year after I left. The rent covers the property taxes on Dad's
place. George has always been a good egg.

I get back in Alice. The kids are covered in crumbs, both passed
out in a food coma. Linds keeps staring out the passenger side
window, refusing to look at me. I think about reaching over to give
her a reassuring squeeze, but think better of it. She'll come around.
We've talked about this before. Just a pretty big shock to have it
actually happen. Alice roars to life and heads back out on the freeway.

In Arlington we stop for a pee break. I'm surprised we made it
this far without one. A blue late model Dodge Intrepid follows us
back onto the freeway. The driver is all alone in the car, his face
obscured by a pair of aviators. At first I'm not sure, but by Boardman
I start to grow suspicious. I try speeding up. I try slowing down. It
doesn't matter. The Intrepid always stays a few car lengths behind.
I'm not sure what to do. I don't want to look suspicious. I don't want
to worry Linds and the girls, all snoozing happily away. The tail stays
right on as we go through Pendleton, and then up and over Cabbage
Hill. My palms begin to sweat and I can feel a tic start to develop in
my eye. What the fuck is the bastard doing? What the hell is he
waiting for? I know what the fuck he's doing. He's watching. He's
watching and waiting. He has all the fucking time in the world.

By La Grande Linds wakes up and looks over at me. I glance
back. She looks worried.

"What's wrong."

I motion her to lean over and whisper so as not to wake the girls.

"We're being followed."

"What?"

I'm not sure if it's surprise in her eyes or disbelief.

"Look in the rearview mirror. You see that blue Dodge."

Linds adjusts the mirror.

"Yeah."

"It's been following us for the past two hours."

"Are you sure? Maybe they're just driving."

"I've tried speeding up and slowing down, he always stays just back a ways."

Linds looks in the rearview mirror again.

"So what are you going to do?"

"I don't know."

The Intrepid is still behind us by Baker. I can tell Linds is starting to get nervous too. The girls wake up and start making a bit of a ruckus. Linds does her best to keep them entertained. By Ontario they've picked up on the general mood. Usually by now they would be demanding another pee break. At one point Stone unbuckles her safety belt and leans forward to whisper in my ear.

"Daddy, is everything okay?"

"Yeah honey, everything is okay."

"Are you sure?"

"Yeah. Just buckle back up your seat belt and play with your sister."

We cross the border into Idaho. Linds leans over, adjusts the mirror again, looks back, and then whispers in my ear.

"He's still back there."

"I know."

"Who do you think it is?"

"Some government flunky."

"Cops?"

"Higher up I'm guessing. Cops would've had to stop at the state line."

"This is freaking me out Paul."

"Me too."

"I'm sorry for not believing you."

"It's okay."

"What are we going to do?"

"I don't know. We'll think of something."

The Intrepid is starting to piss me off. This whole fucking thing is starting to piss me off. I want to punch someone in the face. This is all a bunch of horsehit. No one should be able to treat me this way. Nobody should have the right to make me feel like a deer on the first day of hunting season. Christ. I'm a god damn veteran. I fought for this country. I haven't done anything wrong. I haven't hurt anybody. They have no reason to be following me. Fuck them. Fuck them to hell and back. It's time to take the bull by the horns. I pull off at the next rest stop. The Intrepid pulls off too and parks about ten spaces down from us. Linds takes the kids to use the toilet. I stalk over to the parked car, my shoulders reared back and my fists clenched.

The driver of the Intrepid is stretching his back next to his car. He's about my height and build. His features are so average that he looks out of place. His haircut is short, tight in on the sides. His aviators obscure a good part of his face. He sees me coming. I see a little flash of fear ripple across his features.

"Can I help you?"

"Yeah you can help me. You can help me by keeping the hell away from me and my family."

I jab my finger into his chest to emphasize my point, driving him back a step.

"Excuse me?"

His voice wavers. What a little punk.

"You have no fucking right to harass us like you are. You tell your bosses that we have god damn rights. This is still fucking America. This is still the god damn land of the free."

"Look buddy. I have no idea what the fuck you're talking about. Maybe you should back off...."

"Shut up. I'm a god damn Marine. I fought for this country. Don't think I don't know how to defend myself. Don't think that I don't know how to take care of little piss ants like you."

I give him a good hard shove and he falls back against his car.

"What the fuck do you think you're doing you fucking psycho?!"

He tries to push himself back up, but I push him back against his car again. He tries a second time and I deck him right in the teeth. I feel one of my knuckles pop. He falls onto his ass, his back against the car door, his aviators half off, his nose pouring blood. A woman screams. I turn and see Linds and the girls next to Alice, staring at me. Everyone at the rest stop is staring at me. Some are scrambling to get out their cell phones. I motion for Linds to get the girls into Alice. I turn back to the man lying in the dirt, but he's already scrambled over to the other side of his car. I leave him be. He's obviously gotten the message. I'll be damned if I'm going to run scared all the time. Sometimes enough is enough. I feel good, but I know I need to get the hell out of here. I jog over, get into Alice, and we head back out onto the freeway. The girls stare at me in shocked silence. Linds stares out the passenger window and says nothing.

We stop in Boise and have lunch at a truck stop cafe. The girls get milkshakes. They forget about what happened. Linds is quiet the entire meal. We load the girls back up, but she grabs my hand so we can speak outside.

"What the fuck was that about?"

"I don't know. Guess I just kind of lost it a little bit."

"Was that really the best thing to do?"

"No, probably not."

"What the fuck is going on Paul?"

"You know what the fuck is going on."

"I'm really scared."

"Haven't I always done my best for you and the kids?"

"Yes."

"Haven't I shown that I'm willing to do anything to protect you?"

"Yes."

"Don't you trust me?"

"Yes."

"Then trust me now. I promise things will get better once we get to Texas."

"I know. I know. Things are just all happening so fast. First the rush to get out, then the car following us, then you punching that guy in the face. I'm just really freaked out."

I draw her in close and hold her tight to my chest. I can feel the rapid beat of her heart through her ribcage.

"Everything is going to be okay. You just gotta trust me."

"You promise things will be better in Texas."

"Yeah I promise. Life will get normal again. Things will be better. You'll see. Okay?"

"Okay."

We head out of Boise. At Mountain Home I notice a gray Chevy Impala merging onto the freeway just behind us. By Twin Falls I'm sure they're following us. I don't say anything to Linds. Irrigation circles flash past. Green patches in a world of yellow. Linds climbs into the back seat with the girls, and tells them about Texas. Stone and Rachel have never been there. To them it's just a name. I watch both them and the Impala through the rearview mirror, trying to pretend to be relaxed. I know I'm not doing a very good job. Linds keep glancing up at me, our eyes locking through the mirror. I'm not fooling her.

A sign announces a split in the freeway. North to Montana and south to Utah. I turn on my right blinker and start for the exit. The Impala turns on its blinker to follow. My body is made of steel rods. The one lane exit drifts away from the main road, a widening stretch of gravel between them. I wait for the last possible moment. I wait for the point where the exit starts to drop down below the level of the interstate heading north. The steering wheel jerks like I'm having a seizure. The girls scream and several cars lay on their horns. Alice bounces on her shocks as she crosses over the gravel. The Impala moves away and out of sight. Linds punches my shoulder and starts cursing. I laugh like a crazy person.

"Ha. Mother fucker never even saw it coming. The oldest trick in the book."

"What the fuck Paul. What the fuck was that?"

"Did you see that bastard? Did you see the look on his face?"

Rachel is crying. Stone just stares at the back of the seat. Linds holds Rachel tightly to her. Her face is bright red and there are tears in her eyes. I can tell she's scared.

"Everyone all right?"

"What the hell do you think? What the hell were you doing?"

"That Impala, it's been following us clear across the state, but he sure as hell isn't following us anymore."

Linds gives me a dirty look through the mirror, and then goes back to trying to comfort Rachel. I reach back to give Linds' leg a squeeze, but she jerks away from me. After a while Rachel quits crying. We get off the freeway at Idaho Falls and go north into the mountains. We hit the freeway again at Bozeman and head east until stopping for the night at Billings. The Motel 6 is run down, but well within our budget. I pay cash. We have dinner at a nearby Denny's and then put the girls to bed.

After they fall asleep Linds lays into me again. She yells and screams for a good half hour. In a neighborhood like this, it's nothing out of the ordinary. I start kissing her right in the middle and we make love in Alice. After that she goes to bed. I smoke a joint and then take a drive out, looking. After about an hour I find what I'm looking for. A sister of Alice's, same year, similar enough color, parked in some dive bar parking lot. I park alongside and switch Alice's Oregon plates for the other Suburban's Montana ones.

I head back to the hotel. Saint Christopher glares at me from his medallion. A traffic light turns red. I stop. A homeless man in a faded Carhartt coat and red stocking cap pushes a shopping cart across the street. I see a blue Intrepid with Oregon plates waiting on the other side. I can't be certain if it's the same one, I should have memorized the license plate, stupid, but it looks like it. Fuck. Mother fucking fuck. The Intrepid's interior is in shadow. This is no time to panic. No time to freak out. The light turns green. I drive casually across the intersection and turn down a side street. I take a few more random turns, then pull into a Wal-Mart parking lot.   Idiot. I should have thought about this before we left. Got a little too rushed. Same principle as the cell phones. Anything that can receive can also transmit. I lay down on the floorboards and get the radio loose. I cut each of the wires one by one. I throw the radio into the bushes at the edge of the parking lot.

There might be more transmitters all over Alice. God knows how long they've been tracking me. I'll have to do a more thorough job when we get to Sweetwater. Really take her apart. It would be best if they didn't follow me there, but it's not the end of the world. Just a stop, not a destination. I've been thinking about this for a while. I sure as hell don't want to live the rest of my life like this. Best not to think too far ahead or too far back. Got to concentrate on the moment. Got to keep myself focused. I drive back to the Motel 6 and snuggle next to my wife under the musty smelling covers. After a couple hours my brain finally slows down enough for me to fall asleep.

The next day seems to go a little smoother. Linds doesn't seem mad anymore and the kids have both calmed down. Nobody says anything about the radio. Linds leads a few sing-a-longs, one's she learned as a kid in summer camp. I move my mouth, but don't really sing. I don't know any of the songs. We head east into South Dakota, and then south into Nebraska. I do my best to keep off the freeways. As we cross into Kansas, Rachel climbs up to the front to sit next to me. Linds and Stone lay curled up on the back seat, sleeping.

"Hey Monkey, how you doing?"

"Good Daddy. How are you?"

"Tired, but doing just fine."

"When we get to Texas are we going to be living in a house?"

"Yep. We're going to be living in a nice single wide where I grew up."

"Is it going to be nicer than the last place?"

"Probably."

"That's good. Hey Daddy."

"Yes Monkey."

"Guess what."

"What?"

"Mommy said that when we get to Texas we can get a cat."

"She did, did she."

"Yep. A big old fluffy cat. Is that okay with you?"

"Sounds just fine honey. Sounds just fine."

The highway rolls past and it gets dark. I think about stopping, but decide not to. I drive right through to Sweetwater. Twenty-two hours at the wheel with just a few stops for meals and bathroom breaks. The sun is just peaking over the eastern horizon when I make the last few familiar turns.

Chapter 31

In total, just 147 corporations control 40 percent of the world's wealth. A mere 737 control 80 percent. Most of these are investment companies. Whose money is it? It's all of ours. Our retirements. Our investments. But we are not the ones with control. The system is gamed so we put it where they want it. Money is made, but it's not for us. Most of this money is invested in index funds. The indexes are controlled by just four companies. There are people in this world that live like gods. To them power is just a game, money is an abstract thought, and people are just ants. They can do anything that they want. There are no laws. No rules. They influence us. They tell us how to think. They push us this way and that with the invisible hands of their markets. They can squish us like bugs. These gods control the government. They decide who will lead and who will fall. They game the system so that they will always win. They live separate lives in ivory towers. Gods live among us. Gods who live in a world we can scarcely imagine.

Even in the shade of the ruined wall the rocks feel hot against my back. Flat rough slabs of hardened minerals poking in random spots. It's useless to readjust my position, no way to be truly comfortable, except to accept that there will be discomfort in any position. Once upon a time these four half collapsed walls would have been covered in adobe long worn away by rain and wind. Once upon a time a roof would have blocked out the afternoon sun and held back the elements. People would have knelt on their knees in the dirt of the floor, throwing Latin towards the heavens in the hopes of a higher being reshaping their destinies. Fools refusing to see that the power rested in their own clasped hands. Denying themselves the truth. Wallowing in a world of lies and delusions.

It's funny to think of all the revered buildings on the East Coast. All the pride and upkeep in the shrines that tell the history of our country. All of the bother, and here I sit in the ruins of a church at least a hundred years older than anything held sacred by those pompous assholes, and no one cares because the builders spoke Spanish instead of English. All that history. All that achievement. Thrown away as though nothing had happened. Left to rot into distant memory. The Romantic people had come first, but the Teutonic had taken it away. All glory to the conquerors. The story had become theirs to tell as they saw fit. The version most pleasing to their eyes. The truth doesn't fucking matter. I take another hit off the joint burning in my hand. The smoke crawls its way deep into my lungs. It feels good.

The sound of an engine. Tires crackling across loose gravel and dirt. A cloud of dust rising over the wall that hides me. The church sits against the side of the hill, just above the line of cottonwood trees that mark the location of the river. Vehicles roll by about every hour, or at least, I think so. Close enough for a man telling time via dead reckoning of the sun. About half are government pickups, painted white and green. Beds covered by heavy-duty canopies with prison doors on the back. Border Patrol. Patrulla Fronteriza. The scourge of those trying to get in. The secret guards trying to keep me from getting out. Down here by the river they're thick as flies on a freshly killed deer. The other half of the vehicles are Border Patrol too. They just aren't marked as such. Who else could they be? Who in their right mind would come down here?

Fifteen hundred feet of hillside rise above the ruined northern wall of the church, blotting out the sky. It had been a steep and difficult climb down. It had taken half the morning. Working my way down stony draws filled with junipers. Sliding down nearly vertical rock falls on my ass. So far I'd say it's been the easiest part of the whole damn trip. It wasn't supposed to take this long. Everything has been much harder than it should have been. I know the reason, but I don't want to think about it. It's a thought that good people aren't supposed to have. It's a thought that would not cast me in an appealing light.

It doesn't matter. The harder I try to push it down, the more it forces its way to the top. I've never been able to ignore the truth. No matter how ugly it is. The reason it was easier was because I did it alone. I would have never been able to get Alice down into the canyon. There is just no way in hell. Maybe there are places you can do it, but sure as hell none that I would like to try in the dark with no headlights. Sure as hell none where it could be done unnoticed. Having to leave Alice behind was a good thing. Maybe the best thing that could have happened. Simplify. The secret to a happy life is to simplify. Attachment is just a ball and chain.

Maybe I could have done it. If Linds was still with me. I could have walked ahead and she could have followed. Just like before. The kids could have slept peacefully the whole way in Alice's padded seats, their dreams shielded from the horrors of the night by American steel. No, not even then. We would have had to work our way down the hill, cross the river, and start to work our way up the other side, all in the same night. There is no way in hell we would have been able to hide Alice on this bottom. The camouflage was not designed for close scrutiny. We would have had to abandon her up on top. The girls would have had their armor stripped. They would have been exposed to the horrors of the world.

Oh, and what horrors there are. On this side an Orwellian government with drones hunting for you every second. Telling you what to do. Telling you how to live. On the other side poverty and drug lords, fighting a war funded by rich white men, their noses covered in a mixture of part baking soda and part endorphin rush to forget what their minds refuse to acknowledge. Poverty can be survived, and at least the drug lords leave alone those who leave them alone. There are still dangers though, there are always dangers. What kind of person was I to try and bring them into such a place? The girls are so young. I might as well rip the dolls from their hands. What kind of father wants to make his daughters less safe? Oh, and Linds, the lovely Linds, tinges of internal rot rising to the surface. Such a laissez faire world is not for her. She wants to wear the robes of liberty, but could never bear the cost. No, Linds is happier as a drone. Happier to follow the cow ahead of her into the slaughter.

But I can't live that way. If I must admit the truth, then I must admit to that. I must spread my wings and fly. I know too much. You can't close back up Pandora's box. What would I be if I stayed? Some kind of Judas goat, willfully leading my fellows into the abattoir, watching them be consumed, only to turn back to lead more in.

Praying for the day that my master's no longer deem me useful. Waiting for the time that the bloody knife is at last for me. Like hell. Like fucking hell. I can't ignore the truth of the matter. I can't ignore what is so obvious in my mind. Freedom has a cost, and I am more than willing to pay the price.

"My family was holding me back."

My voice sounds loud and firm in my own ears. The voice of a man who knows the way. I let out a laugh and notice a turtle in the corner gazing up at me. It's a box turtle. About the size of my two palms put together. It sits in a puddle of water, mostly mud, evaporating despite the shade of the ruined wall. It blinks its eyes slowly with careless ease despite its precarious position. Soon its haven will be gone.

"What are you looking at turtle?"

I laugh again and throw a pebble that bounces off the turtle's shell. It does not react. It just sits and stares with solemn eyes. It seems like the turtle is smiling at me. Shit. I must really need some more sleep. I got a little when I first got down off the hill and found my little hidey-hole. A couple hours of uninterrupted slumber. No dreams. The first time in god knows how long. It was best to rest. I can't cross the river until nightfall. It must not have been enough. Fuck it. Might as well go with it. No one around to see. I smile back and crawl over on hands and knees, plopping my back down against the wall next to the turtle in his shrinking pool of water. The turtle doesn't move. It just stares up at me with its little all knowing grin.

"Shit son, you got yourself in a pickle don't ya? Hell, probably not enough water in there to last you to the end of the day. Probably be best if you got your ass back to the river."

The turtle doesn't say anything. He turns his head to watch a passing bird.

"What the hell you even doing out here all by yourself? Strange place to find a turtle. Crouched in a little pool in the middle of nowhere. Of course I guess it's no stranger than me being here. At least I have an excuse. Is that it turtle? Are you just like me? You looking to run away? You trying to get away from something? Is that why you aren't down by the river where you belong? What did you do turtle? What did you do that was so bad you had to run away?"

The turtle looks at me again, slowly blinks his eyes, and then turns his head to study the wall.

"Okay turtle. None of my business. You keep your secrets. We're not so different though you know. I had to run away too. Hell of a thing. All just because I couldn't keep myself from speaking my mind and did what I had to do to provide for my family. I guess those are two different things to be exact about it, but not much difference now."

My joint is all smoked out. I crawl to my backpack, pull it back over, and start rolling a new one.

"I mean hell, it seems like such a little thing. Just a little belly aching on a couple chat forums. No harm done. No foul. Shit, is it a crime to have opinions? To think a little for myself? Apparently. Fucking bastards. I mean, yeah sure, I helped do some tracking of stuff that was probably none of my business. Kept my eyes peeled for how things moved. Helped database what people knew. I don't see how it's any different then those people who get into train spotting or ship tracking. No need to go all silent service about it. Fuck, it wasn't like I was even doing anything with it. Just collecting. How am I responsible if someone uses it for something more? None of my damn business, even if it would have been a damn good idea. No reason to fly off the handle. No reason to red flag me. You know what I'm saying? Fuck. I can hardly see how I'm worth the time or resources. Waste of taxpayer money if you ask me. Don't get me wrong, I'm flattered, but seriously, what the fuck."

I light my newly rolled joint, inhale, lean down, and blow a cloud of smoke into the turtle's face. He pulls his head down into his shell. I laugh.

"A bit for you my little friend. Share and share alike. People like us, we got to stick together. Got to help each other out. For instance, I have to let you know, I'm obligated to tell you, that you're royally screwed man. You are truly fucked. I don't know why the hell you're here, but you sure as hell can't stay, and the only other place around you can go is back to the river. Let's be realistic. You sure as hell aren't going up that hill. I can't see why you're even still wallowing in that mud hole. I mean, c'mon, show some brains about your situation."

The turtle looks at me, and then runs his eyes over the rough stacked stones of the four walls around us. There isn't that much left. The highest point is seven feet in one corner. The lowest is three feet in the middle of the north wall. Easy for me to climb over, but an insurmountable cliff to my companion. Where the doorway once would have been is a jumbled pile of its remains. A mound of stones probably four or so feet high across the entire space, mixed with random boards and rusted loops of barbed wire thrown on by some jack ass with no sense of history. I look down at the turtle quizzically and take another hit, blowing his share down on him.

"How the fuck did you even get in here buddy? Is that it? Is that why you're sitting here all alone? You can't get out? That's stupid. Of course you can get out. You got in didn't ya? If you got in you sure as hell can get out."

In the distance I hear the thrum of a helicopter. Just close enough to hear, but far enough away for me not to care.

"Then again, sometimes I guess we fall into things in such a way that we don't really have many options for getting out. Not without some help at least. Kind of sad really. Sometimes the places that seem the most like refuges, are actually just prisons when we really get a look at them. Funny how that happens. Ah well, shit world and all that."

I finish the joint and crush it under my foot. It's just starting to get to be evening, and it's going to be quite awhile before it's time for me to sneak away. I stare down at the little box turtle as he maneuvers himself to a slightly wetter spot in his puddle that is now just a bit of mud. Shit thing to happen to the little bugger. Just got himself into a bit of trouble and trying to do the best he can with what he's got.

"Don't worry buddy. I won't let you die. When I head out tonight, I'll take you with me. Leave you at the river. Little turtle miracle just for you."

The turtle doesn't answer, but he does go still. I imagine him smiling again. I pull a few granola bars out of my bag and eat them. I drink half a bottle of water and pour the rest over the turtle. I lay down flat, my head on my backpack, readjust my pocket-knife in my right pocket, and close my eyes.

When I open them again it's dark out. The Cheshire cat smile of the moon sits high over my head amongst a swirl of stars and milky way. The air around me is still warm, it's going to be a hot night. I sit still and listen. No sounds except crickets and the gurgling flow of the river. I wait for a bit, until I feel comfortable that no one is around. I pull myself up and look over the wall to the south. Nothing. I crouch back down and pull a t-shirt from my bag. I pick up the turtle from the mud. His legs kick uselessly in the air.

"Quit fighting you little devil. Can't you see I'm trying to help you?"

I wrap the turtle carefully in the t-shirt, soak it all with half a bottle of water, put it in my backpack, and pull up the two zippers on either side so that a space at the top is left open. Wouldn't want my little friend to suffocate.

"You better not pee in there."

I shoulder the backpack and crawl over a low point in the wall. I jog the short distance between the ruined church and the line of cottonwoods. Halfway across I feel the hard packed dirt of the road beneath my feet. I feel better when I reach the trees. More comfortable. Less exposed. The leaves are still green, but will soon be turning gold. The leaves seem to glow in the night, the trunks deeper shades of black in the darkness. Dirt gives way to rounded stones. The river flows right in front of me. My heart beats with excitement. There, right across from me, sits a bank that looks exactly like the one I'm on. Just the same, but completely different. Right there is everything that I've always wanted. Freedom, love, perfection, Amy. A better life, with just a patch of waist deep water in between. Just a few more steps, and then the questions and pondering will be done, my decision will be made.

The river gurgles to itself. Speaking its own language and flowing unaware of its own importance. I slide down a small embankment next to a thicket of cattails. Cold water grips up to my knees. I start to move forward. The sound of voices close by. I freeze. Whispers in Spanish. Splashing sounds. Multiple people moving forward. I push myself into the cattails, hoping the rustling won't give me away, and peak out down the river.

There must be fifteen of them or so, just twenty feet away from my position. Sneaking in, just as I'm sneaking out. Most are men, but there also a few women, and two children. One of the kids is so young that he's being carried by his mother. They are trying to be quiet, but they are terrible at it. I sit, and watch, and wait. I just have to let them pass, and then I can continue on. My crouch puts more of me in the river, and I can feel myself begin to shiver. God, getting your balls wet is always the worse. The group slowly makes its way across, and the first wet boots touch down on American soil.

The spotlight snaps on, illuminating the group with the intensity of a miniature sun. Dogs begin barking, men begin yelling, and the engine whine of quickly approaching vehicles fills the air. The Mexicans scatter, a few rush to get back across the river, the rest try to run further in. Men in green uniforms, guns drawn, give chase. My heart pounds in my chest. Several pickups crash through the undergrowth to the riverbank, their headlights shining across the churning waters. This is bad. This is really fucking bad. I've fucked up big time.

Paul-paul-paul-paul-paul-paul-paul.

The cadence of my name is rapid and panicked. The white brightness of the headlights is blinding. I can't move. I'm paralyzed. Tied down. Helpless. My vision floats above me. I see myself lying in the cattails. The helicopter swoops in low, battering the ground and blowing water and dirt out from under it. A searchlight traces across the shore, illuminating the cattails where I hide for a moment, before moving on, jerking across the scene. It's like watching a picture show. I'm invested, but not there. One of the women runs through the water and throws herself into the cattails next to me. Her breath is fast and heavy, her hair is wild and half plastered against the side of her head. She notices me right next to her, eyes me for a second, and screams. She throws herself back the way she came. The helicopter searchlight flashes across her and holds steady. She tries to climb up on the bank, but a burly border patrol officer runs out of the trees and throws himself at her. The two go rolling into the water, and for a moment he's holding her head under as he struggles to get a pair of handcuffs on her. Another officer comes down to the shore and watches. The helicopter light moves across my hiding space again, but nobody notices. Cursing loudly, the officer in the river finally manages to get the handcuffs on the senorita, and pulls her over to the shore. His comrade helps pull her up, laughing his ass off.

Bright white light dazzles my eyes. My body jerks and my perspective snaps back to its proper place. Water and cattails. Flashlight beams move across the riverbank, poking into any obvious hiding spots. I crouch lower in the river. Stiff with cold and adrenaline. Ready to spring. Ready to run. A hunted deer. Farther back in the trees, sounds of running feet, struggling, yelling. A pistol shot. Two more. Mexicans sit in the dirt, hands cuffed behind their backs, illuminated by pickup headlights, surrounded by laughing and boasting men. Trading stories of their latest hunt. The helicopter light plays over the cattails once again. I can't stay here. They'll catch me. They'll get me. Shit. Fuck. Tonight is not my night. I can't get across. They'd see me in an instant if I tried. I have to get out of here. I have to get away.

Everyone's a little ways from me, all the action is down the river. I push my way to the up-river side of the cattails. I crawl up on to the bank. In a crouch I quickly move back in amongst the trees, careful to be as quiet as possible. The sounds are dying down. Mostly just voices. Men talking. The occasional curse. Two flashlights bob their way towards me, their owners moving as though they are just having a little stroll. I dive behind the trunk of a nearby tree, down into the undergrowth. The lights keep coming closer. The beams flash across my hiding space. I freeze. They move on. I pick up a rock and throw it towards the river. The clatter echoes in the darkness. The two lights turn to follow and the owners hustle to check it out. I sneak off in the opposite direction.

At the edge of the trees I look down the road. Two hundred yards away three white and green pickups sit dark and quiet. I rush across the road and dive back behind the cover of the ruined church wall. I sit. My back against the hard stones. I slip off my backpack and take the pistol out of the front pocket. I cock it, the sound like a firecracker. My breathing sounds like the bellows of a forge. How can they not hear it? They must be able to hear it. My finger sits against the cold metal of the trigger. I'm too close to be taken now. The fuckers aren't getting me without a fight.

Distant sounds of men talking down the road. The helicopter flies back and forth next to the river. Doors open and close. The squeak of shocks. Engines start. Headlights come on. The sound of vehicles moving away down the road. One set of lights and sounds comes closer. It idles by at slow speed. A spotlight flashes across the outside of the ruined church. The pickup moves past, turns around, and then idles by again, slower than the first time. My heart is a bass drum in my chest. A steady thunderous boom. The squeak of brakes as the pickup slows, and then a growing growl as it picks up speed and heads down the road after the others. I let out a breath I hadn't realized I was holding, and puke up a mixture of granola bars and water onto the ground next to me.

Chapter 32

For decades, efforts have been made to cloud and distort the truth behind some of the most important events in United States history. Those with enough sense saw through the clever ruses, but thousands more were taken in. The full scope of what many described as conspiracy theories was not well known until the defection of a high level KGB agent named Vasili Mitrokhin in 1992, who brought with him an extensive archive of over twenty-five thousand pages of KGB documents, collectively called the Mitrokhin Archive. The documents shed new light on the JFK assassination, the CIA, the Martin Luther King Junior assassination, the origins of the AIDS virus, and even J. Edgar Hoover's sexuality. Theories, rumors, and suppositions. All fed by a massive KGB disinformation campaign to spread distrust of the US government. Though the Soviet Union has long since been dead, the results of their efforts continue to reverberate to this day.

The sun peeps over the eastern horizon, peaking in to make sure it's safe to bring itself out all the way. The world below is nothing but shadows and golden hues. The city lights of Sweetwater glow to the southwest. Roscoe to the south. The straight rows and flood lights of the airport in between. To the northeast stretches a multitude of red blinking lights. An army of tall white sentinels, spinning their long arms in never ending circles. I shiver. It's cold up here. It was hot down on the ground. I'm glad I brought my sweatshirt. I take a puff off my joint and look past my dangling feet at Alice two hundred and fifty feet below. The first bits of solar warmth brush across my cheek.

None of this was here when I left. The windmills were just an idea. A cafe rumor discussed by aging fossils who had nothing left to do but drink coffee and gossip. Now there are over a thousand of them. Giants just waiting for their modern day Don Quixote. I've had the impulse to climb one since we got back. An itch in my skull. A little voice in the back of my head, just telling me to do it. I've done my best to ignore it. After all, this is the same voice that looks at Alice's running engine and tells me to touch the belts. It's an impulsive voice. A stupid voice. Not one that should be listened to. However, when I woke up for no good reason at 4 AM this morning, I knew that I was going to do it. I just felt like if I was ever going to do it, I better do it now. Besides, what's life without a little impulsive stupidity?

Getting in had been easier than expected, just an everyday padlock, nothing a pair of bolt cutters couldn't handle. They probably figured that the climb would be enough of a deterrent for most. Not that bad really. Just a little mind over matter. Step by step and all that jazz. It is well worth the effort. I feel at peace up here. All the problems. All the preparations. All the shit. It's on the ground far below. Up here I'm free to sit back and enjoy the sunset without worrying. Up here I have no responsibilities or obligations.

The tired old sun heaves himself up and over the horizon, or is it herself. What is the proper sex of the sun? Probably should go with itself. It's a damn object, not a person. I take another hit off my joint. It's starting to get good now. I can feel a nice buzz starting. A crow flies by beneath my feet, chased by a group of black birds. The smaller birds wheel and dive, pecking at the crow and driving him out of their airspace. I watch them turn into black specks. The windmill arms churn in their lazy spin. I look down at Alice again. Jump says the voice in my head. A switch clicks. I feel dizzy. Sick to my stomach. My brain sends out flares of warning. I can feel myself falling forward and then down, down, down through the air towards the ground below. The wind whistling in my ears. My joint drops. I grip the steel bar that runs around the edge with both hands. A lump rises in my throat.

The voice in my head starts screaming. Get down. Get down you mother fucker. What the fuck are you doing you fucking idiot? Closer to the back a second voice chimes in. You should just jump. Imagine how it would feel. The other voice screams louder. What the fuck, are you nuts? It doesn't fucking matter, you'd be dead. That would be it. Nothing more. What the fuck is wrong with you? Get down before you fall. Get down now.

I pull my legs back up and press my belly onto the cold white metal. I drag myself back to the open hatch and crawl back inside next to the turbine and gearbox. My entire body is shivering. I'm close to hyperventilating. I crouch for a moment, trying to gather myself back together. Down. I need to get down. But that means I have to climb the ladder. A two hundred and fifty foot ladder. Shit. God damn it.

I wish I brought a safety harness. I should have brought a safety harness. It doesn't matter now asshole. You got yourself up. You have to get yourself down. I put my legs over the edge and start down. It doesn't matter. I can't live up here. I got myself up. I have to get myself down. One step at a time. Just don't think about it. Easy as hell. Yeah right. When my foot hits the ground I calmly step back outside. It's warm down here. My t-shirt beneath my sweatshirt is soaked through. I sit for about fifteen minutes with my back pressed against the white metal of the windmill, and then get in Alice and start her up. I still need to do my morning run, get the day started.

The man's teeth are far too white, and his hair too nicely combed. Perfectly parted on the right side, greased down to keep the flop in place. He holds the carburetor in his hands, examining it closely like it's some kind of rare art piece. The kind of in depth look that tells you that somebody has no idea what their looking at, but want you to think that they do. He mumbles softly to himself as he turns the carb around and around, squinting at it in the darkness of the barn. His hands don't look like the hands of a man who would buy parts from an unlicensed parts dealer. They look soft. His nails are clean. I don't know. He's just some average guy. That's the problem. He's too average. Perfectly average. Out of place average. Nobody is ever that average. I wish he would hurry up and get out of here.

"You going to buy it or what?"

The man stops his fiddling and looks up at me. His eyes are a light green. He smiles with his too white teeth. It makes me uncomfortable. It's the smile of someone who knows something that you don't.

"Yeah, sure, sure, I'll take it. How much?"

"One hundred and fifty bucks."

"I couldn't get you to put it a little lower?"

"This isn't some god damn bazaar. I say one-fifty, I mean one-fifty."

"Okay, no problem. I'll take it. My wallet's out in the car."

"Cash only."

"Yeah, sure, no problem."

We walk out the big doors into the sunshine. It's hot out, but then again, what day in a Texas summer isn't hot. Over by the trailer, Stone and Rachel run in the sprinkler. Rachel giggling up a storm. Stone somber as ever. They both wear shoes so they won't hurt their feet on any of the sandburrs or puncture vine growing between the patches of dead yellow grass. Roger Snuggleton lounges on the porch, watching them through half closed eyes. The man walks over to his Toyota Camry, the most average car possible, leans in and gets his wallet. His overly white teeth are smiling as he counts out the bills.

"I can't tell you how happy I am to find this carburetor. My brother and I have been rebuilding this car for years, and you wouldn't believe how expensive some of the parts can get. I'm going to give him a call when I get home."

The man puts the last of the money in my hand and looks up, staring me in the eye.

"My brother lives up in Oregon. You ever been to Oregon before?"

I stare back at the man, my eyes focused on his, trying to discern what kind of person sits beneath the veneer of average Joe bullshit.

"No, I've never been to Oregon."

"You should go if you ever have the chance. Great place. He lives up in a town called Gresham, right up there next to Portland."

I keep my voice as deadpan as my face.

"You don't say."

"Oh yeah. Heck, I'd move up there myself if I didn't want to stay close to my kids, but their mother has already made it hard enough to see them as it is."

"Uh huh."

The average man looks over my shoulder. I can feel his eyes crawling across my kids. My hands tighten slightly into loose fists.

"Those your kids?"

"Yeah, those are my girls."

"Little angels I bet."

"Yep."

"Good for you. Always good to have the father around. Learned that one the hard way. Used to get in a lot of trouble when I was younger. Never really thought things through. Heck, maybe if I kept myself on the straight and narrow back then I could have been part of my kids lives a bit more and they wouldn't be such little fuck ups."

Cold trickles of sweat slip down my spine.

"Probably so."

"Yep, always good to have the father around."

"I have other shit to do today."

"Oops sorry about that. Sometimes I'm a bit of a jabberer. Thanks again for the carb."

The man looks at Stone and Rachel again, then gets in his car, turns around, and heads back up the driveway, a cloud of dust chasing him off. I stand and watch him go and then walk back into the barn. We don't have much time.

Alice doesn't need that much more, just a few little tweaks to make sure everything is adjusted right. Nothing big, just a bit of tightening here and there to settle my own nerves. When I go in for lunch Linds can tell I'm agitated, but she doesn't ask any questions. Rachel babbles on about her morning. Stone stares at her plate of Top Ramen. After lunch I start loading Alice up, keeping track of everything in a notebook. After a bit Linds comes out to the barn to watch, her arms crossed.

"Paul, what are you doing?"

"It's time Linds. It's time to go."

"Paul, slowdown, talk to me. Go where?"

"Down to Mexico, just like we talked about."

Linds stands blinking. Her forehead creased in concentration, her face and stance agitated. I keep working. I don't really have time for the same old arguments again.

"Why now? What's suddenly changed?"

"That guy Linds. That guy said some stuff."

"The guy who bought the carb this morning?"

"Yeah, that guy."

"What did he say?"

"It's not what he said. It's what he implied. You know, reading between the lines. If we're going to get out of here then we got to do it sooner rather than later."

"He just seemed like some guy Paul."

"Of course he did. That's the whole point Linds, but just look at the pattern. Two weeks ago the computer quits working. Last week the phone gets disconnected. Today some average looking guy comes around implying that it would be a shame if the girls didn't have a daddy. We don't have long."

"Christ Paul, that computer was a piece of shit. You bought it out of the fucking nickel ads. God knows how many viruses it had from looking up all the crap you do. And of course the phone got disconnected. We didn't pay the damn bill. Are you sure you're not getting all worked up over nothing, just a bunch of coincidences."

I put the box I'm carrying down and walk over to my wife. I gently grab her upper arms and look into her eyes, her beautiful pale green eyes.

"Don't you trust me honey?"

"Of course I do Paul. I wouldn't be here if I didn't. But none of this really makes any sense to me."

"I know it doesn't. I know it's hard to understand, but you just have to trust me honey. Can you please trust me?"

My wife's eyes fill with fear and I realize that I'm gripping her shoulders a little too tightly and shaking her a bit. I let my arms drop.

"I just need you to trust me."

Linds stares at me a little more, like she's looking for something, and then lets her gaze fall down to my feet.

"Yeah Paul, I trust you."

I gently lift her chin with my hand so she's looking at me again.

"That's good honey. That's good. You know where the bug-out bags are?"

"Yeah."

"Go through them again, and add anything that you and the girls want to take. We leave at sun up tomorrow."

"Okay."

Linds turns and start walking back to the house.

"Don't worry honey, everything is going to be just fine."

She stops and looks back at me with scared waifish eyes. She's still the most beautiful woman that I've ever seen, every bit as good looking as our wedding day, but she looks tired, so very tired.

"I know it will be Paul. I know."

Packing Alice takes the rest of the afternoon and a good chunk of the night. Linds brings me out a beer and a plate of mac and cheese for dinner. I wolf it down standing up while she watches and hand back the plate. I smile and she tries to smile back. She goes back to the house, and I go back to work. So much to get done. So little time. God I hope they don't come tonight. Please god tell me they aren't going to come tonight.

It's close to midnight when I get everything done. I'm beat and sore. I'm not as young as I used to be, even with all the exercising I've been doing. I go into the dark house. Everybody is already in bed. I get undressed, set the alarm clock and lay down in bed. Linds is snoring and does not wake up. My side of the bed is cold. The damn cat snoozes next to her between us. I worry that I might not be able to sleep, but drift off as soon as my head hits the pillow.

I wake up before the alarm goes off. Careful not to wake Linds, I get up, take a leak, and get dressed. In the kitchen I brew myself some coffee and eat a bowl of some sugary chocolate cereal Linds bought for the kids. I don't like coffee, but I need the caffeine. The single wide is quiet. It's peaceful. It's been nice here. I wish we could stay. With a little time and effort, we could have built a nice life here. But those are the breaks. I walk across the living room to the door to the kids' room and put my ear against it. I can hear them breathing inside, lost in dream land. How are they going to react to all this? Is it going to be a terrible trauma, or just some new grand adventure? They seemed to adjust pretty well last time. That's the good thing about kids. They adjust pretty damn fast. I hear footsteps and see Linds walking into the kitchen in her pajamas, an old t-shirt and sweats. Her hair is a birds nest and I can tell she isn't wearing a bra.

"That coffee still hot?"

"Yeah. You better hurry up and get dressed. We'll need to wake the girls soon and get the hell out of here."

Linds pours herself a cup of coffee and takes a sip. She stands in the kitchen, looking at me, clasping the mug with both hands, her fingers flexing and twitching. She's nervous. She wants to say something. We've been married a long time. I know all her tells.

"Honey, don't just stand there. We need to get moving."

"I've given it a lot of thought Paul."

"We really don't have....."

"Me and the girls aren't coming with you. I know there's nothing we can do to stop you from going, but we're staying here."

I stare at my wife as though I've never seen her before. She looks scared. She's trying her best to hide it, but she's frightened. Her little girl eyes, set in a prematurely aged face, dart from my eyes to my chin, to my feet, and back again.

"Honey....."

"We're not going with you."

"Honey. We have to go. We have to go now."

"No we don't Paul. I let you take us from Portland. I'm not letting you take us from here. We can all stay here. You can stay here."

I feel tense. My shoulders hurt. It's too early in the morning. My brain isn't firing on all cylinders. None of this makes any sense. What the fuck is she doing? What the fuck does she think she's doing? I feel my words turn to pleas in my mouth.

"Honey, we have to go. We have to get out of here."

"No we don't Paul. None of this makes any sense. Can't you hear how crazy you sound. All this spy movie crap. None of it makes a bit of damn sense to me."

"We've talked about this all before."

"I know, and none of it made any sense then either. I'm just tired Paul, tired of all this bullshit. I've gone along with it because I love you, but I just can't do it anymore. I'm not going to do it anymore."

Tears are flowing down her face. My own eyes are filled with water.

"You're not taking my girls from me you stupid bitch."

"Then stay here Paul. Stay here with us."

"You know I can't do that. You know I can't fucking do that."

"Yes you can Paul. Yes you can."

"What the fuck are you doing? Do you know what's going to happen? What's going to happen to me? Is that what you want? Do you want me to fucking disappear so you can go back to fucking whoever the hell you want? No worries? No problems?"

"God damn it Paul. I love you. I love you so fucking much."

"Then cut out all this bullshit. Cut out all this crap. We have to go."

"We're not going with...."

"Fuck you whore. Where would you be without me? I supported you through rehab. I did things I swore I'd never do. All for you. All for fucking you. All to keep this family together, and now, now that I ask you to do one thing for me, what is it? Nothing. You're selfish. You're just a selfish bitch."

Her face contorts through the tears. I can tell she's mad now. Just as mad as me. We've gone past the point where we can go back. The storm has been unleashed and we're just going to have to weather our way through.

"No, fuck you Paul. Yes, I'm not perfect. Yes, I've fucked up. But it's not like I haven't put up with your crazy shit. It's not like I haven't put up with your insane demands. I'm tired Paul. I'm just fucking tired of all this bullshit. You're off your god damn rocker. You've lost your god damn mind."

"God damn it you bitch. You're not taking my fucking kids away from me. You're not taking my god damn kids."

"We're not going with you."

"You're fucking coming god damn it. I'm trying to do the best thing for this fucking family."

"We're not going with you."

"All I've ever done is try to do the best for my fucking family. All I've ever wanted is a better life for my god damn kids. You're trailer trash. You hear me, nothing but a god damn piece of white shit trailer trash."

"We're not going with you."

"You're not taking my fucking kids away from me. Not again."

"We're not going with...."

Everything goes blank. Something incomprehensible erupts from my throat. I lunge forward. The lights come back on. Linds is laying on the floor, her mug next to her, coffee sprayed across the floor, counter, and wall. One hand is held against her face. Her uncovered eye is filled with fear and shock. Tears are streaming down my face. I look down in horror at my clenched fist. Never. Never have I ever. Oh god. Oh god. What have I fucking done? What have I fucking done?

I turn and run, out into the cool morning air. The eastern horizon is just brightening. Muted stars still hang in the air. What have I done? What have I done? What have I done? My body seems to be moving in automatic. I'm running. Running as fast as I can. Across the dead remains of the lawn that was once my father's pride and joy. Into the barn that needs a new coat of paint. Climb into Alice. Start the engine. Hit the gas. Out on to the driveway. Around the corner on to the main road. The speedometer climbs upward. Nightmare. This all just a nightmare. None of it is real. God let me wake up soon. Please god let me wake up soon.

Chapter 33

It's coming. It's obvious to anyone that looks that it's coming. The last few steps on a road we were set down eleven years ago. We've all been played, dancing to the piper's tune. There will be no shots fired. No rows of men in black with jack boots beating against the pavement. They have been more insidious than that. It was a gently rising tide. We hardly noticed until the salt water started pouring down our throats. If I had a time machine. If I could go back. Hell, what would be the use? People believe what they want to believe. There would be nothing I could do. Divide and conquer. Direct the hate. Direct the energy. Make them choose sides in a game where it makes no difference. Give each of us magical devices with which we cannot do without. Magic of the modern world that tracks our every move. Listens to our every word. Stay in the world of illusions and live in peace. Terrorize those that insist on seeing reality.

The sound of a car door opening and closing. The steady hum of the engine. The intermittent unintelligible crackle of the radio. Footsteps. Footsteps coming towards me. I push myself back tighter against the south wall of the ruined church. I try to make my prone body smaller. Just another rock. Nothing to see here. My grip tightens around the stock of my pistol. My palms are sweaty. My finger twitches against the trigger. I blink to try and clear the sweat from my eyes. I stare at the patch of blue sky at the lowest point in the wall. White fluffy clouds glide peacefully past. The footsteps come closer. The flash of the crown of a cowboy hat. The jingling of a belt buckle. The sound of a zipper going down. The flow of water.

"Hey, hurry the fuck up, we don't have all day."

The window of the Border Patrol pickup must be open. I can hear the voice of the agent still in it as clear as day.

"I'm hurrying. I'm hurrying. Keep your shirt on."

The radio crackles again. I can't understand what it's saying. The man in the pickup answers back. His voice too quiet to follow.

"Hey Doug, just got an update on Pearson."

"Yeah, what about him?"

"He came out of surgery just fine. No complications."

"What were they doing this time again?"

"Putting a rod down his fibula."

"I thought it was his tibia?"

"No, that was the first time. They were hoping they wouldn't have to do the fibula."

"That's all lower leg, right?"

"Yep."

"Poor bastard. That has to hurt like hell. He'll be laid up for awhile."

The jingling of the belt again. The sound of a zipper going back up.

"Probably so. Fucker will probably get even fatter."

"Jesus Sam."

The sound of footsteps heading away.

"What? If the bastard wasn't so fat he probably would have been able to jump out of the way."

I don't hear the reply. It's lost behind the sound of the door opening and closing. The engine revs up, and the pickup drives away. I breathe a sigh of relief and let my hand with the pistol fall to my side. I stretch my legs out and sit, getting myself back together. I put the pistol back into the front pocket of my backpack, and pull out everything I need to relax. It takes less than a minute to get the joint packed, rolled, and lit. I take a deep inhale, hold it down deep inside of me, feel my heartbeat slow, and exhale. The turtle looks up expectantly at me from his muddy corner, sitting in a shrinking pool created by the contents of two water bottles. I inhale again, and exhale into his face.

"Fucking pigs. All this time and effort. What a fucking waste."

It's hot again today. Even in the shade. It's a strange sense of deja vu. Everything seems the exact same as yesterday. Nothing has changed. It's as though yesterday never happened. I'm thirsty, but I don't drink any water. I need it for my little friend. I need to make sure he survives the day so I can take him to the river tonight. I should have done it last night, but in the all the excitement I just forgot. Holy shit what a crazy night. Okay, that's not completely true. Maybe I didn't just forget. Maybe I just didn't want to be alone. Maybe I just needed a friend a little bit more. Just until I get across the river. Until I can leave all this madness behind me. I owe him. I owe my little buddy.

"It's like I was saying turtle, it's happened a hundred times before. First they engineer an enemy to fill us all with fear. Then they use that enemy as an excuse to take away our freedoms one by one. People give them up willingly. Sacrifice them on the altar of safety and security. Don't even realize how much is lost until it's gone. Slowly. They always work slowly. So nobody notices. Like a frog in a boiling pot. Turn up the heat slow. Little fucker won't even jump. Some people just want to control things. It's how they get high. People like that don't like chaos. Chaos is the byproduct of freedom. You know what I'm saying?"

The turtle doesn't say anything. It just sits and watches me.

"This case is no different. 9/11, the Patriot Act, gerrymandering. It's all part of the same thing. It's all about power and control. Get the people scared. Get them to give you the okay to shit all over them. Treat them like children. Hell, it's what most people really want deep down inside anyways. No responsibilities. No worries. Just let big brother do the thinking. You just sit back, relax, consume, and make some more consumers. Easy-peasy. No worries at all."

The turtle looks confused. I can tell he isn't totally getting it. Probably this damn heat. It makes it hard to think.

"I know what you're thinking. What the hell does gerrymandering have to do with it? It's simple. Takes the voice out of the people. Make it so a certain party always wins a district. Suddenly it becomes just about the money. Someone doesn't play ball, just take away their money. Give it to some asshole who will. Fuck representative government. Get some big bucks in there. Sure you can donate to a campaign. Sure the big money and corporations can't give directly to a candidate, but they sure as hell can do their own promotional or smear campaigns. Thank you very much Citizens United versus

Federal Election Commission. Christ, they don't get much more blatant than that."

The turtle opens and closes his mouth. I blow some more smoke into his face. I wonder if he's a female or a male. Beats the shit out of me how you sex a turtle. I bet Tom's dad knew how to do it. Poor dead fucker. Ah, the hell with it. I'll just assume it's a male.

"Sure, some people might point out the Tea Party. Group like that really throws a wrench in the gears. Hell no. People who say that aren't getting the damn picture. This ain't about favoring one group over another. This isn't about ideology. This is about polarization. This is about shutting things down. Keeping things from working. A bunch of Tea Party yahoos, they just help assure that things aren't going to work. Nice little group. Makes a lot of noise. Causes a lot of problems. No worries. They're not blocking the big stuff. They're not turning back the clock. Hell, the legislative branch is just a joke now anyways. It's all about the executive and the judicial. That's where the power is. Keep the judicial from getting in the way so the executive can do whatever it is they want. Take a little more power piece by piece. Fuck, people applaud them for it. Finally, somebody getting something done in government. Two possibles are easier to control than five hundred or so. Give the illusion of choice. Make people create differences in their minds based on petty platitudes and the grayest of ethics. This time everything is going to be different. Give me a fucking break. It's the same no matter what box you check. Fucking sheep. It doesn't fucking matter."

My hands are shaking. It's been awhile since I've said a lot of this out loud. Not since I used to spend nights trying to explain to Linds how the world works. Not since I used to still post in the forums. Back when I was still figuring it all out. Bunch of fat men up in ivory towers. Greedily hoarding slips of cotton that have value only because we believe they do, and then, only because those same greedy bastards tell us that it's what we need to believe. Ivory towers with foundations of faith. All their power based on our imaginations. Larry got it. Larry understood. He just decided not to care. Better to be assimilated then to go against the flow. When the fuck did he change?

"Rights. Everyone talks about their fucking rights. A bunch of atheists blathering on about god given rights. Ridiculous. There are no rights. We created them. We can destroy them. Nothing there. Poof. Gone. Just like that. There's one right in this world. The right of all living things. You have the right to whatever you can keep others from taking from you. The rest is just imaginary. Free speech. The right to trial. All of it is just crap. Hell, all we're doing is empowering them. Isn't it obvious? When one demands something is a right and demands that the government give it to them, it just becomes a new way to control you. Give us all fucking healthcare. Great, now a few fuckers decide exactly what that means. You can live longer, but only if they decide you can. Law of nature. They can only control what we let them control."

I take another hit to calm myself. I'm getting too worked up. Talking too loudly. I need to calm down. I flick the butt of the joint into the mud next to the turtle. The coal gives out with a hiss.

"I thought that Occupy thing at least had a chance. Bunch of people out in the street. Bunch of people getting mad. They seemed to at least get the sense of things, even if they didn't really understand the details. That's what they're really afraid of. People losing faith. People throwing it all down. Down with what they call society. Down with all of it. For a little bit I thought I might not have to go on the run. For a little bit I thought the world might work out after all. Bull shit. The moment I heard about the first rapes in those camps I knew it was over. Fucking idiots. Don't leave the shit in and tell me it's going to make better milk. The moment they let the crazies take control it was all over. Simple messages. Individuals are smart. The masses are simple. Keep it simple stupid. Fucking idiots. That's no way to turn people away from their chosen god. Government, society, whatever you want to call it. People don't want pure chaos. You got to keep it on the level. You can't tell people that everyone is inherently good. They know better. People want a higher power. No one wants to be responsible and think for themselves. People want fucking leaders. People follow fucking leaders. Leaders don't rant and rave. Leaders have visions. Sure, sure, tear it all down, but what do we put in its place?"

My belly gurgles. I had some water and granola bars for breakfast, but they're no longer cutting it. My body is tired of granola bars and water. It wants something more. It wants a hamburger with all the fixings. It wants a crisp apple. It wants brussel sprouts cooked on the grill in butter and vinegar. I should have brought some vitamins. Man can't live on just granola bars and water. Just one more mark against this fucking world. One more mark against people who just can't leave well enough alone.

"I was too smart. I couldn't keep my mouth shut. The shit is going to hit the fan. It's coming soon. Hell, you can't tell the difference between cops and soldiers. Fucking cops look more like soldiers than I did when I did my bit. The knife's going to get pressed up against our throats and the majority of people aren't even going to care. Oh boy, but those of us who tried to do something, tried to get out the word, we all have to watch out. We're all going to get disappeared. Guys like me, free thinkers, it's time for us to get out."

"Bullshit."

The sound of another voice knocks my thought train off its tracks. I look around frantically. Peak over the side of the wall. Nobody else is here. I'm all fucking alone.

"Bullshit."

I look down. The turtle is staring up at me. His eyes full of defiance.

"What do you mean bullshit? All of it is the god given truth."

"I don't know about that. None of it really matters. What I'm talking about is why you're here. All this crap. Nothing but a bunch of god damn excuses. A bunch of bullshit."

"What the fuck are you talking about?"

"You're not running because you're some hero who dared speak out."

"Yeah, then why am I running?"

"Because you're a coward. You're just some chicken shit coward off on a lark so he can feel special."

I laugh.

"Fuck you turtle. You don't know the things I've done. The things I've had to sacrifice to get here."

"I believe you've done some fucked up shit. I won't deny you got some knocks coming. It's all this overarching stuff that's bullshit. I mean hell, how long you been out here?"

"I don't know, around seven nights or so?"

"How far is it from the highway to here?"

"Probably around forty miles."

"Yeah, you're obviously a threat the government can't ignore."

"Hey, fuck you man. You're just a fucking turtle."

"Oh yeah, fuck me. Sure, I'm just a turtle, but at least I have the common sense not to make life more difficult for myself."

"What's that supposed to mean?"

"Christ, do you need your hand held for everything? Look, I will admit, ignoring all the bullshit, that you've done some stuff where it might not be a bad idea for you to make yourself scarce. But you have to admit that you've done nothing to make this easy on yourself. I mean c'mon, any competent asshole could have gotten themselves over the border by now. You're not an idiot. You have military training. Surely you can get your little head around the situation enough to see the truth of the matter."

"What the hell are you trying to get at? You're just talking in god damn circles. I spent months preparing for this trip. Fucking months."

"And yet here you are, seven days to cross forty miles. Nothing left but a bag of water and granola bars."

"A lot of shit happened."

"I get the sense that has been your line most of your life."

"Now see here...."

"Christ, don't start with that kind of crap."

"So what would you suggest then, oh sir high and mighty turtle?" What should I have done differently?"

"What any sane person would have done. Assessed the situation, judged the true reason why they were doing it, and gotten it done."

"Oh, so now I'm a crazy person."

"You're the one who said it, not me."

"I'm not fucking crazy."

"Said the man having a conversation with a turtle in the middle of the desert."

"So maybe I'm cracking up. I've been through a lot of shit."

"Shit of your own creation."

"Fuck off."

My voice is too loud, but I can't seem to control it. It echoes off the hillside.

"I just want to hear you admit it."

"Admit what?"

"Why you're out here."

"I told you, I had to run, the government's going to lock up all us freethinkers."

"Bullshit, you're just a little nothing. No one of any merit gives a shit about you. It's all just an excuse, a reason for why you can't succeed. If the game is rigged against you, then you don't have to take any personal responsibility. Don't give me that crap."

"So my kids can have a better life. So they can live in a better world."

"Yeah, where's your kids at? I'd love to meet them. We both know none of this shit is for them."

"Fuck you. You don't talk about my fucking kids."

My throat feels tight. Tears run down my cheeks. My hands are balled into fists. The vein in my temple pounds.

"Just fucking admit what we both know?"

"I don't know what the fuck you're talking about."

"Just admit it."

"Admit what?"

"That all you have is fucking excuses. That all of this is just so you can abandon all your obligations. Leave it all behind so you can chase after some ideal dream world that only exists in your head."

"Fuck you."

"Admit the fucking truth. You know it. I know it. Just fucking say it out loud already. You can't handle having a family. You can't handle having others depend on you. They need you and you can't stand it. You want to be loved, but it all has to be on your fucking terms."

"Amy loves me. Amy has always loved me. She's never turned her back on me. She's never judged me or loved me less for the things I've done."

"She's nothing but a voice on a god damn phone. You think being with her will be any different than being with your wife and kids."

"Fuck you."

"Hell no it won't, and you know why, because in your mind you have to be the center of the god damn show, everyone else is just there to support you. If they want to love you, if they want to be loved, it all has to be by your rules, your reality. It's all fine and dandy as long as they never need you to be something you don't want to be."

I'm losing control. I can feel it. My body seethes. My vision pulses with every beat of my heart. I can hear a familiar sound in the distance, but I don't care.

Paul-paul-paul-paul-paul-paul-paul.

My body jerks. The whole world spasms. Branches fall from the trees. Rocks rattle down the steep hillsides.

"Fuck you."

"It's all great until they need you to step up and sacrifice for them."

"Fuck you."

"Why, because you deserve a little happiness, because the world has been hard on you. Join the fucking club."

"Fuck you."

"Admit it you selfish prick."

"Fuck you."

"Admit it."

"Fuck you."

My hand shoots down and grabs the turtle around his shell. His neck cranes and he tries to bite me. His stubby legs flail helplessly in the air. I stand up, screaming obscenities. My arm rears back. The turtle shoots forward. It sounds like a large egg breaking when he hits the wall. I can see blood in the sunshine. I collapse down into tears, curled in the fetal position, pounding the dirt with frustration and hate. My voice is hoarse, barely just a whisper.

"Fuck you. Fuck you. Fuck you."

The sound of the helicopter grows distant. Fading as quickly as it came.

Chapter 34

In 1973 a psychologist named David Rosenhan conducted an experiment where he sent eight people of sound mind and body to twelve different psychiatric hospitals to feign auditory hallucinations in an attempt to gain admission. Every single one was admitted and diagnosed with a psychiatric disorder. Once the patients were admitted they started acting normal again and told the staff that they felt fine and no longer had hallucinations. All were forced to admit to having a mental illness and to agree to take antipsychotic drugs as a condition of their release. When word of the experiment reached Saint Elizabeth's mental hospital in Washington DC, in an attempt to disprove Doctor Rosenhan's assertions, they challenged him to attempt to pull the same stunt on them over a three month period. Doctor Rosenhan agreed. Over the next three months out of the 193 people admitted to the hospital, staff identified 41 as imposters, and a further 42 as suspicious. Dr. Rosenhan had sent none.

"Paul. Paul. Get your ass out of bed."

My mother's shrill voice echoes up the stairs, jolting away nightmares of yelling and tears. I leap up and rush out of my room and down the hall, my four-year-old legs pumping wildly. Past the open door of my parents' room, my mother's big standing mirror giving a brief flash of a roundish face covered by a bird's nest of black hair. Down the narrow stairs. Half running. Half falling. Into the kitchen. Greeted by a wafting wall of pancakes, eggs, and bacon.

My father sits at the table reading the Sunday comics, coffee cup in hand, cigarette in his mouth, his brown eyes roving back and forth with quick darting movements. He's wearing just a t-shirt and boxers. My mother stands at the stove, wrapped in her robe, a spatula in hand, deftly overseeing two frying pans, one cooking pancakes, and the other scrambled eggs mixed with the grease from the bacon. She sings quietly as she works, her words melting into a muted mumbled tune.

The sun shines on the other side of the kitchen window with a false impression of warmth. It's January, it's cold outside, but the kitchen is warm, nearly to the point of it being uncomfortable in my flannel pajamas.

The eggs go into a bowl with salt and pepper. The last pancake gets flipped and added to a plate filled with its fellows that she pulls from the oven. A second plate from the oven holds the bacon, cooked both hard and flat for my mother and me and floppy and greasy for Dad. Down on the table it all goes, along with a jug of reconstituted orange juice. My mother puts two pancakes on my plate, and adds the butter and syrup. The butter is soft, she had placed it next to the oven while she cooked, and the syrup is warm, the bottle dunked in hot water in the sink. She serves my father. He smiles and kisses her on the cheek before going back to his comics. Her family served, she sits down to join us.

We eat in silence, as we often do, but not the morose dismal silence that has seemed to become the norm. No, this is the silence of contentment and domestic bliss, occasionally broken by my father's laugh when he reads a good one. The good ones he reads out loud, except for one which he whispers to my mother, turning her face red as her hand covers her smiling mouth.

"What is it? What's so funny?"

Both my parents look at me, snickering at their private joke, and eying each other in a non-verbal sparring match to decide who will have to answer. My mother loses, or perhaps she just gives in.

"Nothing honey. Something just for adults."

I frown at the often heard excuse, and then go back to my pancakes, watching the syrup soak in and trying to picture in my mind all the things on the edge of my comprehension, wondering what things would be funny to my parents, but unfathomable to me. I don't get very far in my rumination. The pancakes are just too good.

With breakfast over my father sets to washing the dishes, and my mother takes me upstairs so we can get ready to go. We brush our teeth, taking turns to spit in the sink, and she sets to preening her long brown hair into a manageable hairstyle. I go back to my room and play with some of my toys. It doesn't take my mother long to get ready. She comes into my room in a flowered dress and flats, her hair done up, and makeup on her face. She pulls out clothes for me, newer blue jeans and a nice sweater, my mother has a thing for sweaters, and my cowboy boots. I don't kick up a fuss like I normally do. It's a pleasant morning. It seems wrong to be the one to ruin it. She combs my hair, parting it down the left side.

My father comes out of my parents' bedroom, wearing a pearl snap western shirt, black jeans, and rattlesnake skin cowboy boots. We put on our nice coats, face the first pummel of the cold, load up into the car, and head into town. The ride is a quiet one. Not the same kind of quiet as at breakfast. A quiet of apprehension. The radio plays for a bit, but my father flips it off. My mother seems to be shaking. My father reaches over and gives her hand a squeeze. She looks at him and gives a half smile. I hold two plastic dinosaurs in my hands, a stegosaurus and a brontosaurus, but I don't play with them. I stay quiet. I stare up at the St. Christopher medallion hanging from the rearview mirror, flashing in the morning sun. The streets of Sweetwater flash past, quiet and mostly empty, only a few people going about their business.

The church looks much the same as I remember it, though it's been a year since we last were here. A red brick building with slanted roof topped by a white painted cross. Father Rafferty stands outside in a green robe, shaking hands with everyone that comes in. My father shakes his hand and they say a few words that are too quiet for me to hear. Father Rafferty bends down, smiling, and shakes my hand. I smile back politely. We file past through the entryway, going into the church proper. My father and mother dip their hands in the small basin of water before doing the sign of the cross. We stay near the back of the church. All of the pews are full on the right side. My mother leads us to the left. I can tell it makes my father uncomfortable. We always used to sit on the right.

The organ starts playing and everybody stands. Father Rafferty walks down the aisle, preceded by two altar boys, one carrying the cross, the other carrying the big bible. My mother sings. My father and I do not. Everybody sits and mass begins. At first I try to keep up with the adults, mimicking their standing, sitting, and kneeling, but I soon give up. Father Rafferty speaks and everyone replies back. I can't understand what they're saying. It all sounds like mumbling.

I sit on the hard cold wood of the pew, clacking my cowboy boots together until my father gives me a dirty look. My eyes wander across the church, taking in all the forgotten details. It looks much the same as the last time I was here, minus the dark wooden box and everybody crying. The church's carpet is a vibrant green, spilling down the stairs from behind the altar and flowing down the aisle towards the door. The candle under the red glass, the one that's supposed to mean God is in the church, flickers. Father Rafferty drones on, holding pieces of bread up in the air. One of the altar boys rings a bell.

The carpet becomes a river of slime. Tiny soldiers line the tall armrests of the pews on either side. Arrows fly back and forth. Catapults are cranked back and burning boulders are fired across the divide, scattering men and materials. Both sides send out boats filled with men. They are quickly swept downstream. One reaches my side and ties itself secure. Soldiers pour out across the floor beneath my feet. Defenders rush to meet them. Battle rages back and forth. The invaders are repulsed. The boat is cut loose and men are pushed back into the slime. They struggle, but their heavy armor drags them below the swiftly moving current.

Jesus, on the big cross at the front, looks down from his height. Seeing all and never looking happy. I feel bad for him. He looks so sad. Light pours through the stained glass windows, leaving a rainbow of colors across Jesus and the back wall behind the altar. I wish someone would take him down. It must hurt to have nails through your hands and feet. It makes me sad to look at him. It seems silly to be doing all this standing and sitting. Someone should just get Jesus down. Maybe that's the point. Maybe they want Jesus to stay up there. It seems like Father Rafferty has everybody under pretty tight control. My mind twists his words and the mumbled reply of the crowd. It all makes more sense this way. It makes more sense why they don't take Jesus down.

That's what the two armies are fighting over. One side wants to take Jesus down. The other wants to leave Jesus up. Father Rafferty wants us to help the side that wants to keep Jesus up. I'm sitting on the side of the church of the army who want to leave him up. I casually brush my hand across the top of the armrest, scraping off all the men and catapults so they fall to the floor far below. I reach forward to do it to the armrest of the pew in front. My father gives me a dirty look. My mother smiles. I sit back.

It helps. The army that wants to take him down sees an opening. More boats are launched. Some make it across. Men pour out. Those that rush forward to stop them are too few. More boats follow. A bridge of boats is built. The defenders are thrown back more and more. Today may be the day. Today may be a day of victory.

People start getting up and filing into the aisle, lining up and moving towards the front. The bridge is smashed. The offensive lost. Those trapped on the wrong side are cut down. Father Rafferty's commands have won the day again. My mother pushes me up into line and folds my arms over my chest so I'm grabbing my own shoulders. She rests her hands on top of mine. Slowly we shuffle forward. My father stays in his seat. His head down. We reach the front and Father Rafferty puts a piece of bread in my mother's mouth and then leans down and says a prayer over me. His face is saggy, his teeth yellow, and his eyes bloodshot. We step to the side, my mother drinks from an offered cup, the altar boy holding it wipes its rim with a cloth after every drink, and we make our way back to our seats.

The mass drones on for a bit more and then ends. The organ plays. Father Rafferty walks back down the aisle, following the altar boys carrying the big bible and the cross. The music stops, everyone stops singing, and we start filing out of the church. Father Rafferty is saying goodbye to everyone as they head outside. He smiles when he sees us.

"I'm so glad that your whole family could be with us today."

My mother winces, but then forces a smile. My father only grunts. We move past out into the cold air. People stand and talk in groups, their breath steaming, but most hustle towards the parish hall next door to get out of the cold. My father turns towards my mother.

"Do you want to go to coffee hour?"

"No, that's okay. We can head for home."

We get back in our car. My father starts it up and we sit and wait for it to get warm. My mother looks at my father.

"Well, that was all right."

"Yeah."

"The church hasn't changed a bit."

"No."

"But did you notice, Father Rafferty is completely gray now."

"Yep."

My father puts the car in gear and pulls out into the street. I play with my dinosaurs. The streets are a little more busy now. My father clicks on the radio, but my mother clicks it right back off.

"Let's get some flowers and stop on the way home."

My father looks over, his face lined with worry.

"Are you sure?"

"Yeah, I'm sure."

"Okay."

My father turns off the route home. My mother reaches over and gives his hand on the steering wheel a squeeze. We stop at the florists and my mother goes in alone. She comes back with a small bouquet of irises. My father puts the car back in gear and we head out.

"You know those flowers aren't going to last long in this cold."

"I know. It just seemed wrong to go and not bring them."

The car ride is quiet. My mother sings softly to herself. The air feels dry. There's a tickle in my throat. I let off a series of coughs. My mother quickly spins around.

"Are you okay?"

"Yes."

"Are you sure?"

"The boy says he's okay."

"Paul? Are you feeling okay?"

"Yes, just a cough."

My mother stares at me for a bit, the way she does when she thinks I'm lying, and then turns back to stare out the windshield. My father turns the car and we pull through the cast iron gate into the cemetery. Dad stops the car and we get out. My mother takes my hand and we walk through the graves, crunching through the frost-covered grass. My father comes behind, smoking a cigarette. We stop at a little grave with a carved angel on it. My mother leans down and starts fussing with the flowers. Dad stands and watches, lighting another cigarette off his first.

I watch for a minute and then run amongst the graves, hiding behind big ones and pretending I'm a falsely accused criminal on the run. The police are hot on my trail, searching for me from grave to grave. One is close by. His back is turned. I sneak behind the maintenance shed. Another one rounds the corner. We nearly run into each other. Pow. Right in the kisser. The policeman goes down, knocked out cold. I think about taking his gun, but no, that's no good. I'm an innocent man, an innocent man would never take a policeman's gun.

I can see my parents not far away. They're hugging. My father's chin is resting on top of my mother's head. I sneak and hide behind another grave. When they find the knocked out cop, they're going to know that I'm here. I have to hurry.

"Paul. Where are you Paul? It's time to go."

My father's voice sounds raw. The getaway car is ready. The policemen are all too far away to stop me. I sprint across the grass as fast as my legs can carry me, juking around graves so they won't be able to get a clear shot. Pistols fire behind me. Some ricochet nearby. I jump in the backseat of the car. My father shuts the door behind me, gets in the front, starts it up, and we slowly drive back out of the cemetery. My mother is staring out her window as the world rolls past. My father looks past her and gives her knee a squeeze.

"Looks like it might rain."

My mother doesn't say anything. She just stares out the window. Her hand brushes against her green eyes and then she turns back to look at my father and me.

"Who wants to stop for hamburgers on the way home?"

I smile.

"I do."

Chapter 35

Reality is nothing more than a perception. I read that in a book once. I can't remember which. Some think that our reality is constructed by our own minds. I don't think this is wholly true. I think for the majority of people reality is created by those who know how to pull the strings. Creators of an illusionary world where each and every one of us is a hero in our own story. Where as long as we stay in line we're allowed to remain within their created reality, free to fight our battles and have our joys, free from ever realizing exactly how pointless it all is. Those who see the world with their own eyes, they are to be cast out. Let them wallow alone in the cold. Forced to face the fact that we all are nothing but a bunch of hyper intelligent monkeys on a speck of dust living according to imaginary rules that we have created for ourselves. Let them live out in the void. Let them view it all with the naked eye. Watch as they're filled with madness, and claw at the door, desperate to be let back in.

My attempts to sleep don't work out so well. I just toss and turn. My lower back hurts. I can't seem to get comfortable. My mind refuses to slow down. It keeps going at a mile a minute. The more I try to turn it off, the higher it turns the volume. Fucking turtle. Filling the air with all that crap. I can't believe I was going to help him. Get him out of a jam. Now my mind is spinning like mad and I can't seem to get it to stop. I need to rest. I need to relax. It's going to be time to go soon. I need to be ready. I need to be alert. I feel all dopey. On edge. Soon. Soon it will all be done. Fuck I wish I had some more pills.

The turtle lies on his back at the bottom of the wall. His limbs hang like they're made of jelly. The edge of the crack in his shell is just visible. The hungry ground has swallowed up his spilled fluids. I wish it would eat him up too. Above him there's a dark patch on the wall. A stain. Dirt and grime scuffed off. I keep looking at it even though I don't want to. I'm glad it's getting dark. That patch will be invisible in the dark. My eyes are filled with tears.

The turtle was right. Dirty mother fucker. How'd he know? How'd he know what I couldn't even admit to myself? I couldn't let go. I couldn't allow myself to see the truth. I was just making things harder for myself. It would have been easier if it was just me. If I hadn't tried to drag everything else along, things wouldn't have been so difficult. But what kind of person would I be if I had done that? What kind of person could rush off towards a better life, without trying to take those he cares about with him? I don't know. Maybe it all just made things worse. Maybe I should have listened more.

My stomach hurts. I feel sick, but hungry. All I had for dinner was a granola bar and water. The same thing I had for lunch. The same thing I had for breakfast. Fuck. I'm sick of granola bars and water. My hands won't stop shaking. I smoked the last of my weed after I killed the turtle. It didn't help. The whole world feels wobbly. Christ. I don't know. Maybe I'm going crazy. For fucks sake, I'm sitting here fretting over a god damn turtle. How do they put it? On the ragged edge. The edge of what? Beats the fuck out of me.

Fuck that turtle. I'm not a selfish bastard. I was trying to bring my family with me? What more does he want? What more could I do? Sure, I made mistakes. No one's fucking infallible. I didn't abandon them. They abandoned me. It was that bitch Linds. That fucking cunt. I should have dumped her ass long ago. What the fuck was I thinking? She was dragging me down. A weight around my neck. Ha, Linds in Mexico, that's a fucking lark. She wouldn't last two days. Hell, the moment anything went wrong she'd just start sucking dick for coke, or worse.

I know why I kept with her. I know why I did the things I did. The kids. It was all for the kids. I don't know. Maybe it would have been easier without them, but I'd rather have them here with me now. I wish I could go back. I wish I could go back and do it all again. I've lost everything. Everything is gone. So why do I still feel so fucking loaded down? I have nothing. No possessions. No responsibilities. Nothing. Why don't I feel free? I know why. There's still one more step to go. I still need to get across the river. Cut the last cord. Amy. I still have Amy. It's time to get going. It's dark. Just the moon glaring down. Twinkling stars. Probably some satellites. They can't see me. Doesn't matter if they can. I'm almost there. I'm almost at the end. Amy. Soon I'll be with Amy.

The road is quiet. There hasn't been any vehicles in the last few hours. The cottonwoods are dark. I work my way slowly through them. I want to get further up-river from the night before. Best not to try to cross in the same place twice. My movements are slow and careful. Each footstep measured and purposeful. No snaps of twigs. No cracks of broken branches. No rattling of the underbrush. I have the time. I might as well take it. I can be careful. I can be invisible. I've come so far. There's no reason to fuck it up now. A pickup moves down the road. I freeze. At a bend the headlights skitter across the cottonwoods, illuminating me for a brief second. The pickup doesn't stop. It keeps moving, farther down the road and out of sight.

We'll live a simple life down in Mexico. I'll get a job somewhere where I can tinker and fix things. There are still places down there that are remote. Where they need someone to fix things because the new things are too expensive, or too far away. Things don't get thrown away down in Mexico. Nothing is wasted. As long as I can prove myself useful, nobody is going to mind me being there. I'm sure Amy will find something too. She's always been smart. She's never been afraid to get her hands dirty. God, it's been so long since I've seen her. We never got a chance when I lived in Portland. Every time I had a free weekend, she was away, flying, seeing the world. It will be a better life. It has to be.

I've gone far enough in these fucking trees. Hell, I've probably gone about a mile. Maybe not. I don't know. I work my way to the river. The shore is lined with round gray stones. It's impossible to work your way across them without making some noise. Just go slow. There's no one around. Everything is quiet. Just the burble of the moving water. It will feel good to relax again. I've been way too damn tense all the time. It can't be good for you. Always being so tense. So ready for the world to kick you in the nuts. Just force of habit I guess at this point. You get kicked enough you're going to get a little defensive.

I stop at the edge of the water. The river gurgles, unaware of its own importance. It doesn't look too deep. I probably won't even have to swim. Amy. Just a little bit more to Amy. One last obstacle. One more test. I've come so far. All I have to do is cross. Then it's over. Done. My old life will be over. My new life will begin. A better life. I'll be free. Free at last. The crescent moon smiles down at me. The stars twinkle. The arch of the Milky Way bridges the heavens. It's a nice night. A good night. Things are peaceful. Thirty feet away an identical shore sits waiting. I just need to cross thirty feet. I just need to take the first step.

My feet don't move. I stand rooted to the spot. I look back over my shoulder at the darkness behind me. Somewhere behind me, somewhere out there, are Linds and the kids. I hope they're okay. Hell, they're probably already back at the trailer in Sweetwater. Crowded around the TV, watching some movie for the hundredth time. It would be nice to be there. It would be nice to be part of that world. It doesn't matter. That bridge is burned. That world of serenity doesn't exist anymore. Maybe it never did. You can never go back. The only hope I have is forward. I need to cross. Amy is waiting. I need to get to Amy. My feet stay rooted. There's nothing holding me back. No family. No friends. No life. Nothing. Just me.

I'm damn sure not standing here for Linds. I wish I could have seen Linds ten years ago the way I see her now. Selfish. Misguided. Ignorant. Swayed more by animalistic impulses than sound thought and logic. Dumb bitch. The things I could have done if she hadn't held me back. The worry. The fear. The anger. The wasted time and effort. What a different world it could have been. Maybe I'm not being fair. I'm not perfect. I'm just as guilty for many of the same sins as she is. Sure, it was a different time, different place, but still the same. Just like Diane, I stayed as long as I could. I just can't do it any longer. Really we're both just products of our upbringing. Neither one of us really ever had a chance.

Stone's fucked. It's probably too late for her too. The scars are already written all over her face. The face of a woman in her fifties on a child that's only eight. Poor kid doesn't even know it yet. She's on the same road as her parents. Cast adrift to do the best she can before it's time. She has no idea that she doesn't have a chance. Linds and I, we did it to her. We should have done better. For god sakes, that was our only job. To do better. To make some normal kids. To give them the chance that neither of us ever had.

Rachel might be okay. God only knows how she always stayed so cheerful. When you're young you can survive anything. The horrors of the world just flow right off you. Your mind is still malleable. It's not until things start to get rigid that you start to get all fucked up. Maybe she still has a chance. I hope so. I would hate to think of Rachel not smiling. Maybe she'll end up normal. Maybe she'll be able to escape. At least there is that. Rachel might turn out okay. I don't know. Maybe I should have done like Diane. Maybe I should have taken the kids and run the moment Linds started to falter. No use wondering about it now. What's done is done. You can't go back. You can only go forward. I've always been a fighter. I've never been the type to just run away. To sit down and accept my fate.

What am I doing just standing here? What was it that Tom's dad told me that time he visited me in prison. The size of the mountain doesn't matter. All you need to do is concentrate on taking the next step. It was the only time he ever visited me. The last time he ever talked to me. The last attempt to save a sinking ship. I had ranted and raved the whole time. He had just sat on the other side of the glass. Calmly talking in a low voice. Laying out what I needed to do. Don't worry about the size of it all. Just take that first step. There's always hope. As long as I'm alive. There's always hope.

The water is cold. First my feet are cold, my socks and boots soaked through. Then my ankles are cold. Then my calves. Then my thighs. It's slow going. The rocks under my feet are slippery. I jump a little when the water reaches my crotch. Instant shrinkage. I reach the middle. It's only waist deep. I knew it. I knew it couldn't be that deep. I stop for a moment. Let my hands run across the moving waters.

"Daddy! Daddy don't go!"

The voice of my youngest daughter echoes from the north bank of the river. A small shadow moves along the river edge. Going this way and that, wanting to cross, but scared to move forward. I shake my head. Just my imagination. There's no turning back now. I'm already halfway across.

"Daddy please! Daddy please don't leave me."

Her voice is broken by sobs. She's crying. My little Monkey is crying. The river current is getting stronger. Trying to knock me down. I can see the little shadow, stretching her arm out towards me. Water trickles down my cheeks.

"I'm sorry Monkey. I can't. I can't come back. I've come too far."

"Come back Daddy! Come back!"

There's nothing I can do. There's nothing to be done. I turn my back on the northern bank and its wailing shadow. It's nothing. There's nothing there. Nothing. I just need to cross. Get to the south bank. I can see Amy there. She's standing there right now. She's wearing a green sun-dress. Her black hair is loose, floating in a summer breeze. She's smiling at me. Beckoning me forward into her warm embrace.

The shadow of Rachel is still crying on the northern bank. Two smaller shadows emerge to join her, then a larger one with a moustache and an old fishing hat. There's movement from the line of trees. Hundreds of them. Maybe thousands. I can hear their voices. Pleading. Begging. Lecturing. It's all too much. What do they want from me? What do they expect? Why can't they leave me alone?

Paul-paul-paul-paul-paul-paul-paul.

Pain stabs through both my arms. A sharp pain, rising from my forearms, climbing up my veins, closing an icy fist around my heart. The helicopter moves down the river towards me. A darker black in the shadows of the canyon. A spotlight illuminates the moving water below. Skittering across the liquid undulations. No. Not now. Not here. There's nowhere to run. Nowhere to hide. Fuck. What am I supposed to do? My body turns. I've always been one to fight. I've never been one to run away. I brace myself against the increasing flow of the current. Amy to my left. The wailing shadows to my right. They are all quiet. There is no sound other than the helicopter. I hurt. I hurt so much. Too much. I feel like I'm being ripped in two.

Paul-paul-paul-paul-paul-paul-paul.

Large beads of sweat flow down my arms. They drip off my fingertips. The dark shadows of the barren hillsides climb endlessly up into the night sky. The whole world falling downward to me at the lowest point. The helicopter comes in right over the top of me. A dark emptiness. A void. Water pushes away from the column of air holding it in the sky. The river doubles its efforts to push me over. The searchlight swings around. Hunting for me. Finding me. The light is bright. So fucking bright. A voice booms over a loudspeaker. It's a strong voice. A voice of authority.

"Paul. It's okay Paul. We're here to help."

Bullshit. It's just a bunch of bullshit. My back braces. All my muscles tighten. I strain against the overpowering force of the light. Deep down I feel a sense of elation. Paul. They called me Paul. They know my name. They know who I am. They've been looking for me. I'm not a nobody. I'm not just another bug amongst ants. Adrenaline courses through my veins. Hot as molten metal. Burning. Burning me from the inside out. I can still fight. They haven't got me yet.

The searchlight gets brighter. I raise my hand to protect my eyes. The light flows around it like water. I can feel every heartbeat throb through my body. Across my chest, down my arms, a vibration to the tips of my fingers. Brighter. Too bright. Pain. Excruciating pain. The distinct lines of the river bank soften and run together. Sharp features obscured into watercolor illustrations. A world melting into blobs of color. The flow of the river keeps getting stronger. It pushes. It shoves. It wants me off my feet. It wants to force me under, hold me down, drown me. The light travels through my eyes, bursting its way into my brain. Lighting all the dark recesses. No sound but the rotor above me. Screaming out my name. I try to move, but I can't. I'm tied down. My feet are lead weights. I can't escape. I'm cornered. Trapped. All I can do is lean forward. Fight the river. Fight the light.

Two hands fall and rest upon my shoulders. A voice sounds in the wind. A voice only found in dreams.

"Let it go Paul. Just let it go."

Each beat of my heart is a distinct echoing tick. A rumbling lub-dup that ripples across the world. It hurts. God how it hurts. I'm bent nearly double. The downward current grows stronger. I feel cold. Weak. My muscles are losing their strength. The hands give my shoulders a squeeze.

"Let it go Paul. Just let it go."

I feel heavy. I let my backpack slip off my shoulders. I hear it splash into the river behind me. The voice keeps whispering its unceasing mantra in my ear. I'm still heavy. I reach into my pockets. My hands won't close tightly. The hydraulics have all leaked out. Out comes my pocket-knife. Out comes my mother's St. Christopher medallion. Both fall into the water with a resounding plop. I feel drained. Empty.

"You and me Paul. We are the same. People like us aren't meant for this world. We see too much Paul. We'll always see too much."

"No."

The scream erupts from deep down in my lungs. The hands start to pull me back. Strength surges back into my body. A last desperate attempt to keep myself from going over. I lunge forward. Screaming. Choking. Spitting. The arch of the Milky Way cracks and falls away. The stars in the sky swell. Dots growing and expanding. Merging into one great light. The color leaches from the landscape. Leaving only white. The whole world is white. The light overhead is painfully bright. I can't turn. I can't move. There's movement all around me. Panicked bustling just out of sight. I hear the voice in the loudspeaker.

"Paul. We're just trying to help you. We're just trying to help."

My lunge falls short. My strength falls back, bleeding out into the river where it's carried away downstream. The river gets stronger. The hands on my shoulders more insistent. The world around me is gone. The shadows. Amy. All gone. No way to go back. Impossible to go forward. I know I can't go back. I know I'll never reach the other bank of the river. It's not there. I'm alone. Just as I've always been. Just as I've been since the day I woke up to find my parents gone and my grandfather and Beth sitting downstairs at the kitchen table. Talking in whispers. Just as I've been since my father came home that evening, and took me upstairs to tell me his lies. I don't have much left in me. I hurt. Everything hurts. The smell of freshly made bacon, pancakes, and eggs permeates the air. Filling my nostrils. I hear humming. An old song. One I haven't heard outside of memory in a long time. The hands on my shoulders are gentle. I can feel warm breath on the side of my face. The remembered voice whispers in my ear.

"It's okay Paul. Stop fighting. If you stop fighting, everything will be okay."

I let myself go limp. My body relaxes. Thoughts, melting before they form, dribble out my ears. I let the hands guide me down. I fall backwards into the river. I don't sink. I float. I drift. I let the waters take me where they will. Diane. Philip. Linds. The girls. Amy. None of it really matters. All are beyond my control. Beyond my reach. There is nothing here but me. Just a branch floating on the water. Nothing weighing me down. The river pulls me away. Leaving it all behind. The light fades. White walls and a white ceiling. The feeling of a hand in mine. My forearms hurt. Distant murmuring. Trying to get my attention. Amy's voice in one ear and Rachel's in the other. Shadows slowly rising at the corners of my vision. No. There is no then. There is no later. There is only now. I let go of the hand holding mine. I feel a jab on my left arm. The shadows fade. The voices fade. The pain in my arms, the white walls and ceiling, it all just fades away. I float on downstream. Nothing holding me back. Nowhere I need to be. My lips curl up into a smile. I'm free. I'm finally free.

About the Author

Shawn Campbell was born in Eastern Oregon in 1983 after a harrowing drive through a fog. He currently resides in Portland, Oregon where he works as an economist and lives with a lovely house plant named Morton. He has had several short stories published in various literary reviews, but this is his first book.

CPSIA information can be obtained
at www.ICGtesting.com
Printed in the USA
LVOW10s1557220118
563525LV00007B/272/P